DRAGON GUARDIAN

IMMORTAL DRAGONS BOOK FIVE

OPHELIA BELL

Dragon Guardian

Copyright © 2017 Ophelia Bell

Cover Art Designed by Jacqueline Sweet

Photograph Copyright © DepositPhotos.com and Period Images

All rights reserved. No part of this book may be reproduced in any form or by any electronic means, including information storage and retrieval systems, without permission in writing from the author, except by a reviewer who may quote brief passages in review.

This is a work of fiction. Names, places, characters, and events are fictitious in every regard. Any similarities to actual events and persons, living or dead, is purely coincidental. Any trademarks, service marks, product names, or named features are assumed to be the property of their respective owners, and are used only for reference. There is no implied endorsement if any of these terms are used.

ISBN-13: 978-1-955385-10-7

Published by Animus Press

UNITED STATES

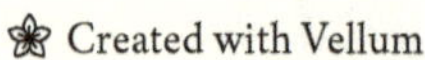 Created with Vellum

Time is the school in which we learn, time is the fire in which we burn.

— DELMORE SCHWARTZ

PROLOGUE

Inside the Nymphaea Haven, Several Millennia Ago...

A cool trickle of water scattered over Aodh's sun-drenched back, slowly making a line down his spine. Icy beads formed, moving at his lover's command in tickling circles down his body. When they reached the apex of his cleft, he clenched his ass and opened one eye to stare lazily at the source of the wet exploration.

Meri let out a throaty laugh and gave him a smile of mock surprise. "Why can't I play with you there? You let Neph do it all the time."

With a growl, Aodh surged up, toppling the nymph and pinning her beneath him against the warm stone they'd been sunning themselves on.

"Because Neph's better equipped to follow through. What have you got?" He held her arms above her head with one hand while he slid his other down her twisting torso. When he delved his fingers between her thighs, he found her as slick and ready as any nymph. Wetter, even, reminding him how she'd taken Neph's seed earlier and was still filled with it now.

"Aodh, stop," she complained, even as her hips pushed up into his hand, forcing his probing fingers deeper into her.

"Do you really want me to stop?" he asked, looking down at her face.

"Yes," she said, though her head moved from side to side in clear contradiction. The little liar always loved playing games with them.

He let out a gruff laugh and latched onto one of her hard nipples, then replaced his mouth with his hand as he slid farther down.

"Maybe you want my mouth more," he said, grazing his lips over her glistening mound.

"Oh, Gaia, that's worse," she said. "Definitely don't use your tongue on me." She spread her legs wide enough for her wet petals to part for him.

Aodh's eyelids fluttered closed at the sight of her sodden folds still creamy with the remnants of Neph's climax. The satyr he'd fallen for wasn't with them at the moment, off seeing to some important Haven business with his sister, but he'd left a lovely gift that Aodh intended to savor.

Meri moaned impatiently, then shivered and let her head fall back when Aodh dipped his tongue in for a taste. Her flavor was there too, but it was Neph he was after and he delved in hungrily, grabbing her thighs to hold her wider for him.

Sweet Mother, the taste of his lover was intoxicating, and he almost wished he could have had Neph's gift unadulterated by the essence of this nymph. Meri's taste was pleasant, and abundant the more Aodh licked her, but her presence was only a necessity.

He plunged his tongue in deep, seeking to lick every last drop of Neph from within her channel and off her slick lips. His beloved satyr's essence coated his tongue as he continued his onslaught of Meri's tender flesh, his arousal driving him to pull a body-shaking orgasm from her quickly so she would return the favor.

He couldn't bring himself to fuck her. Not yet, though Neph didn't have the same reluctance. The satyrs and nymphs in the Haven were much freer with their attentions. Dragons were generally just as free, but the significance of Meri's presence in their secret meeting place in the temple gardens beside the Nile was too significant for him to get past.

He wanted Neph as his mate. And even though the feeling was mutual, they'd be breaking laws and denying traditions in declaring their desires to the higher races. As two of those races' leaders, they had to set an example.

Breeding was an issue for the nymphaea, which meant Neph needed a female to do his duty to his home and his race. Meri might be that female.

"You could just fuck me," Meri said when Aodh rolled over and tugged at her shoulder to signal he was ready for her mouth on him. "My pussy's tight. Just ask Neph—he loves it."

"Can't risk it. You know that," Aodh said, though he knew there was no way he'd accidentally impregnate her without marking her. Their arrangement was secret, merely a cover for a deeper melding with Neph once Meri was safely pregnant with Neph's child.

Resting her hands on his thighs, Meri let out a sigh. "Listen, I know I'm not here for you to love, either of you. I'm not blind or stupid. Neph wants a deeper bond with you as much as you want it with him, but you need me to make it happen so you can keep up appearances. I'm all-in for my own reason—I want a baby. What nymph wouldn't be honored to be the chosen mate of a Dionarch and be the mother of his children? But you should know making sure *he* can pull this off when he and I are in public together depends on how close you and I are in private."

She stroked a skilled hand up the length of his shaft. Pleasure shot through him, making his body hum and his aura pulse around him. He propped himself up on his elbows and glanced down at her.

"Go on," he said, curious about her direction.

She pressed a kiss to the tip of his cock, sucked the head between her lips, and teased the underside with her tongue for a moment... just long enough for him to war with the impatient need for her to take him all versus his curiosity about what she might be about to suggest.

She released him with a pop and slowly stroked his rigid length.

"He needs to look like he loves me, but we both know he doesn't. He loves you. But if you and I were more closely bonded, it would make it as if we were one person. One soul in two bodies. He can have you when he has me, and he can have you when he has you. Happy Neph all the way around."

Meri went back to sucking him before Aodh could comment, his mind shutting down in response to her mouth. Happy Neph all around was all he could think of, and the idea made *him* happy. Happier than Meri's delicious lips and tongue working him to climax.

He lay in a buzzed stupor for several moments afterward, then gradually opened his eyes to see her swirling, expectant gaze.

"What exactly do we need to do? Are you talking about melding? Because Neph and I are already about as deeply melded as we can get."

"You aren't this deep. He won't share this with you because it's too sacred a bond, which is sad, really. But I care about the two of you and want you to be happy, so I'll make the sacrifice. All you need to do is give me a taste of your blood ..."

Aodh shot up and scooted away from her. "Absolutely not. *Our* blood is sacred ... mine and my siblings. It isn't possible for me to share it."

"Not possible? Or are you just not willing? Wouldn't you shed your blood for love, like we do? Every loving bond between a nymph and satyr pair is bound by a blood meld. There can be no deeper bond between us. Neph hasn't offered you that bond, has he?"

Aodh frowned, his heart in turmoil. Neph had melded with him so many times they shared their senses easily when they made love, like it was second nature. But when his lover was away, the satyr kept his mind shut off from Aodh. As one of the six members of the Dragon Council, Aodh understood the burden of responsibility, but his burden was not as great as his more powerful siblings'. Ked and Belah bore the heaviest burdens of their kind. Aodh's own responsibilities required less thought, more action; he was the dragon who oversaw the teaching and training of all the dragon Guardians, as well as the crafting of his people's temples and artifacts.

"I don't blame him for his responsibilities, Meri. I would never ask something of him that he wasn't willing to give."

"No, but wouldn't you give him something of yourself, if you could? If you knew your blood could be a gift to him, would increase his happiness, wouldn't you give it? Giving without asking in return is the ultimate proof of your love."

Aodh's chest tightened and he looked away for a moment, staring at the nearby fountain burbling up from the center of the lush gardens they lay in. He reached beneath the water with his mind through the portal into the Haven that lay on the bed of the river, seeking out the bond he had with Neph as unobtrusively as he could.

He found his lover's consciousness and hovered just on the outside, not wanting to intrude, but Neph seemed to sense him there and shifted his focus from whatever Haven-related task he was performing. A deep, welcoming warmth enveloped Aodh's being at that small bit of acknowledgment. No words were shared, but Neph's love was clear before he got back to business.

"I would give him my very soul if I thought we could get away with it," Aodh said.

"Then share your blood with me. You won't regret it."

CHAPTER 1

AODH

The Island of Ceylon, Inside a Temporal Bubble

Forget Fate—Time had just moved to the top of Aodh's shit list.

As an immortal, he'd taken time for granted. It was as plentiful as the air he breathed. But being trapped in a prison on an island in the river of time meant little expectation of enjoying more of his infinite life with his mates.

His life was no less infinite in this place—it was literally an island, and one he'd visited many times. Or *would* visit, he supposed. He didn't quite have the same broad perspective of time that the nymphaea had. But there was no mistaking that Nyx had locked him in a time bubble that day she'd sent him away from the Haven. He had no way to escape, and no expectation of being found anytime soon.

Because thanks to fucking Time, he now had even more than he wanted. The future he'd come from was more than three thousand years away, by his estimation of where ... or *when* he'd wound up. Even if Nyx came to her senses or, Mother forbid, Neph found out and came looking for him, it could happen at any time within that vast window of his past that now, paradoxically, stretched ahead of him like some well-trodden road he'd just as soon not walk down again.

Once was enough. He was ready to get on with his life, but the getting on part started where he'd left off, not … *now*. Whenever now was.

His time might be infinite, but the space he had on this island wasn't. Shortly after arriving, he'd tested the boundaries, shifting and flying as far as he could until he hit the edge. The magical barrier surrounding the island hadn't provided any resistance, and for a moment he'd believed he could just fly past the shore and into the world beyond, but within seconds he found himself turned around and aimed back the way he'd come without so much as a tilt of his wing.

He'd tested every direction, and finally determining that there was no escape within his power, he'd decided to get the lay of the land and spent a few hours flying a circuit around the borders. He recognized the place within only a few miles of winging above the island's moonlit shores. Ceylon wasn't vastly different from the last time he'd seen it, though parts of it looked distinctly less worn down, and it was missing the odor he recalled from when the dragons had first instituted their hibernations and retreated to the ancient temple on this very island.

Nyx had wanted him clear of Meri's influence, and she had certainly succeeded in her goal, because everything about this place suggested he was a few centuries too early for the nymph to even exist. She'd only been a few decades old when he'd fallen into her trap like some hapless fool. At the time, Meri had been one of the newest additions to the powerful squadron of the Haven's Thiasoi soldiers, hand-picked by Nereus himself. That meant she was in the circle of trust, one of the rare positions of honor granted only to those dozen assigned protectors of order within the Haven.

Her lack of attachment to one of the Thiasoi satyrs had meant she was perfect for their needs. A little too perfect, it turned out, once Aodh learned how she'd orchestrated the entire relationship to suit her own purposes.

He landed in a secluded cove that reminded him of the once-accessible entrance to the Haven. He dug his talons into the sand and shifted, staring out at the starlit water, still trying to process this turn his life had taken. As wild and open as this island was, it was still as much a prison as the room he'd been trapped in at the Stonetree Lodge no more than a day or so ago.

He stared up at the stars blindly for several moments. When he focused on the bright pinpoints in the black velvet, he had the perfect clock right there in the heavens, but what he saw didn't improve his mood. The arrangement of the constellations and the tilt of the Earth's axis only confirmed what he dreaded—Nyx had sent him far enough into the past that his presence would be meaningless to the enemy his blood might serve to lure. In fact, if his interpretation of the stars was correct, he was a good four centuries before Meri had even been born.

He clenched his fists impatiently, wishing for some outlet for the rage that bubbled forth. More than three thousand years—all the mistakes he had made stretched before him now, yet he could take no steps to change them as long as he was trapped here. And for how long. he had no clue, but given the vindictive Dionarch's command of time, he wouldn't put it past the Nyx to leave him to rot for centuries —he could very well be trapped here until he caught up to his own present, one plodding century at a time.

The island was familiar to him, at least, though the last time he'd visited, it was at least five centuries older. The vegetation was still lush, but the landscape now was harsher, having not been softened by age.

Ceylon was significant to his race, though it had been all but forgotten over the ages. His mind turned over the ancient memories. They hadn't cared about the place in some time, having far greater things to worry about than their ancient hibernation grounds. Dragons endeavored not to dwell on the past as a rule, and he and his siblings were no different. But something itched at the back of his mind. Some lost nugget of history that might be meaningful if he could just grasp it.

The hibernations … they'd begun not long after he and his brothers made their ancient pact to resurrect their sister. Their enemy had grown too strong, too ruthless for them not to take serious precautions. There had been six hibernations since the first. Six temples within which their children slept to protect each generation until they grew powerful enough to protect themselves.

The most recent was the temple in Sumatra, built by the Guardians of the last generation. Their ancient tradition had begun with the very first temple. Except they hadn't built the first one. Only five of the six temples had been built by the Guardians for the younger generation. The first temple had already existed, though they had no explanation for its presence or its design. The legend was that Fate and the Mother Dragon had created it for them in their time of need, and that the immense power infusing its many rooms, and even its very walls, was a divine gift intended to protect their young while they weathered the storm of attacks from their enemy.

That temple was on this island.

～

AODH STARED down at the slab of unmarred stone, struggling to reconcile his memories of the temple with what lay before him. The first dragon temple had been the only one with a visible above-ground structure, which had been painstakingly carved out of a granite mountain. *This* mountain that Aodh stood atop now. Yet here he was in the spot where a temple should have existed, and there was nothing but solid rock.

He shifted and took to the air for yet another circuit around the huge formation. There had to be a clue somewhere … a doorway perhaps. A magical cloak that had hidden the structure from his kind until they'd required it for their first hibernation. That event was still several centuries in the future from the time he'd been trapped in, and the temple had most certainly existed then.

He could recall every smooth, polished surface of the floors and walls, the carved stone columns that lined the corridors and supported the barrel vaulted ceilings. The intricate designs adorning the massive doors to each of the chambers intended for the first generation of newly designated Court dragons to hibernate within.

He and his siblings had found the temple when they decided to protect the future generations of dragons from their enemy's relentless hunting and capturing. Older generations were strong enough to stand against the Ultiori hunters Meri had corrupted and controlled, and the army of mind-controlled soldiers that she used Nikhil's vast military skills to command.

This island had drawn them in, not only due to its location being closely guarded by one of the ursa clans, but by its relative remoteness even from the other races. It had seemed ideally suited to dragons in much the same way the monastery's island had when they'd built that mountaintop refuge. In fact, the residents were some of the most receptive humans they'd ever met, once they arrived. It was as though they'd already recognized Aodh and his siblings as gods, tripping over themselves in order to serve.

The temple had shocked them with its ideal location, size, and magically protected barriers that opened only for them. The power infusing the place was so familiar it had to have been built by a dragon, but if it hadn't been any of them, their only conclusion was that the Mother Dragon had prepared it for them, with Fate as her guide.

So where was the fucking thing?

He wore himself out hunting the rugged mountain for something—*anything*—to indicate that the temple existed in this spot. He could envision it in his mind's eye, yet not even a hint of dragon magic existed where the temple should have been. Only stone and dirt and trees.

Landing at the peak of the mountain, he let out a frustrated bellow that echoed around the entire island prison. He dug his claws into the stony ground beneath him, kicking up boulders and flinging them into the air. He paced around what should have been the domed cupola roof, but was only dirt-covered rock.

As he paced, his tail swung from side to side in angry sweeps, tossing aside every loose object in his way. The not knowing ate at him. He had no way out of this place and no indication he'd be released at all. As far as Nyx was concerned, he was better off dead, only he couldn't die. She likely intended to leave him here permanently.

His mind churned over the implications of that thought. If he remained here, eventually his time would overlap with events he recalled. Except he remembered the day he'd entered the nonexistent temple with his siblings, and he hadn't been here. Only the perfect temple had stood in this spot, completely empty and waiting for the youngest generation of dragons to begin their hibernation within.

His talons hit something too hard to break and he realized he'd been unconsciously clawing into the earth beneath him in his rage. He angled his head to the side to peer with one big eye down at the ground. Something gleamed through the dirt, and he expelled a blast of hot wind from his nostrils to blow the dirt away.

His pulse picked up at the sight of the vein of crystalline quartz that shot through the stone. He remembered the shape of this stone and the way it let light filter into the temple below. Drawing back a fisted talon, he smashed it against the mountaintop with all his might, but only met unyielding stone with no hint of an echo to indicate what he stood on might be hollow.

With renewed energy, he worked to dig away the dirt and rocks from the area. After several hours of work, he'd clawed and swept several square dragon-lengths of the mountaintop clean so that the solid stone beneath was visible.

Taking a deep breath, he summoned as much power as he dared, then launched himself in the air a few hundred feet and angled his head down while he hovered, his massive wings holding him aloft. A gust of blue-white fire blasted from his mouth and hit the center of the stone beneath him with an impact that sent dirt and stone flying out in a massive cloud.

The entire mountain trembled, pieces of it crumbling away from the monolithic slab of stone. When Aodh ceased his blazing inferno, he landed with a heavy thud, gaze fixed in the center of the stone where his fire had been focused, his breathing shallow with utter disbelief.

An unmistakable starburst pattern adorned the stone where his fire had hit, a result of the quartz cracking and a vein of solid gold beneath it instantly melting and flooding into the cracks. It gleamed bright yellow, dimming to orange as it cooled, but the pattern was as familiar to Aodh as the scales on his own tail.

That starburst was the apex of the roof of the temple—a structure they believed had existed forever. Except if he'd been the one to create that pattern, that could only mean one thing.

He was the architect. Not the Mother or Fate, though Fate was most certainly the engineer behind this predicament he found himself in. Aodh himself had just put his mark on this island as the first dragon to set foot here, and though the paradox twisted his mind into uncomfortable knots, he knew better than to fight Fate. Just as attempting to fly through the barrier of his prison would only send him back in from the other side, running away from Fate's plan would only send him full circle, straight back into the trap he sought to avoid.

With a deep growl of resignation, he set to work. Most temples took an army of skilled Guardians several decades to complete. As the sole architect and artisan, he estimated this particular temple would take centuries.

At least he knew he'd have something to do for the next four hundred years.

CHAPTER 2

NEPH

Returning to the beginning was the exact opposite of progress, by Neph's definition. Yet here he was, glowering at the same icy creek that had been his exit point from the Haven mere days ago. His sister Nyx had truly gone mad if she'd locked even *him* out of their home.

When he'd absconded from the Haven with Calder and his mates, his only thought was protecting them from his sister's insane rampage. After a desperate stint of drifting around the world to all the potential portals that would take him back home, he'd discovered his sister had managed to block every last one. It had never occurred to him that Nyx would also bar her own brother from reentry. Yet here he was, still trapped on the outside, in the human world.

He felt like some kind of vagrant, having to try every last secret portal that only he or Nyx knew of to get back into the Haven.

"All right, sister. If this is how it has to be, so be it."

He could still feel her through the River and was not comforted by the wild churn of madness that answered him. Nyx was barely coherent now, having descended even deeper into madness since he'd left. He expected her to still be enraged—ever since losing Nereus, she'd been somewhat less than rational when the visions gripped her—but their connection granted him visuals more than thoughts, and what he saw confused the hell out of him.

In the short time he'd been gone, it seemed she'd already lost control of the Haven entirely to her daughter, though how it had happened he couldn't tell. Nor *when* it could have happened.

He suddenly had a strange sense of disorientation. Nothing felt right about this scenario. Not that Assana wasn't a capable leader of the Haven—she was the commander of the Thiasoi, after all. The image of his niece looked far more world-weary and sad than she had the last time he'd seen her. She sat upon her mother's throne with a dragon mate by her side, and not just any dragon, but the immortal Red who'd once befriended Nereus before Nyx had chosen the satyr as her mate. There had been a time when he wondered if Gavra would seduce his sister, when he even dared to hope the seductive Red would succeed. If he had, then Neph would have had some leverage to go public with his relationship with Aodh.

Clearly Fate had had a different plan for them all, if Assana had completed such a bond with a dragon that powerful. But there was something more that resonated across the distance that separated Neph from his niece. The pair of mates were linked, Assana's divine essence permeating Gavra as strongly as his filled her. They were blood-melded, and that fact had magnified her power exponentially. More than enough for her to keep the Haven safe until Neph could find a way back in, but when the hell had she had time to do this if not within the barely two days since he'd been gone?

He might have thought he was viewing Assana's future—

he'd looked into his loved ones' futures often enough in the past, but made it a policy not to dig unless he believed it affected the safety of the Haven directly. Yet the quality of this image was too crisp and distinct; it had the immutability of the recent past—something that had already happened and could not be changed.

He squatted down beside the creek and dipped his fingers into the water, grimacing at the chill but needing the additional link to the River to help him understand. The River gave him no clearer image of the Haven, only Nyx locked up in her grotto as though it were a prison, his niece sitting on the throne accompanied by her powerful mate, and a strange and unexpected sight in the center of the Haven, right at the Source.

An immense and glorious tree grew there now, piercing the misty veil that separated the Haven from the ursa Sanctuary above it and emerging from the very center of the lake that fed Gaia's Falls. The tree had Gaia's power written all over it, and while its presence was alarming, a flickering vision filtered forth from his memories of futures to come, giving him a sense that the tree belonged there, straddling all three worlds: Earth, Water, and Sky.

Still, there was no apparent route back inside for him.

With a sigh, he stood and rubbed his hands together briskly, breathing into them to infuse some warmth through his cold digits. He hated the cold, so he chose a more appropriate form to travel in that wouldn't require clothing to keep warm. One of the more hardy creatures of this forest who visited the nearby river would do.

A moment later he stood on four gray-furred paws, his thick pelt protecting him from the chill and his wolf's senses pricking up to scent the wind.

The scent of humanity was close, and he turned on his heels until he could make out a somewhat clear path through the woods away from the creek. Staring into the distance, his sense of unease grew when he took in the pristine, unmarred blanket of snow covering the forest path. Nothing but pure white without a single divot to indicate anyone might have passed by recently. He sniffed again, seeking the familiar, and eventually picked up the fading scent of his nephew and the young satyr's dragon and ursa mates.

Shaking off the sense of dread, he headed down the path following their aroma. The snow was almost a foot deep, with an icy shell on top that crunched beneath his fur-covered paws.

A bitter wind blew through, carrying tiny dry snowflakes that tickled his whiskers. His big paws crashed into the deep snow, kicking up tufts of it as he went.

After several minutes, he came over a rise and rounded a dense, green thicket of rhododendrons. A trail of smoke filtered up against the gray sky, and he picked up his pace as the cabin it belonged to came into view, a sprawling dwelling constructed of hewn logs with a porch that wrapped around its perimeter. Inviting dormers peered out from the second story like expectant eyes. The building exuded the promise of warmth and safety, something Neph hadn't expected to ever crave, but the cold had managed to seep through even his wolf's pelt and he ran quicker, desperate to get out of the damn cold.

He bounded up the steps onto the cabin's porch, shifting into his human shape as he moved, and immediately set his fists to the door, banging to be let in.

"Calder! Are you in there? It's Neph. We need to talk!"

A big shape filled the narrow, diamond-shaped panes of the door's window, and a second later it flew open, revealing a huge, bearded man with a tangled mane of gold hair. He stared at Neph in confusion, but the warmth that blasted from inside felt too good for Neph to care that a stranger had opened the door. Neph groaned and attempted to push past the big man, but was met with a pair of giant paw-like hands at his shoulders, holding him back.

"Hang on there, friend. I don't know you, but I sure as shit know this ain't your house. Want to try an introduction first?"

"Who the fuck are you? Where's my nephew? Let me the fuck in." He pinned the other man with the power of his spinning stare and the blond frowned, his grip on Neph's shoulders weakening. He seemed to waver on his feet as though losing balance, then blinked rapidly and shook his head.

"Don't know what the hell you are, man, but that won't work on me. I'm as steady as an oak in a heavy wind. Give me your name and I'll let you in to tell me the rest of your story. I'm betting since you're standing out there in nothing but skin, you've got a good one."

Neph gritted his teeth and forced himself to focus on the man. His huge frame and thick beard suggested ursa. Pale blue eyes, blond hair, and the obvious bulk of his big thighs—not to mention his very presence outside the Sanctuary—likely meant he was a Windchaser. One look deeper into the man's eyes told him everything else he needed to know.

"Arcadius Windchaser," Neph said. "I'm not your enemy. My name's Neph. I'm one of the Dionarchs of the Haven, and my goddamned sister's locked me out."

The ursa's eyes widened, his brows shooting up. "A fucking Dionarch? Since when do you guys ever leave the Haven?"

Neph scowled. "Since today. Can I come in now?"

The ursa released him and stepped to the side, pulling the door open wide and gesturing into the house with his free hand.

"Should I bow or something? Not sure what the protocol is."

"I don't fucking care," Neph said, rushing into the warmth of the cabin. He darted a quick glance around and grabbed a blanket that lay over the arm of a chair. Wrapping it around himself, he moved directly to the big fireplace and stood as close as possible, letting out a long groan as the warmth seeped into him.

"Your kin ain't here," the ursa said as he shut the door and approached Neph. He paused and leaned his big, flannel-clad shoulder against the heavy slab of wood that made up the mantel above the fireplace. "They ain't been here in a few days, in fact."

Neph's skin prickled with unease at the news. He pressed his lips together and looked at Arcadius. "How long? Exactly when did they leave?"

Arcadius frowned and scratched his beard. His gaze lifted to the ceiling. "Let's see, the Queen sent me out the same day Gaia's Falls dried up. I was to deliver a message that Nyx ... your sister, that is ... was holding the Source for ransom. And her payment was the two male dragons visiting us."

"Just the males?" Neph asked, knowing full well that Aurum's sister Numa was still in the Sanctuary. Perhaps it wasn't as bad as he thought.

Arcadius shrugged. "As far as I know. I don't ask questions ... I just do what I'm told. I brought the message to their sister. Didn't even know where she'd be—just that she was out here somewhere, and it was my mission to find her and tell her where her brothers wound up. I got lucky that she was here."

Neph settled down onto the worn sofa, his shoulders sagging as the weariness from the last few days of stress finally hit him. "I dropped them out here because it was the safest exit I could access quickly. Nicholas's bloodline directed my drift when I carried them out. So you didn't take long to find them. How long since they left?" He was ready to throttle Arcadius for taking his time with the answer.

"Oh, well, that was just three days ago, and they'd been here at least three days before that. At least enough time for that dragon to bake a freezer's worth of food. Brother, I don't know what I'd do without all that food she made. I mean, I can hunt and cook, but nothing like the gourmet shit that dragon put away."

Neph's stomach dropped. Six days. He'd known he could lose time by drifting too frequently, but had no idea it would be that much time. It'd been centuries since he'd even left the Haven. Struggling to keep his voice even, he said, "And where are they now, Arcadius?"

"Well, you can call me Cade, seeing as how I've seen you naked. They left right after I arrived. Said they would take the Queen's message to the other dragons so I didn't have to. They asked me to stay put in case anyone else left the Sanctuary. I was damn surprised to have anyone knocking on my door, much less a goddamn Dionarch. Lost, at that." He chuckled.

"Where did they go?" Neph asked, sitting forward and gripping his knees through the blanket.

"The turul Enclave. It's only an hour or so from here. They said someone named Nikhil is there and that he'd help them find the other fella's father and the lost Thiasoi. Said someone named Nereus is the best way to fix Nyx … that'd be your sister."

"Yes, I know who my sister is. She's the reason I'm fucking here to begin with. I have to find them. If they're going after the Ultiori, there are things they need to know."

Cade nodded slowly and eyed Neph from head to toe. "You're gonna want a better outfit to go back out in this shit. I'm about to bake one of those pot pies Aurum left. Sit and eat, warm up and get your bearings. The storm'll blow itself out by morning and you can travel in sunlight."

Confused, Neph darted a glance at the window only to see a completely white cloud of violently blowing snow. He shivered involuntarily.

Cade chuckled. "There's clothes in the closet upstairs that'll fit. The Queen said to make myself at home here, seeing as how I'd likely be stuck through the winter. Go ahead and do the same. Supper will be ready in an hour or so."

CHAPTER 3

NEPH

The Windchaser's weather sense held true. By the next morning, the snowfall had ceased and a clear blue sky looked down on the pristine white world beneath. Neph didn't waste time once he'd outfitted himself with warm clothes and gear from the upstairs closets in the house. He tried the men's clothes in the two bedrooms, but found the only clothes that fit were the ones belonging to the youngest male who'd lived here. Jasper was the ursa's name, Cade had said. The ursa Queen's younger cousin was a big man whose shirts must've easily fit Cade's broad shoulders, but were baggy on Neph's more streamlined frame. It didn't matter to him as long as they kept him warm.

Once he drifted to the mountain cliff that bordered the turul Enclave, only a few moments passed before a falcon soared into view, its russet feathers glinting in the winter sunlight. The huge bird shimmered as it landed, its torso growing and elongating as it took a more human form. The wings remained, as did the feathers that covered the bird's feminine curves.

The familiar face that emerged when the bird's head flowed into its new shape surprised him.

"Sophia North. I'm not sure I deserve the honor of having you greet me. You've aged well."

The striking, dark-haired woman smiled, her eyes glinting with the kind of knowledge another of his sisters—the Diviner—kept tight to her chest. Neither were females to be trifled with.

"So have you, Neph, but there are deeper signs of our age beyond our appearance. The fact that you're outside the Haven will no doubt take its toll on us all. But the truth is that I came to greet you because the others are busy making a plan of attack. It's good that you're here—you may want to talk your nephew out of the stunt he's planning. The way is open for a few more minutes. You may drift to him or fly. Your choice."

Beyond the edge of the cliff, a rippling in the air betrayed the presence of the opening in the barrier that shielded the Enclave. If Neph tilted his head just so, he could see the cliff-side structures on the other side of the chasm. Tilting the other direction, all he saw was another cliff that looked just like the one he stood upon.

"I don't have time to fly, if I can help it. Thank you, Sophia. I hope we have time to catch up later, but you'll have to forgive me if I'm in a hurry now."

He gripped her by the feathered shoulders and kissed her on the cheek. The ancient turul matriarch had always been a close friend, though one every bit as devious as his sister … more so, if his suspicions were true and she was in fact an agent of Fate even more elusive than the Diviner herself.

Sophia gripped his hand and held tight, pulling him closer and preventing him from leaving. "You are not meant to go with them, Neph. You may not have had time to see for yourself, but you will look, and when you do, you'll see. Fate's plan for you lies in that cabin you left behind."

His brows drew together. "In the cabin? But …" He shook his head, realizing it was a trick of words. Seers like Sophia North often spoke in riddles, or too literally to easily take a statement at face value. The only thing back in that cabin was a big ursa, whose entire life and history Neph had glimpsed the moment they'd met, and most of Cade's future had nothing to do with a lost satyr like him.

"I'll take your message under consideration," he said with a nod, then aimed his focus through the open portal to the impression of his nephew he sensed far on the other side.

The group didn't see him at first when he drifted into the busy dining hall. Hundreds of turul and dragons congregated, surrounded by packs and gear, apparently in preparation to leave. He easily blended into the mess and silently observed for a few moments as he made his way around the room to the front, where his nephew stood beside his mates and several others.

Calder was carrying on an intense conversation with another man as they leaned over a table, pointing at what appeared to be a map on its surface. Something about the other man triggered a chilly feeling in Neph's gut. If he could just see the man's eyes …

"Can we help you?" someone asked when Neph stopped on the opposite side of the table and stared pointedly at the stranger his nephew was talking to. He looked toward the speaker—an intense-looking man with stormy eyes, cropped black hair, and a glowing dragon mark on one side of his neck.

"Neph?" another voice asked, and gradually everyone stopped talking, their attention shifting to him. The second speaker he recognized by his deep green eyes and black hair, and let out a sigh of relief.

"Nicholas. It's so good to see you're safe."

The big ursa chuckled. "Thanks to you. What the hell are you doing here?"

He glanced at Calder, who finally tore his focus away from his conversation. His eyes widened. "Dion's balls, Uncle. Why aren't you back in the Haven?"

Calder trotted around the table and pulled Neph into a big hug, then held him at arm's length with a worried frown.

"Nyx ..." Neph began, but was cut off by a collection of curses as his nephew's mates came to stand by his side.

"We heard what she did," Aurum said. "Should we be worried that you didn't make it back inside?"

"I have to trust that Assana will do what she can. She's a strong girl. You all need to find Nereus."

"Come with us," Calder said. "We need every able-bodied creature we can recruit for this, Uncle. Nikhil's intent on going on the offensive against the Ultiori. Finding my dad is only the start of it."

Calder glanced at the man he'd been speaking with, who still stood on the other side of the table, arms crossed. Now that Neph could see the man's eyes, the chill increased. This man was touched by the River, and not in a good way. The remnants of his past clung to him, stains of the blood he'd spilled over centuries ... millennia ...

"You ..." Neph said, his voice low and menacing. "You're the one she corrupted."

"Might want to take a step back, brother," a male voice said, and a pair of hands belonging to two different men gripped his shoulders and held him.

Nikhil took a deep breath, regarding Neph for a long moment. Then he nodded and dropped his hands to his sides.

"Let him go, Iszak ... Lukas ... He's right to hate me, and wise to be cautious. Neph, I hoped we would meet because now that I'm free of Meri's spell, my mission is to *end her*. I'd hoped Aodh would get me into the Haven so we could speak, but it seems he's there and you're here, so I guess this was meant to be. Tell us Meri's secrets so we can destroy the bitch once and for all."

"You're fucking blood-melded to the bitch, and you don't know already?"

Nikhil closed his eyes for a beat, seeming to draw strength from within. He slowly shook his head as he opened his eyes. "She first melded me when I was weak. I was almost never in control during all the years we were melded. That's done now." He unbuttoned the cuffs of his shirt and slowly rolled up his sleeves, then pulled open his collar. His neck and wrists displayed brilliant glowing blue marks. Dragon marks the likes of which Neph had never seen, and filled with even more power.

"You belong to a dragon," he said.

"I have always belonged to a dragon," Nikhil said. "Meri stole me. Now that I'm back where I belong, I intend to make sure she pays for everything she made me do. Will you help?"

Soft murmurs flooded the room as Neph's identity was shared among the group. He glanced around, taking in all the creatures. Dragons and turul mostly, but there were a few humans too. Two of the humans he instantly recognized as dragon-blessed. Most were mated. In a rush of images, he saw all their futures too quickly to fully process, but the kaleidoscope of lives was so complete without a single gap, it was clear there was no space for him.

At least until he returned his gaze to the closest group. He met the eyes of the dragons who were his counterparts as leaders of their race. Belah, Aurum, and Ked stood side by side. Within their futures, he saw the place where he belonged. That unfilled space belonged to their three missing siblings, who he easily envisioned right beside them where they belonged. And beside Aodh's vacant spot were two other conspicuously empty places … too empty for Neph to deny.

There was only one dragon whose future he was tied to, and that dragon wasn't in this room. No one in this room required his presence to complete their journey.

"I will tell you what I can about our enemy, though I regret it won't be much. I knew Meri as a skilled Thiasoi fighter and an ambitious nymph. I believed she might make a worthy mate at one time."

"You loved her," Nikhil said. Not accusingly, but as a simple statement.

"No. I loved what she could offer me and Aodh. That was all."

He gritted his teeth against the tightness in his chest. Everyone was listening so intently he could hear heartbeats and nothing else.

Under his breath, he said, "You all remember how strict our laws were at the beginning. Love wasn't recognized as true unless a child was produced from a union. Did Fate even grant the turul an excuse if two males found each other? Were there ever true mates of the same gender who otherwise would never have been recognized as mates?"

A clear, female voice rang out. "Never in our history has Fate's mark shown a turul a mate that wouldn't be accepted. This generation is the first to choose one who wasn't either human or turul, or of the opposite gender."

Neph shot a look over his shoulder and saw Sophia moving through the crowd toward them.

"Meri was meant to carry our child, nothing more," Neph continued. "And she was willing, but she thought to begin a blood meld without a bond of love. I would never have blood-melded her. I didn't take that step with Aodh only because of the limitations on our relationship. We could never be public about it, even with her as our third. As Dionarch, I couldn't let my feelings cloud my judgment. The Haven mattered too much. It matters even more now."

"Does she wish to return home?" Nikhil asked.

"You tell me. My guess is she wants power. Her blood meld with Aodh gave her a taste of immortality. She's found a temporary means of persisting since then, but that would never be enough. Even if she managed to acquire the body of an immortal to inhabit, she would always have to share it with their spirit, or some remnant of their connection if it was an even swap. The only thing powerful enough to grant true immortality is the Source, but there's no way in hell we'll let her get back into the Haven."

Nikhil nodded. "That's comforting to hear, but what I know about her is that she's nothing if not dedicated to her goals. If she was willing to have a child with two immortals, that tells me she was likely after this goal long before she blood-melded Aodh. Producing a hybrid baby was the purpose of her experiments as long as I've known her. She made it *my* goal for some time, feeding on my craving for a child of my own. I have reason to believe she succeeded in at least creating a hybrid embryo ... but that was the last thing that happened before I defected, so I have no way of determining if my suspicions are correct. Whether the child was viable or not, I don't know, nor have we been able to confirm. If she wants the Source to help give that child immortality ... it would be the first step in building an entire immortal army that would be impossible for us to beat."

"An immortal army," Neph said. "But no one can access the Haven now. The Sanctuary is locked down until the Equinox. No one is getting in."

"How could she make it happen, is what I need to know," Nikhil said in a level tone. "Think."

Neph shook his head. "It isn't possible. The Source itself

is how we travel in and out. When the portals are active, they're connected to the Source ... powered by it. But thanks to my sister, the Source is almost entirely shut off from the rest of the world now. Only the Sanctuary has access, otherwise the ursa would die."

"Which was what Nyx was threatening to do if the Queen didn't send her our brothers," Belah said.

"They'll be fine," Neph said. "The fact that Nyx didn't request your sister suggests that she's interested in them as mates for the nymphs. She's been desperate for more satyr offspring for ages, but hadn't yet managed to talk me into it. I don't take mating lightly."

"Your sister isn't a danger to the Source, is she?" Nikhil asked

"On the contrary. Nyx's madness is entirely focused on keeping Meri out of the Haven and away from the Source. She was willing to risk a war with the ursa to protect it, in fact. If there's any weakness, it would lie with the Sanctuary's barrier and the portals inside. Cade tells me the guardians have all been called home so there are no protectors on the outside."

"The barrier is strong." Aurum scowled at him. "My siblings and I made sure of that when we entered. Anyone not attuned to the barrier will be killed if they try to pass through on the Equinox. It's impenetrable any other time."

Neph's eyebrows shot up. "You've added fire magic to the Sanctuary's barrier? That's good. In that case, it will be nearly impossible to breach. I doubt even I'd be strong enough to get through. I think we have little to worry about now, until we can learn more details of what she has planned."

Calder stood up a little straighter. "That's the next step. If we're going to ensure the Haven and the Source are secure, we need both you and my mother inside and in control.

Preferably of your own minds, too. I have a plan to find my father, which I think is the first step. If we can rescue him and get a message back to Mother, she may regain her sanity enough to allow us back inside. Come with us to find my father."

Looking into his nephew's eyes, a troubling image appeared of the younger satyr unconscious and connected to tubes, floating inside a transparent tank of liquid. Five other satyrs hung suspended near him, all in the same state. One of those other satyrs' faces made his heart lurch in his chest. His closest friend and his sister's mate, Nereus, was trapped in there. It was the clearest vision he'd had of his old friend in ages, no doubt brought on by Calder's determination to carry out his plan.

This vision of his would happen, whether he liked it or not, but he wasn't meant to be part of it. The only thing he could influence was Calder's understanding of the future he was headed toward, and provide him with the tools to survive.

"This path you've chosen is dangerous, Calder, but I can see there is no other path for you. Unfortunately, my path lies in another direction. If Assana succeeds in getting the dragons released from my sister, I want to be close to the Stonetree portal in case Aodh exits. My journey is by his side, that much I'm sure of. I can give you one gift, however."

He took a deep breath and looked at Aurum and Nicholas, who had moved to stand by the side of their mate. Perhaps that vision of Calder trapped in a tank like some lab specimen was only a short snippet of the worst moment. He had seen numerous visions of people's deaths during his brief scan of the room—some would die during the course of this mission, others in the distant future. Babies would be born and matings forged. Their races would be stronger with each new bond.

He hadn't seen Calder's death, and for that he was grateful. But there was one thing he could do to ensure his nephew survived what he had seen.

"You must blood meld your mates before you leave. If the love between the three of you is as true as it seems, a melding as intimate and permanent as a blood meld will strengthen your powers exponentially. Meri won't expect it because she never properly understood how a blood meld was meant to work." He directed his next comments to Nikhil. "She overpowered your mind by brute force. If there had been love between you, the outcome would have been far different. You've shared blood with someone stronger since, haven't you?"

"He has my blood. He's had it from the start," the blue-eyed Belah said.

"And yet not even that prevented Meri from influencing you?" Neph asked.

"I let the taint of betrayal drive me," Nikhil said. "I don't back down easily once I've decided on vengeance. It took Belah's blood and her undying love to bring me back, along with a turul's song."

"Use the turul to your advantage, then. If they could break her spell on you, they'll be invaluable. And Calder … when you do find Nereus, which you will, a drop of your own blood could revive his mind. You are Nyx's son and her power runs through your veins. All he will need is that small taste to remind him who he is."

"Are you sure you won't come with us?" Aurum asked.

"Perhaps later I can join you all, if Assana succeeds in bringing her mother to her senses without us. If that happens, we should take the fight to Meri, and I'd love nothing more than to join you all when you attack."

"We're headed to the first dragon temple, in Sri Lanka,"

Nikhil said. "It's the most secure location that can house the army I'm building."

Neph nodded. "I know the island well. We used to have several portals there. If there's flowing water within the temple, a drop of Calder's blood in the water will allow me to locate you easily via drift. Good luck."

As much as he hated leaving his nephew to carry out this mission without him, Neph was anxious to get back to the cabin. He couldn't see what awaited him in his own future, but he knew Cade's future was likely to be just as dull for some time. The pair of them would make good company while they bided their time.

"Uncle, wait," Calder called just as Neph stepped out onto the chilly balcony, preparing to drift back to the cabin as soon as Sophia opened the barrier for him again.

Calder approached him alone, his brows drawn.

"What is it?" Neph asked.

"The blood meld … Are you sure we really ought to do that? It's been against Haven law ever since Meri was expelled. I don't want to go down that path if it's going to jeopardize my relationship with my mates."

"It's likely to have the opposite effect," Neph said. "Do you love them? And do you believe Fate has tied you to them?"

Calder chuckled. "Aurum does. And I do too. Nicholas … well, he's never exactly hidden his feelings."

"A blood meld will only make you stronger in every way. Don't worry about what the rest of the Haven thinks … The safety of our home may depend on you taking this step. If the love is truly as strong as you say between the three of you, there is nothing to fear. The bond is permanent. Even without love involved, the power of shared blood never leaves. It can only be overridden by a stronger bond."

"Like the bond you have with Aodh … That's how you broke

Meri's spell over him, isn't it? I remember the day it happened. You and Mother caught Meri when she flew off as the dragon. You gave him a drop of your blood to banish her from his mind. Why didn't you ever complete the meld with him?"

Neph swallowed and shifted his gaze into the distance. The old memories rushed back uninvited. Old regrets.

"I couldn't," he finally said. "And it's one of my greatest regrets. To publicly claim a dragon as my blood-melded mate —especially a male dragon who I couldn't breed with— would have turned the entire Haven against me. The blood meld would have signaled our exclusivity, even though we'd have been willing to accept a third. And after Aodh's mistake, we had no choice but to banish him from the Haven."

"But it was Meri's doing."

"I know that, but she'd already had all the female Thiasoi convinced otherwise—that Aodh was the instigator. I knew he was better off away from the Haven. Meri's actions should have resulted in execution, but we banished her as well."

Calder nodded, and Neph was grateful that his nephew didn't bring up that old mistake. It was something they'd all become painfully aware of as soon as they recognized Meri's stamp on the atrocities that began less than a century after her expulsion from the Haven.

"For what it's worth, I hope you find him soon," Calder said. "I regret not staying with Nicholas and Aurum to begin with. If I had, none of this shit with Mother would be happening."

He gave Calder a long-suffering smile and a pat on the shoulder. "Your path was written the moment you were born. You should know this by now. Do the right thing as a satyr who loves his mates. Blood meld them and make your bond an everlasting one. You may need their power on your mission to infiltrate the enemy's base."

Calder stiffened. "You've seen something, haven't you? Tell me before I go."

Neph shook his head. "You know the visions don't always make sense. All I know is that you will find your father. What happens beyond that is up to you."

Calder gave him a curt nod, his throat working with barely checked emotion. Neph pulled him into a tight hug and squeezed. "If I believed my path was beside you, nothing could keep me away. It's time for me to return to where Fate wants me."

CHAPTER 4

VRISHTI

*V*rishti was grateful for the clothing Emma had loaned her when she passed through the Stone-tree portal into the bitter chill of winter on the other side. When she'd first entered the Sanctuary a few weeks earlier, she'd come from one of the warmest, wettest spots on the planet, so she hadn't brought the type of gear necessary to trek through the winter wilderness of Appalachia.

The dense forest around her had a thin layer of snow still covering the ground, though if the gray clouds were any indication, it might soon be replenished. She easily found the path Emma had described and followed it down the mountain, her boots crunching along the frozen ground and the dead leaves as she went.

She hiked for an hour, pausing periodically when she caught a glimpse of the majestic views through the bare trunks of the trees. She wasn't in the remotest place in the world, but it certainly felt like it. She saw no signs of humanity until after more than an hour when she finally spied a thin trail of smoke rising up from a valley in the direction the path was taking her.

She stopped and took a deep breath, suddenly filled with trepidation about the meeting she was about to have. The meeting she both hoped for and dreaded, if Nyx had been right and the Dionarch's brother was staying at the cabin the ursa Queen's father and uncle had built in these woods.

"He's going to understand," she told herself, though she wasn't sure if she believed it. How much should she tell him, anyway? Would he laugh at her when she said Aodh had promised himself to her? Aodh and Nyx's brother had thousands of years of history behind them. Even if they were estranged, that counted for a lot, especially compared to some naïve, virginal woman who'd shared one kiss with the man they'd be looking for. One kiss! Sure, it wasn't her first kiss, but it hadn't been far from it.

And would Neph even be willing to entertain the idea of what she was going to propose? Could *she* find the guts to even ask?

The toe of her boot snagged on something hard and she let out a squeal, flailing her arms to try to catch her balance. Just as she was about to fall on her face, a strong arm wrapped around her waist, yanking her backward.

"I gotcha," a rough voice said against the back of her neck.

Vrishti stiffened, her heart racing to the edge of panic. The arm released her and she turned around so fast her heel caught on the same errant root and she nearly toppled again. The man grabbed her arms and steadied her a second time.

"Whoa, kiddo. Steady there." He held onto her for a second longer and then slowly released her once she stopped moving, as though she might tip over if he wasn't careful. This gave Vrishti a second to take in the huge man's bearded face and shaggy blond hair. Just about all she could see in the midst of the mess were laughing eyes the color of glaciers. She thought he might be smiling under that thick beard, but she wasn't quite sure.

"Are you Neph?" she asked, blurting the question out before she could censor herself. She'd been so focused on her eventual meeting with the satyr it hadn't occurred to her whether she might run into anyone else.

The man's brows shot up and he barked a laugh. "That thin-skinned bastard? Hell no. He sticks to the indoors in this weather. Satyrs never could handle the cold. I'm Cade, Windchaser ursa, through and through."

He stood back and stretched out his arms, giving Vrishti a full frontal view of his very, *very* naked body. She gaped as she took in all his muscular, furry glory, right down to the thick length of flesh hanging between his thighs. After a second, a big hand drifted down and covered it up and her eyes shot back up to his.

"Don't pay no mind to him. He shrinks up in weather this cold."

Vrishti's mouth fell open, but she caught herself before she could comment on his so-called shrinkage. If what she'd seen had been a shy penis, she'd better avoid him when he warmed up.

When she didn't manage to find words, Cade leaned toward her and said, "So, you're here for the old stag, eh? I was headed back that way anyway after making a circuit around the stones. Somehow had a feeling something would be different today, and I wasn't wrong because here you are. What's your name, kiddo?"

"Vrishti Rainsong," she said. "And yeah, I'm looking for Neph. You must be the Windchaser who came to bring the message to Aurum and Nicholas. How are they?"

"Not sure. They were in a hurry to move on once I gave them the news about Aurum's brothers. I guess it's my turn to ask you … is everything all right at home? They set things right inside? Did the dragons make good?"

He started walking and she fell into step beside him as

they headed down the mountain, still awed by his utter lack of modesty or sensitivity to cold—at least aside from his *shrinkage.*

"Sort of. The Sanctuary's safe and so is the Haven. I'll tell the whole story once we get to Neph since it's all stuff he needs to hear anyway, if that's all right."

"Good, because that poor bastard's been bouncing off the walls since he got here. Gives new meaning to cabin fever."

"Is he … is he all right? I met his sister and she went a little nuts, so I worried whether that was something that affected them both because they'd been separated, you know?"

Cade frowned and rubbed his beard. "Well, if you mean is he sane, then I suppose. If I had to guess what's troubling him, I'd just say he needs to get laid, but that's no surprise seeing as how he is what he is."

"What he is?" Vrishti asked.

"Yeah, the ruttingest rutting stag in history. Only Dion himself ever had more play this guy. Funny thing is that even though he acts like he's all full of pent-up lust, he hasn't so much as glanced at my ass. Been perfectly behaved save for the stiffy he sports half the time. Puts me to shame. Which is why I'm perfectly happy he hasn't asked. Much as I'd love to help him out, my backside isn't ready for another commitment of that … ah … *magnitude.* Tell me, why'd they send a Rainsong out, anyway? I'd have expected another Windchaser."

Vrishti took a second to register his question after the fascinating commentary on Neph's legendary libido. For the first time, she was surprised that this ursa didn't know who she was.

"I'm Sathmika's daughter …" she began slowly, not sure how much she really wanted to divulge just yet, but this big ursa seemed genuinely curious.

"The Summer shaman," he said thoughtfully. "I knew she had to have a secret love child out there somewhere. It's like all the shamans made some kind of pact. I wouldn't be surprised if Solina and Brigit did the same thing. That doesn't explain why you're here, though. And what it's got to do with Neph."

"You are curious, aren't you?"

"Hey, I fully expected to be stuck in that cabin alone for the winter, but somehow people keep showing up. Well, I was the one who showed up first, but then when Nick and his mates left, I had a whole couple days to ponder my solitude before Neph crashed my one-bear party. Said he was waiting for a friend … Didn't say who, but I got the distinct impression that friend was a male. Figured it was one of those dragons, and he didn't look happy about having to wait. Except he did look awfully excited just the same. Fucking confusing fucker."

Vrishti laughed as Cade shook his head. "You're the most talkative recluse I've ever met."

"Known a lot of recluses, have you?" he asked, a spark of humor in his eye.

"One, at least … My dad was pretty solitary. Unless I was at home, he didn't really socialize. I think he secretly always wished he could be with my mother again."

Cade was quiet for a moment before saying, "I take it he didn't get that chance."

She swallowed and shook her head. "He made it through the portal at the end, at least, but Mom says if he was dying, the power of the barrier would have absorbed him. That his spirit is part of what protects the Sanctuary now."

They remained silent, Cade's mood bordering on broody.

"I'm sorry," she finally said. "I didn't mean to ruin the mood. Dad was a recluse, but he wasn't much of a talker even when I was home. All he wanted to hear about was how my life was going, so I did the bulk of the talking. Not a lot happened in the village where I grew up, so he loved hearing my stories from school. I guess I'm glad I get the chance to listen for a change."

Cade shot her a warm smile, which really just amounted to a crinkling around his eyes and a slight upward curve in his mustache, since she couldn't see his mouth.

"Don't tempt me, kiddo. I can talk your ear off all night. Neph isn't one for conversation, so if you're around for a while, I'll have plenty of stories to make up for it."

"I'd like that," Vrishti said. "If I'm around for a while, but I don't know if I will be."

Cade frowned, then let out a sigh. "Story of my life, I guess. People come into it, then leave again. I suppose there are worse places to spend my solitude, though. I get plenty of visitors even if nobody stays, and it's beautiful here. You should see these woods when they're alive. Every season is magic. Especially winter, though you wouldn't know it now. Just wait until tomorrow—we're getting snow tonight, so you'll see the magic when you wake up."

"But if you're alone all the time … Don't male ursas have to worry about their pheronesis every month?"

Cade snorted. "Kiddo, when you get to be my age, a quick yank is enough to settle that right down, but I can always go down to the human town and find a willing partner for a night. Females have it harder until they mate. I'm sure you're no stranger to the issues."

Vrishti darted a quick glance at him, biting her lip. Cade narrowed his eyes and stopped in the middle of the path. "Tell me you've hit your estrous and are done with it. You're the prime age for your first one. Your mama wouldn't have let you leave the Sanctuary without getting through that."

"I didn't exactly give her a choice," Vrishti said. "There's too much at stake for me to sit in there and do nothing.

Besides, I knew that you … and … and Neph would be here, and …" She trailed off as his shaggy brow descended, and backed up a step at the ominous look he gave her.

"Kiddo, I may be trained to help you, but your first estrous is a big deal. You'd need *two* of me to get through it, if you're Summer's daughter."

"But Neph …"

Cade's eyes widened and he let out an amazed laugh. "You think you're gonna rely on the stag to help? You get within a mile of a satyr that powerful when you're in heat, *helping* will be the last thing on his mind. Satyrs *fuck*, kiddo. It's just how they're built, and this one hasn't been laid in far too long." He stood, shaking his head at her with his hands on his naked hips, then stared up at the sky. "Gaia's tears, this must be a test. Fate's fucking testing me, the old bastard."

"I haven't hit it yet … not even close," Vrishti said meekly. "If anything, I was hoping to have it happen with you because I need access to that power. I know a spell to help Neph get home, but I won't be strong enough to cast it without hitting my estrous."

"Is it really just about getting him home?" he asked, his eyes narrowed again as he regarded her.

Vrishti pressed her lips together.

"Didn't think so," Cade said. "And I take it you'd rather wait until we're at the cabin before you talk. Fine. Come on, we oughta keep moving."

He brushed past her and lumbered down the path at a pace that had Vrishti jogging to catch up. Out of breath, she asked, "How much farther is it?"

"'Nother half hour." His clipped tone told her he was done with conversation.

She'd just barely arrived, and already she'd fucked things up. She'd been hopeful when she crossed through, but her optimism was quickly eroding the longer she jogged after the big ursa.

Her mother had tried to talk her out of going, at first. Then when Vrishti had refused, Sathmika had offered to send a pair of ursa males with her "just in case."

But it'd been the same pair who had serviced her cousin Revna, and she had trouble even looking at the pair without imagining all the filthy things Revna had described about their time together.

In the end, Sathmika had kissed her goodbye and said a brief spell that had left a tiny sunburst mark in the center of Vrishti's chest. She could still feel the mark pulsing with power.

"For protection, baby," was all her mother had said when she'd asked what it meant.

After about twenty minutes, the path emerged onto a gravel road that Cade followed up an incline. Vrishti was winded and sweaty beneath her layers of warm clothing. She tugged off her hat and scarf and unzipped her parka, shrugging out of it. They had to be close.

Cade glanced back at her and chuckled, slowing to a walk again so she could catch up.

"For an ursa girl, you sure do bundle up."

"I'm a Rainsong," she muttered. "Not used to cold weather."

"I guess there is that. The Queen's mates hated it last year when they had to man this post until they got Windchasers to take over. Those boys of summer do have thin skins, but still, you're ursa. You've got nothing on that stag where hate of the cold is concerned. Which reminds me, I need to get more wood chopped so his delicate constitution isn't offended. Gotta keep the man warm, and I'm not about to offer a snuggle at night. You go on in and introduce yourself."

He paused in front of a huge block of wood that looked like a tree stump and wrenched an axe out of the edge of it.

Vrishti stared at the idyllic cabin with its pretty eyebrow dormers and rambling porch that wrapped around the perimeter. The building wasn't quite the cabin she'd envisioned. She'd pictured something built out of solid logs like the clan lodges inside the Sanctuary, but this house had been meticulously constructed, every detail showing the immense care that had gone into its design.

"Emma grew up *here?*" she asked.

"And her cousins," Cade added, then brought the axe down hard into a big block of wood, sending two halves flying off to either side. Vrishti took a few steps forward to stay out of the path of more chunks, but couldn't bring herself to walk up the steps onto the porch. After what Cade had told her about Neph, she was even more anxious about meeting him.

When the door swung open, she jumped and stepped behind the rear fender of the big pickup truck in the driveway.

"Cade, you cooking tonight or am I? We've got frozen venison or frozen venison. Every goddamn thing is frozen. I found more pie in that freezer, though. Says 'blackberry' on it. Does that sound good?"

Cade shot a look over his shoulder as he positioned another block of wood for chopping. "You know how to work the stove, man. Go for it. Set a timer this time so shit doesn't burn. It'd be a damn shame if we burned down the Queen's house."

Vrishti stared at the man who stood at the top of the steps, trying to reconcile Cade's assessment of him with the actual visual. He was beautiful … as beautiful as Aodh, if she'd been shown a photo negative. He had shining black hair that looked like he'd just gotten out of the shower. The wavy locks brushed his shoulders, curling at the ends around the collar of a deep blue flannel shirt. He was the spitting image of his sister, but with far less delicate features. Swirling blue eyes were deep set in a strong-boned face, his wide jaw extending to a cleft chin beneath full lips.

"Put some fucking clothes on, Cade. I'm freezing my balls off just looking at you."

"I'm chopping wood for your goddamn fire, you frigid bastard. I'll do it how I want … warm enough from the exertion at any rate. Besides, the lady doesn't seem to mind, do you, kiddo?"

Cade shot her a grin and Vrishti nearly ducked behind the truck to avoid Neph's attention for just a little longer. Now that she'd actually *seen* the man, she really couldn't bring herself to talk to him.

But it was too late. Neph's dark brows rose and he finally turned to look at her. In that instant, Vrishti's insides turned to jelly. Dizziness overwhelmed her in a way it never had in the moments when she'd talked to Assana, or even to Nyx. They both had the same strange swirls in their eyes, but they were nothing compared to the immense power of Neph's that seemed to suck her straight into an abyss.

Gravity failed her then, and the next thing she knew, she was on her back listening to the sounds of a pair of men cursing and calling her name.

CHAPTER 5

NEPH

He hadn't seen her coming. He'd been so blind to her, he nearly hadn't seen her when she was standing right in front of him, either. But when the beautiful young woman lost her balance and collapsed, there was no mistaking her presence anymore.

Cade rushed to her first, calling her name. It took Neph another second of staring in surprise before he jumped to action.

"Vrishti, kiddo. Snap out of it," Cade said, and Neph immediately picked up her name and said it too. He ignored the cold gravel under his denim-clad knees, still too shocked by her appearance to care that the cold was seeping into his skin.

"Vrishti, you're all right, you're here," he said, earning him a shocked look from Cade. He had no idea where the words had come from—they'd just made sense. When Cade moved to scoop her up into his arms, he pushed the big ursa back. "Let me. You still need to get dressed."

Neph lifted her easily, leaving her small pack behind on the ground. Cade's lack of clothing meant nothing to him, really. He just wanted to hold her. It was a strange instinct, but one he couldn't deny having. That it could only mean one thing was the last thing he wanted to think about right now. He'd focus on that once he got her inside and made sure she was all right.

Pushing backward through the half-open door, he kicked it closed behind him and headed toward the living room. The fireplace crackled with a huge fire that he'd fed only moments before stepping out onto the porch to … shit, he couldn't even remember why he'd gone outside now.

She blinked up at him groggily when he laid her down on the overstuffed sofa. Sweat beaded on her brow and she let out a soft moan when she met his gaze.

"Seasick …" she muttered, her face growing pale and taking on a distinctly greenish tinge that he was sure had nothing to do with her ursa heritage. She shook her head, swallowed thickly, then closed her eyes and moaned the word "sick" again.

"Fuck," Neph muttered when he figured out what was wrong. He rushed to the kitchen, dumped the bowl of cut potatoes onto the counter, and hurried back with the empty dish, reaching her side just in time for her to roll over and retch.

After emptying her stomach, she managed to sit up, but kept her head bowed and her elbows on her knees. Her color seemed a little more normal now, a warm brown with a ruddy glow that betrayed a love of the outdoors. Dark curls had escaped her thick, black braid and coiled sweetly around her cheeks. He resisted reaching out and touching one, just to see if she was real.

"Your eyes," she said in a faint voice he almost didn't hear.

"What about them?" he asked.

"Looking at you is like … sailing in rough water … I've never been good with boats. Always get seasick."

He let out a sigh of relief. That's all it was?

Standing, he headed to the small downstairs bathroom and disposed of her sick in the toilet, then rinsed out the bowl. He glanced up at his reflection in the mirror, into those familiar chaotic depths that hadn't been calm in eons. His eyes were even wilder now, mirroring the churn of emotions inside him at her arrival.

No wonder she'd gotten sick after looking at him. He gripped the counter and forced himself to take a deep breath and calm the wildness inside him. It was no easy feat. He'd been angry for weeks, and despite being as even-tempered as any satyr could get—you learned not to give a shit about most things when you were as old as he was—he still had a hard time calming himself now.

His world felt like it had been falling apart for ages. A slow and steady, but inevitable crumbling that had begun the day they'd banished Meri from the Haven instead of executing her. He'd exiled a part of his own emotional foundation that same day and had paid the price ever since.

Now that his sister had lost her shit and taken over the Haven, he had nothing. One last mad dash to protect Nyx from herself had only gotten him locked out of his home. His nephew was safe, at least, so Nyx wouldn't have that on her conscience.

He supposed it was fitting, now that the world was finally giving up and falling into pieces around him, that he'd be trapped in exile the same as he'd done to Aodh all those years ago. Forced out of the Haven with no hope for return, no welcome in store.

Except for this girl … as a satyr so tightly connected with the River that he could see events backward and forward for ages, he should have seen her coming. That he didn't only meant one thing … Vrishti was here for him, and her presence was so significant his life was bound to hers as inextricably as it was to Aodh.

Slowly the mad storm around his dark pupils calmed, until he even managed to reach a clear, serene aqua again. The shade reminded him of the cove at the mouth of the Haven, with its crystalline waters and pale, soft sand. He hadn't seen those eyes in the mirror in a while, but he had to get his shit together if she was here now.

Whoever she was.

Vrishti … an ursa female. A very beautiful ursa female, as far as he'd been able to tell, despite the wan look he'd left her with. But any more than that he had no way of knowing without actually asking her.

"Feeling better?" Neph asked on his way back through the living room. He didn't stop to look at her this time. Even though he was sure there was no danger in making her seasick again, he suddenly felt off balance in her presence. He tossed the bowl into the kitchen sink and turned on the oven to preheat, then went back to chopping vegetables.

When she didn't answer, he looked up from his task to see her staring at him, wide-eyed and unmoving.

"Vrishti … are you well?" he asked. She appeared to have recovered, and had shed a few more layers in the last few minutes. She was no longer green or clammy; her skin had returned to a healthy shade with the pink glow of someone who'd recently come in from the chilly winter air. She wore a snug gray Henley and well-worn jeans that were threadbare in the knees. She'd taken off her boots and stood in thick stockinged feet in front of the fireplace, looking like she'd been about to go somewhere, but had gotten frozen in place.

"Sorry," she said, dropping her gaze to her feet. "I … um … came because … you're Neph. And, well … um… Aodh … ah … *fuck.*"

Neph couldn't help but smile at her awkward stammering. It had been a long time since he'd been around a woman who hadn't already known him for thousands of years. But he had to break the ice somehow if he was going to get anything out of her.

"Vrishti, look at me." Thinking quick, he grabbed a couple carrots, made a few quick cuts, and then fixed the pieces to his face … two in the ears, two in his nostrils. Then he screwed up his mouth and stuck out his tongue in the goofiest manner he could think of and crossed his eyes.

She hesitantly lifted her face and abruptly burst out in laughter.

"Oh my god!" she blurted out as she doubled over in hysterics. "That's the funniest thing I've ever seen. Please … please stop!" She glanced up at him once, let out another giggle and shook her head. Tears streamed down her cheeks as she held her stomach, this time it was spasming with mirth rather than nausea, at least.

He'd done his job. He retrieved the carrot sticks from his face and tossed them into the sink.

"Better?" he asked with a smile.

Vrishti sighed and nodded. "I'm sorry about that. I just freeze up around exceedingly pretty people."

"It must be impossible to look in the mirror, then," he said, eliciting a bright blush.

She rolled her eyes. "Give me a break, have you seen yourself? I mean … wow." She came toward him, some of her earlier hesitance returning, but she seemed more curious now and less completely overwhelmed.

"It's just a face," he said. "I have many. This is just the one my parents gave me, and the one I don't have to put any effort into wearing."

She slid onto a barstool across from him. "Oh, I like it. Never change."

"I'm a water shifter, Vrishti. Changing is what I do." He

focused on her face and shifted his own features to match, right down to the tiny dark mole that adorned her upper lip.

"Okay, now *that* is going too far. Not funny." She scowled at him. "I like you better as you."

He reverted to his natural human face, wondering how she might react to the face when it was part of his primal form. His features never changed … only his body and his personality, every desire brought fully to the surface.

"Good," he said. "I like me better as me too, but sometimes a different face is required. Now, are you going to tell me your story now that you can string together a full sentence?"

He turned away while he waited for a response, focusing his attention on the chunk of deer roast he'd pulled out of the huge chest freezer in the cabin's cellar. With a touch, he made quick work of the crystallized water molecules inside, returning them to a liquid state. Then he put the roast into a pan surrounding it with the vegetables he'd chopped and shoved the whole thing into the oven.

When he looked back at Vrishti, she was frowning at him.

"What?" he asked.

"You're not a very good cook."

"I'm not a very picky eater. This is what we have every night."

When she continued giving him a dubious look, he added, "There's pie. It was already made. All I have to do is bake it. The pies in that freezer are delicious."

"I'm not sure if I trust your definition of delicious," she said, "But as long as you didn't make it, maybe it'll be good."

"You haven't even *tasted* the meat yet. How do you know it won't be good?" When she lifted her eyebrows and opened her mouth to speak, he held up a hand to stall her. "Wait, don't answer that. I forgot how seriously ursa take their food. You are more than welcome to alter the meal any way you wish." He stood to one side and gestured to the oven.

Shaking her head, Vrishti rounded the bar and pulled the barely warmed pan back out of the oven, then rifled through the cabinets. After a flurry of movement and flying spices, the air was filled with a cloud of delicious aromas. Within moments, she'd put the pan back in the oven with a satisfied nod.

"There," she said.

Neph stood with has backside against the sink, finding it tough to breathe—not due to the spices, but from her sudden proximity to him. There was room for two, but he wasn't a small man, and her enticing curves were all he could think about. She was in her element, clearly, moving with easy grace that betrayed her years of practice at this very task. It was a mesmerizing transformation from the shyness she'd displayed earlier.

The very second she discovered him watching, she stiffened and blushed and the moment ended. She retreated to her barstool again, mumbling something about it being good enough for now.

"I'm sure it's better than good enough," he said. "Here's something I know I can't screw up … In fact, it's one of the things I am best at." He reached for a bottle of wine, uncorked it, and poured her a glass of aromatic red liquid, then filled one for himself.

She relaxed with her first sip, giving him an apologetic smile. "I didn't mean to get in your way. It was just a sin the way you treated that meat. I couldn't just let that happen."

"It's good that you took action. Honestly, Cade's been griping about my cooking since I got here, but he still insists we take turns. When you live the life that I've led, cooking for yourself is pretty low on the list of priorities."

She took a deeper sip of wine, her cheeks already flushing from the spirit.

"I almost can't believe I'm here. That Nyx was right … you're right where she said you would be. I just wish she'd told me where Aodh was."

Neph went rigid, then leaned across the counter toward her. "What do you mean, where Aodh is? He's in the Haven, isn't he?"

"No. Oh, shit, you don't know. I should start at the beginning."

Neph braced himself for the worst. Knowing how Nyx had been behaving when he'd left, what Vrishti had to share couldn't be good news, and as she talked, it became clear how bad it really was. Eventually Cade joined them, silently tuning into her story as they set the table and served dinner.

Neph continued refilling her glass and she continued to drain it, still talking during dinner and only pausing long enough to accept Cade's profuse and enthusiastic gratitude for a meal that didn't taste like shoe leather for a change.

She seemed to be evading some key detail in her story, however. At no point in her explanations of the past week or so since Neph had left the Haven did she explain her presence here now. If anything, he became more and more certain that the Sanctuary was where she should be, not here with him. Except for the obvious instinct that she *belonged* here with him, logically, rationally, it made no sense.

Finally, she took a breath and stood to clear dishes. Cade jumped up and grabbed them from her.

"You sit, kiddo. I've got cleanup duty tonight since you cooked."

Neph shot Cade a dirty look, but the big ursa just shrugged.

Vrishti reached for the wine and refilled her glass, giving Neph the sense that she was drinking for fortification more than anything now. She was working up to something, and he needed to let her get to it at her own pace.

He took a sip of his own wine and regarded her. The intoxicating liquid was nothing compared to her. Her awkward innocence yet bright, sharp mind were endearing … arousing in a way none of the nymphs he'd ruled in the Haven had been. Her lack of presence in his visions of the future was every bit as enticing as any wet dream, because that only proved to him that she was too close to him … too significant an entity in his own life for him to know exactly what she really meant to him and how she might impact his life going forward.

She was a wild card, and one he craved stripping down and mounting more than he could believe.

She'd paused her story and looked away, fidgeting with the stem of her wineglass. She'd gotten to the end, at least to the point of saying, "And here I am," but still hadn't explained the why of her presence here.

"Why are you here, Vrishti?" Neph said.

"Because you're the only person who can get to Aodh. We can't let him stay locked up wherever Nyx put him."

"Even if I could get to him, which I can't, Nyx had a good reason for sending him away. He's like a magnet for Meri."

"But if finding her is such a challenge, isn't that a good thing? He should at least have the option to choose. He's hidden from her before without Nyx's help. Besides …"

She dropped her gaze again and bit her lip, seemed to steel herself and gather her words, then looked him straight in the eye. "He's mine. My … chosen mate. Would you leave your mate locked up if you knew how to save him?"

There was no bite to her words, no accusation, yet he felt the stab of them deep. He wouldn't leave Aodh trapped in whatever time Nyx had sent him to, but it wasn't so easy a problem to remedy.

"My abilities aren't enough. Yes, I am capable of reaching him where my sister trapped him, but not without my link to the Source. And as long as I'm out here, I have no access to it. The Sanctuary's portals aren't breachable from this side by anyone but an ursa, and even then, the two of you can't get back in until the Equinox. It just isn't possible for me to use that power to access the flow of time without a link to the Source."

Vrishti took another long swallow of wine, her eyes wide and intense. "What if I told you I could give you a link to the Source? I know an ursa spell that lets me access that power."

The hesitance in her voice was the only thing that kept him from jumping up and demanding that she show him now. He spread his fingers and pressed his palms flat on the surface of the table, staring across at her.

"If you have a spell that does that, I want to see it. Then we can decide if I can reach Aodh."

"I can't," she said. "Not yet. I haven't reached my estrous yet, and I won't have enough power for the spell until I do."

"The spell is tied to your fertility, isn't it?" he asked, beginning to understand her fear of divulging all the details. If she hadn't reached her estrous, there was a strong chance she was a virgin. More than strong, judging from her behavior. The power wasn't just the simple command of the life energy that permeated the world and all living things—a power even a male ursa like Cade could access at will, if they were trained for it.

"I have to … um," she began, then shot a fearful look at them both as though she'd just realized she was sitting in a room alone with two very virile males.

Cade was the first to break the silence, and he did so with a loud laugh. "Kiddo, you've dug yourself into a nice little hole here, haven't you? I'll help you out, since you're very new to the whole ursa gig. All that sweet power that builds up inside females before their estrous comes straight from the Source. That's why it's so damn dangerous. But the only way to let it out is for you to have an orgasm. Or even better, a whole *lot* of orgasms. I never knew it could be harnessed and reused … Mostly us males just channel it back to Gaia. So you're telling us that you have a spell that lets you do that?"

Cade's clinical explanation did nothing to cool Neph's rising lust. Vrishti had come to *him* with this request, one that she knew required her to give herself to him. Or did she know?

"You understand this means we'll have to fuck?"

Gaia's tears, simply saying the words made his cock painfully hard.

Cade cursed. "Let the kid get her bearings, for fuck's sake. Nobody's fucking anybody."

"It's all right, Cade," Vrishti said. "I … I'm aware of how I access the power. I only had an idea of how *you* would access it, but now I know. If it means rescuing Aodh, then I'm prepared."

Neph let out a sardonic chuckle. "I don't think you are." He stood up from the table. "Let me show you exactly what you need to be prepared for, because the only way for me to use my full power is in my primal form." He swiftly unbuttoned his shirt, then his jeans, stripping deliberately out of each item of clothing, ignoring Cade's fountain of profanity. She had to see.

Vrishti sat stock still, her mouth slightly open and her eyes growing wider.

"You don't have to …" she started. "I mean, I get it …" She raised a hand when he stood naked in front of her after walking around the table.

"This isn't what I need to show you," he said, then summoned his primal shape and shifted. In a smooth flow of magic, his body grew. Giant horns sprouted from his head, curving back from his temples in coiling ram's horns, and his lower body spawned a coat of thick, black fleece. "This is."

Even in his human shape, it'd been impossible not to be aroused by her. His simple nakedness a moment earlier had heightened her reaction to the point that he could easily scent her desire. But now his cock had grown in both size and need with the surge of his primal instincts. The thick length protruded from its nest of fleece at his groin, massive shaft curving up in a smooth arc that pointed directly at Vrishti.

"Are you prepared for this, girl?" he asked, voice dripping with every ounce of lust that filled him. He gripped his shaft and gave it a long stroke, enjoying how she licked her lips. He'd happily bend her over the table and fuck her now, but despite that wild craving, he still knew better—though he would have tormented her more with his satyr shape if Cade hadn't stepped himself between them and shoved Neph backward.

"You fucking son of a bitch! Get yourself under control, man. I said, *nobody is fucking anyone* in this house. Not tonight. Not after all that goddamn wine, and especially not without her saying she's good and goddamn ready for it." He turned to look at Vrishti, and in a more comforting tone said, "He is right, though, kiddo. You are far from prepared for his crazy ass."

Neph relaxed and let his shape recede back to the less powerful, but more palatable human form he lived in most days. The swell of desire didn't dissipate, but he ignored it and hoped that at least his eyes would remain calm enough for her to look at him without getting nauseous. He swiftly pulled his jeans and shirt back on. Even with the roaring fire, there was still a coolness in the air that he was constantly aware of. If only it would cool off his craving for her.

He sat back down across from her and gave her a hard look. "You're inexperienced, not only with the power you're seeking, but with the means to create it. You're a virgin. You've never been serviced through an estrous—any female ursa who has been through that experience wouldn't have that scared kitten look you're giving me now. One orgasm from a fertile female in the middle of estrous carries enough power to bend time. Nyx and I are the only creatures in existence who can use that power, but that should highlight to you how reckless you're being by even showing up here. It has less to do with tempting me than simply knowing your own body. When you orgasm, how wet to you get now?"

She opened her mouth and closed it again, reached for the wine, but he was quicker, snatching it away from her. "No way, kitten. You can't escape in the wine anymore. Not until you lay it all out for me. If I'm going to do this, I need to know exactly where you are. Have you ever even had an orgasm?"

Her throat worked silently as she swallowed and shook her head. Neph's hands went to the table again, pressing into the surface so he didn't ball them into fists and punch something.

Taking a deep breath, he said, "All right ... I can't fucking believe I'm doing this for that bastard, but I hope when we get to him he says thank you. Here's what you need to do ... You're going to go upstairs, take off all your clothes, get into the shower, and turn the nozzle to the massage setting. Then aim the water at your pussy."

Her gaze remained fixed on his face, her eyes as wide as they could go. She fidgeted slightly in her chair and he inhaled reflexively, hating himself for how his mouth watered and his dick pulsed at the potent scent of her arousal.

"Hold it on you for a count of ten and then stop. Get a hand mirror and look at yourself in the light, see how wet you are, how hard that tight little clit is, and touch yourself until you feel like you might explode. Feel that orgasm hanging by a thread and leave it there. It'll be torture, but that's the point.

"Then when you get up tomorrow morning, do it again. I don't want to see you with clothes on until you come to me begging for my cock to make the hurt go away, because when you do hit your estrous, kitten, my cock is the only thing that'll make it better. Don't look at Cade … He's a strong male ursa, but he's not strong enough for what you've got buried in you. If you really are powerful enough for what we're going to do, I'm the only one who can help you. Besides, where we're going, he can't follow."

Vrishti's brow crinkled and he sensed the question coming. She'd barely gotten out the "why" when he answered.

"You've got to push yourself. Your body's sexual responses are slow. If you'd been masturbating since you were younger, you'd be ready for your estrous sooner. We don't have time to sit around and wait. Trust me, I've seen some of the shit that's coming. You say you have the power, then you need to trigger your estrous so we can get to it."

"In the shower …" she said.

"C'mon, kiddo," Cade said, nudging her shoulder gently with a big hand. "I'll show you where you'll be sleeping. There's locks on all the doors, so don't worry."

At the big ursa's urging, Vrishti stood and followed in a daze. The pair trudged up the stairs that circled around in a spiral behind the fireplace. A moment later, Neph heard water running and then Cade returned, shaking his head.

"Don't know what the hell her mother was thinking, letting her out of the Sanctuary with so little experience.

Females aren't even allowed out for their pilgrimage until after their first estrous."

Neph emptied the remaining wine into his glass and swallowed it in a few quick gulps. "I don't recommend hanging around for the next few days, if you want to maintain your own sanity," he said to the other man.

Cade sat back in his chair and crossed his arms over his broad chest, eyeing Neph. "You think I'm leaving her at your mercy? The fuck I am. I may not be enough for her on my own, but I can sure as shit make sure you treat her right."

Neph raked both hands through his hair and speared the other man with his gaze. "You don't get it. This is Fate's doing … her being here, I mean. I should've seen her coming. I would have, if she were just after a simple quest to save a friend. But that isn't the case … not by a long shot. She's here because my ex is the mate Fate has marked for her."

Cade narrowed his eyes. "So, what the fuck does that have to do with how you treat her? Is that ex of yours even going to be enough?"

"He will, but she'll have two regardless. Because I'm hers too."

"How do you know that? You said you didn't see her in those visions of yours."

"Process of elimination, sort of. I can see your future clear as day. I can tell you the day you die, in fact. But my own future is a complete blank. I didn't see her. I can't see her future. And I can't see the future of the man she wants us to find. What that means to me is that the three of us share a future so closely bound my powers of foresight are nullified. And nothing has ever fucking scared me so much as knowing, yet not knowing."

Cade relaxed and shook his head. "All right, man. I'll be scarce over the next few days. If you need me, I'll be at Alec's and Julia's. Just promise you'll be gentle with her."

"She's my mate, Cade. If I fuck this up and she leaves me, I may as well die."

"But you're immortal …"

"I know, man. I know."

And after pushing away one mate all those ages ago, Neph already knew what it felt like to walk through life feeling like a dead man. Not only was Vrishti here, offering him another chance at family and fatherhood with a truly worthy female, but she was also offering him a way to mitigate that ancient mistake. That simple fact made loving her a given, and there was nothing in the world that could make him jeopardize that.

CHAPTER 6

VRISHTI

*V*rishti stood under the pounding pulse of the shower, unable to get Neph's image out of her head. Not the beautiful man she'd been too stunned to speak to in the kitchen at first, but the majestic, sexual beast he'd changed into later to make a point.

Naked bodies were a thing she'd barely gotten used to after the scant few weeks she'd spent in the Sanctuary, but the residents there, particularly around the Rainsong Clan Lodge, leaned toward nudity as a rule. So she'd seen her fair share of huge, naked ursa males recently. Cade had only shocked her because of how cold it was in the woods where they'd met.

Neph was something entirely different. He wasn't just a naked man … even when that was all he was. No, when he transformed, he became something else—a creature whose entire purpose was sex. Cade had been right. Neph was made to fuck, and she couldn't stop picturing that giant shaft and what he might do with it. To her.

Getting turned on wasn't an issue. She'd become more aware of her body's cycles and strange new fluctuations since entering the Sanctuary. She'd finally learned how to shift just before she'd left. She could reach her inner beast simply by sinking into that awareness, as though it were second nature to be something other than what she was. She was no stranger to craving a transformation of her entire body, and her bear form was a welcome escape from the uncomfortable desires of her human flesh. Ever since the day Aodh had kissed her and said those beautiful words—the ones that made it as clear as day how much he wanted her—she couldn't fall asleep at night without imagining his hands on her.

But she'd never seen him naked and aroused, so in her head it was only his hands on her body, his mouth on her skin, and his voice whispering in her ear how much he wanted to bury himself inside her until she screamed his name.

And she'd certainly never touched herself while having those thoughts. She'd just let the desire crash through her, clenching her thighs to stave off the worst of it until she fell asleep. But the need would rise in the dead of night with the dream of Aodh's mouth on a part of her body that had never seen the sun, much less the gaze of a man.

Often she would wake up and find she'd unconsciously summoned a bed of flowers to grow around her, straight from her mattress. That was when she learned she could channel that desire into creating living, growing things, and had focused her studies from that point forward on under-standing how that magic worked. She still had a lot to learn about the magic, but it had at least given her an excuse to avoid dwelling on the desires that triggered the magic. Now she had no choice but to face those desires head-on.

At least Neph hadn't asked her to get naked in front of him. But to do what he asked, simply knowing he'd told her to do it, was too much.

Wasn't it?

To have Aodh back, safe, her promise kept … She'd already risked everything by leaving the Sanctuary to try to find him. Was her virtue too big a sacrifice? She'd known it was going to happen one way or another, but for some reason, the logistics hadn't occurred to her. Somehow the concept of sex was still alien to her despite her aching need. It was something that happened separate from her … to her body, but not to *her*.

To give herself an orgasm … or, no, that wasn't what he'd told her to do … She was to play with herself to the point that she was close, but not actually come. That was just a little too much to conceive of.

But she had to do it. Nyx had said that her brother would have all the answers, that Vrishti might not like them, but she had to do as he asked if she wanted to find Aodh. *"Finding your love is never easy once you've lost it,"* Nyx had said, pressing her hands to the invisible barrier of the magical cell that held her. *"I'm the perfect example. Neph will know what to do. Obey his commands if you wish to find your dragon."*

Her hands shook as she reached up and grasped the handle of the shower head and removed it from its bracket. The hot water beat harder against her skin the closer she brought it. Sharp pleasure burst through her nipple when one strong jet passed over it, and she gasped.

The goal was to tease her estrous into showing itself. Pleasure was how to reach that goal, but not too much … not enough to actually orgasm.

Experimentally, she aimed the shower stream at her nipple again, deliberately moving it into a slow circle and focusing on the warm spread of sensation that moved down her body, pooling between her thighs. Without even trying, she pictured Aodh's mouth again. He'd barely touched her beyond that one farewell kiss, so his mouth had been burned into her mind. The sharp sensation of the shower jet became his lips and teeth sucking and toying with her nipple.

Vrishti sighed. Good. It felt so good. Even better with the fantasy of his touch, of his pale eyes gazing down at her with both adoration and wicked lust. She redirected the flow to her other nipple, aiming until the point of discomfort. The jet blasted a hard, unrelenting pressure, and Neph had asked her to put it between her thighs.

Just like that, Aodh's face faded and Neph's replaced it with that carnal glare he'd given her while in his primal form, his hand fisted around his massive shaft. Her vaginal walls clenched hard, and she moaned aloud at the overwhelming ache that took up residence in her core.

"No," she groaned, wishing for Aodh's image to return. She couldn't pleasure herself thinking about another man, even if she had to eventually fuck that other man to save the one she loved. She shook her head and opened her eyes, hoping that by being more present she could get this done. She stared down past her heavy breasts and round belly to the thatch of black curls between her thighs. If she couldn't have Aodh, she would do this for herself. Not for either of the men—the one who was lost, and the one whose help she needed to save him.

This was her problem, her task, her quest. If training her body to do what she needed it to do was what it would take, she should be all in for *herself*.

"Right. You can do this," she murmured, then dropped the nozzle and reached for the soap. She drizzled a measure of body wash into her hands, then lathered them up and cupped her heavy breasts, exhaling softly to focus. This should be like any other learning experience, similar to how she began each day over the past few weeks of lessons to understand how her magic worked. She'd been trained to find her center, to focus on the present, avoid distractions and be *in* her body. From her body, she could access the magic of Gaia through her connection to the Earth.

This should be no different, yet when she rubbed her nipples with soapy fingers and watched herself do it, she must have been *too* focused on the act, because she didn't feel the same spark of desire she'd felt from the jet of the shower-head while her eyes were closed. The sensations were nowhere near as pleasurable as when she'd imagined Aodh doing it to her. Still, it *was* nice, and her body responded.

When both nipples were hard, dark peaks, she bent to pick up the nozzle again. A count of ten, Neph had said. Holding her breath, she braced her feet wide and aimed the stream at the top of her cleft. She bit her lip and stared down at the pulsing jet as she slowly lowered it, the hard pressure of two of the trio of streams parting her lips for her and the third suddenly blasting right atop her tender clit.

Sensation surged through her and she cried out, nearly dropping the nozzle from surprise. Hands still shaking, she regained her balance and reached down to adjust the water so the flow wasn't quite so strong.

She found her clit again with the stream and forced herself to hold it there.

"Ten … nine … eight …" Heat grew exponentially with every second, her entire body alive with sensation. Cool air hit her skin now that she wasn't beneath the hot water, but all the heat was concentrated between her thighs. "Six … five … fo-ohh God …"

It was just too much. The pressure built up deep inside her, right where she felt it when she drew on her magic to do a small spell. She needed release, but she had to see this through the way Neph had commanded.

"Three … two-ahh … one." She dropped the showerhead and grabbed at the window ledge just above her for balance as she caught her breath. Her entire body was alive with want, her core throbbing in time with the pulsing of the jet she'd held against her flesh.

With a shaky hand, she dipped her fingers between her thighs and found herself slick with moisture. Her clit pulsed under her light touch, hard and swollen to twice its normal size so that it peeked out from her outer lips enough to be visible.

She absently turned off the water, the sharp awareness of her own physical sensations distracting her from everything but following through on Neph's instructions. Tossing a towel onto the lid of the toilet, she sat heedless of the water dripping off her and spread her legs, then reached for the hand mirror on the bathroom counter.

Her reflection flashed into view for a second and she halted the movement of her arm, staring in surprise at the flushed woman who looked back at her. She had wide, dark eyes and full lips parted with desire. Vrishti knew what hid behind those eyes, but didn't dare admit it yet. But learning a new thing was within the scope of possibility to her, even if that new thing was her own body's reactions to touch—to pleasure.

The body she saw in the reflection was sensuous and beautiful, but she only saw pieces of it at a time—the wet, black tendril of hair clinging to her cheek, the dewy curve of her shoulder, the slope of her breast down to the darker brown pebbled circle of her nipple. She tilted the mirror lower and watched more of her appear, reflected back to her as though it were another creature being displayed in that small, round looking-glass. Her belly with its smooth, caramel-colored skin offset by the dark black of the hair that covered her pubis.

And there, nestled amid that dark nest, was the shining pink tip of her clitoris. It seemed to have its own heartbeat now, its own mind that screamed *want* at her. It wanted to be touched, and so she spread her thighs a little wider until her outer lips parted, giving her a clearer view of her own glistening pink sex.

She traced a finger along the edge of one outer lip, tilting her head in fascination as she opened herself. Her lips parted like a flower opening to the sun, and she finally understood how very sexual all those beautiful paintings were that she'd admired in her Art Appreciation class in college. How very feminine in a much more primal way than she'd ever understood until now. They weren't flowers in those paintings after all, were they? This was what they had depicted. Her sexuality and the very core of her power was right here, bound up in that swollen little bundle of nerves and in all the copious fluids that flooded from her opening to soak the towel beneath her.

Slowly, she dipped her index finger between her lips and pushed it into her opening, biting her lip at the slight pinch as her invasion stretched her. There was no way a cock as huge as Neph's would fit in there without pain. Could she prepare herself for him? Or was the pain part of what was required? No, that made no sense. It wasn't pain that fueled the magic, it was pleasure. She knew that much from her studies, though now she finally had the empirical understanding to back it up.

Pleasure was what she was after now, what incited that build-up of power in her core, and her finger felt nice sliding into her channel, then back out again to drive that need higher. She pushed a second finger in and her clit tightened and throbbed harder. She hadn't even touched it, yet it ached for contact, for release. She feared now that if she actually *did* touch it, even the slightest amount, that she would come apart at the seams. So instead, she focused on her opening, sliding her fingers in and out, in and out, until her breathing quickened and her muscles clamped down, craving more.

Only to the edge, she reminded herself. She was too enthralled with the sight to stop yet, however, gripping the mirror tightly in her right hand while she watched her fingers slide into her opening. Lifting one leg, she bent her knee and propped her heel on the edge of the toilet lid, then lifted the other and raised it high enough to rest her foot on the corner of the counter beside her.

This forced her to lean back against the tank, but she had a clearer view of her entire nether region in the mirror, now that she was spread wide enough to see. Her labia parted and her fingers sank in deeper. She experimented with a different motion and gasped when her fingertips hit a soft spot on her inner wall, which she prodded gently. Pleasure shot straight to her clit and her legs twitched. Her heartbeat hammered and her body hummed with that building need that she had so far only ever felt in her dreams of Aodh.

She abruptly stopped moving her fingers, but in the mirror she could see the shining flood of her juices running down from her spread opening and coating the tight rosette of her asshole. She withdrew her fingers, caught up in the fascination of discovery now, curious to see what other reactions her body might have to different stimuli. Only a small part of her brain still clung to the idea of treating this as an experiment; the rest of her just wanted to feel more, now that she'd opened the door to this knowledge of herself.

Her fingers glistened with her slick juices and she slid them down past her perineum to circle around the darker, creased skin that surrounded her rear opening. Perhaps that was the key to building pleasure but not crossing the point of no return. It felt nice … ticklish at first, then just *good* once she'd traced a slick circle around her hole a few times. With a swift little poke, she shoved the tip of her finger inside.

"Oh, fuck!" she yelped at the sharp and unexpected jolt of pleasure that went through her. Her clit thrummed with renewed need, but complete release remained just beyond that thin barrier of control she managed to keep testing.

Biting her lip and acutely aware of the salacious things she was doing to her own body, she twisted her finger around, simply *feeling* the slight sensations that resulted from different movements. She could feel *everything* back there. Every time her knuckle passed that tight ring, she felt the little bump and rub, and it felt good. Not quite the concentrated, unbearable pleasure of the shower's jet against her clit, but a different kind of pleasure that she sensed had the same potential for mind-blowing release if she let herself go that far.

She wanted more. If her goal was to get to the edge, she *needed* more, but she needed both hands free to go further.

She set the mirror down, deciding she could look again afterward. Her ass was still slick with the juices of her arousal and her finger easily penetrated without any other assistance. Now that her other hand was free, she began teasing again, starting with her nipples, then sliding two digits between her folds and deliberately grazing over her stiff clit to test her endurance.

Her needy little bundle pulsed with desire, and she pressed the heel of her palm against it as though the pressure would help stave off the inevitable. It helped only slightly, but it was enough for her to push a second finger into her backside. That hurt a tiny bit, which pushed the rising tide of ecstasy back a little more, but the current swiftly regained momentum when she released the pressure of her hand from her clit and grazed a finger over the swollen bundle.

An involuntary exhalation escaped her lips and her head buzzed, feeling just as swollen with sensation as every single inch of flesh between her legs. Another soft stroke over her clit and the swelling sensation increased.

Close, but not over, she reminded herself, but sweet Gaia

did she want to go over so badly now. Her entire womb felt like it was about to burst with the pleasure of those two simple sensations … the two fingers sliding in and out of her ass, not even that deep, and the feather light touch of her other finger over the sensitive skin of her clit.

She didn't even have anything in contact with her vagina, yet she knew without a doubt she would lose herself with only a little more of what she was doing now.

The reminder of that emptiness in her core where her fingers had been earlier incited a sudden image of a huge cock, only this time it was attached to a naked, lust-ridden Aodh and not the huge Satyr she'd seen earlier. *"... bury myself inside you so deep ..."* reverberated in her ears, and her already weakening hold on her self-control faltered. The wetness flooding her pussy increased, and she very nearly lost her mind.

"No!" she cried out, yanking her hands away from herself and sitting up, the mirror flying off the counter as she knocked it to the floor with her foot. She clamped her thighs together and pressed her bare feet to the floor, doubling over as she resisted the overwhelming need to fall over that edge of pleasure.

She stared down at her face looking back at her from the mirror. Her eyes were wild with pent-up desire, but she looked different somehow. There was an awareness in that look that hadn't been there before. A want for something she hadn't known she wanted, not even after those late night dreams of Aodh.

The dreams had been nothing more than abstractions of desire, her craving for his presence tied up with her memory of their first and last touch—her body filling in the blanks in the only way it knew how, but without the aid of actual physical sensation to drive it all home.

Now she knew what true pleasure felt like. Or what the

beginnings of it did, anyway. And she wanted more. The light brown eyes gazing back at her from the mirror on the floor told her as much, but they also expressed the fear she didn't want to admit she had. The fear that allowing herself to find that pleasure before she found Aodh ... to cross that barrier without him ... would be a betrayal of the most important promise she'd made him. That he would be her mate ... and that she would be his.

She rose and shakily wrapped herself in the terrycloth robe Cade had handed her before leaving her to bathe. Turning on the hot water faucet, she leaned on the counter to regain her bearings, deliberately avoiding looking at herself in the mirror again. When steam billowed up from the sink, she washed her hands, then wet a cloth and carefully cleaned the arousal from between her thighs, avoiding too much direct contact with her clit. She'd cooled off a bit in the last few moments of self-flagellation, but her body still felt like a live wire and she didn't trust that she wouldn't accidentally throw herself off that ledge.

No wonder people talked about taking cold showers when they were turned on. She contemplated standing under a cold stream now, but knew it wouldn't help, given her ursa resistance to cold.

By the time she exited the bathroom and softly stepped across the hall into Emma's old bedroom, her desire had subsided and exhaustion nearly dragged her down. She fell onto the big bed and buried her face in the pillow, demoralized and yet strangely excited. The contradiction of emotions only made her feel worse.

She had to do this for Aodh. For love. And she owed it to herself to know her body better. There was nothing *wrong* with what she was doing, so why did it still feel like a betrayal? It wasn't like she was in love with Neph. Her magic worked a certain way, that's all. Any other ursa would do the same and not think twice about it. Her cousin Revna used her magic all the time.

"But she doesn't fuck anyone to use it," Vrishti said into the dark. That was a poor argument. Revna might not fuck anyone, but she sure as shit took pleasure in using her magic.

Vrishti had seen it in Revna's eyes when she'd cast a powerful spell one day. "It's like having an orgasm, if you do it right," Revna had said to her. But until she finally had a proper orgasm, Vrishti wouldn't ever know what it was supposed to feel like if she did it right.

Now she had an inkling of what that was supposed to feel like, and she was forced to keep from going that far. This was torture. But it made sense despite the discomfort she was in now.

She rubbed a thumb over the slightly upraised mark her mother had left in the center of her breastbone. The power of Summer would be hers at the Equinox, but she already had a link to it and could call on it if she needed to. Unfortunately, Summer's power wasn't quite the same as the power of the Source, and the Source was what Neph needed to access in order to use *his* powers to take them to the time and place where Aodh had been imprisoned.

Vrishti closed her eyes and sighed as she traced the sunburst of power on her chest, aware of both that power and the power of the Source that still thrummed between her thighs. Every drop of desire that flowed from her was for Aodh, and she would take herself to the edge as many times as it took to access the power she needed to find him.

CHAPTER 7

NEPH

Sheets of thin ice covered the creek, obscuring the flow of the water beneath, but Neph could still sense the current with his eyes closed. He sat silent on the bank, letting his mind become part of the current, following it all the way to the bigger river it fed and on to the ocean. The meditation told him nothing new, because the connection this creek had once had to the Haven had been severed shortly after his arrival. Still, the exercise calmed him and helped him focus.

At least he had found his nephew and could sense the other satyr's power through their shared connection to the River. There wasn't much to learn from that connection other than that Calder had grown even more powerful ... the kind of power that could only be gained via blood melding with one's mate. *Mates*, he corrected himself.

He'd considered joining their search for Nereus, but every vision he had made it clear there was no place for him in that quest. Vrishti's arrival had only reinforced that his purpose lay elsewhere. Aodh's ancient connection to their enemy may come into play somehow, and that meant he and

Vrishti had to follow through on her mission to find the dragon.

He'd spent thousands of years questioning Fate. After expelling Aodh from the Haven, he'd no longer believed the bond they'd had was anything more than wishful thinking spurred on by several decades of secret trysts and hundreds of sessions melding with the dragon. He should have left well enough alone … They'd had a good thing. Why had he insisted on inviting a female to join them?

Meri would only have been a mask for them to wear. Another lie to tell—to themselves and everyone around them. But Vrishti's arrival had reminded him to look for Aodh's timeline, and with that simple search, he'd been forced to revisit those old memories, and was surer than ever that Aodh and Vrishti both were fated for him.

Vrishti's raw determination to find the dragon was refreshing, but also terrifying. She was innocent, barely even understood her own nature as it was, and yet was willing to dive into his world with her eyes wide open. Somehow it gave *him* the drive to try too. Though at some point, he would have to explain to her where the two of them fit together in all this. For the time being, he would let her believe they were only after a shared goal to find her chosen mate. Soon they would be three, and when they were, she would have to understand that Fate intended them to be three. Not just two.

Baby steps. Vrishti's innocence required that he take things slowly. Her willingness to follow through with triggering her estrous was proof of her determination, though it would require a level of intimacy with him she may not be ready for. He doubted she'd easily be able to accept that Aodh wasn't the only male meant for her.

He stood and stretched, adjusted the thick wool scarf around his neck, and rubbed his gloved hands together to generate a bit of warmth. It was still early, with the gray dawn light barely beginning to illuminate the blanket of snow that had fallen the night before. The entire forest was soft and silent and he turned, taking slow, measured steps back the way he'd come, careful to place his feet back into the same footprints to avoid disturbing the near-perfect serenity of the morning.

Vrishti would be hungry when she woke. And she'd likely still be hesitant to do what was needed to trigger her estrous. The prospect both worried and aroused him, which was an incredibly confusing combination. As innocent as she was, he found it difficult to justify the things he must ask her to do, and he had to remind himself yet again that she'd embraced this quest and would likely keep trying no matter what.

But despite the fact that he would have full command of time itself once she could provide him a link to the Source, they still had to move quickly. Time did not stop flowing, even once they started diving into the River at different points, and the more they distanced themselves from their *true* present, the more power would be required to access those points, and the more time they could lose as a result.

They would both need strength, and at least feeding her was one thing he could do today to ensure they had it. Hopefully his choice of breakfast would satisfy her. He was decidedly better at cooking that meal than he was at supper, at any rate.

On the way into the cabin, he loaded up his arms with firewood, which he deposited into the inset box to the side of the fireplace. He tossed a couple big logs onto the fire, then shed his coat and boots. It was still chilly in the house, and he would need it warm if he was going to tolerate what he expected he'd need to do later.

"Hoping, you fool. Just admit you're hoping it comes to

that," he muttered, holding his hands out over the rising flames that licked over the fresh logs. He'd commanded Vrishti to spend her time here naked, learning that physical comfort, particularly with her own body, was one of the keys to unlocking the tight shackles she had on her sexuality. Most ursa females were long past sexual discovery at her age.

He'd seen the look in her eyes when he'd stripped and shifted in front of her the night before. That sharp spark of arousal that had overcome her had swiftly been shut down by some misplaced sense of propriety that made him wonder who had raised her. That was no matter now, but at least he knew he could incite lust simply by being naked around her, so if that was what she needed, he would happily give it to her. Just not until the fire had warmed the place a bit more.

The flames licked higher and he fed another log into the fire. Soon enough he was able to shed another layer as he pondered the potential outcomes of the day, until he was in only his jeans and a tight cotton t-shirt. He expected to shed the rest soon, but opted to avoid shocking her first thing in the morning. Then he set to work cooking.

As expected, the scent of frying bacon was the thing that finally roused her somewhere on the second floor. His ears twitched and tingled when her feet hit the floor above and the creak of the wooden joints betrayed her movements. He kept cooking, tracking her noises while he fried several eggs and made toast. She moved across the hall to the bathroom, probably brushing her teeth and hair. Then she made her way to the top of the stairs and stopped.

He heard nothing but her breathing for several moments, then her steps retreated back toward the bedroom she'd slept in. Then returned and halted once more at the top step.

His mouth quirked to the side. Indecisive girl.

"Breakfast is ready!" he shouted in her direction. But rather than come down, she retreated again.

"Coming!" she called from down the hall near the doorway to her room.

Neph shook his head, laughing softly to himself at her ridiculous ruse. Finally her footsteps made it to the top step and came farther, but he frowned when he heard the soft swish of fabric accompanying her movements.

She entered the living room and crossed it, smiling nervously at him. Her wavy black tresses shone from a fresh brushing and her eyes were bright with a strange inner excitement that made him itch to understand. Had she followed all his instructions the night before? This morning? He inhaled slowly, hoping to catch a hint of whether she had … But if she were aroused at all, he couldn't tell over the scent of fresh bacon.

But she wasn't naked, which was obvious, and she was also obviously pretending that she didn't know she'd broken the rules already.

"Smells delicious!" she said, sweeping up to where he stood with his hands full of two plates, one filled with toast, the other with the aromatic bacon. Her gaze tracked the dish and he caught the soft rumble of her belly. She reached out to steal a piece, but he lifted the plate just out of her reach.

"No you don't," he said, narrowing his eyes at her.

"What? You just said breakfast was ready. Why can't I eat?"

Her eyes were fixed on the plate and the pink tip of her tongue darted out to lick her lips.

"You can eat when you take that off," he said, nodding at the patchwork, kimono-style robe she was wearing cinched tight around her waist.

She dropped her hand and froze, her gaze finally tearing away from the bacon to look at him. The caramel skin of her throat rippled as she swallowed.

"It … it's too cold in here …" She glanced over her shoulder toward the fireplace.

"Bullshit," he said. "I could happily strip with that fire blazing, so I *know* you can handle the temperature. If you want my help, you have to follow my rules, Vrishti. Strip."

Vrishti glared at him and tugged at the belt of her robe. "I can't fucking believe I'm taking my clothes off for bacon."

"Good girl," he said, smirking at her and carrying the food to the table. He studiously avoided looking directly at her, hoping his nonchalance about her nudity would help keep her comfortable. Out of the corner of his eye, he saw her pull the ties of the robe free. Her breathing sped up slightly and she hesitated for a split second before letting the silky fabric slide down her arms and catch on her hands.

"Um … I don't suppose I should hang onto this?"

"Just toss it wherever," he said. "You won't need it."

He retrieved the eggs, the bowl of sliced fruit, then the carafes of juice and coffee. All the while, he sensed her agitation.

Finally he glanced at her as he pulled a chair out from the table. "Sit," he said. "And you can move your hands, kitten. It's nothing I haven't seen." She had her palms cupped gently over the tips of her breasts. He didn't have the heart to tell her that what his attention was drawn to most was between her thighs.

Silently she complied, and seemed grateful when he said nothing else but simply filled her plate with food.

He let her eat, allowing himself only peripheral awareness of her supple curves as she fed herself. Her breasts were full and dark-tipped, reminding him of chocolate. Idly he wondered why he liked to compare female body parts to food, but he'd always done it with Aodh too, so it wasn't restricted to women. His tongue was his favorite way to explore a lover, after all, hedonist that he was.

When she sat back and sighed, her breasts jiggled alluringly and her hands immediately went to cover them again.

"Okay, this is why clothes are good," she said, forcing him to realize he'd been mesmerized for a moment. "Nothing you haven't seen before, huh? If that's the case, why stare so hard?"

"I'm sorry. You're … very different from a nymph. More …" He struggled for the words to express exactly what he saw when he looked at her, and finally shrugged. "Just more."

Her face fell and she hunched over slightly. "I know there's more of me. You don't have to remind me. I met Assana … saw all the other pretty little nymphs running around half-naked in the Haven. That place is like supermodel central."

"That isn't what I meant," he said, confused by her withdrawal. She had seemed defiant, strong-willed, in that moment when she'd disrobed. This transformation into self-consciousness was a step backward.

"Then what *did* you mean? Huh? I'm more *what*?"

"More sensual. I've been surrounded by nymphs for centuries. They certainly have some strong commonalities. That's all I see anymore. Their physical perfection is designed to seduce. You're nothing like them. You're so much more." He forced himself to stop before he blathered on about what she really represented to him. Baby steps. Get her to accept her beautiful body as a source of pleasure, not shame.

"Either way, I'd like to get dressed," she whispered, her arms crossed tightly over her chest now.

Fuck, he wasn't off to a very good start. Impulsively, he stood up and stripped off his shirt.

"Nobody's going to be dressed," he said, tossing the shirt aside and unbuttoning his jeans. Vrishti stared up at him with the same shock she'd had the night before when he stripped. "Don't worry, it's just going to be me as a normal human-looking dude. I'll save my primal form for when we actually need it."

When he stood in front of her naked, she was chewing on her lip, unable to take her eyes off him. "Um … you're …" She pulled one hand from under her armpit and gestured vaguely toward his hips.

"Hard? Yeah, that's because you have a beautiful shape, Vrishti. Fucking arousing as hell to look at." Definitely not because every single instinct that drove him wanted to breed her. "The sooner you accept that you are a sensual creature, the better. We are Gaia's children. That primal current ties us together. Denying what you are keeps you isolated from the power you're capable of. You know this already … otherwise you wouldn't have come to me and asked for my help awakening your estrous."

She lifted her gaze to his, and his heart clenched at the fear he saw in her eyes.

"I'm just not ready for all this. Oh, god, I'm sorry." Her bottom lip trembled and she sucked it into her mouth as tears welled in her eyes. Abruptly she raised her hands to her face, clearly more ashamed by her tears than her nakedness.

"Fuck, don't cry." Neph crouched down by her chair and pulled her hands away from her face. "You don't have to do anything but *feel* right now. Just experience the world naked. Not even the whole world, just this little piece of it. It's just you and me in this cabin. Right now, I'm going to wash dishes. You can help, or you can relax by the fire with a book. Just *be* here now, Vrishti."

"Be here *naked,* you mean." She glanced down at herself and took a deep breath, followed by a soft sniffle. She looked back up at him with a shy, sideways smile that made his dick pulse and his heart pound at the same time.

Neph chuckled. "Yes, naked. But be aware of the sensations you experience." He reached up and traced a thumb lightly over her jaw. "Stay in the moment, Vrishti. Be aware of when something feels good or not. Let yourself enjoy the good without the burden of too much analysis. I'm the king of hedonism, so in a little while, we'll have a snack and maybe open a bottle of wine. There are plenty more of those pies in the freezer … I think Aurum must have made them while she was here, because I've never tasted anything more delicious."

Vrishti let out a shaky little sigh. "Wine and pie might help," she said. "But isn't it a little early?"

"It's never too early to indulge when you're trying to learn how to do it right. I'm happy to teach you how to let loose, but we need to start slow. Once your estrous hits, on the other hand … there will be no holding back."

"My estrous …" She nodded and let out a frustrated huff. "God, I wish it'd just happen already. I wish this were easy for me, I really do."

Neph grabbed the back of the chair and pulled it around so she was facing him directly. "It will get easier. Trust me, within a day or two—hopefully even less time—you'll wonder why it was ever so difficult."

Her face scrunched up, but he was relieved when she dropped her hands to her lap and tangled her fingers together instead of concealing her lovely breasts from him.

"What if it doesn't happen that soon? What if it takes longer?"

He gently rested his hands on her knees and slid them down to her calves. She tensed slightly, her eyes widening at the contact. At this proximity, he was acutely aware of the scent of her arousal, as well as the way her nipples tightened.

"Kitten, if it takes any longer, it'll be my fault, not yours, and I should resign as Dionarch. Any satyr worth his cock knows how to seduce a female, even a reluctant one, within a matter of minutes. We could do this faster if my goal was to fuck you, but it isn't, so it may take just a little longer."

"Is … is that what you're doing? Seducing me?" she asked quietly.

"That's precisely what I'm doing, albeit in a very unconventional way. The goal is to trick your body into needing a good fuck so much your estrous begins. We need you fertile to access the magic."

He stood and continued his description of their goal as though he were simply outlining an itinerary for the day while he picked up the dishes from breakfast. Vrishti fidgeted in her seat for a moment before finally sitting on her hands to hold them still. He glanced up at her from the kitchen as he worked on the dishes. "Why don't you relax on the sofa? Try to clear your mind. Watch the fire. When I'm done here, we can talk a bit more."

She nodded and stood, her gaze darting shyly to him as she turned to walk toward the open living area with the roaring fire heating the space. Neph paused, empty dishes forgotten in his hands as he admired the luscious curves of her backside, the narrower arch of her waist, and the wavy mane of jet black hair that draped down over her shoulders. That ass … the mere sight of it … had his cock stiffening to a painful degree.

Baby steps, he reminded himself, clenching his eyes shut and forcing himself to refocus on the task at hand, grateful that the counter obscured the very prominent evidence of how turned on he was simply by her presence. He was perfectly capable of *not* having a hard-on in the presence of a beautiful woman, but this game he was playing with her might be the end of his sanity, and he'd be better off locked away in the Haven with his insane sister.

Vrishti settled herself on the sofa, reclining slightly against one arm and staring at the fire.

"Where did you go this morning?" she asked.

He blinked back at her in surprise. "Ah … this morning?"

"Yeah, I saw you walking down the road all bundled up. You don't have to tell me. I just thought we could maybe have a conversation about something other than my … fertility, or whatever."

"I went to the creek. There used to be a portal to the Haven there. That's where I arrived when I brought my nephew and his mates out. I guess I keep hoping there will be a glimmer of the Source when I go and I'll be able to go home. Mostly I just meditate while I'm there, though. It's peaceful. Even more so right after a snow like last night."

"The rain is what I think of most when I think of home," she said. "I like this place, though. It's comforting. Feels like a real home … like a family belongs in this house. Not at all like this … waystation, or whatever it's become." She gazed around the comfortable, heavy wood furnishings, the mismatched cushions, random blankets, and worn rugs that covered the hardwood floors.

Neph followed her gaze, trying to see the place as she perceived it. The love here was unmistakable in every log that had gone into building the place. The stones that made the huge fireplace had been pulled from the creek—he still sensed the touch of the Source on their surfaces, even though they'd been out of the water for decades at least. The trees that had been cut to build the cabin had all come from the very forest that surrounded them, drinking the water that Gaia's Source shared with the outside world. There was certainly magic here, but he guessed that wasn't the magic Vrishti noticed.

"They are family, though, aren't they?" he said. "The ursa queen and her cousins grew up here. Her brother is mated to my nephew. She is family to me. Her brother is also mated to Aodh's sister."

Vrishti smiled and darted a bright, playful glance at him. "She'll be like what … a sister-in-law? I have no idea how that works, but thank you. I don't feel quite so bad about masturbating in her bed now."

Despite her sardonic tone, Neph lost his grip on the soapy dish in his hand and it crashed into the sink. Dion's balls, how did this female manage to throw him off so easily? He took a deep breath that caught in his throat. Clearing the obstruction with a cough, he glanced at her and said, "And how did that go?"

She pursed her lips and darted her gaze to the fire before speaking. "I'm trying to wrap my head around it all. I think I'm starting to understand why you asked me to do that. I mean … from an analytical standpoint, I guess. My body's reactions are interesting."

"You should stop analyzing," he said. "Feel. Just feel. Your pleasure depends on more than simply the physical responses your body has to touch. It's in your head, too."

"I can't help it," she said softly. "This is how my brain works. I have advanced degrees in biology. Well, botany, actually, but still. I'm a scientist at heart. I like knowing … learning how living things work."

He finished wiping down the counters and dried off his hands as he rounded the bar counter and leaned his hip against it, facing her. "And what did you learn about how your pleasure works?" he asked. He still held the dish towel strategically in front of his raging erection. This was going to be a long couple days.

Vrishti's cheeks flushed. She crossed her bare legs, stretched out on the sofa before her, and rested her palms on the tops of her thighs.

"The showerhead was a little too much, but my fingertip felt nice in places. My … my nipples feel good when I touch them. And …" She bit her lip and lowered her gaze, then turned her head to stare into the fire again.

"And …?" Neph said, hoping she'd continue, but she only shrugged. "All right, then tell me what went through your head that moment when you thought you'd go over the edge … You didn't, did you?"

Vrishti shook her head. "You said not to, so I didn't. I was thinking about him … Aodh. I pictured him making love to me. That's what made me have to stop or I knew I'd come."

Her statement stung. Neph shifted his gaze to the fireplace as well in an effort to refocus on the conversation, but the image of his old lover tangled with this beautiful young ursa had dug into his mind, likely as vivid as her own fantasy had been. It did nothing to dampen his desire for her, but a dull ache took up residence in his chest as an odd counterpoint to the ache in his groin.

She was in love with Aodh, not him. The dragon was who she wanted.

He turned back around, found another thing to clean to avoid looking at her while he gathered himself to push on.

"Describe your fantasy. Tell me what you were doing while imagining it."

She remained silent for a moment, her hesitance a thick presence in the air between them. Finally, she cleared her throat.

"I did what you asked. Used the shower to … stimulate myself, but it was just too much, too fast. When I got out of the shower, I found the mirror like you said and … and I touched myself while I looked. I liked how my fingers felt inside me, but when I imagined *him* taking their place, his mouth on me, his hands on me, his *penis* inside me …"

Neph's focus was so intent on her the swift pounding of her heartbeat and her rapid breathing may as well have been his own.

"You've been intimate with him already, then," he said.

"Not like that. I mean … he kissed me once. He told me he wanted to be inside me, but I've never even seen him naked."

"Close your eyes, Vrishti," he said, glancing over his shoulder at her.

"What? Why?" She stared back at him, wide-eyed.

"So I can fulfill your fantasy, or most of it, at least." If he was going to do this right, he had to accept that what got her going might not be him. Not at the moment, anyway. He wanted Aodh every bit as she did, though his own fantasy was slightly reversed. The big white dragon liked to be topped, and Neph had always been more than happy to oblige him. But he would wager that Aodh would relish fulfilling Vrishti's fantasy if he were here.

"What are you going to do?" she asked.

"Just close your eyes," he said, coming back around the counter and standing before her, this time not making any effort to conceal his erection.

"Are you going to fuck me?" she asked, her voice catching on the word "fuck."

"Not until you beg me to. I am going to make you feel good, though, if you'll just do what I ask."

She took a deep, shaky breath and nodded, her full, round breasts making his mouth water the way her nipples perked up at his words. Finally, her dark lashes fell, her lips parting at the same time and quick breaths coming as though she were starved for oxygen.

Dion help me, he thought as he focused his power on shifting into the shape he knew would provoke the desired response from her.

CHAPTER 8

NIKHIL

Pidurutalagala, Sri Lanka
Present Day

The concentration of magic grew stronger the closer they got to the center of the island. Nikhil stared down over Belah's blue-scaled shoulder, his hair whipping in the wind as she glided in a tightening circle over the jungle below. Iszak and Lukas kept pace on either side, their energy palpable through the shared bond of their dragon marks and the magic of the North Wind that now filled Nikhil's lungs.

Ked and Aurum flew to either side as they descended to what would be their new headquarters as they geared up for an all-out assault on their enemy. They'd already begun the week before when Calder had agreed to be the bait to their hook.

Meri wouldn't be able to resist recapturing the powerful satyr once she discovered she'd lost him. The one detail that had worked in their original failed trap was that she'd believed she'd locked Nikhil into that room with Nicholas, and she had no further use for a puppet whose strings had been cut. As far as she knew, Calder had escaped, and she'd been enraged to the point of blind fury, which had ultimately seen Calder and Nicholas trapped and left for dead inside the abandoned facility in Canada.

Nikhil had instructed Calder to keep up that ruse and pretend that he'd escaped all along. Now that they had ensured Meri could no longer strip him of his connection to the River, they would have no trouble locating him wherever she took him.

The gold starburst pattern on the roof of the temple caught the bright sunlight and flashed in Nikhil's eyes. Beneath the polished dome cupola of the temple roof, the stairway inside came into view as they descended. Belah arced around, and wide stone balconies nearly covered in thick, viny growths became visible surrounding the cupola. The throng of flying creatures aimed for these entryways to the temple, landing and immediately shifting or dismounting as they streamed in from the air.

Nikhil had ordered the entire army to follow them here and now stood back to observe as every dragon and turul they could recruit flew in and proceeded to follow Ked and Aurum down the staircase into the temple itself.

"Do you need us?" Belah asked when the last dragon had departed down the stairs with a final salute to Nikhil. Only his mates remained behind, Lukas and Iszak standing nearby with sharp eyes scanning the horizon.

"I can manage on my own for this," he said. "I'll meet you in the throne room below when I'm done."

The two turul nodded and departed, but Belah hesitated. "This is old magic," she said. "The oldest. This temple existed long before the first hibernation. The magic's been concentrated over several millennia, grown stronger as time passes, as though dragons have lived here all along, though we know it's remained empty. That alone speaks to the timeless power of this place. If you can't harness it ..."

He frowned at the worry in his lover's gaze, her pretty brows knitted together and her fingers tangled before her slightly swollen belly.

"This is only dragon magic, little beast. Trust me to know what to do with it after all this time. It's just a piece of what I plan to use to fortify this place. Your power is better reserved for the baby. We'll need you too much later. Go rest."

He pulled her in and cupped the sides of her jaw, kissing her gently on the forehead. When he reflexively slipped his hands down to encircle her throat with his long fingers, she let out a soft moan and her eyelids fluttered closed. His cock stiffened to a painful degree and he gritted his teeth. He ached to take her here. He'd had too little of her since their reunion, and none of her to himself, every moment having been shared with her other two mates.

"Go," he said gruffly. "We will have time when this battle is won."

But she didn't move, and he didn't release her. With a rough jerk that surprised even him, he pulled her to him and crashed his mouth against hers. Their lips collided with bruising force, the kiss a hungry dance of lips and teeth and tongues. She dug her fingernails into his neck, raking up to his scalp as she sank into him with a desperate groan.

Nikhil still hungered for her like a man starved, even after she'd given him what he'd always wanted from her. *Especially* after she'd given him that. The marks on his wrists and around his neck gleamed in the dimming light of sunset, as strong a signal to his desire as the hard arousal that pressed against the hollow between her thighs. But he didn't have time for this. His centuries-old craving for this woman ... his pet, his wild little beast ... would have to wait a little longer.

Forcing himself to release her, he stepped back with fists clenched at his sides. Her gaze burned with longing that reflected his own need, but she nodded.

"Hurry," she whispered before she turned to go.

Spinning around, he surveyed the jungle canopy that spread out beneath this mountaintop temple. The faint cloak of power shimmered several yards away. From the ground and the air, no one without dragon blood would be able to see it, but it was old and most certainly wouldn't protect the place from Ultiori hunters if they got wind of its existence. The jungle had all but taken over the monolithic structure, and even to a trained human eye, it would appear as no more than stone ruins covered in vines. It had been constructed with the painstaking care of all the dragon temples, however, and imbued with powerful magic during the process.

This temple, the first of all the dragon temples, was the perfect spot to set up their base of operations.

Nikhil stretched his arms out in front of him, bent his hands at the wrists, and faced them palm-out, feeling for the field of power that surrounded the temple. With the power of all four races infusing his being, he focused, drew magic from the winds, from the setting sun, from the earth beneath his feet, and the deeper flow of an underground aquifer he sensed far below. The power flowed from his palms, latched onto the existing barrier, and fortified it. A shimmering dome extended up and around as he continued to pull the magic through his body.

Then he closed his eyes and focused on the warm power of the marks that branded his neck and his wrists, and drew on the new power that filled him, the power he would not have had without the acceptance of Belah and her mates. He stretched his arms out to the sides and tilted his head back, relishing the sharp bite of pain of his shackles, the symbols of this new power.

From his fingertips on one hand shot brilliant streams of light, and darkness from the other. The light of the soul-deep love for his goddess, his *Tilahatan*, and the darkness of their shared desires that had only been magnified by the pair of mates she'd chosen in his absence.

Sweat beaded on his brow as all the pain and love and devotion he'd held for so long fueled this last push of energy into the field of magic that would not only cloak, but permanently protect their new headquarters. No one would pass through without his say-so, from either side.

When he opened his eyes, he stared up into the black velvet of the night sky dotted with millions of brilliant white stars. The barrier was done. Now to get to work.

He descended the narrow staircase that led down into the temple. Warm light filtered from recessed pockets in the walls, illuminating his path. Several long flights down, the stairs finally ended at a hallway. The scent of food reached him from somewhere nearby and he perked up, realizing that he was starved after the long trip first from the turul Enclave, then from the dragon Monastery to reach this ancient spot. There was movement through a large, arched doorway beyond, where he guessed the great hall was situated. Belah's sister must be busy preparing a feast for throngs of soldiers he'd recruited over the past few weeks.

He would allow Aurum this initial indulgence, but after tonight, the gold dragon would have to delegate the task of cooking to others. He needed her too much for their primary task during this mission.

"Do you wish to sit?" a gentle female voice asked, drawing Nikhil out of his planning. He turned to see a petite woman with brilliant green eyes that slanted in her olive-toned face. He frowned at her.

"What do you mean?"

She nodded to the center of the room at the huge jade

throne that rested there. "You were staring at it," she said, one eyebrow raised. "I'm more than willing to take charge—it is my responsibility as Queen, after all, but considering the company I'm in and the goal we all share now, it seems like you are better suited for that particular position of power at the moment."

Nikhil let out a soft snort. "Sitting isn't my style," he said, then regarded the young female dragon. "Racha, is it? Thank you for rallying the dragons and bringing them all here. I wish we could have recruited more turul, but Sophia informed me the Enclaves are too spread out. They're on alert for any needs we may have at least, and will be ready to move at a moment's notice."

She nodded. "The rest of the Court and I are at your command. Is there anything you need?"

"A war table," he said, eyeing the platform where the throne rested. "That throne is useless to us."

"Consider it done." Her eyes flashed with green light, and seconds later a handful of big, pale-haired Guardians came into the room. White smoke billowed out of their mouths as they surrounded the throne, drifting in a cloud to encompass the hunk of green jade, and the stone began to change shape.

Before his eyes, the throne disappeared, replaced by a huge stone table the width of a large dragon. Wisps of smoke concentrated so tightly on the surface it looked like dozens of small snakes darting around as a map took shape. The rugged landscape of the map shifted swiftly, areas sinking deep while others rose up from the flat shapes of continents. Ethereal smoke filled the deep depressions, grew clear, and settled with small ripples to indicate liquid.

The Guardians had created a scale replica of the entire planet by the time they were done, then seemed to hesitate, congregating and whispering.

"This is more than I need," Nikhil said. "It's amazing, frankly. What else is there?"

The dragon who'd been introduced as Roka looked up and said, "The higher realms, sir. We can mark the locations of the entry points, but we only know the landscape of the Dragon Glade."

"Then show me what you know and we'll figure out the rest."

Roka nodded, and a fresh plume of white smoke billowed from his nostrils. The others joined in, and within a few more moments there were four small globes hovering above the map of the Earth, each a swirling mass of color he knew represented the element commanded by each of the higher races. A blue globe for the Haven, a white one for the Enclaves, a green one for the Sanctuary, and a red one for the Dragon Glade.

Beneath the hovering globes, the map lit up with multicolored lights, showing him where the portals were for each of the worlds. Only the Dragon Glade had a single point of entry, but the seven hibernation temples were also marked. Four green marks glowed for the different Sanctuary portals, four white ones for the turul Enclaves. The Haven's access was nonexistent, however.

Nikhil cursed. They needed Calder for this. No one in his army knew a thing about the Haven, and that was the one place they needed to focus on.

When he looked up, he realized a crowd had gathered, dozens of eyes regarding him expectantly. One pair in particular, deep green flecked with silver, caught his attention.

"Nicholas," Nikhil said. "Is your link to Calder ... safe?" He still had a difficult time even thinking about the blood meld his surrogate son had taken part in a week earlier.

Nicholas nodded. "It's strong. He assured us it's unbreakable. Aurum and I have a link not only to him, but to his sister in the Haven and to her mates as well. Calder may not be able to report in often where he is, but we can report for him."

"Where is he now? Is he still in Madagascar?"

"He's been captured as planned," Nicholas said, his jaw clenching just slightly, betraying his frustration at not being near his satyr mate. "They have him in transit now, headed north, as far as we can tell, but he has no idea what the destination is."

"And you and Aurum have the capability to drift without him?"

Nicholas gave him a patient smile. "We *are* him, *noshi*. The blood meld made us one soul. Our powers are merged now, so yes, we can both drift to wherever we need to go."

Nikhil froze at the old paternal endearment the young ursa used for him. His gaze fixed to Nicholas's face and a solid stone seemed to block his throat. He was not the boy's father, but perhaps was the closest thing to one that Nicholas had ever had.

"And your mind …" Nikhil began, forcing the words past the tightness and failing. He shook his head. "Never mind. Everyone out except for Nicholas and Roka. I need you two to finish this map."

The observers departed, chatting among themselves, leaving Nikhil with the young ursa he'd long considered his adopted son and the dragon Guardian from the Court. The white-haired Roka stood back with arms crossed, waiting patient and silent. Nicholas, however, came forward and placed both hands on Nikhil's shoulders.

"My mind is strong and is my own. What Meri did to you is nothing like a true blood meld is meant to be. She *raped* your mind, *noshi*. The bond I share with Aurum and Calder is purely consensual and built from love. Gavra, Assana, and

Silas have the same kind of bond, and we are all stronger for it. *We will beat her.*"

"Good," Nikhil said, unable to keep the rough edge of relief from his voice. "Because the three of you are the key to getting to Meri and neutralizing her once she's shown us the location of Calder's father, if the man is still alive."

"Finding Nereus is the best path to protecting the Haven. At least we all agree on that."

"It's a defensive measure only. Our aim is still to destroy Meri, but understanding what she may be after helps us strategize. If we are correct about her goal, she will try everything to reach the Source to use its power. But she is still unpredictable and holds immeasurable power as long as she still maintains control of the Ultiori and all the facilities the organization owns. Even after reclaiming my memories, I know there are gaps in my knowledge about the organization. She kept me in the dark most of the time she controlled me. Gave me the illusion of power while I pursued my own agenda of revenge against the dragons."

"I thought your agenda was to create a child and you lost interest after finding me," Nicholas asked.

"Oh, I still wanted a child. One that would resemble what I imagined a child of Belah's might look like. Meri seemed to prefer encouraging the violence, however. I think that's where the breakdown in our link began. She pushed that rage too far. And when I learned Belah was in the world again, the contradiction between Meri's influence to have me kill and my desire to be with Belah finally made me snap. Of course, without Belah or Evie North's song, she'd have been able to regain control. But I would have been little use to her. And now that I know I *have* a daughter … Well, let's just say that there's only one thing I have to do before my life is complete."

Roka shifted positions off to the side, uncrossing his arms

and dropping his hands. Nikhil redirected his attention to the big, white Guardian. "Are you implementing operation Wildcard?"

Nikhil's eyebrows rose at the mention of the mission he'd sent his Elites on now that Calder was in position as an Ultiori captive. "How do you know about that?"

"I listen," Roka said, but didn't elaborate.

"I'd like it to be a surprise for Belah. So if you don't mind, please don't mention it outside this room."

"Yes, sir," Roka said, and Nikhil gave him a sidelong look, but the big dragon was clearly a man of few words. Despite his high rank among the Court, he was at his heart a soldier, which was clear to Nikhil by his keen attention and solid bearing, not to mention his deference to his superiors. He appreciated the Guardian's economy of speech and knew he would follow commands without question.

The project Roka had mentioned excited Nikhil, but so far only Ked and Kol knew of it, which meant one of them likely mentioned it to Roka. He turned back to the map, his gaze gravitating to the glowing dot in the center of Australia.

Somewhere in the world right now, his two oldest Elites were en route to that spot—the newest dragon temple to be built and the one where his daughter Asha currently lay in hibernation.

The very second he'd given Naaz and Neela permission to embark on their journey, they'd left. Naaz hadn't granted him a backward glance, but Neela hesitated before following her twin brother. The lithe, beautiful, dark-skinned warrior he'd trained and raised as his own had looked back at him as though she needed his blessing to go.

"Zorion is yours, Neela. Go find him."

She'd come back to him and gazed up into his eyes. "I'm not thinking about Zorion right now, Sayid. You know what is missing. What we must find at the end of this. I need to know what happened to the baby Meri took from me."

"The child died. Miscarried like the others," he'd said, but Neela gave him a sad look and shook her head.

"You and I both know that isn't true. She was our blood. Yours and mine. The sooner you admit that bitch used you for stud duty as much as my brother and the other Elites, the better. We were *all* her slaves. I am happy you are with Belah finally, but *we* made a baby too. Don't forget her once Naaz comes back with the daughter you truly wanted."

Nikhil closed his eyes, still stinging from the disappointed look Neela had given him before turning to go. Operation Wildcard was their secret—Naaz and Neela had ached to be reunited with their dragon mates for centuries, ever since Nikhil hid the pair of treasures away from them. He'd only recently discovered the two ancient sarcophagi were none other than the pair of immortal dragon children that had been stolen from Belah so long ago.

His head swam every time he thought of them both, but he should have long been over the implications by now, especially considering he'd fathered another child with a woman he'd long thought of as a daughter herself. It didn't matter that Meri had been in his head when it happened, making her vile promises even as he made love to Neela inside her prison cell. They were all old enough to be well past the perceived perversion of *how* the children were made. They weren't even children anymore, after all.

At least Zorion and Asha weren't. He snorted softly. Zorion ... whatever he was. The ancient offspring of a pair of immortal dragon siblings, stolen away because of how potentially destructive his power could be. Well, Zorion was about to be introduced to the female Fate intended for him, and if he knew Neela, she'd take advantage of whatever powers Zorion had to offer in order to find the baby that had been taken from her.

He didn't like the idea of a wildcard in his army, didn't quite trust that Zorion would accept his commands, but he had instructed the twins to convince their mates to stay put until called upon, and he at least trusted *them* to do what he asked.

Nikhil directed his attention to the map once more, forcing himself to avoid looking at the glowing dot in the center of Australia and wondering how close Naaz was to waking Asha. He'd protected his daughter and her brother for eons, not even knowing their identities for most of that time. Some deep understanding of their significance ... their value ... had driven him to hide them away, however. The discovery that the pair had been his own lover's lost children made it all make sense.

Now it was time to awaken them, though the truth was that he could have done so at any point in history. He could have allowed Naaz and Neela to follow through with their instinctive need the very day they'd discovered the pair of hibernating dragons in one of the most remote, magically secured chambers Nikhil had ever come across. The fact that Naaz and Neela had the power to enter should not have been a mystery. He knew now that they had always been meant to awaken the pair.

If it was meant to be, why did it still make him itch?

Belah's scent reached him a moment before her gentle touch soothed its way down his arm. He turned to see her blue-eyed gaze, and her slight, inquisitive smile.

"What troubles you, Nikhil? It isn't like you to appear ..." She paused and leaned forward, then whispered into his ear, *"Helpless."*

Pressing his lips together, he shook his head. This was supposed to be a surprise.

"Nothing's troubling me," he said, and was unsurprised by her raised eyebrow.

She regarded him silently, her power a barely perceptible tingle inside his mind, reminding him that she could easily read his thoughts if she chose to. He *was* her pet, though she let him be the master. But if he couldn't tell her, who would he tell?

"I met with the twins before we embarked. When you and Iszak and Lukas were gathering the turul to bring them here, I found Sterlyn and Marcus and called the twins back to the Monastery."

Her eyes widened and her mouth dropped open. "The twins … you mean *my* twins? My godchildren? Why …?" Confusion and a hint of hurt crossed her face, her brows drawing together.

"I'd hoped to surprise you twofold. But secrets are dangerous, and maybe this will still be a surprise. Naaz and Neela are the reason I found your son and our daughter. They are Zorion and Asha's mates. And so I sent them to do what a hibernating dragon's mates are meant to do."

Tears immediately sprang to her eyes, making his heart lurch uncomfortably in his chest. He wasn't used to these extremes of emotion and wasn't sure quite how to react, but he pulled her against him, giving into the impulse to hold her tight.

"Why are you crying? This is good. At least, I thought it would be good …"

"It is!" she said, pulling back and staring up at him. "It's more than good. It's the most wonderful thing I could imagine. And you knew this all along? That the twins were fated to be with my children?"

"Not at first. It wasn't until the second generation of dragons woke from hibernation that the Ultiori put together how things worked. Then I understood why the twins reacted the way they did when I took your children away from them. At the time, I only cared about controlling them … keeping them loyal, even if it was under duress. I owe them this."

"And yet you're troubled by it," she said.

Nikhil chuckled. "'Troubled' is an understatement. There are other things I'd prefer not to speak of yet, but the idea of giving up this control I've maintained for so long … I have barely begun to know my own daughter. In my mind she is a child, even though I know in reality that is far from the truth. What if Naaz is too much like me? I know he isn't my blood, but he is like a son. I trained him. And Zorion … I know his father too well. I'm not sure I trust him. Am I going to regret this?"

He trailed off, perplexed by the amusement on Belah's pretty face. When she lifted a hand to touch his cheek, he leaned back, frowning at her.

"You're her father. Asha is the only child of your blood. Of course you're going to feel overprotective. And Neela is like a daughter to you. You do realize that both these women are more than capable of taking care of themselves? You have nothing to worry about, but it is no surprise you do regardless. This is merely what it means to be a parent. So get used to it."

He twisted his mouth and stared back down at the map, unable to suppress a growling expletive. How the hell did he get used to this feeling of helplessness?

"*Noshi*, the Haven is mapped, as is the Sanctuary," Nicholas said, drawing him out of his brooding.

Grateful for the distraction, Nikhil moved around the huge table to stand between the big ursa and the dragon guardian.

"Show me, son," he said. As he leaned in and listened to Nicholas's explanation of how the new maps worked, he caught Belah looking at him, her gaze shifting between him and Nicholas. Realizing what he'd just called the boy, he gave her a half-smile and shrugged.

This was what it meant to be a parent. Half worry, half pride in the accomplishments of his children, even if they weren't of his blood. The child growing in his lover's womb would hold no less prominent a place in his heart than the man who stood beside him, or his true daughter who still lay asleep somewhere on the other side of the world.

And if Neela was right and another daughter existed, he would move mountains to protect her too.

CHAPTER 9

VRISHTI

With her eyes closed, all of Vrishti's other senses came alive. She thought she heard Neph speak a soft curse—or was it a prayer? Then she heard him move, the air in the room growing cool and damp like a thick fog had blown through before the heat of the fire warmed her again.

She tensed, digging her fingertips into the tops of her thighs as she tried to track his position by sound. He moved closer, then her skin cooled, telling her his body stood between her and the fire, blocking some of the heat. She turned her head, faithfully keeping her eyes closed, but aiming her senses in the direction of his breathing. Then that sound lowered and she guessed he must have crouched next to the sofa at her side.

Fingertips gently touched her cheek, a thumb slid over her jaw, and then his hand cupped the back of her head. Her heart pounded, and she couldn't decide whether she was terrified or incredibly turned on, even though the touch was completely innocent.

"Open your eyes, love," he said, only the voice was not his

smooth-as-silk seductive one. It was rougher, more guttural, and as familiar to her as her own breath.

Her eyes flew open and she let out a sharp cry. "Aodh? Wait … how …?"

She sat up and reached for him. The shining white hair was his, the pale eyes were his. The strong lines of his face, the square jaw and thick neck. Everything was right, but it couldn't be this easy.

"This is what you wished to see, is it not?" he asked, and she finally understood.

"Neph … you … you're *him*."

He closed his eyes, and a soft smile played at his lips that seemed a little sad, but when he opened them again, all she could see was the same raw desire she'd seen in her dragon's gaze the last time they'd seen each other. That day when the ursa clan leaders had trapped the three dragons in magical cells, she'd gone to him, but a barrier had separated them and they hadn't been allowed to so much as embrace.

But this wasn't really him. "You don't have to do this," she said.

"It's your fantasy. If seeing him is what you need to trigger your estrous, we need to try. Enjoy it. Enjoy me, and take advantage of your ursa nature while we're at it. I am at your command every bit as much as Aodh would be, were he here for real."

"But you're still not him," she said. "You can't fake it."

His face grew serious in a way that was so much like the expression the last time she'd seen Aodh.

"I am yours, Vrishti," he said, his intonation and accent the perfect replica of Aodh's. "If you choose me as your mate, I am at your command as much as any ursa male would be. It doesn't matter that I'm not an ursa."

She slid her hand down the side of his face, marveling at the likeness. She could get lost in those pale eyes that reminded her of the snowstorm she'd seen through her window the night before. She grazed her nails lightly over his stubbled cheek, remembering how she'd wished to touch him that last day and feel the roughness of that unshaved cheek against her skin.

This was about indulging herself now, wasn't it? That was what Neph had said. Just feel … enjoy the moment. And he had given her the perfect gift to awaken her pleasure. But she didn't want a one-sided experience. Could he fake all of it that well?

"I want you to take pleasure from me, too," she said. "Make me believe it. If you want a command from me, that's it. Make me believe I am pleasing you."

"My love, everything about you pleases me."

He raised his hands again and cupped her cheeks, one thumb grazing over her lower lip. His gaze fixed on her mouth and Vrishti was sure her heart couldn't beat any harder. Would he kiss the same? How faithful could Neph really be to Aodh's true nature?

She was about to burst with desire to know when his warm lips finally brushed over hers. She thought he might tease at first, but then he let out a low growl and surged forward, claiming her with a kiss so hungry she was immediately thrown back to that first moment. The first time Aodh held her in his arms, he'd kissed her exactly like this.

Only that time, they'd both been fully clothed.

Vrishti responded with a soft moan of her own, clinging to his shoulders. His muscles rippled beneath her palms as he moved, large hands sliding up her back and pulling her closer. Her knees pressed at his belly and she reflexively spread her legs to allow him to draw her into him. He was so big, he made her feel small by comparison. Not even Neph was quite big enough to do that, except in that intimidating primal form of his.

This is Neph, she reminded herself, but when she pulled away from the kiss and the lust-filled silvery irises of her dragon peered back at her, she gave in fully to the fantasy.

His lips descended to her throat and she sighed, arching into his kisses. He wrapped both hands around her waist, easily holding her while he worked his way over her collarbone and down her chest, trailing a wet tongue along her sternum. The sensation tickled in a strange way, and she glanced down to see that his tongue was far from the human shape she'd felt when he kissed her. It was forked, the dual tips grazing up over one nipple and toying with it until she twitched from the pleasure.

"D-do dragon tongues really look like that?" she asked.

He latched onto her nipple with his lips, but they spread into a smile as he nodded. "I know this body as well as I know my own," he said. "Every inch is true to him. The way I use it is true to him, especially the way I intend to worship you with it."

She lost focus when his talented tongue and lips shifted to her other breast, his big hand cupping and kneading as he sucked. Acute, throbbing heat ignited between her legs, the wetness coating the tops of her thighs.

This was so much better than her fantasy. She couldn't take her eyes off him, though his touch made it hard for her to stay focused on reality. She stared in wonder as he moved lower, his mesmerizing eyes glancing up her torso as he went. He slid his hands down to her hips, fingers spanning her belly and thumbs lightly brushing the dark curls that covered her mound. He pulled back slightly and gazed down at her.

"Did you get this wet when you fantasized about me last night, love?" he asked, his gaze fixed on the dew of her arousal.

She didn't know the answer, but couldn't form words, so

she only shook her head. His touch was so close to her core, his mouth only inches away, close enough she could feel his breath and wanted more.

Slowly, he brushed his thumbs lower until the pads rested at the top of her cleft. She bit her lip, waiting … anticipating his touch. God, she wanted him so much.

He lifted his gaze to her and said, "Tell me what you want, Vrishti. In your estrous, you will need to communicate clearly what your needs are. Say it out loud."

She closed her eyes and moaned, arching her back and pushing her hips into his touch. He pressed back down, pinning her to the sofa.

"Words, love. Use them."

"S-spread me and touch me, please," she whispered.

His eyes burned brighter and he licked his lips. But instead of touching her core as she'd hoped, he gripped both her thighs and squeezed. "Show me the way you showed the mirror last night. Let me see how you touched yourself."

She was lost with need and could only nod and comply, latching onto his command like a lifeline. She bent her knees and spread her legs, propping her heels up on the cushions. His gaze returned to her core, his forked tongue darting out to lick his lips. Then he leaned back on his heels and gave her a nod.

Her juices ran down between her cleft, and when she dipped one finger gently between her folds, she gasped at how soaked she was. Far wetter than she'd been the first time. But her dragon was watching this time, and she didn't want to disappoint him.

Keeping her eyes fixed on his face, she slowly stroked herself, sliding a finger lightly over her clit, careful not to give herself too much stimulation. She knew she had a limit and was swiftly reaching it, but she wanted this experience to last as long as possible. Moving her hand lower, she gently probed for her opening and pressed a finger in, repeating what she'd done the night before with the mirror as her only audience.

His brows drew together and his gaze grew hooded. His shoulder bunched and she glanced down his long muscular torso, discovering that he'd just fisted his huge cock and begun to stroke himself while he watched her.

A soft gasp escaped her at the sight and her gaze flew back to his face. He smiled. "Two can play at this game," he said. "Keep going."

She nodded and couldn't help but smile back, for the first time beginning to have fun with this strange and unexpected turn. She turned him on enough that he was touching himself. Could she provoke him into bringing himself off? Someone should get an orgasm out of this whole thing.

Licking her lips, she continued to tease her opening. She pushed a second finger in, wincing slightly at the stretch of her untried entrance, and fucking into herself just enough until she found the sweet spot she'd discovered the night before.

"Sweet Mother, you are perfect," he said, and her attention fixed on him again, marveling at how perfect *he* was. She remembered the dragons' speech patterns after traveling with them, and this creature who was so mesmerized by her arousal might well have been Aodh himself, materialized straight from his prison.

She pulled her slick fingers from her channel just before she lost it and recalled what she'd done next the night before. The first test had merely been an experiment, but she knew now that it would feel good. She rested her fingertips just beneath her opening, her gaze fixed on his face worried how he'd react if he saw her touch herself there.

"By Gaia's grace … I mean … oh fuck, yes, touch yourself

there, Vrishti. Keep going. Keep making yourself feel good, baby."

Her brows twitched at the slip in his mask. Dragons didn't praise Gaia. That was strictly an ursa or nymphaea thing. But she didn't care. The illusion of Aodh's arousal was a potent incentive to begin, but the reminder that Neph was the one actually losing himself at the sight of her somehow made it all the sweeter.

She slid her fingers lower, a little shocked at how slick and wet her rear entrance was. The inclination to close her eyes and lose herself to the sensation nearly claimed her, but she forced her eyes to stay open so she could watch his reaction. He licked his lips, the tip of his tongue a normal shape this time, and then let out a growling curse when she finally pushed one fingertip into her tight, puckered opening.

The level of power she had over him hit her then. He was lost to the sight, his fist stroking in swift beats up and down his thick length while she fucked her fingers into her tight ass. She wanted to see him completely lost to prove to herself that she had control.

Lowering her other hand, she spread her folds wide so he could see every bit of her.

"This was when I pictured you fucking me, Aodh."

Merely speaking the words made her core clench, a warning that she was close, but it had the desired effect on him. His eyes went wild, his head fell back, and he let out a long groan of pleasure. Vrishti froze, her own body hovering on the edge of an experience she could still only imagine or dream of, but his reaction told her everything about how it felt to find that peak.

His knuckles went white from the strength of his grip. She stared at his pistoning fist, his fingertips digging into the underside in a way that seemed almost painful, but it was clear he felt nothing but pleasure. After only a few more swift strokes, his body tensed and his hips bucked upward.

"Vrishti …" he groaned as his semen erupted from his tip in thick white ropes, coating his belly. The voice was Aodh's … there was no mistaking it, but the wild swirling of his eyes told her the sentiment was most certainly not coming from the dragon.

They stared at each other, panting in rhythm. After a second, she removed her hands from between her thighs and slowly closed her legs. Her pussy was still tight with desire, but she needed to cool off or she'd go over the edge like he did, and then their entire mission would wind up taking longer. She frowned at that thought. Would it really be so bad?

"I'm sorry," Neph said, shaking his head. "That was really not fair of me to do right in front of you."

He seemed dazed and all the more endearing as a result. Would Aodh have apologized too? She guessed he would have. In fact, she would bet money that Neph was far less likely to feel remorse for such a thing. He really was pushing the transformation for her sake.

She stood on shaky legs, retrieved the dishtowel from the back of one of the barstools, and brought it back to him. Simply walking was arousing to her, with her entire nether region fully engorged and soaked from their game. He glanced up at her with a grateful smile when he took the towel and began to clean himself up.

"Don't apologize. I think you are magnificent. And at least one of us got to have an orgasm. Um …" She halted, unsure whether she should even ask the question. He knew what they had to do, so she should trust him, right?

"What is it?" he asked, glancing up at her, his eyes having returned to the pale static glow she recognized as Aodh's.

"What would happen if I accidentally finished? Would it ruin everything?"

"Not exactly. Your estrous would take longer, though. At least it would happen at its normal rate ... at the time your body would have naturally reached its fertile peak. This ... ah ... *exercise* is simply designed to make it happen sooner. Trust me, it *will* happen soon, and once it does, you can have as many orgasms as you wish."

His gaze slipped up her body and back down, his tongue darting out as he focused on the cleft between her thighs. Her clit pulsed in response to his focus.

"You are so perfectly *him*," she murmured. "Even his tongue." She reached out and brushed her fingertips over the side of his face, then smoothed them over the nearly translucent, silken strands of his hair. Even on his knees, he was huge, his head coming to her shoulders and his chest wide and thick with muscle. She slid her hand down his neck to his shoulder, squeezing as though she didn't quite believe the illusion. She *didn't*, of course, because she knew better, but he was so real.

"I am him in just about every sense but the one that matters," he said softly. "But what I know of Aodh ... well, let's just say that I know the man better than he knows himself in a lot of ways. This ..." He gently gripped his now flaccid cock. "... in particular. I am intimately acquainted with every inch of this body, so it's not a big stretch to assume this shape."

Vrishti stroked over his shoulder to his chest and moved to stand in front of him. He shifted his knees apart to make room and she stepped in, gazing down into his eyes as she stroked the smooth, hot skin that stretched across his pectorals. He was pale, but his flesh had a sheen of warmth to it, and was smooth beneath her touch.

"Is it all right if I touch you?" she asked. "I've never seen

... well, never been this close to a naked man who I actually wanted." Heat flushed her cheeks at his upraised eyebrow, pale like the hair on his head.

"Does it give you pleasure, Vrishti?" he asked in a deep, suggestive tone.

"Yes," she whispered.

"Then may I ask the same question? Is it all right if I touch you?"

"Y-yes ..." she said, uncertain of what she might be agreeing to, but eager to find out.

Aodh ... Neph ... whoever he was ... only rested his hands at her hips and squeezed gently. She smoothed her hands down his arms, marveling at the ropey strength in them, then stepped closer and bent down to brush her lips across his cheek.

He stroked his hands up her sides, thumbs grazing the undersides of her breasts, then let them roam back down to her hips and slide back to cup her ass. His touch was light and unintrusive, as though he merely wished to pet her, to experience the same pleasure the softness of his skin gave her as she let her hands explore his body.

She lowered her head a touch more, teasing her lips at the edge of his mouth, and he shifted just enough to meet her, capturing her lower lip gently between his. A little sigh escaped her just as he slipped his arms around her back and pulled her close, tugging her off balance so she was forced to slide down into his lap. He held her cradled against him, head bent to hers, their lips tangled. His tongue was the only thing that moved, teasing at the seam of her mouth until she opened and allowed him in.

Her body hummed with ecstasy just from that soft invasion, and though he no longer caressed her elsewhere, she was acutely aware of every place their bodies came in contact. She inhaled through her nose, unwilling to breach the kiss for even a breath, and moaned at his fresh, cool scent —precisely the same scent she recalled from her brief moment in the dragon's arms the first time.

They remained entwined like that for what felt like hours, simply holding and kissing, his touch no more than a light caress of her jaw or shoulders as he worshiped her mouth with his. His body responded, however, and he took a moment to readjust himself when his cock pressed dangerously close to her core. When she reached between them to take him in her hand, he pulled her away, twining their fingers and holding her hand against his chest.

She lost time like that, lost any sense of anxiety or worry, any impatience. The rest of the world fell away in Aodh's arms. In her mind, they'd retreated back to that solitary mountaintop when he'd first kissed her, only now they were as she'd wished they could be—naked in each other's arms, on the verge of making love.

She never wanted this moment to end.

Her stomach thought otherwise, however. When the first vibration gurgled between them, he faltered and she gripped him tighter, but the moment was over.

He pulled back and took a long breath, smiling at her. "I suppose that's our signal to break for food."

"We just had breakfast, though. I can wait."

But something instinctively felt wrong about that statement. She raised her gaze to the windows. Bright sunlight streamed in, reflecting starkly off the virgin snow outside. She sat up and looked around to the big grandfather clock that stood opposite the dining table.

"It's past noon. What the hell?"

He chuckled softly. "Time flies when you're having fun. Let's get you fed. Then we can resume this, if you wish."

"Jeez, if I'd known all this involved was being fed and

kissed breathless all day, I wouldn't have been so nervous about it."

"I did tell you it would get easier. How do you feel?"

"Horny and hungry."

"Good. Two things I'm an expert at fixing."

CHAPTER 10

NEPH

Shifting focus to food again did little to calm the whirlpool of desire that sunk deep into Neph's soul. He could barely catch his breath after having Vrishti in his arms for all that time. The fact that he'd been perfectly content just kissing her went against his very nature.

It was what Aodh would have done, he tried to tell himself, but knew damn well that was a lie. Vrishti had followed his instructions, bringing herself to the brink of orgasm several times, yet not crossing that line even once. He had seen it in her reluctance to stop touching herself once she'd begun, and that look had driven him to his own orgasm. He had no doubt that if he could see her aura, he'd see a cloud of energy around her ripe enough for a dragon to absorb. Aodh wouldn't be able to resist taking her over that edge.

But Neph didn't work the same way. Indulgence was his forte, and indulging in *her* meant sharing in as many sensual delights as possible. Fucking would be the pinnacle, and while he generally didn't practice delayed gratification, the reward at the end of this would be worth the wait.

He had to force his cock to agree, however, and stood in front of the open fridge for somewhat longer than necessary until his stubborn appendage finally relaxed. Being naked around her was as much of a turn-on as seeing her naked, even though what she saw at the moment wasn't even his own body.

As far as she was concerned, he was Aodh. At least, if she was humoring him with the fantasy. He needed to embrace his old lover's quirks again, even the ones he'd found irritating. He'd spent ages inside the dragon's head. Once upon a time, sharing thoughts with Aodh had been a welcome retreat from his responsibilities as a Dionarch. A pang of regret sliced through his chest. How had he gone so wrong?

He made himself focus on the interior of the fridge and his gaze finally settled on the ideal lunch. By the time Vrishti returned from freshening up, he had the table set once again with a small feast worthy of her nature and her voracious appetite. She indulged herself in food like a true hedonist, in a way that would make Dionysus proud. Every bite she took of the hearty leftover venison sandwich was accompanied by sweet, joyful noises. She dove into the slice of cold blackberry pie with equal abandon, and after polishing it off, she swept up the remnants of purple filling left on the plate with her finger, sliding the appendage into her mouth and licking it clean.

Her eyes lit on his as she sucked, lashes lowering slightly as she held his gaze. She must have seen how singularly focused he was on her mouth, because she narrowed her eyes and drew out the tormenting action. She slowly pulled the finger out of her mouth with a pop and then darted her tongue out to lick the length of it one more time.

Then she grinned at him.

Neph shook his head and laughed. "Sweet Mother, you are a temptress. Are you *trying* to get fucked, Vrishti?"

She inhaled sharply and her cheeks flushed a bright pink. "You are good at being him," she said. "I keep forgetting that you aren't."

"The idea is for you to forget," he said. "Let go and enjoy the fantasy I've made real for you."

Her face screwed up in irritation. "Except I can't forget that what I need is for my body to do its thing. The waiting is driving me insane."

He stood and cleared the empty dishes, shaking his head and chuckling softly. "It will happen. The more you relax and simply indulge in what gives you pleasure, the closer you'll get. Are you still hungry? There's more pie ..."

Her dark eyes twinkled mischievously. "I'm full, but if you'd like to watch me eat more pie, I'll happily indulge *you*."

"I'll pass," he said. "As much as I love watching, I do have my limits." He turned on the faucet, grateful for the mindless task of cleanup to give him a distraction from looking at her for a few moments. He took a deep breath and soaped up the dishcloth, setting to scrubbing the dishes while he thought of reacquainting himself with the Source and the long-unused power of drifting through time as well as space.

His thoughts were completely derailed by the sensation of Vrishti's soft hands sliding around his waist and her naked breasts pressing into his back. His blood flow returned full force to his cock and he closed his eyes, enjoying the feel of her.

"You're so much more than just a fantasy," she said, laying her cheek against his shoulder.

He hooked his fingers between hers and drew her hand to his lips. "I am yours, whether it's fantasy or something else. Every part of me belongs to you, down to my soul," he said. He clenched his eyes shut tighter and swallowed. Every word was the truth as Aodh would have spoken it, but his own truth was woven so tightly with it he couldn't tell the difference.

"I know," she whispered, brushing her lips against his right shoulder. "I just can't not touch you. I don't even know how to process all this, but it feels more amazing than I could have imagined. I so want to pretend, to let myself believe you're him, even though I know better."

He exhaled slowly. Gripping her hands, he turned and opened his eyes, then smiled down at her, summoning every buried memory he had of his old lover and setting aside his own desires to show her what she needed to see to be fully invested in the fantasy.

"Vrishti, my love, when I said I was yours, I meant it. That you've chosen me is the greatest honor. Your being a dragon's fated mate makes our endeavor a tricky one, though …" He licked his lips as his gaze shifted down to where her soft breasts brushed against him. "My instincts wish to taste the glorious energy you can only give me by releasing your Nirvana. Waiting for it is killing me, but I know it will be all the sweeter for the delay."

He shifted his hands up her sides and brushed his thumbs up the lower swells of her breasts. Her breath hitched and she froze as he barely grazed the underside of her nipples.

"I confess I wanted your orgasms for lunch," he growled, bending his head to brush his lips over her neck. He grazed his teeth against the sensitive skin just beneath her ear. "I wanted to fill myself with your essence until I overflow. I still want that. You understand what that means, right?"

She let out a shaky exhale and nodded, her dark eyes wide with desire when he pulled back to look down at her. "Your brother Gavra told me something once … I saw him at the Rainsong Lodge after he helped service one of the females. He said he never … ah … fucked them. Their pleasure was what sated him."

"I am starved for you, my love," he said, thrilled that she was finally giving into the fantasy enough to mention Aodh's brother. "So I have to live with food as a substitute. But maybe I can have just a taste to tide me over until supper?"

He gripped her by the waist and lifted her up, turning in one smooth motion to deposit her on the countertop. Before she could protest, he had both breasts cupped in his hands and one dark nipple in his mouth, his tongue rejoicing at the pebbled texture. He moved to the other, giving it an equally reverent taste, then fell to his knees, pushing her legs apart.

Summoning his favorite feature of his old lover, he parted Vrishti's folds and buried his forked tongue between, kissing her slick, silken core with as much fervor as he'd kissed her lips for hours earlier. She let out a cry of surprise and leaned back on her elbows, her hips bucking up into him. The cry swiftly shifted to a moan and when her thighs began to quiver, he forced himself to pull back.

Vrishti stared up at him, breathless and flushed, her chest heaving.

"I can't fucking get enough of you," he murmured, rising slowly and shaking his head. He leaned on the counter, caging her between his arms and staring down at her. "The very second your estrous hits, I will be inside this sweet pussy, buried so deep you cry my name. Say it now, for me, love, just so I can have a taste of that too."

She licked her lips and took a breath. "Aodh," she whispered. Her voice caught, but the swift rise and fall of her chest was evidence of the depth of love tied to that name.

She sat up straighter and lifted both hands to cup his face. In a stronger voice, she said, "I love you, Aodh. So much."

The knife of regret grew to a burrowing ember of pure jealousy. Neph gritted his teeth, reminding himself who *she* was seeing, who she was talking to, and it wasn't him. In a mad effort to cover up his anger, he kissed her, conquering her mouth savagely. He hoped the kiss conveyed passion and love rather than the overwhelming need to possess.

It made no sense, if he still had any love left for the man who he pretended to be. And he did, which was what made it so impossible to process. He would see this task through as much because he had to make things right with Aodh as because he needed to experience Vrishti falling apart under his touch.

CHAPTER 11

VRISHTI

The pretense forgotten, Vrishti surrendered to the claim Aodh had on her heart, her body, and her soul. Every touch was exactly as she'd dreamed, his warm, hard body enveloping her while his tongue penetrated her mouth, teasing at her tongue the same way he'd just teased her core to the very edge of release.

He slipped his hands down her body and cupped her ass, pulling her tight against his hips so the hot rod of his flesh was lodged between them. She wrapped her legs around his waist and undulated against him, marveling at the contrast of velvety smooth texture and hot, hard steel so perfectly pressed against her core.

Neph responded in kind, pushing his hips into hers and matching her rhythm. Her muscles clenched, an almost painful ache taking up residence between her thighs. The need nearly overwhelmed her, and excitement burst inside her chest. Was it happening now? Had her estrous started?

She let out a sharp gasp and pulled back.

"What is it?" he said, staring down at her with concern beneath the barely contained lust in his eyes.

But the second he stopped moving against her, the sensation subsided and her elation along with it. "N-nothing. I thought ... Never mind."

"You thought it was starting. It will be obvious when it does, love. A simple orgasm won't ease the ache. You'll need to be fucked by a male to find relief. What did you feel?"

Her heart still pounded so hard she had trouble catching her breath. "An ache ... like pain but nice, if that makes sense. Like a muscle that's been overworked and needs a good hard massage."

"Hmm, that's just your body's way of telling you it wants to come." He grinned down at her and leaned back a little farther, letting his big hand drift down her side, idly grazing her nipple with his thumb as he went. He dipped his hand lower, sliding it between her thighs and spreading her folds open with two fingers, careful not to touch her clit directly. His gaze darkened and he glanced down. "You're a lake down here," he said.

"You do that to me, I guess," she said on panting breaths. "Isn't that where the magic comes from, though? When it does happen ... when I have access to the power of the Source?" Her voice trembled with need as he stroked her slick lips and grazed his fingertips around her opening.

"You're the one who knows the spell, my love. The way you described it, I believe that yes, your juices are the key. The *amrita* you release when you find your Nirvana will be summoned from the Source itself."

It made sense, considering all her other spells were powered from that desire. She'd never been entirely certain where the power originated, but she sensed its buildup even now and inadvertently let a measure of it surge from her hands. Deep green vines webbed the wood block of the counter she sat on, and tiny leaves of ivy erupted from little shoots along the surface. The ache in her core subsided, only to rise once more when he slicked his fingertips up to her clit again and swirled them in a slow circle while shaking his head and giving her a disappointed look.

"No magic, Vrishti. Keep it inside until you feel like you'll explode. That's how this works—how we force your estrous to the surface."

His fingertips tormented her, one slowly dipping deeper into her core, pushing past her tight opening. His finger was thicker than hers, the stretch even more exquisite than it felt when she'd touched herself, and her muscles clenched around him, grasping and aching for more friction. His attention remained focused on her entrance and the slick, glistening folds that his finger slowly disappeared between.

"So tight," he murmured. "I can't fucking wait to feel you wrapped around my cock." He pulled his finger out of her, then pressed two fingertips to her entrance and pushed inside again.

She let out a soft moan and rose to meet his thrusting digits. More … she needed more …

"Look at me," he said, cupping the back of her neck with his free hand and tilting her head back. Vrishti forced her fluttering eyelids open and stared up into his.

His fingers sank deeper, their tips rubbing gently on that soft spot inside that she'd discovered could push her to the edge in an instant. She wanted him to take her there, to feel him inside, stretching her while she lost herself to the pleasure.

"Please," she said, spreading her legs wider and lifting her hips into his slowly thrusting fingers. "I need more."

"No, Vrishti." He tightened his grasp on her nape, immobilizing her head. She was his prisoner in that moment, a slave to the pleasure he inflicted on her, and he refused to give her the key to her freedom. He pushed her to the edge and seemed to instinctively know when she was about to lose her mind, because he withdrew his fingers and he caressed her slick outer lips until her breathing slowed.

Just when she thought she'd regained control of her body, however, he pushed his fingers back into her and grazed his thumb over her clit. He leaned down and brushed his lips across her jaw, pressing them at the sensitive skin beneath her ear.

"Hold onto this feeling, love. The more control you have over it, the more power you can harness later. I need you to come to me. Find my prison. Save this power to do that."

"I … I won't come. I promise. I mean I *will* come to you. I won't … ohh ..." She bit her lip, losing her train of thought and too hyperaware of the press of his fingers into her and the delicious stretch of him inside her virgin opening. She'd always imagined it would hurt, but this didn't hurt at all. The pressure was exactly what she needed to ease the aching clench of her muscles, while at the same time driving her body into a tailspin of greater desire. She dug her nails into the wooden counter top beneath her, as though clawing for purchase on her body's reactions to him. She could hold on. And she would.

For Aodh.

But the hot gusts of Neph's breath against her neck betrayed his own barely contained need, and Vrishti's heightened senses fixed once more on the hot column of flesh still pressed against her thigh. Without looking down, she lifted a hand and slowly brushed her palm up along the hard length all the way to the slick, weeping tip. For a split second she pictured the thick shaft sinking into her where his fingers were. Her body trembled and she let out a soft moan as her control over her reactions wavered.

He pulled back, removing his fingers from inside her again. His gaze fell on her face, his rough grip on her neck never lessening.

"Does touching me turn you on so much?" he asked.

She licked her lips, tried to nod, but couldn't move. "Yes, I … I was thinking about how you would feel inside me."

His lids lowered and he stared at her sodden, swollen core as though contemplating the idea himself, then slowly shook his head. "Not yet. When I'm inside you, I won't be able to stop until we're both coming so hard we can't think."

"But you're allowed, even if I'm not. I want to make you feel good. I want you to come for me." She angled her hand to grip him by the base of his cock.

His hand dropped to the counter, freeing her neck. He let out a harsh grunt when she squeezed him, but he didn't object.

"Vrishti … Sweet Mother, I want to be inside you now."

"But you can't. You just said you'd lose control. Lose control for me like this." She stroked her fist up his length, marveling at the rigid feel of him under her palm. Her fingers weren't long enough to wrap around him entirely, but her touch made his entire body shake nonetheless. The sight of Neph—of Aodh—overcome with pleasure at her touch caused a tingle of pure elation to flood her body.

For a second, she worried she might come just from witnessing *his* crumbling control, but the sensation simply became a warm rush that settled in her chest rather than between her thighs. She sat up straighter and reached down to cup his delicate balls in her other hand. His hips tilted into her, pushing her own hand against her core again. She released his balls and pulled him tighter with her heels, letting his sack press against the wet heat between her thighs while she pressed his cock against her belly and continued stroking him.

His shoulders bunched as he hunched over her, his lips brushing against her throat, then up her jaw, seeking out her mouth. She moaned into his kiss, struggling to stay focused on her task with the onslaught of his tongue easily distracting her.

"Faster, baby," he murmured, and she felt his hand cover hers, his long fingers wrapping around and squeezing hers against his heat. He controlled her movements, stroking both their hands up his length and down again, showing her the tempo he desired. When she nodded her understanding, he released her and she kept going, tightening her grip and speeding up her pace.

"Like this?" she asked, recalling the way he'd thumbed his tip when he'd made himself come in front of her earlier, and repeating the action herself.

"Yes," he whispered. "Just like that. I'm so fucking close."

He thrust into her hand, his velvet heat sliding up her belly in an increasingly frantic rhythm. He lifted one hand and cupped her breast, clutching it as though it were a lifeline, then bent and pulled her nipple into his mouth, sucking hard. She gasped at the sudden resurgence of her desire and almost faltered, but her mission was near completion.

She needed to feel him lose himself. Needed to know she'd been the one to cause it, to know that she could do to him what he did to her. She wrapped her other hand around his base and with both hands on his shaft sped up the tempo more, smiling when his gaze flashed to hers and she saw nothing but his utter surrender to her touch.

His teeth grazed his lower lip, and she thought he'd been about to say her name when his head flew back and the word became a guttural cry. His cock seemed to vibrate under her touch, the thick, hard flesh pulsing as semen shot from the tip. Streams of thick, white fluid jetted out, landing on her belly and her breasts, on his hand where it still clutched her. Several droplets spattered against her face and landed in her hair, and he kept coming.

She let out a gasp of surprise, but didn't stop stroking

him, only leaning back to try to avoid the full measure of what was left.

Finally his hand wrapped around hers, halting her movements. "I'm done, kitten. You can let go."

He smiled down at her lazily and she blinked up at him. Neph's new endearment sounded odd coming from Aodh's mouth, spoken with Aodh's voice. She released him, her insides suddenly a twisting coil of confusion. It was all only a fantasy, albeit a very convincing one, but still, it wasn't real.

What *was* real was how good she felt having just stroked his cock until he'd lost it and came all over her. What was real was the sudden, shocking realization that she didn't like the way that word sounded coming from a different man. "Kitten" was Neph's word for her, and even though it'd been barely a day since he'd first used it, she couldn't imagine hearing it from any other. Not even Aodh.

But he didn't seem to have noticed that he'd broken character. It was still Aodh's pale gaze that slipped down her body, admiring the mess he'd just made. He swiped a semen-covered thumb over her nipple, smearing the fluid and making her gasp from the slick texture. Then he lifted his gaze to her face and grinned.

"I'm an artist," he said, chuckling and lifting his hand to brush at her lower lip. The slick sensation made it clear that there was more of his orgasm coating her cheek, and some of it had apparently made it to the corner of her mouth. "Open up, love. I want you to taste me."

His gaze fixed on her mouth and she complied, parting her lips and darting her tongue out to slide over the wetness he'd left there. His expression darkened with fresh lust as her tongue hit his thumb and she teased it around the tip, tasting the salty-sweet fluid that coated it. Wrapping her lips around him, she sucked his thumb into her mouth, cleaning the digit carefully with her tongue and enjoying the strange, cool sensation that traveled down her throat when she swallowed.

Abruptly he pulled his thumb free and bent to capture her mouth with his, licking his essence off her lips before plunging his tongue deep inside. The sudden invasion made her gasp, and she let out a muffled cry of surprise when he lifted her in his arms and began walking through the house.

"Where are we going?" she asked when he finally lifted his head, releasing her mouth so she could speak.

"Shower. I always clean up after myself, and I made a good mess of you just now."

She giggled. "You did. I guess that means you liked it?"

"It was no substitute for what I'm sure your tight snatch must feel like, but you outdid yourself, love."

He continued up the stairs with her clinging to him and didn't release her until they were already in the shower with flimsy curtain drawn and the hot water beating down on them both. He kissed her once more, then lowered her from his arms, clinging to her from behind as though reluctant to let her go.

Vrishti reached for the soap, but he wrapped his hand around her own.

"That's my job," he murmured against her ear, shifting closer until his warm skin brushed against her back and his fresh arousal pressed into her ass.

She released the bottle of body wash into his hand and watched in anticipation as he squeezed a measure of aromatic gel into his palm and lathered up. Then he cupped her breasts with both soapy hands and squeezed, sliding his palms around the heavy globes to thoroughly clear the remnants of his orgasm from her skin. One hand moved up her chest, soaping over her sternum and sliding up her neck before moving back down to join the other hand at her breasts again. He toyed his slick fingers over her nipples, squeezing and pulling at them until the sharp jolts of pleasure made her gasp and involuntarily push her backside into his hips.

"Feels good, doesn't it?" he said, nearly growling the words into her ear. He released her breasts and drifted his hands down her torso, moving in slow, deliberate circles as he went. With one hand at her hip, he cupped her mound with the other, still circling it as he slipped his fingers between her folds.

The water sluiced down her body, washing away most of the soap, but his fingers still found little friction. He shifted to the side, leaning against the tiled wall so that his legs bracketed hers. He braced his feet against the opposite side of the small tub and bent his knees so that he was at eye level with her. His long, muscular thighs held her caged between them and she was acutely aware of the thick erection that brushed against her hip.

"This is about you now, Vrishti. Try to ignore my cock. Turned on is a perpetual state when you're naked. Remember, if you get too close and need me to back off, say so."

Close? She'd been too close all day, and his idly stroking fingers were swiftly bringing her to the edge yet again. Her clit felt impossibly swollen. Hell, every muscle in her core was so engorged she felt like she had a softball lodged between her thighs, and his touch was only making it harder to think.

Then Neph slid his other hand down her back, palm still soapy and slick as he reached the cleft of her ass. She couldn't help but let out a soft whimper when his fingertips teased at the apex and stopped. Rather than move farther, he gripped her cheek and squeezed, spreading her open.

She reflexively clenched, and he tutted in her ear. "Relax, love. I already know how much you like this. You showed me this morning, remember?"

Oh, god. She had, hadn't she? She'd fingered herself right in front of him while he worked himself to orgasm the first time.

"You liked watching me do it," she shot back.

He smiled, and she nearly lost herself to that look. Aodh hadn't smiled often during their time together, but when he did, he lit up like the sun. Had he smiled more frequently when Neph knew him?

"I loved it, and I'm going to love seeing you come apart when I do it to you." The fingertips still absently sliding between her folds in front began stroking her clit in tiny circles. She opened her legs, not sure whether she was hoping to find relief from the movement or get more contact. Heat built swiftly between her thighs, but yet again he stopped when she was so close to the edge she could taste the other side.

"Kiss me, Vrishti," he said in a gruff voice. "It'll help keep you grounded."

Grateful for the command, she hooked an arm around his neck and leaned into him, found his mouth in her haze of pleasure, and groaned as he accepted her hungry kiss. It helped to have some sensation focused on a different part of her body. She could focus on where their mouths were joined, and the overwhelming pleasure building in her nether region seemed just a little more distant, less ever-present.

At least until his fingers pushed inside her again and began fucking in and out, skillfully massaging that tight ache that made her crave something even bigger to fill her up. She groaned into his mouth and accidentally bit down on his lip. He grunted softly, but didn't pull away. He slid his fingers lower down her backside, one tip probing.

God, she wanted more. She could sense the looming limit of her will swiftly approaching, but needed to see how far she could go, to feel everything he could do to her to get her there without pushing her over. She lifted one knee and rested it atop his, spreading even wider for him.

He let out a soft murmur of approval against her lips and pressed his soapy finger harder against her tight rear entrance, swirled it in a tiny circle, then pushed again without breaching the barrier.

Vrishti groaned a soft plea into his mouth and he chuckled in response. "Not too close yet, are you, love?" he said.

"No, please just do it. Put your finger in my ass."

"As you wish," he said and once again his fingertip pressed at her opening. "Relax. Let every muscle go, baby. If I ever put my cock here ... which is going to happen, I promise you ... you'll need practice letting me in."

She clung to his neck with both hands, pressing her cheek to his jaw. With eyes clenched shut, she concentrated on relaxing the muscles between her thighs, bearing down against the pressure of his finger at her backside.

"That's my girl," he murmured, slowly pushing his fingertip into her. At the same time, she felt a thicker pressure at her core as he added a third finger to the two he'd been fucking her with. "I think you were made to have two cocks fill you up, love, the way you respond to this. Are you sure I'm enough for you?"

The question made no sense to her. With his fingers plunging in and out of both her pussy and her ass, she wasn't coherent enough to comprehend more than the shaky hold she had on her self-control. Her body was at the edge of complete surrender, and she wanted more pleasure, but wasn't sure if she could let herself have it.

A swelling sensation began in her womb, so much like the sensation she had when she summoned her magic ... or when Aodh visited her in her dreams, only this time it was even stronger, more impossible to deny.

"Stop! Oh, god, stop! I can't ... can't take anymore!"

He immediately withdrew his fingers from her and pulled her into his embrace. The hot water beat down on them both for several moments while her tension eased, and though the heavy ache between her thighs didn't go away, it at least didn't feel like it was on the verge of exploding.

She just stood there, grateful for his sturdy body supporting her. After a few moments she was conscious of his fingers massaging her scalp and the gentle combing of them through her long, tangled wet hair. The scent of shampoo filled the steamy enclosure. She looked up at him and was greeted by a half-smile.

"I got some in your hair, too ... Figured we needed to take care of that before we got out, at least."

She nodded, feeling shell-shocked and drunk, as though the build-up of desire was somehow toxic. Without thinking, she grabbed the shampoo bottle and tipped it over his head, squeezing a healthy measure on top of his scalp. Then she dropped it and lifted her hands to begin working it in.

They spent the next few minutes washing each other's hair, and she had the urge to ask whether Aodh even really needed to bathe or if he just magicked himself clean. But then she wondered whether Neph needed it or if his watery magic kept *him* clean. But she didn't say anything, because for some reason it seemed like drawing attention to Neph's disguise would ruin the moment, and she really, really liked the way he was touching her now, even though it was the least sexual way he'd touched her all day.

"Rinse," he commanded, turning her in his arms and reaching up to unhook the shower head from its bracket. She tilted backward, supported by his arm, and closed her eyes, letting him rinse the suds from her hair. Then she stood and took the shower head from him. She stood facing him, about to aim the spray of water at his head, but dropped it instead.

"Don't I get rinsed?" he asked.

She stared back at his soapy body, suds trailing down the side of his face, over his thick chest, and slipping down his ridged belly.

"I think I missed a spot," she said, reaching for the body wash again. She tilted the bottle over his erect cock and drizzled a generous amount on the head of his shaft as though she were adding chocolate sauce to ice cream. Then she dropped to her knees and gripped the magnificent column in both hands, instantly stroking at the tempo he'd showed her earlier.

"Sweet fuck …" he said, his head falling back against the tiled wall behind him. His belly quivered and he looked back down at her. "You don't have to. I know how unfair it is."

"Do you not want to come again? Does this at least feel good?"

He cursed again. "Vrishti, what I want is to bend you over and bury myself inside you until we both come ten more times. This is beyond amazing, but it's a poor substitute for the real thing."

He pressed his lips together, his stare fixed on her face. Within those familiar depths she was sure she saw the telltale hypnotic swirl that belonged to Neph. A slow smile tugged at her lips and she raised up a little higher so that her breasts pressed against the insides of his thighs.

"I want the real thing too," she said, slipping his cock between her breasts and pressing them together. "But that doesn't mean I don't love the substitute."

He grunted and licked his lips when she started sliding her flesh up and down his shaft, the soap lubricating the movements. "This substitute … can't fucking argue your point, baby." He reached down and toyed with her soapy nipples, sending a fresh flood of warmth between her thighs. God, she'd be happy when she could finally lose control of her body and let herself be taken to the edge by his touch, to have him do exactly what he said he wanted to do, but now he was the one she wanted to see fall apart as many times as she could make him.

The head of his cock pushed up between her breasts, pink and glistening and covered with soap. All it would take was a tilt of her head to take him between her lips, something she'd craved since her first taste of his seed. She paused just long enough to reach down for the forgotten shower head and aimed it at his tip. Remembering the intensity of the sensation when she'd used it on herself the night before, she adjusted the dial to the pulse setting and watched his expression as she ran the stream up and down his length.

"Feel good?" she asked.

"It's nice, but not as amazing as having your gorgeous tits wrapped around me."

She nodded. The majority of the soap was rinsed off. She leaned back in, careful to leave the tip of him clear of her soapy breasts. When his cock was solidly wrapped in her flesh again, she darted her tongue out and licked the shining underside, toying her tongue into the slit.

"Fuck yes, suck me," he said and exhaled sharply when she wrapped her lips around his tip, stroking her breasts up and down his length in an even rhythm. She kept her mouth on him the entire time, taking him deeper on the downstrokes and licking around his velvet tip on the upstrokes. The brief taste she'd had of him earlier drove her need to bring him off again; this time she was greedy, though, and wanted every drop of his seed to wind up in her mouth.

"Baby, you're about to get a mouthful. If you don't want … oh, *fuck* …"

Before he could finish, she closed her mouth around his

thick head and sucked harder, hungry for him to let go and give her what she wanted. It only took another few strokes and a flick of her tongue against the underside of his head and his cock bucked between her breasts. His hands shot out and gripped her shoulders, then one went to her head, holding her in place as his orgasm surged from his tip in hot, smooth streams.

She swallowed, her body thrumming with victory as much as all her pent-up arousal, then licked her lips and grabbed the shower head again. This time when she stood, she aimed the spray at the soapy tendrils of his hair, amused by the utterly dazed look on his face. It seemed she'd need to be his caretaker for a bit this time.

She got them both dried off and led him to the bedroom, deciding that a nap was in order. He didn't object and seemed more than happy to climb under the covers with her with a soft rumble of sleepy contentment.

"You're amazing, kitten," he said as he curled himself around her from behind and pulled her into his naked chest. Within moments he was breathing deep and even, the hand that gripped her naked breast now limp. But Vrishti lay there in the waning winter light, tormented by indecision and conflicted over the promise she had made to a man she realized now that she barely even knew.

CHAPTER 12

AODH

Chanting voices drew Aodh out of a sound sleep. He cracked one eyelid, peered down his white-scaled snout, and let out a soft puff of smoke in the direction of the worshipers. Over the past decade and a half of his incarceration, the locals had gradually determined they had a god in their midst and decided to start leaving him offerings. Today's smelled delicious—three full-sized goats, freshly roasted, several fat water fowl, and a collection of baskets filled with fruit.

The abundance must mean it was the New Year, which would mean he'd been on this island for closer to twenty. Had it really been only twenty years?

He observed the collection of humans beside the large spring outside the entrance to his cave. Several years ago they'd built a small, rudimentary temple to him from the fallen jungle trees. Upon the columns that supported its roof, they carved what appeared to be his likeness—a serpentine creature with rocks in its claws and teeth.

He should have taken precautions to avoid being seen,

but after a year of hiding, he grew frustrated at how slow the temple construction was progressing, and would continue to do so if he could only shift and work at night. Conserving his energy for shifting between forms was just slowing him down. As a dragon he could get more done, and he didn't need to rely on the humans to refill his well of magic as frequently.

The New Year meant it was time, though, and the breath he'd expelled acted like a drug, inducing calm euphoria in the worshipers, who began playing soft drums while several started the ritual dance to honor him.

This year there were six dancers, and he watched with lazy interest as they performed the now familiar steps to their dance. Each couple paired off, male and female acting out a courting ritual. He'd never actually communicated his specific needs to them … never spoken to them at all, for that matter. They'd somehow deduced what he needed after a pair of lovers attracted his attention one day in the forest.

The couple had been terrified of him at first, when he'd happened upon them in his true form, but they'd been emboldened after his first dose of magic breath to return to their lovemaking and allow him near enough to watch more closely. They'd returned a day later, bolder still, their auras glowing enticingly with the power of their arousal. They repeated their trysts nearly every day for a week, the woman's gaze fixing on him while her lover pierced her from behind.

"You can have me too," she'd said.

He hadn't taken her up on her offer, but the potent swell of their energy just before they climaxed had drawn him close enough for a taste. On the verge of a descent into feral madness, they were lucky he hadn't simply devoured them, but there was something about their reverence for the pleasure they shared that made him want to keep them around. He'd simply crept close enough to hover over them, then darted his long tongue out to tease down the woman's back, then beneath her belly to the place where the pair were joined. His large tongue teased them both until they climaxed in an explosion of power that flooded his body and cleared his mind.

The offerings and rituals hadn't begun until a little less than a year later when the couple returned one day to show him the bundled newborn in the woman's arms. Somehow they'd connected her conception to his participation in their lovemaking, which was ridiculous. He had no way to influence fertility the way the ursa did. But the longer he observed the locals, the more he realized their overall health had improved since his arrival. His breath had healing properties, and good health certainly could affect fertility indirectly.

Whatever they chose to believe made little difference to him. He was simply pleased that they trusted him enough to feed him regularly so he didn't have to bother shifting to forage for himself. Dragons weren't exactly the stealthiest of hunters, after all.

Now that Aodh was a full-blown god in their eyes, he took to the role with aplomb, keeping a steady fog of smoke swirling around the spring and their altar, swaying in time with the beat of their drums. He marveled at how easily most humans would gravitate to intimate, sexual contact once he'd worked his calming magic on them. The seductive power of a Red's smoke could draw that desire to the surface, but simple relaxation and peace could have the same effect of release from inhibitions, allowing them to surrender to their deeper desires.

The way they responded to his magic was certainly less frantic and desperate than they'd behave if they were affected by a Red's smoke. Aodh's white smoke caused contented smiles to spread across their faces, and as the dance progressed, they undulated in a swaying, erotic dance that had them fully naked and coupling in a languid tangle of limbs.

He always waited until their auras were fully merged, their energy a brightly glowing bubble that surrounded the entire orgiastic group. Only then did he rouse and venture closer, dipping his horned head to watch with his long tongue darting out to flick in quick tastes over their sweat-anointed skin.

Some of their flavors were familiar, his tongue delving in to aid their pleasure. One of the women let out a breathy moan, her aura shivering with a tinge of fear when he drew close, but her pleasure spiked when he found her core and tasted her. A new flavor washed over his tongue and the man whose cock had filled her moved away to give him space.

He peered closer, his big heart skipping a beat when he saw the woman's lovely face, her ebony waves spread out against the dark-skinned torso of one of the men who was fully occupied with a different woman. The orgy went on around her as Aodh stared and she looked back up at him.

"Vrishti ..." he murmured in his resonant voice. All movement halted, the entire small clearing grew utterly silent. It was the first time he'd spoken a word in the two decades since they'd begun to worship him. Shit. If they knew he could speak, they might want answers he wasn't prepared to give.

He let out a harsh snort, blinked at the woman, then reared back and roared. She wasn't his mate, wasn't even close to the woman he was locked away from now, who he had lost hope of ever being with again.

Screams reached him from the clearing but he was beyond caring how he appeared to them. He launched himself into the air, crashing through the canopy of trees above and soaring as high as he could into the sky before the edge of his prison caught him like a net and held him tight. He kept flapping his wings, roaring all the while in frustration at this trap which ensnared him.

Finally he gave up his futile attempt to break free and flew in circles until his wings ached from exhaustion. Only then did he return in the pitch-black of night to the entrance to his cave. He'd missed out on this year's offering of power, which would have lasted him the year, but the food remained. He devoured it, and was about to crawl back into his cave and down into the center of the mountain to continue his relentless digging and carving of the interior when the glimmer of a human aura caught his eye from the edge of the clearing.

He paused and focused on the faint shimmering glow that signaled apprehension and recognized the same reddish tinge of fear that he'd seen in the woman's aura earlier. The woman who wasn't Vrishti, though her resemblance was uncanny enough to remind him how he had failed.

A twig cracked as she took a hesitant step closer. He stilled and watched her approach until she reached the center of their small ritual altar and knelt, casting aside her sarong, then lowering her forehead to the ground.

"I have come as a sacrifice to you, Vishvakarman. Please don't punish the village for whatever I did to displease you."

Her voice was hoarse and thick with fear and remorse. The salty scent of her tears reached his nostrils and his heart sank. She didn't deserve his wrath for simply not being the woman he wished for every night as he drifted off to sleep.

He turned and made his way back down the slope to the altar, then gently nudged at her shoulder with his snout.

She let out a yelp of fear and huddled tighter into herself.

"Do not fear me, please. I will never harm you or any of

the others." Softly, he expelled a small plume of smoke that encompassed her curled up form. She gradually relaxed as she breathed and ventured a glance at him from beneath the arms she'd draped protectively over her head.

"You won't eat me?" she asked in a shaky voice.

He let out a soft chuckle. "Humans have far better uses to me than serving as food. If I ate all of you, who would bring me such delicious treats? But even that isn't my favorite thing about you."

"It's true, then?" she asked, sitting up. "That you absorb our Nirvana when we achieve our bliss?"

"You have it right, little one," he said, leaning down and gusting out a puff of warm breath that tossed her hair back in a tangle around her shoulders. "And I fear I interrupted you from achieving yours earlier."

Now that he had time to look at her more closely, it was obvious she was nothing like his beloved Vrishti. She was leaner and darker-skinned, her breasts smaller, her hips narrower. But she was lovely and also much younger than Vrishti, the softness of youth still far from receding due to the harshness of her environment. She was every bit a woman, though, and the scent of sex still clung to her from the ritual he'd so thoughtlessly interrupted.

She closed her eyes and took a deep breath, her nipples stiffening under a fresh gust of air from his nostrils. "You may take it from me now, if you wish," she said, opening her eyes again and meeting his gaze directly. Her aura flared with hopeful anticipation, but that same thread of fear still marred the alluring glow of the bubble that surrounded her.

"I will not take from a woman who fears me," he said. "The others don't react as you do. What's wrong, little one? What frightens you?"

Staring up at him, she said, "You frighten me. Your size, your beauty. Your teeth and claws. The roar of your voice when you're displeased. You are a god, and it is wise to fear a god."

"Can I tell you a secret?" he asked.

She nodded, never once shifting her gaze from him. Her eyes widened when he summoned the last dregs of his remaining magic and shifted, his huge body shimmering and shrinking before her in the dim glow of moonlight. The girl gasped and covered her mouth with both hands.

"I am just a man if I choose to be," he said. "Nothing to fear." He lowered himself to the ground in front of her and sat cross-legged in the center of the altar. "Tell me your name."

"I … I'm Priya. Priestess in training. My mother was the first to give her Nirvana to you, before I was born. I fear I've caused shame to my family by displeasing you."

He let out a long sigh. "That was my mistake. You didn't displease me, Priya. You only reminded me of someone … my mate … who I was forced to leave behind when I came here. I thought you were her, and when I realized you aren't …"

She frowned, her aura finally losing its thread of fear. "Vrishti," she said.

Aodh nodded, his heart clenching at the mere mention of her name again. "You see, I was the one who brought shame on my family. Being here is my punishment, and it would be unfair of me to transfer that punishment to the innocent. I deserve this sentence and all the discomfort it brings."

"May I comfort you?" she asked. She leaned forward on one hand and rested her other on his knee, sliding it up his thigh to his slumbering cock and brushing her knuckles along the length of it. Arousal shot through his body, and welcome though it was, he grabbed her hand and brought it to his lips.

"If I made love to you, I would only be picturing her. It

wouldn't be fair to either of us. But there is something you can do for me."

"I only wish to please you."

"Please yourself, Priya," he said, gripping her hand and lowering it between her thighs. Her wet heat brushed his fingers as he placed her hand over her mound. She inhaled sharply, her other hand shooting up to grip his shoulder for support when he pushed her fingertips against her clitoris and rubbed in a tight circle.

"Y-yes, I can do that," she said, taking over the movements causing her aura to swell with sweet energy the color of the sunrise.

"That's right, little one," he said, brushing his lips over her cheek and sliding his hands up her sides to cup her breasts and toy with them while she pleasured herself. Within moments she was at the brink, and his soft urging to give her Nirvana to him sent her over.

The welcome flood of power sank into him, but was only a small measure of what he needed to last until the next year's offering. His rigid cock begged for more, but the rogue appendage didn't know she wasn't the woman he really wanted. He could draw more orgasms from her now if he chose, except she already looked exhausted after the evening spent terrified of being eaten by him.

He pulled her into his lap and held her in her sated, lethargic state. After a few moments, she let out a little sigh. "It might be better if you'd eaten me," she lamented.

"Why?" he asked, suppressing a laugh. "I will use my tongue on you, if you wish. I just wanted the pleasure of watching you satisfy yourself."

"Because they all believed I was meant to be the high priestess after my mother died. Now they think I've displeased you and that only my life will return your favor to the village."

"We'll have to figure out a way to change their minds. You are the daughter of the first female to share her Nirvana with me since I arrived here. You should be my priestess, but to truly become one, I must bond you to me. It will be like a mate's bond, but different, and your people will know you are worthy when they see you return to them."

"Tell me what to do."

"Kneel for me once more," he said. She slipped off his lap and shuffled to face him on her knees. Her gaze traveled up his body as he stood in front of her. He mentally prepared himself for the gift he'd decided he owed this lovely woman. It had nothing to do with the fact that she had an uncanny resemblance to the woman he loved. She'd overcome her fear of him the same way her mother had, and offered herself unconditionally. The woman was prepared to be *food* for him, if he'd chosen to take her that way.

Dragons had been bonding humans to them for ages. Entire families existed with magically enchanted bloodlines that compelled them to loyalty and secrecy. He couldn't help but wonder if what he was about to do would be the beginning of it or just a perpetuation of the practice. But it always started somewhere, and it always started with blood.

He couldn't help but chuckle to himself at the irony. He should have refused to share his blood the first time it was asked of him. At the time, he'd allowed his blood to spill out of love. Ultimately, he'd lost that love.

Now it was both for love as well as a sense of duty to this woman and all she'd offered. And perhaps a way to serve as a beacon to the only man out there who had any hope of finding him and bringing him home.

"You must take my essence first. My Nirvana. Do you understand?"

She nodded, her dark eyes sparkling with excitement at the prospect. She reached for him and he took a step toward her, his cock already stiffening before she'd ventured a caress along his length. From this angle, she could have been Vrishti. The full lips pressing a gentle kiss to the tip of his cock could have been his lovely, innocent ursa mate's. The more he pictured her on her knees, the more this other female transformed in his mind, and the harder his cock became until he ached with need to be deeper. He gripped the back of her head, tangling his fingers in her thick hair.

"Vrishti…" he murmured, letting his eyes flutter closed as she engulfed him in her warm, wet mouth, her tongue gliding along the underside of his shaft.

To her credit, Priya only murmured in approval around him, gripping his base as she sucked him deep.

He lost himself to the pleasure for several moments, simply giving into the fantasy that Vrishti was really here, that this beautiful, generous worshipper was the mate Fate had sent him. It took considerable effort to pull himself back from the brink of complete denial. The orgasm rose nearly to the breaking point when he opened his eyes and concentrated, staving off the sudden rush of climax for a moment longer so he could complete the second half of the task.

While she was occupied with her mouth around his cock, diligently sucking him, he manifested a single sharp talon from one finger, breathed a lick of bright white flame over the point, then made a slice with it across the center of his opposite palm. Blood welled red and he held it over his shaft, holding back the flow until the moment when she pulled back and her lips were wrapped around his swollen head.

Then he squeezed a single droplet that fell and landed on the top of his cock to be consumed by her on the next downstroke. On the next upstroke, he let go of his control and rejoiced with a sonorous roar as his semen erupted into her mouth. She kept hold of him as he spilled his Nirvana into her, gazing up at him with reverence and swallowing every drop.

The moment the bond was sealed, he knew, because her eyes flashed with silver light behind the rich brown of her irises, and the color lightened instantly, becoming a silver that matched his own eyes with only a limbal ring of her original color left behind.

Her lips slipped off his cock with a soft pop and she let out a gasp of surprise. "I can feel the bond. It's like a second heartbeat in my chest."

"Your bloodline belongs to me now, Priya. You and all your children are under my protection. And your children's children." He bent down, kneeling to face her once more and taking her hand in his. "But to ensure your people accept that you are my priestess, I need to give you something to show them."

They would see her eyes and likely believe based on that alone, but the color often didn't persist through generations without a renewal of the bond. The talismans were therefore a requirement.

Cupping her hand in his, he opened it to reveal her empty palm. He lifted his cut hand up and held it over hers, squeezing again until a slow trickle of blood fell, filling the lines in her skin. When there was enough for his needs, he halted the flow. Then he exhaled a breath of pure white smoke, directing the potent magic to the blood. The two mixed—breath and blood combining into a palm-sized medallion of pure white stone marbled with pink veins. Before the tendrils of breath faded, a snakelike figure of a dragon appeared like an "S" on the surface.

"This is your proof, Priya. Proof that you are the chosen one. You and your line will serve me first. You may recruit other acolytes and you may perform additional rituals at the seasons' shift for further boons to be granted to your people, but your line will be the only messengers I will communicate with. When you have your first child, take a hammer and split this talisman into two. The pieces will each become one whole talisman and will be the sign of your family's bond to me and my own line. My line will know yours by the talisman and the bond."

He sent her away into the gray dawn, admiring the strength and purpose she carried with her now, so similar to the determination he'd seen in his own Fated female when she'd last said farewell to him.

THE YEARS that followed were spent painstakingly carving away the interior of the mountain with claws and teeth. Sometimes he would spend months lost to his task, not even aware of the passage of time until the gradual dissipation of power reached his mind and he found himself craving blood more than conversation.

He would creep out of his cave and was always rewarded by the gifts he found. For a week at a time during each solstice and equinox, he received a series of offerings of first food, then eager acolytes ready and willing to perform their rituals while he looked on and took the power he needed. Within each group there was always at least one member who wore a talisman and had glowing silver eyes.

He never showed himself in his human form to them again. Eventually the temple's completion grew closer and he'd lost track of the years he'd spent. Generations had passed and the population of humans on the island increased, each seasons' rituals attended by more people until he knew it was time to fade back into mythos. The temple was as exquisite a creation as any he'd ever built, every detail as true to his memory of the creation as he could make it, even realizing that he had made it to begin with.

He was about to collapse the cave and let the worshipers continue with the power of their ideas to carry them into the quickly evolving future when he thought of one last task to complete before considering the temple finished once and for all.

He crawled out of his cave on weary legs, blinking up into the bright sunlight. A well-worn path now led up to the mouth of the cave, twisted vine railings bordering it to ease the climb of pilgrims seeking to come pray to him. Half a mile down the mountain there was now a larger structure where the old altar once stood. A hermitage where the priests and priestesses and acolytes lived.

Priya's bloodline still led them, loyal to his message and his memory, though he emerged so infrequently that was all he was to them. Only the occasional brave youth from Priya's line would venture deep beneath the mountain to seek him out as a rite of passage. He let himself be found and always gave them a gift to take back: a freshly renewed bond and a new talisman for their firstborn child.

He waited outside the cave, and it didn't take more than a few hours for his presence to be noticed. The priestess who greeted him was dressed in a golden embroidered sari and sat atop an ornately decorated elephant who trumpeted her own greeting to him.

Both priestess and elephant bowed their heads to him when he rose to his full height and spread his wings.

"Thank you for coming, Duhita," he greeted her, sending her a plume of magic smoke as was his custom over the years during rituals and visitations.

"My pleasure, Vishvakarman. Are you in need of a special ritual? Please tell me how we may serve you and honor our families by doing so."

"Gather everyone who is willing. I have grown weary of my life on this island, and now that my temple is complete, it's time for me to sleep within it. But before I shut myself inside, I have one more task, and need as much power as I can gather from my followers."

"I will see to it now. We shall come to you at the peak at sunset."

That evening's ritual was unlike any they'd performed for him before. More than two dozen priestesses, priests, and acolytes participated with even more surrounding them, playing their instruments and keeping time with the bodies entwined in intimate congress. They continued for hours, and Aodh circled the tangled humans, lending his breath and his tongue to their pleasure, absorbing the energy he needed until the sun broke over the horizon in the east and every member of the group but Aodh was limp and exhausted.

He blew out one last potent breath over the entire group, infusing it with a suggestion that his presence the night before had been but a hallucination—a vision sent from the ether to give them wisdom, and not a dragon in the flesh sharing their pleasure with them. Then he conjured a cloak for the exterior of the temple to make it appear no more than a vine- and tree-covered mountain before he crawled back into his cave. As he descended, he flicked his tail in broad sweeps at the walls and ceilings of the cave, collapsing it behind him.

If the ones who he wished to find him actually came, they would need no door to reach him.

Once back in the core of the mountain, he wandered through the vast, empty halls of the pristine temple, barely registering the exquisite work of art he'd created with his own talons and magic. The center of the temple held a gradually widening spiral staircase beginning at the very peak of the mountain beneath the gold-starred cupola roof. He entered it at the great hall where he'd placed the requisite green jade throne to await the queen who would rule the first generation of hibernating dragons.

He descended several flights past all the empty chambers where the other dragons would sleep while they awaited their Fated mates to arrive and awaken them. Far beneath where the earth grew warmest was a secret chamber he'd built to spend the rest of his days in while he waited in what hoped would not become a futile effort.

Within this chamber was a carefully constructed pool containing water from a hot spring that bubbled up from far beneath. The huge, elliptical chamber held nothing else but a pair of carved figures he'd created in the hopes that their likenesses would somehow call them here through time. But he'd decided that wasn't enough …

If he was forced to bide his time here, he wanted a secret way out whenever he finally reached his own time again. A way to safeguard his kind with each passing century.

The other temples had yet to be built, but he knew their locations and their construction as well as he knew this one. Each of them would have a similar hidden chamber with a spring like this one that had originally been merely symbolic and meant to tie the dragons to the elements as they slept, so that the essence of all the higher races would be remembered. The steam from water heated in the fires within the earth's own belly rose up around him, carried by the invisible currents of the secret ducts built into the vault-like temples. It symbolized the dragons' loyalty to the other higher races and their intention to persevere against their enemy.

All he had to do was carve the glyphs into the stone between his lovers. Six circular patterns, six of his most potent lungfuls of magical fire to bind the spells that would only activate when the chambers in those other temples were finally built.

The guardians who built each chamber only knew they must be built and sealed, the symbolic core of power to bring good fortune to the dragons who slumbered above. He'd already left the plans for all the other temples in a locked chest within the queen's chamber. Not even he would question them when he discovered them … After all, he hadn't, had he?

He snorted, his breath making the freshly carved glyphs glow brighter for a moment. Like his siblings, he'd seen this temple and everything within it as a divine gift in their time of need. Well, here he was, the so-called god of architecture readying himself to hibernate in the secret cell within his own prison. Proof that the divine powers he knew existed really had very little interest in the lives of their creations.

If you wanted something done right, you had to do it yourself. So he had, and now he was tired. Not just tired, but soul-weary, his heart aching for the contact of the two people he'd longed for to the exclusion of all else for the past two centuries.

He settled himself across the steaming pool, his snout resting at the edge, breathing the aromatic steam he'd infused with as much of his own magic as he could to infect himself with; the magic that would eventually result in stasis meant to last until a fated mate arrived to awaken him.

Through the pale haze of magic, he gazed at the pair of statues. The long-legged satyr with the most beautiful cock Aodh had ever encountered rested on one side, his huge horns arcing up to the ceiling above.

On the other side facing him sat Vrishti with her knees bent and legs spread, her core open and ready like some luscious fertility goddess awaiting the seed of her lover.

They were his, and despite his detour, he had to believe Fate had not lied. Somehow he would be with them again. As he drifted off with the sight of the two statues filling his vision, they seemed to come alive in his mind, the satyr figure rising off his seat and stalking to the lovely ursa maiden and burying his cock deep inside her. When she climaxed, the room flooded with the gushing wetness of her power, and he finally understood why the Source needed to be protected.

Power that strong must be kept safe at all costs.

CHAPTER 13

CALDER

The hunter's huge fist sailed at Calder's jaw for the second time. He braced himself, resisting the reflexive urge to liquefy in order to absorb the impact without pain. Knuckles cracked into his cheek with a sickening smack and agony sliced through his head. Deep inside his mind, Aurum and Nicholas both winced and their worry tightened his chest.

"There must be a secret portal to access the Haven. The sooner you tell me how to access it, the sooner I will put you out of your misery." Meri's chilly voice slithered into his ears, sending a razor slice of icy fear down his spine. He shook it off and flexed his jaw. It was a trick of her power and no more. She couldn't really hurt him, now that he was blood-melded to his mates.

The big hunter raised his fist again, ready to strike on his mistress's command. Calder eyed him warily, wondering how many more strikes he'd have to endure before she gave up for the day, or before she let slip some clue as to the whereabouts of the satyrs she held captive.

"I told you, my mother's gone mad and locked down the

Haven. I barely made it out alive. Releasing Nereus is the only way back in."

"Your father is dead, along with all the rest of the Thiasoi soldiers I captured. Try again."

She was determined to stick to that story, it seemed. He shrugged. "I don't know what the hell you expect me to tell you. We've been over this for days. You siccing your thugs on me isn't going to change the truth. Mother's batshit crazy, Uncle Neph is MIA, and I'm locked the fuck out of the Haven. My father is the only thing that can fix her. If he's dead, then I guess we are both shit out of luck."

Meri rounded on him with a howl of rage, her dark hair flying. She flew at him, snarling like a wild thing, her eyes a cyclone of fury, her nose nearly pressed against his when she grabbed his head raked her nails across his cheek deep enough to draw blood. She bent her head and licked a long, wet line across the bleeding wound she'd just given him, then sat back and sneered.

"I will get to the Source one way or another," she said through gritted teeth. "If you won't give me the secret, I have better uses for you." She turned to her lackey. "Hold his head still and open his mouth."

Before Calder could blink, a large hand gripped him by the hair and wrenched his head back painfully. Another grabbed his chin, forcing his mouth open. He bucked against his restraints. This was how it had to be, but hell if he was going to let her take him easily.

She climbed on top of him, her knees digging into his groin painfully as she knelt on his lap and held her wrist over his mouth. He let out a strangled cry of protest, tears springing to his eyes, but all he could do was watch while she opened a vein in her wrist with a barbed ring and her blood flowed.

This is what we want.

The repeated reminder was little consolation when her blood hit his tongue and the magic instantly flooded him. He clung to consciousness, but her power inundated him like a landslide, too quick and violent for him to maintain purchase.

Let go.

Every fiber of his being struggled against the onslaught of her power and the dark tendrils that crept into his mind. He could push her out, he knew, but as unpleasant as the experience would be, they needed her to believe she had full control over him.

"We aren't going anywhere, Calder." Aurum's golden voice reached him like a beacon beyond the darkness that flooded his consciousness. Nicholas's solid, unwavering presence was right beside her, keeping watch over the deepest part of his soul and the shared well of power they would use to defeat Meri when the time came.

After one last-ditch struggle he told himself was for appearance's sake, he let go and the darkness finally took over.

Rather than be bound by her trap, his soul retreated into the safety of that secret place, like a pebble sinking to the ocean floor. The cloudy darkness of Meri's power blotted out the light above, but he was safe within the arms of his lovers.

"This is only the beginning," he reminded them. Aurum and Nicholas both nodded.

"We're ready for whatever she has to throw at us," Nicholas said. His expression shifted inward and he turned his head, as though listening to something beyond the range of Calder's hearing.

"What are Nikhil's orders?" Calder asked.

"Watch and wait. The fact that she hasn't tried to kill you suggests she still wants you for something. That she doesn't need

you conscious for whatever it is likely means she wants your blood."

"That would be her M.O.," Calder said bitterly. *"But for what, I don't know. She has enough power with her own blood if she can still use it to knock me out like this. Female blood has always carried the most power."*

"All we know is that she's hiding something big. Hopefully if she thinks you're under her control, she'll slip up and say something. As soon as we sense it's safe, we should restore enough of your consciousness to at least listen in."

Calder hated the lack of control he had over his own body. All he had was a vague awareness of movement, as though his center of gravity had shifted and was now being carried. Thanks to his tie to Gaia and the River, at least those primal senses couldn't be overridden by Meri's power, but none of his other senses functioned at the moment, all having been obliterated by the darkness she'd flooded him with through that single drop of her blood.

"She's moving me. When it stops ..." He frowned, because she *had* just stopped, but she couldn't have taken him very far. A cold, familiar pressure filled his consciousness, like a flood-gate had been opened and a strong current rushed in. *"Oh, shit."*

The world went black again and his awareness of his lovers washed away. Everything else in the universe dissipated, in fact, including the blood Meri had just fed him to take over his mind. He was in the drift, going who knew where because she was the one in control of it and had a tight hold on him.

It lasted longer than any drift he'd taken, stretching on without end until his lungs ached from lack of breath. His body would acclimate itself to the River if he stayed in it long enough, but until the reflex kicked in, he'd be close to panic as though he were drowning. The worst part was that his connection to Aurum and Nicholas was gone; only a vague essence of their power remained inside their secret place as though they'd been the ones carried away by the flood.

He reached out a desperate thread of power to locate them. With the River's power, he shouldn't have lost them any more than he should have lost the link to the Thiasoi all those years ago, but wherever Meri had taken him, he had no connection.

His awareness of his body returned with a jolt. Cold hard floor pressed against his side, the pain in his head returning with a vengeance from his beating. He let out a rough groan and opened his eyes, blinking into flickering shadows that coalesced as his vision cleared.

A pair of sleek-booted feet came into view, their shining leather creaking as the owner crouched.

"Fuck," Meri said. "How the hell are you awake already? Please don't tell me you're as stubborn about giving in as your father is."

Calder closed his eyes, feigning nausea, but needing to process what she'd just said. As stubborn as his father *is*. Not was. Swallowing past a dry tongue, he opened his eyes again.

"What the fuck are you planning to do with me, Meri?"

She tilted her head and cast her gaze down his prone body. His wrists and ankles were still bound. He had the power to easily slip his bindings—she must have known that. Testing her reaction, he did just that, letting his cells become fluid enough for the ropes to pass through before he became solid again. He flexed his fingers and sat up, looking around at the nondescript concrete room she'd drifted them into.

"There's no way out," she said. "Try to leave, if you wish to learn for yourself."

Her utter lack of interest in what he did next told him she wasn't lying, but there was a small chance she could be bluffing, so he called her on it. Reaching for his link to the River, he focused on the drift, but no sooner had he dematerialized to become one with the flow than his body smacked into a solid wall of magic, preventing him from drifting past whatever structure she'd brought him to.

The impact left him stunned and writhing on the floor, his entire body awash in so much pain he felt like he'd just walked through fire. When the agony finally faded enough for him to see straight, she was standing above him, gazing down imperiously, her arms crossed over a midnight-blue silk blouse that accented her full breasts. She'd certainly chosen an attractive host this time around.

"I can see I need to work harder to subdue you. I wonder if your blood is as sweet as your father's." She swiped a hand through her sleek brunette hair and stepped closer, placing one booted foot on either side of his hips. A pair of big men clad in scrubs approached from behind her, one of them carrying a rope.

"You know bindings can't hold me. I'll find a way out of this place somehow," he said.

"If you had the power to even stand, you'd be running. That misguided escape attempt weakened you too much, and you know it."

He gritted his teeth, willing power back through his tingling limbs, but she was right. He was as weak as a newborn, his limbs shaking limply when the pair of men gripped each of his wrists and yanked his hands above his head to bind them together. Something hot seared his skin and he let out a surprised yelp, staring up at the bindings.

"What the fuck are you tying me with?"

"The same magic that powers my barrier also infuses the ropes. You remember being locked in that cell before, right? Not even your ursa boytoy had the strength to break out. Every creature has a weakness. Earth and Sky just don't mix. Neither do Fire and Water."

The heat that sank into his skin finally made it click. Dragon magic … Fire. That's what she'd used to hold him, weaken him. And somehow even his blood bond to Aurum had been severed, though he still had some resistance to Meri's power if simply drifting had managed to wash away her mind control. But he wouldn't be able to do that again.

Her gaze flicked to the man at his head, and without a word he knelt, holding Calder's bound fists to the floor. He felt another pair of strong hands at his feet, tying his legs together and holding them still as well.

Then she smiled down at him and bent her knees, lowering herself until she was on all fours above him. This new human body she inhabited was younger and taller than the gray-haired doctor he remembered—the one who'd locked him and Nicholas in that cell and left them for dead. This one resembled the nymph's true form more than any other he'd seen her take, which must have been why she chose it.

She chuckled softly as she lowered her face to his and turned her head, brushing her lips over his cheek. "You look enough like your father that I can pretend. Let's see how your taste compares."

Her warm breath gusted against his ear, making him shiver with disgust, but when her hips pressed into his, her core rubbing back and forth over his groin, his cock responded.

He let out a hiss of irritation at the uncontrollable reflex.

"You can't fight your nature, Calder. Why don't you just let it happen?"

"Why, so you can fuck me, you fucking whore?"

"Who said I wanted sex?" she said into his ear. A second later a sharp pain sliced into his neck and her warm mouth pressed to his throat. He could hear her swallowing, could feel the current of his blood flowing from his body into her mouth. All the while her hips writhed against him and his primal self responded, his cock hard and throbbing with the need for release.

She rose up and smiled down at him through blood-tinged teeth, then licked her lips and let out a sensual moan. "Just as savory as Nereus. Now let's find out if your essence tastes as good."

She proceeded to slide down his body and he arched, trying to buck her off, but her two guards tightened their grasps on his bonds. She reached his midsection and unfastened his pants, gliding her fingertips into his zipper as she tugged down the tab with her other hand.

He closed his eyes, wishing like hell it didn't feel so fucking good when her lips wrapped around him and she sucked him deep. She had been his father's equal in fighting skill when he'd first known her, back when he had still admired her poise and prowess—and occasionally entertained a pubescent satyr's fantasies of bedding her when he came of age. But that had been before she'd changed ... betrayed her race. It should be no surprise that she'd retained the skills he'd always imagined she had, which rivaled those of any nymph. Maybe not equal to a dragon, but his cock didn't seem to make any distinction despite the waves of revulsion that had his head buzzing with dark denial when his orgasm tore from him in a flood she eagerly swallowed.

In a flash, she moved back up and clutched his head savagely in both her hands, her lips still glistening with saliva and remnants of his climax.

"I have every drop of your fertile essence inside me now. You will not shed my hold again." Her fingers dug into his temples, her thumbs nearly choking him as they pressed hard against his throat. As the unwelcome meld began, darkness flooded his mind, but it wasn't the bleak shadows of unconsciousness. It was her power taking over, slithering in like an inky, multi-headed snake, filling in and immobilizing every corner of his consciousness until he was paralyzed in his own mind, barely able to form a solid thought.

The darkness pulled him under and he let himself sink, grateful when he finally managed to slide beyond her reach into that secret place that he shared with his lovers, only they weren't there now. All that remained of Aurum and Nicholas was a single raven's feather and bright golden talon.

She couldn't reach him this deep inside his mind, but wherever she'd taken him was beyond their reach too.

CHAPTER 14

NIKHIL

"*W*hat do you mean, you've *lost* him?" Nikhil yelled.

Their Trojan horse was supposed to be foolproof, the blood bond between Calder and his mates unbreakable, or so they'd claimed. He had no reason to doubt them, either, not after being under a blood bond of sorts himself for most of history. He'd had few moments completely free of Meri's presence inside his mind until Belah's blood and Evie's song had dragged his soul away from her dark clutches.

"We don't understand it, *noshi*," Nicholas said. He held Aurum close, her face buried in his chest. The beautiful golden-haired dragon had let out an ear-splitting roar of distress a moment ago before falling into a heap on the ground. Now she was inconsolable, her despair sucking most of the light out of the room so that even the brilliant green jade of the map table appeared drab and dull. "He was there one moment—in Madagascar where they captured him. Then we sensed him carried in a drift. Then he was just gone. It was like a door slammed shut between us."

"No trace?" Nikhil asked, unable to believe their so-called permanent bond had been so cleanly broken.

"Not of Calder himself," Nicholas said. "We're still linked to the River, we still have his power, just not *him*. His essence is still part of us, but his soul …"

"You can still contact his sister in the Haven?"

Aurum's sobbing quieted and she turned to look at Nikhil, her red eyes brightening for the first time in several minutes. "My link to my brother is still strong. His mate must know something … or her mother."

Nicholas gave him a grateful look and led Aurum out of the room. This was a major setback if they couldn't maintain contact with Calder throughout his mission, but they had other tasks to complete.

One of his teams was systematically tearing down the Alexandria Institute's—and the Ultiori's—network. It would make it difficult for the organization to band together, or even function in the human world. Without Elites to lead their mercenaries and without the necessary resources to function, they'd have trouble fighting back against Nikhil's infiltration of the organization.

There were protocols in place to deal with such events, but as the Institute's former security head, Nikhil knew how to circumvent them. If Calder was as important to Meri as they all hoped, she'd be too distracted by his acquisition to maintain control over the dismantling of her network.

But she had always been working toward some end-game related to her breeding experiments. If she was close to reaching that end-game, she may not care about maintaining her control of the Alexandria Institute's facilities. He had to be prepared for the eventuality that she had come that close to her goal to be willing to sacrifice the entire Institute to reach that final step, whatever it was.

He stared down at the map, rubbing his temples to stave off an encroaching headache.

A gentle hand slid over his shoulder, the touch easing some of his tension. He reached up and placed his hand over Belah's and sighed when she slid her other arm around him from behind, pressing her breasts into his back.

"My sister will find out how to reach Calder again, even if she has to circumnavigate the globe to do it."

"We don't have time for that," Nikhil said wearily. "Everything we've learned so far suggests the Equinox is our deadline to get to her. If Meri's planning something big, that will be the day she carries it out."

A throat cleared behind them and he turned, tucking Belah into his side as he moved, unwilling to relinquish her touch just yet. An auburn-haired human woman dressed in well-worn expedition gear stood a few paces away, below the dais that held the huge table with their world in all its detail. She arched a brow and smiled.

"I didn't mean to interrupt, but I think my team and I found something you'll want to see."

The spark in her eye instantly set him on alert. "What do you mean, you and your team? We're on stand down until we hear from Calder. No one does anything except on my order."

The woman chuckled and crossed her arms, tilting her chin up. "You can't expect a team like mine to come to a temple like *this* and sit on our asses."

He felt a gentle vibration against his side and looked down to see Belah smiling and barely suppressing laughter.

"What are you laughing about?" he growled. "Do you know this woman?"

"Yes, Nikhil. And I should have introduced you two before now. This is Erika Rosencrans. Erika and her team were the ones who awakened the current brood. In fact, she and her mate helped me find you."

"Hey, don't blame me for that," Erika said, dropping her hands to her hips and drawing his attention to a belly as swollen with pregnancy as Belah's. "If anything, it was indirect. Something tells me you two would have found each other no matter what. But the fact remains that my team and I kick ass at finding ancient dragon shit, and we've found something new—or rather, very, very *old*—that you are not going to fucking believe. Want to follow me and I'll show you?"

Erika tilted her head toward the door with a cocky smile and turned to leave the room. Nikhil followed her to the end of the throne room where the massive spiral staircase carved out of the mountain itself descended deeper beneath the temple. He had led a few thousand dragons and turul here because the temple was the most secure location that could house an army the size of his, but it was an artifact of ancient dragon lore, so he shouldn't be surprised that someone had felt the urge to explore the place. He'd commanded a half dozen shadows to ensure its security should anything breach his cloaking barrier, but otherwise had had no interest of his own in anything but the major access points from outside, of which there was only one—the cupola rooftop where they had entered.

On the way out through the door, the big red dragon he knew as Geva fell into step just behind her, piquing his interest further. Belah squeezed his hand and her soft laugh tickled inside his mind.

"You're more than three thousand years old. Surely you've met other females like Erika."

"None that were on my side. Not since you, my love."

"Don't get any ideas. Geva may look deferential, but he is every bit as possessive of her as she is of him."

A laugh erupted from him unbidden, making the others turn back and look in surprise. He bit back more laughter and shot an amused look at his lovely blue goddess.

My love, between you and our mates, I have my hands full. One demanding female is quite enough. Especially when she comes with not one, but two possessive sidekicks.

His skin tingled with a brush of cool wind, signaling the presence of the North brothers falling into step behind him.

"Trust me, we will happily keep you busy, *sir*," Iszak said under his breath. "When time allows. What did she find?"

Their group descended the staircase two-by two all the way to the lowest level. The air heated and dampened the closer they came to the doorway at the bottom, and the incongruous scent of winter snow accompanied it. They filed into the cavernous space, spreading out around a circular pool several yards in diameter filled with crystal clear water.

The water was the source of the scent, he realized, and was also filled with power evidenced by the buzz of euphoria that seeped into his body.

"Aodh," Belah said, squatting down to dip her fingertips into the steaming water. "I don't understand. It's his power that infuses this water. I'd know it anywhere. But he never knew about this chamber. He couldn't have."

Erika shook her head. "Not unless he was here when the thing was built about three thousand years ago, give or take a few centuries. When did you guys first use this temple?"

The light wavered and shifted between darkness and golden light as Belah's siblings entered. Ked's power sent an uncomfortable buzz through Nikhil's skull that faded with Belah's touch. When Aurum moved to her brother's side, the light in the room returned to normal, and it was as though everyone released a pent-up breath at once.

"This was the first hibernation temple," Ked said. "You

ought to remember when we first went to ground. You chased us here, but the temple already existed then."

Erika trailed her fingertips through the steaming water. "I hate to break it to you guys, but this room has been here a lot longer than the first hibernation, which from everything I've learned must have been around the sixth century BCE. Our equipment dates it around three and a half millennia ago. There are remnants of dragon scales that old, plus some other evidence … biological … in the water."

"What about those?" Nikhil asked, motioning to the pair of intricately carved statues on the far side of the pool in the shadows.

Erika stood up from the edge of the pool where she was squatting and walked to the other side. "That's what I wanted to show you, actually. Not the statues, but these six markings on the floor between them."

The rest of the group followed her around the pool.

Nicholas stopped short a few paces from the statues. "Holy shit." He grabbed for Aurum's arm and pointed at the larger of the two statues—a huge likeness of a satyr, actual size, crafted in perfect anatomical detail.

Aurum let out a soft squeak and Belah froze in response.

"What is it?" he asked.

"That's Neph," Belah said. "The nymphaea Dionarch who visited us at the Enclave before we left."

Nikhil's eyebrows shot up and he looked more closely, finally seeing the likeness in the statue's face. He'd only had a brief visit with the man who had come to ensure his nephew Calder and his mates were safe before insisting on returning to the Black Mountain forests to wait … for Aodh, he'd said after confirming that the white dragon wouldn't be able to follow through on his promise to get Nikhil into the Haven.

"Strange to see a statue of a satyr inside a dragon temple,

don't you think?" Erika asked. "And who's the fertility goddess? Someone special?"

"Those are my brother's mates," Aurum said. "He didn't like to admit it, but we all saw it. Gavra and Assana confirmed that Vrishti's begun searching for him. I don't know what this statue could mean, though. She's young. Barely more than two decades old. There's no logical reason for her likeness to be here for so long. Besides, we have a link to Neph now, and he says she is with him. They are trying get to Aodh as we speak."

"Guys, the statues aren't the important thing here," Erika said. "Look down, dammit. These glyphs on the floor fucking glow with power if you touch them."

She bent down and rested a hand on top of one of the six designs carved into the floor at the feet of the statues. Immediately all six glowed and a low hum filled the room, causing the hair on the back of Nikhil's neck to stand on end.

She lifted her hand and the glowing stopped, as did the humming.

"I wonder …" she said, then moved to step within the hexagonal shape within the circles.

"Erika, don't," her red-haired mate said, jumping into the circle with her. The second he entered, the entire circle lit up beneath their feet, and with a pop of air, they disappeared.

Collective gasps and curses sounded from around the room.

"Someone tell me where the fuck they went," Nikhil growled. He targeted each of the six humans who had been in the room when he entered, finally staring at the pretty blonde with the braid who was scribbling madly in her notebook. When the room quieted, she glanced around and then froze when she caught his intense gaze.

"Ah … Best guess from the translations …"

Belah interrupted her. "They were teleported to another

temple. Wherever Aodh is, he somehow managed to infuse this room with his magic, including creating this portal. Each of those glyphs are old draconic. They are keys to the other dragon hibernation temples, all of which he had a hand in designing and building. All except for this one, which is why this room is so confounding. This temple was here long before we needed it, and *none* of those six temples existed yet. That glyph ..." She pointed to a glyph that glowed bright blue, "Leads to the temple where my children sleep even now, which was only just completed and sealed within the last year."

A brighter glyph pulsed green—the one that Erika had touched before stepping into the circle and being followed by her mate. A second later the couple appeared again, Erika laughing and Geva scowling.

"That was fucking *epic!*" She hopped out of the circle. "The temple in Sumatra is where it goes. Aww, honey why are you frowning?" She patted Geva on the cheek. "Didn't ever think you'd have to go back there, did you?"

"Are you certain?" Nikhil asked, pushing past the others to squat down beside the circle. "If this is true, we could have secure exits from the temple to all these other locations."

"I've translated two of the glyphs so far. Sumatra is one, Madagascar is another ..." the blonde with the braid tried to say again.

"Sweetheart, you don't need to do the rest, I can tell you what everything says in this room if you just ask," Belah said. "Come on ..." She reached out and took the young woman by the hand.

"If we can get to the Madagascar temple from here, we can pick up Calder's trail," Nicholas said, shooting a look at Nikhil. "We shouldn't wait too long to follow. This will give us an advantage. Especially if the Lamia's taken him to her base."

"Jesus, I still picture a razor-toothed beast eating babies inside a dank cave whenever you say that," Erika said.

Nicholas snorted. "That's not too far from the truth, really."

Ignoring them, Nikhil stood back from the glyphs and nodded. "We will use the portal but not until we ensure the temples on the other end are secured, understood? We'll begin with Madagascar."

Wasting no time, he kissed Belah on the cheek and stepped into the circle with Nicholas and Aurum. The gold dragon glowed so brightly her brother's darker, unpleasant buzz was completely drowned out, replaced by warmth as pleasant as a summer sun. Aurum bent down and pressed her palm into the center of the glyph with the orange glow, and a moment later, a rush similar to the drift pulled Nikhil through space.

CHAPTER 15

NIKHIL

They landed in a dusty cavern almost identical to the one they'd left, except this one was missing the pair of statues the other had.

"The power is weaker here," Aurum said. "Definitely not built by Aodh, but it's linked. He was the one who always oversaw the construction of the temples. My siblings and I had our own tasks. How did we never know about these chambers? They must exist in every single hibernation temple."

Nikhil gave the room a swift, scrutinizing look, and seeing nothing more than dust, he moved to the door. It was a heavy block of solid stone with another glyph etched in the center of it. He traced his fingers over the pattern and it responded instantly, lighting up with a blue glow that was reflected by the glow of the marks at his wrists and around his neck.

"What's that about?" Nicholas asked.

"It must be tied to blood," he said. "I wonder if the glyphs respond to anyone who isn't a dragon or mated to one."

The trio made their way up a flight of stairs similar to

the one in the other temple and came out into a vast, empty throne room. The space echoed eerily with their footsteps. Somewhere in the distance a clattering sound echoed and was followed by the rhythmic fluttering of small wings.

"Someone's here," Aurum said. "They're in pain … frightened."

"Who would have access to the temple?" he asked.

"Only Guardians can open the doors from the outside, once the ascension is over. The temples remain cloaked after the fact, but the spell is no more than camouflage."

"So anyone with a vested interest could locate one if they knew where to look," he said. "When I led the Ultiori, tracking down where you guys slept was one of our missions. We never had much luck beyond narrowing it down to a half dozen islands, including this one. You didn't give Calder this location before he drifted to Madagascar, did you?"

Nicholas shook his head. "He didn't come to Madagascar for the dragon temple. The Haven used to have an entry point here before Nyx shut everything down. Since Meri's aware of all the various routes of access, he hoped it would lend credence to his story if he seemed to be arriving through a portal that happened to be near one of the bases of operation you mentioned."

"Then someone must have gotten lucky," Nikhil said, following Aurum up a staircase and down a long corridor.

An agonized groan echoed through the elaborately carved stone halls. Nikhil darted a glance to the ceiling, and the flickering glow of an aura filtered through the floor above them. Aurum let out a soft curse and broke into a run.

"Is it human?" Nikhil asked, speeding up to pace her with Nicholas on their heels.

"Dragon," Aurum said as they reached the closed doorway

to the exterior where he could see the aura of a huddled shape hunched down in the corner just outside.

Aurum smacked her hand against a glyph beside the door, which lit up in bright gold. The stone slid open to reveal a blood-soaked shoulder with what looked like a deep gash rending through intricately inked muscle. The figure the shoulder belonged to was dressed in ripped black clothing, and when they drew close, appeared to be holding his belly.

Aurum held her hands up, halting their trio and nodding at them both. Nikhil nodded back, accepting her silent command and watching her walk softly toward the bleeding figure. Ahead of her he spotted the shimmering golden cloud of breath she'd expelled as it caught the errant evening light from the jungle outside and swirled its way toward the stranger as though it had a mind of its own.

Aurum's foot knocked a loose pebble and the figure immediately jerked, head turning sharply and eyes widening in shock. The person scrambled around and half-stood. From this angle, Nikhil could see it was a man who'd clearly been involved in a bloody skirmish of some sort. Cuts covered his arms, his shirt was barely scraps remaining clinging to his body by the blood that had seeped through his wounds. His jeans were almost as destroyed.

"Who the fuck are you? This place was supposed to be empty. How'd you open that door?" His eyes darted to the heavy, carved jade door they'd just come through.

"We're friends," Aurum said, holding out her hands in a nonthreatening gesture. "How we got here doesn't matter. How were you hurt? Let us help you."

Within the next few seconds, her smoke reached him and he seemed to relax slightly. He shook his head. "You're in danger. They're after me ... about half a dozen hunters. I got separated from my squad after we escaped the Ultiori camp. I knew this place was here and thought I'd hole up until the hunters gave up looking, but I couldn't get the damn door to open."

"Sealed temple doors require a Guardian to open from the outside. You're a Shadow. Surely you could have hidden from the enemy anywhere."

The man's bloodied skin rippled and he let out a long groan. "Not enough energy to fade. I'm having a hard time keeping it together enough not to shift out in the fucking open. I hoped if I could get inside and shift, I could stay put long enough to heal and for my team to track me down. Our squad's Guardian is in the wind. I thought I'd be able to open the door."

He darted a look over his shoulder and let out a curse.

"How close were they?" Nikhil asked, hurrying past the man and sprinting up the long staircase.

"Only about fifteen minutes … which was ten minutes ago. They're fucking ruthless! What the hell are you doing? Don't go up there and wait for them. Let's get inside! There are too many for us to face."

"Get him back to Sri Lanka!" Nikhil yelled back down to the others. He reached the top of the staircase, emerging onto a flat sandstone roof that looked down onto a jungle below. Sounds of booted footsteps and rustling branches reached his ears through the thick foliage at the bottom of the hill this secluded temple entrance was hidden on.

He waited and watched, his gaze darting to every movement, his hearing tuned into any sound that didn't fit within the context of the jungle. He flexed his fists, his adrenaline already flowing in anticipation of a fight.

When the first tiny figure came into view far below, a surge of power crackled through Nikhil's limbs, the energy burning hot in the marks at his wrists and neck. The gaze of the person making his way toward the top of the mountain shot to the spot where Nikhil stood, fixing instantly on him.

His marks were a beacon, but that was good. The sooner they reached him, the sooner he could make them hurt. While he relished the moments he inflicted pain on Belah to give her pleasure, he still craved the opportunities to release his own beast and let it run rampant.

The first man called out a warning, then a battle cry. They were at a tactical disadvantage with their position, but clearly weren't smart enough not to stupidly assume Nikhil was the only one here waiting to fight them. The rest of the hunters emerged from the forest and spread out, charging up the hill in an attempt to flank him.

There were six, just as the injured dragon had said, and within the blink of an eye and the span of a drift, they were on him, popping into view a scant yard from where he stood at the top of the steps.

Nikhil drew his dagger, let out a snarl, and lunged. As he leapt, he pushed the magic that infused is blood down his arm and into the blade. The steel flared with bright blue fire as he swiped it across the first target's face, aiming for his eyes. Then he drifted, rematerializing several feet away behind the other men. His first victim howled in pain, dropped his weapon, and covered his face. Blood flowed through the gaps in his fingers.

Nikhil laughed, his entire body vibrating with pure pleasure at the hunter's agony.

"You've never had to face me before, boys. Are you sure you want to stick around?"

The five who still possessed sight whirled around, their eyes widened in shock.

"Sayid," one man said. "Dr. Waters said you were dead."

"Wishful thinking," he taunted.

"Because you betrayed the Ultiori," another man snapped. His lips curled into a sneer. "She wasn't happy about that. Said if we ever ran into you to kill on sight. Said we'd be rewarded. I'd like that reward, because she always has a nice juicy bonus between her thighs."

The five soldiers circled him while the sixth continued wailing from his debilitating injury. The continued flood of agonized shrieking fueled Nikhil, his fingertips itching with the power that filled them and the need to cut again.

"You don't know me that well if you think this is going to be easy." Nikhil studied their movements, waiting for the right moment. Beneath him, hurried footsteps retreated, signaling that Aurum and Nicholas had obeyed his command to take the damaged dragon back to their base through the portal. He was on his own.

This was going to be good.

He flexed his free hand, relishing the fresh surge of power, and slowly turned, following the movements of his opponents. How cocky were these men? He hadn't trained them personally, but they'd clearly recognized him. They no doubt knew him by reputation, but that didn't mean they knew how he fought.

He wished for a sword. A larger weapon would have been ideal for a fight with this many opponents. But swords were impractical to carry and weighed him down too much when he drifted. The large bayonet-style dagger he carried was the heaviest thing he could drift with. It was clearly enough to put one man down even without killing him. A human man, at least, and every Ultiori hunter started out human.

One of the men feinted in a misguided attempt to catch Nikhil off-guard. He barely even blinked, but the stunt caught the others' attention for the split-second he needed. Without a sound beyond the gust of air leaving his lungs, he leapt at the man who seemed to be in command of this squad.

The blue blade brightened, the light quickly turning red as he swiped it across the man's throat, cutting in a wide arc that might have appeared careless, but wasn't. On the back-swing, he buried the blade in the thigh of another man with pinpoint accuracy.

Jugular, then femoral in a single swing. Two men down, or soon to be once they bled out.

He used the man beneath him as leverage, anchored his hands on the ground and flipped up and off, landing squarely on his feet facing the remaining three.

This would be trickier now that they were on guard. They came toward him, slowly closing in. While they couldn't actually hurt him, capture wasn't beyond the realm of possibility, and that absolutely was out of the question.

The sudden silence in that moment made his blood go cold. His first victim no longer sobbed from his wound. He couldn't fix his senses on the position of that man who he hadn't had time to outright kill. He silently cursed. If he hadn't craved inflicting pain so much, he'd have given the man a mortal wound at least. There was no way he'd bled out from being sliced across the eyeballs. So what had happened to him?

The other three closed in and he braced himself, dagger at the ready. Then they paused, eyes going cloudy for a beat before clearing again to a solid, complete, midnight black that reflected the world like dark orbs of polished obsidian.

"You thought you could hide from me, didn't you, fool man?"

He had only a moment to register the familiar mad timbre of the words before his feet were knocked from under him and he went down with a heavy thud onto the hard stone. A pair of slick hands pressed to his throat and he looked up into the bloody, blinded eyes of his first victim, whose actions were now dictated by the additional eyes of the men who Meri now controlled.

He slashed upward with his dagger, but he was too slow.

Another man fell on him, knees pinning his weapon arm to the ground while the other two pinned his other limbs.

No. This could *not* happen so close to the start of their mission. No amount of surging blue fire could stop Meri once she had control. Their pain mattered little to her as long as she got what she wanted. Every hunter in her employ was expendable.

"Oh, baby, don't look so sad," the feminine voice cooed from the lips of the scruffy, swarthy figure looming over him. "I missed you. I think we can work things out, once you come home. I have even more power now than I had when you left. Remember that satyr I thought was so useless? The one you seemed to like so much? Well, I caught him again. Turns out he's far more powerful than he let on. And I have a small surprise for you. I wanted to show you, but you left so unexpectedly I didn't get the chance. That Blue bitch's baby is nothing compared to this. You always wanted your own spawn. Well, you can finally have it if you return to me."

Nikhil struggled in their grip, his stomach on the verge of rebelling simply from the sickening sweetness of Meri's tone.

The world turned fuzzy and a rushing sound filled his head. He yelled in protest at the telltale signal of a drift beginning. Then a roar filled his ears and he braced himself to be pulled into the rush with his captors.

The weight suddenly disappeared from his legs in a flurry of black fur and golden scales. His other limbs were freed a second later as the bodies went flying. Nikhil slashed upward with his freed knife hand, burying the blade once and for all into the blind man's throat. He fell limp, releasing Nikhil's neck, and the undertow of the drift ceased.

Jumping up into a crouch, he stared around. A massive golden dragon pinned one man with her taloned foreclaw and tore into his chest with the second bloodied claw. Then he turned and stared with horror as another man lunged with drawn blade onto the massive black-furred bear that held the last man down.

"No!" Nikhil yelled, sprinting toward Nicholas. Aurum turned and immediately let out a panicked roar. Neither of them were fast enough. The hunter buried his blade into Nicholas's back and clung to the hilt, twisting it hard.

Too late, Nikhil reached him, launching himself at the man's back, grabbing him by the chin and swiping his blood-covered blade across the man's neck. He tore the man away and threw him to the ground.

The big bear didn't move for a moment. Then with shimmering green magic, he shifted beneath Nikhil. The blade clattered to the ground and Nicholas grunted.

"Can you get off me a sec? I think I wrenched my shoulder."

Frozen, Nikhil just stared down at the bare, muscular shoulder. There wasn't even a scratch on it, but the bones jutted out in a grotesque fashion, pushing at the muscle and skin until it was white.

He rolled off, allowing Nicholas to shift his naked body off the mauled corpse beneath him.

Aurum shifted and rushed to her mate's side. "You scared the shit out of me!" she said, but her words were directed to Nikhil.

"He had a blade. I was too late …" Nikhil said dumbly.

Nicholas chuckled, then winced. "One of the bonuses of being blood-melded, it seems. Flesh as impervious as a dragon's."

Aurum shook her head. "You can still dislocate a joint, though."

"No thanks to four hundred pounds of dead weight landing on top of me. Ow."

Nikhil marveled at the pair, who were clearly all in one piece and had quickly come to his aid.

"Thank you," he said. "She would have happily locked me in a cage for eternity if she'd captured me."

"We'd have rescued you, *noshi*. The dragon we took back to base has some intel you'll want to hear."

"We'll head back as soon as I secure a barrier around this location. Drag the bodies inside and burn them. We don't want any other hunters following a trail to reach this place."

The pair hesitated and glanced at each other. "We aren't going back with you," Aurum said.

"Why not?"

"This island is the last place Calder was before Meri drifted him away. It's the best place for us to begin tracking him to wherever we lost our connection. I can sense his essence here as strongly as if it were my own. We can't waste time."

Nikhil gave them both a curt nod, barely blinking when Aurum refocused her attention on Nicholas and swiftly jerked his arm back into its socket. The ursa grunted, his face going pale for a second before he let out a long breath.

"Are you all right to travel? That will ache for a few days."

"All I need is a night with my girl and I'll be good," Nicholas said with a grin. He stood, and within a breath Aurum had him clothed in cargo pants, boots, and a t-shirt, much like the hunters they'd just killed. Before his eyes, she shifted as well, until she was just as indistinguishable from the hunters as Nicholas.

"We're starting at the Ultiori compound," she said. "We will try to get word to you as soon as we know something. Kol gave us the locations of the various cells of Shadows and Guardians in the direction we think we need to go. We're hoping to catch up with the injured dragon's squad mates."

Nikhil nodded. "Boreas guide you," he said, and watched them walk down the hill in the direction the hunters had come from.

As they left, he realized what he'd just said and couldn't help but laugh. The turul saying hadn't been part of his vocabulary before, but saying it gave him an odd sense of belonging that he hadn't had until this moment. A dragon and an ursa had just defended him from attack by men he had once commanded. Had killed for him.

He set to work summoning the magic required to create a barrier around the entrance to this dragon temple. Then he dragged the corpses down the steps and into the temple itself, shutting the door behind him. He'd station Guardians here and in each of the other temples the portals went to. They would provide useful access points to the rest of the world.

And he and the others could set about recruiting more of the higher races to fill out his army. If today was any indication, Meri had indeed grown stronger. Who knew how many soldiers she could command with a thought? They needed to be ready.

CHAPTER 16

VRISHTI

Chilly air hit Vrishti's skin, rousing her from a comfortable sleep filled with dreams of all the orgasms she wished she could have while waking. The funny thing about the orgasms in her dreams—they somehow never left her quite satisfied. They were as elusive and insubstantial as a mirage, and she always woke up wanting, but had never wanted a climax so much as she did now that she knew how to achieve one, but was not allowed to have it.

She blinked up into the darkness, disoriented by the unfamiliar surroundings. Shadows of wooden beams shot across the ceiling above her, cast by winter moonlight from outside. She turned toward the dim light to a frost-rimed window and the snow-blanketed forest beyond. She'd kicked the down comforter off in her sleep, it seemed, which was unlike her. Reaching to the side, she gripped the corner and tugged, but it didn't budge.

Her stomach turned a flip as the prior afternoon rushed back in a blur. Neph naked, transforming himself into the lover she most wanted to be with, and then all the glorious things they did, naked, to each other.

He was still in bed with her, and now she remembered that last lethargic thing he'd said after she'd made him come in the shower then led him to bed. She'd managed to lose herself to the fantasy of being with Aodh, until the moment Neph had broken character and referred to her by his own pet name for her.

Kitten.

She propped herself up on her elbow and looked down at the barely recognizable mound of blankets beside her. A black-haired head and the side of a smooth, sculpted cheek was all that was visible amid the puffy comforter-covered lump. The rest of him was curled up in a tight ball, completely wound up in the blankets. *All* the blankets. And he was shivering.

Vrishti's lips twisted into an amused half-smile. Sure, it was cold, but not *that* cold, was it? The fire in the fireplace must have died down during the night, but she didn't even have goosebumps.

She carefully slid off the bed and fumbled about in the dark for the robe before remembering she'd worn it downstairs that morning and left it there. Probably better that she didn't put the thing on, in case he woke up and chided her for not staying naked as instructed. Her nipples pricked, only partly from the chill air. For the first time since discovering her nature, it hit her how little she minded being naked. The cold didn't bother her, but it clearly took its toll on Neph.

She quietly padded out of the room and down the stairs. The living room was cast in a deep, warm glow from the embers in the fireplace, but the fire had burned down to coals hours ago. She grabbed a poker and shifted the charred remains around until tiny flames flickered to life against a remaining chunk of blackened firewood. Then she added several dry logs on top and waited, watching the fire rekindle and begin to burn with renewed heat.

As much as she didn't mind the cold, the warmth felt amazing and she continued standing in front of the blaze, letting the heat sink into her naked skin. It almost matched the remnants of need that still pulsed insistently between her thighs. Taking a deep breath, she forced her thoughts away from that for the moment. Her estrous was taking its sweet time, but she needed a break from the effort.

She lifted her gaze from the fire to the knickknack-covered mantel in front of her. It boasted all manner of odds and ends: an assortment of little hand-carved sculptures; blown-glass figurines; pebbles and bird feathers and other found objects; and at one side were family photos.

She stared at the pictures with a smile, realizing that the cute children in them must be the ursa queen, Emma Stone-tree, and her cousins. There were several images lined up on the mantel and hanging from nails driven into the chimney itself, all with the same pair of men and the three kids at various stages in their young lives. One girl was always just a little taller and had a big, happy grin, while the smaller boy and girl to either side seemed a little more hesitant to pose for the camera. In most of the pictures, Vrishti recognized the cabin itself in the background, though it was much bigger now than in the photos. They must have added on over the years to accommodate the growing kids.

She glanced around the room, sighing softly at the enticing sense of belonging and comfort in this place. She was family too, and was grateful for this mini-sanctuary outside the Sanctuary. She would have to remember to thank Emma for this when she returned. *If* she returned … She had no idea what to expect from this mission of hers, only that the man currently huddled in the bed upstairs was intent on helping her access her magic so they could complete it.

Her stomach flip-flopped again, partially with hunger. They'd had lunch then fallen into bed after that amazing shower and slept the evening away. It was well past midnight now, and she hadn't eaten since. Food hadn't seemed to matter as much when all she really wanted was *him*.

She glanced at the ceiling. Neph. Not Aodh, as he'd pretended to be all afternoon. Aodh was who knew where … or *when* … And as much as she'd enjoyed pretending, she was a fool to let that pretense go to her head.

The fire blazed and crackled, and she added another big log that she hoped would keep them warm through the morning. Then she rummaged through the fridge for a quick snack before heading back up the stairs.

Her hunger pangs had dissipated, but her stomach still churned as she made her way down the hall. She crept back to the room where Neph still slept, recalling how he'd wrapped himself around her just before drifting off. She'd never slept with a man, and it seemed odd how easily she'd given over to the comfort of his arms. And how eager she was to return there, even though he wasn't the man she was doing this all for.

She paused in the doorway, her heart pounding in her throat. The room had heated while she was gone and Neph now lay on his back, the covers kicked off onto the floor. He still slept soundly, his broad chest rising and falling in slow, even rhythm. His strong, lovely features were serene, and she couldn't help but be reminded of the saying, "Still waters run deep." The nymphaea were water shifters, after all. No wonder he was so damn sensitive to temperature.

Whatever he was dreaming about must have been hot, judging from the erection that jutted up between his thighs. Vrishti chewed on her lower lip, staring at his cock. She'd seen him naked and hard that first night, but only for the few moments before Cade had yelled at him.

Now she had a clear view, albeit in shadows, of the sheer size of him. She stepped closer, pausing at the foot of the bed by one of the sturdy bedposts and marveled at the differ-ences between this sleeping man and the figure of her other lover he'd taken on during the day for her benefit. The contrast was striking now that she had a moment to take him in. Neph's hair was black, his features more angular, his eyes slightly slanted, and his skin more golden-hued than the stark white of the dragon he'd pretended to be.

His dick was just as glorious, but also shaped differently —more uniform in thickness, whereas the cock he'd shown her and let her pleasure the day before had been thicker at the base and tapered to a flared mushroom head. Neph's own cock was girthsome throughout, curved in a subtle arc, the end wrapped in a foreskin with the shining tip barely peeking through. Her palm tingled with the urge to touch, to caress what she knew would be hot, silken skin. Would he taste the same as he had while pretending to be the dragon?

Her core tightened with a fresh wave of desire, wetness coating her upper thighs. She didn't want to wake him, but this was an ideal opportunity to push her body to its limits again in an effort to trigger her estrous.

Cupping one breast, she thumbed her nipple and dipped her other hand between her legs. She found her clit hard and swollen, just as she'd left it when she'd fallen asleep in his arms. She stroked herself gently, closing her eyes with a sigh and leaning her head against the big bedpost.

Just enough to get close, that's all ... Think of Aodh and how he'll feel when you find him ...

But she found she couldn't picture Aodh just then. All she pictured was the image she'd just been gazing at of Neph lying naked with a huge hard-on. One she'd give anything to be able to climb on top of and feel sinking deep into her aching channel.

She opened her eyes as her fingers worked at her swollen

flesh, and froze. Neph was awake, his dark, hypnotic gaze fixed on her and his hand gripping his cock.

"Come back to bed, kitten," he rumbled. "Let me do that for you."

Vrishti swallowed and nodded, then moved mutely around the bed and climbed in beside him. He turned onto his side and tugged her close, turning her so that her round backside was tucked tight against his erection. She let out an involuntary moan and her core clenched with the rising ache of need.

"This is my job," he murmured in her ear, sending a shiver of pleasure through her entire body. He gently cupped her breast and pinched her nipple, toying with it for several seconds until she squirmed. Then he slid his hand down between her thighs and let out a low growl of approval at the flood of wetness that greeted him.

His touch became hypnotic, his fingers teasing between her thighs until she could barely stand it, moving up to caress her breasts, then simply roaming over her body until the unbearable ache for climax dissipated. Then began again, never stopping until she finally drifted off from the sheer exhaustion of every nerve in her body aching for release.

CHAPTER 17

NEPH

*N*eph's cock throbbed painfully against the warm cleft of Vrishti's ass. He longed to bury himself inside her, impatient for her body's cycle to kickstart and her estrous to begin. Her soft curves pressed against him were the most decadent indulgence for his senses. Even with the ache of pent-up desire, he somehow didn't mind simply touching her—driving her pleasure as close to the peak as he dared before easing her back down again.

After a good hour of such teasing, she finally dropped off on a whimper, her body giving up for the night and succumbing to a more pressing need for rest. Sleep was an indulgence he could do without, especially if it meant he could simply lie here with her and feel her delicious curves tucked tight against him for hours.

He considered rolling onto his back and taking care of himself, but swiftly dismissed the thought. He didn't want to wake her, didn't want to lose this close contact with her for even a moment. Not to mention something about the tense longing felt right. Not just *fair*, since she had to wait for her orgasm, but *right*.

It's you who drove that habit into me, you old bastard. He sighed at the silent thought, one that at one time in ancient history would have been heard by Aodh.

The dragon had once spent every second of free time in the Haven with Neph, or just outside it in their secret hideaway beside the Nile River. They'd been so closely melded they shared almost every thought. And one of those thoughts Aodh had shared was how much he loved the taste of Neph's Nirvana when he'd been compelled to hold back his climax for as long as possible. Aodh would have feasted on Vrishti's Nirvana if he could be here.

He frowned into the darkness. Aodh would have also wanted to be the first to take her there. The first to bury his cock in her virgin pussy, because he'd always said there was something particularly intoxicating about a virgin's Nirvana, the first time she came while being fucked.

His cock twitched against the soft cushions of her backside. As much as he wished he could save that treat for his old lover when they finally reunited, there was no way around it. Her magic ... the access to the Source that he needed ... would only come from the kind of orgasm he could give her by fucking her in his primal state.

With a soft rumble of fresh arousal, he brushed his lips over her bare shoulder and inhaled her sweet scent. He was being far too generous ... He relished the idea of being her first. Reveled in it. Aodh would have his chance, and by then Vrishti would be well-trained to hold back her climax until the last possible moment. The dragon may miss out on her virginity, but he'd benefit in the long run.

The best Neph could do would be to give *her* the dragon her first time. At least for that first, crucial stroke. He could be Aodh when he first fucked her, then shift into his primal form once she was primed to take a full-sized satyr cock. One that would pull the flood of the Source from her body when she climaxed and enable him to harness that power to carry them where they needed to go.

He hummed at the vivid fantasy and squeezed Vrishti's nipple. The sleeping Summer princess murmured a soft, incoherent sound of pleasure before quieting again, her breathing deepening.

Yes, that would be ideal. That way he could absolve himself of at least a little guilt, and would be able to tell Aodh he'd had her in spirit, even if he hadn't actually been there. If the dragon agreed to meld again, he'd be able to relive the moment through Neph's memory.

He frowned at a sudden realization. He could be Aodh, *had* been Aodh for most of the day, but he wasn't presently shifted into his old lover's shape. Somehow during the night he'd slipped back into his own human shape and hadn't realized it. But Vrishti hadn't said a thing, and had eagerly tucked herself in his arms and passionately given herself over to his attention. She'd responded as openly and eagerly as she had all day without the slightest protest.

The pounding in his chest rushed to his ears. She responded to *him*, not the dragon she professed to have claimed as her mate. Of course Neph knew her fate was bound to him as tightly as the dragon. There was no doubt in his mind that the three of them belonged together. But he needed her focused on Aodh as much as he was for them to get to the dragon. If her desire for Aodh waned, it could make getting to him problematic because Neph hadn't set eyes on Aodh in thousands of years. While Vrishti may have never bonded with the dragon, she'd voiced her claim. Somehow he needed to make sure she didn't lose that determination to make the dragon hers.

On that thought, he flooded his body with magic, altering his shape into the dragon he knew so well. In Aodh's familiar form, the feel of her body was every bit as delicious against his and he spent the rest of the dark, snowbound night simply holding her and watching her sleep.

This is for you, friend. So you'll know what she means to us both once I can finally share these moments with you.

When dawn filtered through the snow outside, he decided he couldn't wait any longer. He'd lain awake all night, aching for her and hoping like hell today would be the day. Decadent plans had formed in his mind as he considered how to tease her to the point of madness enough to trigger her estrous once and for all. He needed to get started, but needed her conscious first.

But nothing as gloriously indulgent as what he had planned could be rushed.

He pressed a kiss to her neck, brushing his lips down over her soft skin and drinking in the apricot scent of her. As he moved lower, he cupped her breast and gently thumbed her nipple until it hardened. Shifting up onto his knees, he eased her onto her back. She sighed and let out a soft little hum, twisting her torso in her sleep until she got comfortable again. The air had cooled, but was oddly not as cold as most mornings and he recalled that she'd been out of bed when he'd awoken the night before. She must have stoked the fire before coming back to bed. All the better for him. At least he could tolerate shedding the covers long enough to enjoy the sight of her naked, sleeping body for a few moments before he went about waking her up.

He hovered over her torso, slowly sliding his palm around the tip of her breast while dipping his head to suck her other nipple in his mouth. Then he flicked each one with his tongue until both were acceptably stiff and pebbled. He reluctantly abandoned the beautiful orbs, working his way down over her belly, kissing and teasing with the tip of his tongue until he reached her navel.

With a firm but gentle grip, he pushed her thighs apart

and summoned the part of his dragon lover he'd always admired most. He slid the thick, forked tongue along her wet slit, using it to part her folds until her swollen clit was visible.

As he pushed his tongue into her opening, she finally roused slightly for the first time, letting out a soft, hitching cry. Her feet slid up and her knees fell wide, opening her up for his tongue to delve deeper. He took the shift as an invitation and moved to kneel between her thighs, pushing them wider and capturing her clit between his lips, sucking until her hips twitched and her fingers clung to his head. Tangy wetness flooded his tongue, and he slowed his licks to savor it.

He tilted just enough to gaze up her torso into her eyes. She stared back, her brown eyes wild with need and her full lips parted and glistening.

"I want to come so bad," she said, then let out a low groan of frustration.

He lifted up onto his hands and smiled. "Today, I have a good feeling."

She clenched her eyes shut and rolled away from him, grumbling. "God, I fucking hope so."

Neph's gaze lingered on her round backside as she trudged out the door and across the hall to the bathroom. While she took care of her morning business, he headed downstairs and started breakfast. She was no doubt starving after skipping a meal, so he wanted to make sure she was well-fed before he moved ahead with his plan. It would do no good to have a starving ursa to deal with when they started a temporal drift. They wouldn't be able to take much with them, considering their method of travel required them to be fucking.

She arrived half an hour later with wet hair and bright eyes, the aroma of her need a fragrant cloud that overpowered even the sweet almond scent of the body wash she'd used. Neph's cock roused again instantly, the fresh ache sinking into his balls when her gaze dropped to his groin and she licked her lips.

She tilted her head and smiled, then met his eyes. "Does his dick really look like that?" she asked, pointing at his hard-on.

Neph froze, caught off-guard by her reference to this body in the third person. "Ah … You mean my dick?"

"What? I'm not so dumb I forgot completely that this is just a magic disguise. I like it. But I'm curious how much of it you made up versus what I'll get to see when I'm with him. You've basically just turned yourself into a full-sized sex toy for me to play with."

She sauntered toward him, her lust-filled gaze raking over him. The sweet, beautiful woman didn't mince words, and that made him all the hotter, especially when she came close enough to feel her shower-fresh heat and cupped his balls before sliding her fingers around his cock and stroking upward.

"A-as long as it's working …" he murmured, losing track of his actions when she pushed him against the counter and fell to her knees. She pressed a light kiss at the tip of his cock and he groaned, nearly losing his grip on the things he was holding. Right … breakfast.

"Vrishti …" he said, setting the two bottles of homemade syrup on the counter and dropping his hands to her cheeks. He squeezed her shoulders and urged her to stand. "As much as I want to be inside that mouth right now, you need real food first."

She gave his cock a wistful glance, then stood. "Then you'll just have to tell me whether you've managed to replicate the taste of him too."

"The taste …" He laughed. "Dion's balls, you need to

know how faithful this representation really is, don't you? Trust me, I know him well enough to get every detail perfect. Even his flavor, which is ambrosia, isn't it?"

"What do you taste like?" she asked. "Will you let me taste you next time?"

"You mean the next time I get to come in your mouth? That I can do." He felt almost hypnotized by the look of abject hunger on her face that he was sure had nothing to do with a need for food.

Forcing himself to stop looking at her, he turned back to the stove and grabbed the platter of crêpes that he'd crafted into convenient rolled tubes. He'd hoped for fresh fruit to go with them, but they'd eaten what they had the day before.

When he turned, her nostrils flared and she finally redirected her attention to the food. There was the hungry ursa he knew must still be there.

"God, that smells so good. Should I set the table or something?"

He gave her a wicked grin. "Today, kitten, you are the table. Lie down."

He gestured with his platter laden hands to the dining table, which he'd covered with a couple thick quilts for her comfort. She cast a confused look at the table, then back at him. He'd moved all but one chair out of the way, but guessed he probably wouldn't even need that. If everything worked the way he hoped, she'd be mid-estrous before the meal was over, and he'd be buried balls deep in her.

She did as he asked, hopping up onto the sturdy, custom-built table, and yet again he admired the skilled craftsmanship of the men who'd lived here. She slowly lay back, watching him the entire time as he set the food down at her head and went to the stereo to turn on music. Appealing to all her senses was his goal today. If seduction was a dance, it needed a suitable tune to accompany it. A moment later, strains of a rhythmic bass beat filled the air, instantly rousing his lust another notch.

He pulled out the chair at her head and sat, bending briefly to press a lingering kiss to her lips. Then he took a crêpe in one hand and a bottle of blood-red syrup in the other.

"Open," he said. She complied, parting her lips, ready for the first bite. He drizzled the homemade raspberry syrup onto her tongue then dipped the crêpe in. She bit it and closed her eyes, letting out a pleased moan as she chewed and swallowed.

He fed her like that for several moments, alternating syrup with crêpe and switching between the four different flavors of syrup he'd found in the fridge. Maple, raspberry, blueberry, and chocolate. On about the fourth serving, the drizzle of raspberry went wide and trickled down her chin.

Vrishti let out a little gasp and laughed. "You missed," she said.

"Did I?" He grinned down at her and bent, darting out his tongue to lap up the mess. He captured her sweet lips, sucking the sticky syrup off before plunging his tongue into her mouth. Without looking, he tipped the bottle up again, haphazardly aiming for her breast. She let out a soft squeak of surprise, her hand shooting up to his arm. He released her lips and looked down at her, grinning again.

"Am I your breakfast, then?" she asked, laughing.

"You better believe it. I'm starving."

He drizzled more of the sticky red syrup in little spirals over her nipples, between her breasts, and down to her navel. Then he stood with a fresh crêpe in hand and dipped it into the puddle between her breasts, swiping up the syrup before stuffing the entire thing in his mouth. Fruity sweetness and buttery flavor blasted his taste buds. He hummed in enjoyment before taking another and repeating the process, this time swirling it around her nipples before eating it.

She laughed at his comical enjoyment of the food. "You're such a tease!"

"That's the point," he said. "Do you want more?"

"I want your mouth on me. You can't leave me covered in syrup."

"One sec," he said, dipping the last crêpe into her navel before devouring it. Then he sat and gripped the edge of the blankets, tugging them toward him until her head rested at the very edge of the table. He kissed her again, relishing the hunger with which she reciprocated, her hands coming up to tangle in his hair and hold him closer. He stood again and leaned over her, cupping both her large breasts, squeezing them together, and slowly licking around and around her nipples. He sucked at the skin he'd covered with syrup in an effort to clean it all off.

Vrishti arched into him, murmuring a soft "yes" as he suckled at her raspberry-flavored nipples. He slowly cleaned the stickiness from between her breasts and moved lower as far as he could go from that angle, able to just reach her navel and lap at the little red puddle he'd left there.

She shifted beneath him, pushing backward, and suddenly she gripped his hips and her lips brushed the underside of his stiff cock. Her body moved again, her knees bending and heels digging into the table for leverage.

"Vrishti, where are you going?" he said, straightening up to look down at her. Her head was tilted off the edge of the table now, damp hair hanging down in black waves. The top half of her face was barely visible beyond his cock, which she took in her hand and licked again.

"I want to taste you for real. Not him. You."

He attempted a protest … he needed to keep her focused on the dragon whose likeness he currently inhabited … but her hand around his dick and her lips brushing his balls sent every other thought out of his head. Then she opened her mouth and sucked one ball in, swirling her tongue around and around, and he nearly lost control.

"You want me to suck you, don't you?" she murmured in a husky voice.

"Yes. Please, yes," he groaned. The bass beat of the music picked up just as she tugged his cock down, angling it into her open mouth. Her head was fully draped over the edge of the table in what couldn't have been a comfortable position, but she still eagerly opened for him and he couldn't help but push in past her lips.

Her tongue was hot against the head of his cock, her lips smooth and wet. It was all he could do to remember his purpose here was to drive *her* wild with need, not the other way around.

He opened his eyes and forced himself to refocus. Her knees were bent, her legs slightly parted. Some of the raspberry syrup had run down over her hips and over the swell of her belly to her curl-covered mound.

He leaned over her, the movement causing his cock to push deeper into her mouth, but she seemed eager to take him, sucking harder as he moved his hips. He cupped her between her thighs with one hand, propping himself on his other arm to help maintain enough leverage to avoid choking her outright with his cock.

He sank two fingers into the sodden heat of her pussy and she moaned, tilting her hips up and spreading her thighs wider for him. So hot, so tight, and with that mouth already driving him to the brink, he couldn't think straight.

She bucked into his hand, meeting the thrusting digits. He pulled out and slid them lower, finding her tight rear opening and teasing around it in circles. She emitted a strangled moan, her body quivering with need and her steady sucking motions halting for a second.

He pulled back and his cock slipped from her mouth.

"Turn over," he commanded.

With a wide-eyed, hungry look, she nodded and flipped onto her belly. He moved in, looking down at her upturned face while she gripped him and descended on his cock once again, taking him as deep as he could go. Gaze fixed on the mounds of her ass, he leaned down again and gripped a cheek in each hand, squeezing and parting them. She moaned around his cock, lifting her hips to his touch and spreading her thighs wider. He dipped the fingers of one hand between her legs again and sank them into her wet channel, drawing her juices up to coat her tight puckered hole.

She shuddered again from the pleasure, and he felt compelled to give her a reminder. "Stop when you get too close."

She responded with a small, muffled murmur around his cock that only sent a pleasant vibration through his body, urging him even closer to release. Then he sank his index finger into her ass. She tightened her grip on his cock and sucked harder, pushing her ass back into his hand as he began to fuck his finger into her.

He marveled at how she responded, how much she seemed to love what he was doing to her. When he pushed a second finger in, stretching her opening wider, she shifted up onto her knees, giving him even easier access and spreading her cheeks wide.

"I cannot wait to bury my cock in you, baby. And when we get to Aodh, he's going to have this ass of yours all to himself while I get that sweet pussy. We'll fill you up so full you forget who you are. Would you like that, Vrishti?"

Her head bobbed on his cock and he made out the

slightest nod and another low moan that he interpreted as an eager yes. She sucked him with renewed vigor as he finger-fucked her backside. Her body shook with the pleasure of his attention, but hopefully she'd only hover at the edge without going over as long as he steered clear of her clit. Suddenly her ass tightened and she pulled away, slipping her lips off his cock.

"Too much," she gasped. "Want to make you come. Want to taste you."

"Be my guest," he said, removing his fingers from her and straightening up to look down his torso at her pretty mouth descending on his cock once more. The sight itself was orgasm-inducing, and it only took her a few more strokes before she had him at the edge. He rumbled her name in barely coherent syllables, growling low in his throat when she cupped his balls. He tensed when she ventured beyond, a slick finger probing at the tight flesh just in front of his own rear opening.

The ecstasy of awareness shot through his body, and it was all he could do not to come just from the gentle exploration she'd embarked on. He hadn't asked for this, but now that she was intent on going there, he wanted it like he couldn't believe. He shifted his stance just enough, spreading his legs for her. She found the sensitive opening a second later, her finger probing lightly.

"Baby, the second you go in, I'm shooting everything I have right down your throat. Just fair warning."

Her eyes widened with excitement and she seemed to smile at his acknowledgment of her adventure. She sucked harder, drawing a groan from him, and a second later her finger pushed past the sensitive barrier of his ass. Pleasure shot through his body at the long-missed contact, and true to his word he let loose, crying out as his balls tightened and his orgasm exploded from his cock.

Lights danced behind his eyes as she continued to suck him dry, her fingertip barely breaching his ass, but teasing in and out nonetheless in a maddeningly delicious rhythm. When she eased off him and sat up, he crumpled bonelessly into the chair, returning her curious look of amusement with a crooked smile.

"You're right, you do taste different," she said, licking her lips. "You taste like some kind of juicy, exotic fruit. Kiwis maybe, but not quite. His flavor is more like mint."

Taking a deep breath, Neph gathered his attention to her words and nodded. "That sounds about right. You taste like apricots, by the way, as long as we're comparing."

She shifted around and sat up, dangling her legs off the edge of the table so they hung between his splayed knees, her shins brushing his thighs. She chewed on her lip and darted her gaze to the side, a cute tell that she wanted to ask a question she was embarrassed about.

"What is it?" he asked, leaning forward and resting his hands at her hips.

"So, what I did that time … was it something *he* likes?"

He sat back with a chuckle. "Kitten, there's nothing you can do that he won't love. As for that … yes, he does particularly enjoy that. Even more if it's this that's doing it …" He gripped his half-hard cock and pointed it at her. "At least once upon a time, he did." He frowned, wondering if Aodh still enjoyed the same things after all this time. Was he truly being faithful to his old lover's quirks? He hadn't seen the man in forever, after all.

"I can't imagine I'd stop enjoying that. But then I haven't been properly fucked yet, so maybe that's just a substitute. Will you really both be able to … you know. Will he mind sharing, do you think?"

She was straying into complicated territory he wasn't quite ready to deal with yet. Keeping her on track, he said,

"He's your claimed mate. The better question is whether you mind sharing him with me. I won't lie ... we didn't part on great terms. What he and I had was special, but I won't pretend he'll welcome me with open arms. If you want us both, you just have to say so and he'll eventually come around."

Her brows twitched and she gave him a dubious look. "How could he not still love you, after what you're doing to help him?"

"I doubt it's as simple as whether he loves me or not. Fate had a hand in what happened between us. I didn't exactly handle things well because appearances mattered too much when we were together before. We couldn't just *be* together. Not without undermining the power we had as rulers of our races. We made a bad decision and suffered the consequences."

He took a deep breath, forcing himself to hold her steady gaze. She had the most serious look on her face, and for a split-second, he worried he'd said too much.

"I think you're full of shit," she finally said.

His eyebrows shot up and his mouth fell open in a surprised laugh. "What?"

"Listen ... I'm not dumb enough to not know you're Neph wearing an Aodh suit right now. I'm also not dumb enough to not realize your sister locked you out and banished Aodh for a damn good reason. She wasn't exactly forthcoming about it when I talked to her, but Assana kept insisting her mother wasn't always like that, and that she didn't feel like she could adequately fill her mother's shoes. I haven't been in this world for very long, but I *have* paid attention."

Neph sat up straighter in his chair and nodded. "All right, fair enough. Tell me what you know."

"Not enough." She gave him a sheepish shrug. "But I don't want to wait until I inherit the spirit of Summer in a few months to learn what I need to know. All I can guess is that somehow you and Aodh are tangled up with this elusive enemy we have. The Ultiori or whoever leads them … I keep getting mixed up details. Something called a Lamia, which is chilling if that means what I think it does. Or there's someone named Mary?"

"Meri … like the ocean, and yes, the Lamia moniker is as terrifying as it sounds. She survives by drinking the blood of potential hosts and stealing their bodies afterward."

Vrishti grimaced and shivered, the sticky red substance that coated her skin seemed more macabre suddenly. "So why did Nyx do what she did? Why did she put Aodh in that prison?"

"Because Meri wants him as a host. Or she wanted him once. She was one of us. A nymph. When Aodh and I were together, we wanted a third to keep up appearances. She was going to be that for us."

"You needed a beard to hide your gay relationship."

He frowned. "I don't see what facial hair has to do with it, and our relationship was plenty lively when we were together. We loved each other."

Her mouth quirked to the side and she regarded him for a moment.

"How old are you?" she finally asked.

He blinked at her. "Ah … older than I look?"

"Neph, my own mother says she gave birth to me when she was almost five hundred years old. I know we live a long time."

"I'm about as old as any gods you've heard of. I *was* many of those gods, at one point or another, when I was younger. So was Aodh."

She shook her head in mild irritation. "You're a little out of touch is all I'm getting at. I was born at the end of the twentieth century, and raised in the human world. Where I come from, you and Aodh were in a homosexual relationship —a secret one—and you needed a female for legitimacy. I take it that plan backfired."

Understanding dawned on him and he smiled. "Yeah, that's pretty close, except I wouldn't classify us as homosexual. We're pansexual. We enjoy sex with all genders, all races. Always have. We just happened to fall in love with each other." More like Fate *made* them fall in love with each other, then spent the next three thousand years fucking with them.

His heart thudded heavily in his chest at the other unspoken sentiment he'd nearly blurted out on the tail end of his explanation. He'd never deny that he loved Aodh and had never stopped loving him, but that empty hole in his heart beside the one Aodh owned was already swiftly being filled by this lovely, syrup-coated ursa female before him. He almost admitted that he'd fallen in love with her too.

"What happened between you?" she asked softly.

He slouched back in his chair and swiped his hands over his face, simultaneously shedding the dragon disguise he wore. She didn't seem the least bit fazed by the transformation, which gave him a little confidence to stick with honesty.

"Meri tricked him and stole his body. She told him I wanted to blood meld with the two of them ... something nymphaea only do when they're deeply in love and wish to demonstrate that love with a permanent bond."

"You two didn't love her."

"Not even close. She was a means to an end, and one we hadn't even decided on yet. I had an obligation to produce children and believed she'd be a good mother. That was all. We had no idea she had another agenda until it was too late. After it happened, Aodh had to leave the Haven and never return. And I had to stay."

"No farewell kiss, I take it?"

"It was a rather abrupt parting, and we haven't seen or spoken to each other since. That was more than three thousand years ago."

"Whoa, all right. That's just a little beyond my ability to comprehend." She fidgeted with her hands at the edge of the table, her lower lip disappearing behind her front teeth.

He sat forward and gave her an earnest look. "Maybe you can understand that my love for him never diminished. I never found another mate worth blood melding, or even procreating with."

Her frown deepened. "I …" She paused and looked directly at him again. "Does this mean you and I are in competition? Am I going to have to compete against you for his love?"

"Dion's balls, I hope not. I don't think I'd stand a chance. Besides, I think you know better than that. You're an ursa. What do you think is the most likely outcome here?"

She swallowed, her expression sinking inward as she pondered his question. Finally she tilted her head and smiled. "That's what you meant when you asked if I'd be willing to share him. Ursa females usually take two mates … a bonded pair. Would the two of you be that for me?"

Neph's entire body buzzed with elation at her question, but he carefully kept the feeling buried. "I can't speak for him, but that would be my hope."

Her pretty mouth fell open and her gaze grew distant. She rubbed the back of her neck and let her hand drop to her breast. A sharp jolt of arousal shot to Neph's dick when she squeezed her sticky breast and delicately brushed her fingertips over her nipple.

"I would like that," she said, her gaze sliding from his crotch back up to his face.

"Would you?"

"Yeah …" she said huskily. "I mean, I've enjoyed having

him here in place of you, but I knew that was all you all along. To have you both … To have you as you, like last night. I want that." Her brows twitched and her face grew pinched as though she were in pain.

"Vrishti? What's wrong?"

"Nothing … I just. I'm going to go get cleaned up. Can we talk more after?" She slid off the table and he shifted backward in his chair to give her space to move past him.

"Sure. We can do whatever you want."

Her smile seemed strained and she practically ran up the stairs, leaving him alone and bewildered by her hasty retreat after such a frank conversation. He let out a deep breath and scrubbed his hands over his face, almost laughing at the thought that for once it had actually been *his* face she'd been looking at when she expressed her desire to have both him and Aodh together.

The sounds of the shower kicking on and the curtain rings sliding across the bar kicked him out of his hopeful reverie and he got up to clean up the mess. He wished like hell that he could see a vision of how things would turn out for the three of them. The lack of knowledge might mean they would be together, but it might not. He could only assume his lack of accessible visions on their futures indicated as much, but the visions were Fate's messages, he knew that much, and he'd learned long ago not to trust Fate. It had been Fate's fault he and Aodh had chosen Meri, after he'd learned *she* also had no discernible presence in his visions.

For all he knew Vrishti could be another enemy, but somehow he had a hard time believing that. Even without actually melding her, he believed he knew her mind. She was honest and open, and would not hide her desires or her love if that's what she felt.

He should offer to meld this evening. They'd shared enough of each other's essence for a strong melding, but he'd hesitated so far for fear it would ruin the illusion he'd chosen to give her to push her to her estrous. He could fake Aodh rather convincingly, but there was no way he could fake the inside of the dragon's head. But if she wanted to learn what made Neph tick, a melding would be the surest way to share who he truly was.

His mind wandered to a delicious fantasy of tasting her again as he dried the dishes. He thought he'd only imagined the orgasmic cries at first, but his eyes shot to the ceiling when they rang out again … an agonized wail that was more pain than pleasure, then his name carried on a broken sob.

He dropped the dish and ran, taking the stairs two at a time. When he reached the bathroom, the shower curtain was closed, her cries coming from inside. He tore the curtain open and found her on the floor of the tub, huddled into herself with one hand between her thighs.

"Please, make it stop! I can't … Nothing I do helps!"

CHAPTER 18

VRISHTI

*V*rishti winced and pressed her palm to her belly. She worried that she'd suddenly gotten her period and was experiencing the worst menstrual cramps of her life. The spasming in her lower abdomen came on strong and acutely painful at first. She ran to the bathroom, but once there discovered no blood. The only red coming away on the tissue was the raspberry syrup Neph had drizzled all over her. The wave of pain subsided, leaving her core simply aching with need for an orgasm, which was nothing new after the past two days of teasing she'd endured.

Shaking off the strange buzzing heat that lingered, she turned on the shower, hesitating with a hand over the hot water knob before opting to leave it cold before she climbed in. Icy water streamed out and it hit her skin, cooling some of the heat. Yes, that's what she needed … just a few minutes to cool off.

She stepped beneath the stream and shut the curtain behind her, simply standing beneath the water and drinking it down, hoping to cool herself from the inside too.

A sudden wave of agony gripped her, making her double

over with the force of it. She let out a sharp cry and shot her hand out to grab at the tiled wall, clutching her other hand around her midsection. The current of the shower hit her skin, every tiny stream pounding at her. It didn't hurt, though … On the contrary, it felt even more tortuous than Neph's touch, every single sharp pulse sending a fresh jolt of need straight to her core, which clenched and released spasmodically.

She pushed her hand between her thighs, pressing her palm against her flesh and rubbing as though trying to simply work out a kink in a muscle, but something told her this wasn't the kind of kink a simple massage could work out. Another wave of agony ripped through her and she fell to her knees with a harsh cry. It wasn't supposed to *hurt*, was it?

With an involuntary, shuddering moan, she pushed her fingers into her soaked channel, finding some relief from the spasming when her fingers stretched her muscles open. But try as she might, she couldn't ease the ache completely.

"Neph!" she yelled, her voice catching on a sob when another spasm wrenched her core. "Oh, god, please help me!"

Her cries barely had the strength to carry over the sound of the rushing water, but when the pain of a fresh spasm hit, the resulting cry felt like it was ripped from her throat. Please let him hear her.

The heavy beat of her pulse hammered in her ears, but beyond it she thought she heard footsteps pounding up the stairs and coming toward her.

When his shadow filled the space beyond the curtain she let out a sob of gratitude. He wrenched the curtain open.

"Please, make it stop! Nothing I do helps … please!"

"I'll take care of you, kitten, just hold on."

He stepped into the bathtub behind her and bent down, resting a large hand against her back. The contact immediately eased some of the pain, but it left behind the pulsing ache of need between her thighs.

"This is it, isn't it?" she asked. "Why does it have to hurt so much?"

She clenched her eyes shut as another wave passed, and opened them again, her gaze fixed on the water swirling down the drain.

"Its purpose is to get you breeding as early as possible. The good news is that it only happens every four years, and it gets easier."

"Oh. Good." She let out a halfhearted chuckle.

"Better news is that it's time for you to come."

"Is—is it going to hurt? Because I can't handle this."

His laughter didn't make her feel better, but the way his hands squeezed her hips made her entire body respond with a tingling wave that was more pleasure than pain for the first time since it had started.

"Come here, kitten. Let me give you what you've been craving. We'll ease into it since it's an ongoing ordeal."

She relaxed and relented to his touch. He pulled her backward and she sank against his warm chest, leaning back between his bent knees. The cold shower still streamed down over them both.

"How long does it last?"

His big hands roamed down her breasts with only a cursory caress before sliding over her belly and between her thighs. He immediately sank two big fingers into her and she moaned in gratitude, spreading her legs and draping them over his thighs to rest on the edges of the tub as he began to finger fuck her steadily.

"It's different for every female," he said. "Your first time is always hardest, but I have heard that if an ursa gets pregnant right away, it's done."

"And if she doesn't?"

"It'll come in waves every few hours until your fertile period passes. Some say a week, others a month."

She let her head fall back against his shoulder, barely comprehending what he said over the steady push of his fingers into her. "Good," she murmured, not even sure whether she meant it in response to his statement or simply how he was making her feel.

A warm, deep chuckle filled her ear. "You haven't felt *good* yet, kitten. Wait until we're really getting into it. I'm going to make you come now to ease the pain, but we're only getting started."

He plunged a third digit into her opening, pushing deep and causing her to writhe and buck her hips up into his hand. He cupped her jaw with his free hand and turned her head, twisting behind her enough to dip his head over her shoulder and capture her mouth with his. Their lips and tongues merged, and he shifted the hand between her thighs until his thumb found her swollen, aching clit and began to rub it in rhythmic strokes.

She let out a harsh cry into his mouth, nearly yelling a warning when the pleasure grew too great. Then she remembered this was what had to happen.

Within a split-second of that worry, she was gone, her body abandoning her to the pleasure of his touch, every cell exploding in light and sensation as the first glorious orgasm took her.

The entire time, he murmured into her ear. "That's right, kitten. Give yourself to me. Give it all to me."

The wash of sensation left her feeling made entirely of light, and it took several moments for her sense of self to return. As the blast of pleasure subsided, she felt less overwhelmed by the aching need, but it was still there, lingering in the background like some half-quenched flame that would soon flare again.

She let out a soft sigh, relaxing against him and twisting slightly to look up into his face. He'd resumed the Aodh mask again, which seemed odd after the conversation they'd had, but she didn't question it. She was far too grateful for the relief he'd given her.

As the momentousness of the event dawned on her, a smile tugged at her mouth, blooming into a full-fledged grin.

"It happened," she said, smiling at him.

He laughed and lifted an eyebrow. "It is happening, kitten. We've barely even begun."

His hands rested on her thighs and he lifted one, pointing a finger at the shower head and making a small gesture accompanied by a foreign word whispered in her ear. The water gradually warmed, the heat a welcome change now that her body temperature had regulated a bit. She became acutely aware of the thick, rigid length pressed against her back in between them and her pulse picked up again.

"What next?" she asked, hoping she already knew the answer.

"Enjoy the respite while you can. The next wave will hit, and then … well, this is when one of the pair of ursa males assigned to service you might offer to stretch that lovely little snatch of yours with his fist."

She tensed and twisted around fully to stare at him in shock.

"No! There is no fucking way you're doing … *that!*"

"Don't worry, I don't need to. I can't impregnate you … at least not yet … so you, my lovely kitten, get my cock. I should warn you that at full size it isn't much different from a man's fist, but when you're in the throes of your estrous, that's what you'll need."

Her core spasmed hard at that comment, and not in an unwillingly tense way … more like a hungry "yes, please" way. She shook her head and looked at his cock, the one she'd enjoyed sucking so much just a little while ago. Then she remembered the other night when he'd shown her his true form and the massive tree trunk of an erection he'd sported.

Her pussy quivered with fresh need at that thought and she nibbled on her lower lip. Neph brought his hand up and cupped her wet cheek, tilting her head to redirect her gaze to meet his.

"It's all right if you like that idea. It's also all right if you're a little scared. We don't have to go there until you're ready, but we *should* try to move things along now that your body's primed for it."

Her abdomen heated and a twinge of pain spiked low in her belly, shooting between her thighs. She winced and nodded swiftly. "I'm ready. I guess you know what to do?"

He smiled and began to stand, gripping her hands and raising her up with him. "If anyone knows what to do, it's me, kitten."

He swooped in and kissed her then, catching her off-guard so she was forced to wrap her arms around his neck. He caught her in his embrace, his hands cupping her bottom and pulling her into his wet body. He lifted her easily, shoulders bunching under her grip as he turned them both and pressed her against the wet tiled wall of the shower.

All the while he kissed her, devouring her mouth and leaving her breathless with resurging need. The ache between her thighs grew more urgent with every slick caress of his hand down her side, over her breasts, every soft nip of his teeth at her lips. His stiff length pressed at her core and he shifted, seeming to sense how close to the edge of another wave of acute need she was getting.

He cupped his hands under her ass again and pulled her thighs wide, hitching them up over his hips.

"Are you ready, love?" he asked in a gruff, deep tone that

disoriented her with the change from his true voice. He tilted his hips back, his cock sliding down her soaked folds until his tip grazed her entrance.

But this wasn't right, and it took her a second to figure out why. Her eyes shot to his pale orbs and water-soaked white hair and she pushed at his shoulders.

"No, not like this," she said. "Not like him."

His white brows twitched and he frowned. "But I thought you wanted him as your first. I know that's what he would want for you."

"Maybe, but it isn't what I want. I mean, I want *him* to make love to me, but you aren't him, even when you're pretending to be. I know it's you. Please, don't be him. The first time I make love to him, I want to know it's him."

Neph stared at her for a beat, then nodded. His features slowly dissolved back into his familiar dark hair and golden skin, his cheeks roughened with stubble and his eyes swirled with some unfathomable emotion, but he refused to meet her gaze for a moment as he completed the shift.

"Ready, kitten?" he asked, his tone more businesslike than before … more than she liked. But this really was about getting to Aodh, wasn't it?

Then the pain sliced through her again, more agonizing than before, and she stiffened in his arms, crying out and grimacing as her head flew back against the wall. She dug her nails into his shoulders and nodded, unable to find breath to voice her need.

Without another invitation, he slammed deep, his thick length spearing into her.

She let out a sharp cry at the surprising pleasure of that first thrust, then moaned as the pain departed completely for the first time, replaced only by the delicious rub of his cock inside her, right in the spot where she needed him most. He pulled out and slammed into her again with fierce precision.

For some strange reason, she got the sense that he was punishing her for something. Like she'd just hurt him, and his relentless pounding was meant as retaliation for that hurt. But after the first few strokes, nothing else mattered but the perfect, stretching penetration of his cock as it slid deep into her with repeated pounding thrusts. She came hard, her body shuddering as she clutched at him, but he didn't let up.

"It's time for us to go, kitten," he growled. "Hold on tight."

Beneath her hands his shoulders thickened, his neck widened, and the muscles of his already sculpted chest swelled, nearly doubling in size. She stared up at his face in awe and amazement as his features also grew, and though they were larger, they didn't change. The only difference was the glorious pair of horns that arced back from his brow, nearly brushing the ceiling above him.

And the sensation between her thighs changed, too. The sense of fullness grew, and he kept pushing into her, each stroke filling her and stretching her wider until she let out a sharp gasp when the pleasure peaked and yet another orgasm loomed at the edge of her senses.

"Hold the magic, kitten. Just a little longer. Come when I say."

"I—I can't," she whimpered, her eyelids fluttering closed at the exquisite pleasure that shot through her with every press of that unbearably thick shaft into her stretched opening.

"You can. Hold tight to me. Look at me."

She opened her eyes, staring up into the fathomless deep whirlpools of Neph's eyes. Some strange hurt spun in that cyclone, which she didn't understand. His expression was completely at odds with the way he made her feel, even without the pleasure he'd given her the past couple days. It made no sense for him to look that way, not when they were bound together like this.

Not with the sudden, sharp understanding that she loved him.

A shudder of ecstasy washed through her, and he let out a low groan that mirrored the one she released. Their eyes stayed locked together and she surged up, grasping the back of his neck and crashing her lips against his. The movement shifted her almost all the way off his cock, but she didn't want that just now. She wanted to look into his eyes and kiss him and tell him what he meant to her, but her body's needs protested, her womb spasming with the need for penetration again.

This wasn't good enough. She let out a frustrated cry and pushed at his shoulders. He stumbled backward, one big leg shifting to rebalance, but his huge, hoofed foot caught on the edge of the tub. Just as she slammed back down on his cock again, the ecstasy too overpowering to stop, the world tilted and they crashed to the floor, the shower curtain ripped, and the metal bar it was attached to came free from the wall in a wrenching twist and crack of metal against wood. Before she knew it they were falling, Neph clutching her as she let out a yelp.

He hit the floor with a crash and a grunt. The impact forced her back down onto his cock, hard. His heavy horns flew back, digging into the wood of the floor behind his head and he let out a harsh groan as his cock was forced deep into her again. Vrishti's mouth fell open in silent rapture at how perfectly he filled her now, and she began to move again, slowly at first, then more frantically when she found the sweet spot about halfway up his dick. She braced her palms on his massive chest and pivoted her hips over that immense thickness that penetrated her, working herself on the ridged head until the pleasure swelled in her belly nearly to bursting.

His eyes flew open and he stared at her with the full power of his gaze.

"Come for me, kitten. Come all over my cock. Give me all that sweet fucking power that's filling you now. Give it all to me."

She gripped his head, tangling her hands in his hair, then wrapping her fists around his horns as she pumped herself on him. The pleasure crashed into her suddenly and she tightened her thighs around him while his big hands guided her hips up and down on his cock. The first wave hit like a lightning bolt and she cried out, slamming down hard onto him as liquid pleasure flooded between her legs.

"That's right, kitten. Give it to me."

She surged up, kissing him again. She wasn't done yet. The climax had her in its grip and she clung to his horns with both hands, using them for leverage as she pumped herself on that glorious, massive shaft, riding out wave after wave of pleasure.

Just when she thought it might finally end, Neph's face contorted, his fingers dug into her hips, and he thrust up into her hard. The friction sent her to another peak and she arched her back, crying out as she rode his bucking hips, no longer caring that there was a world that existed outside the joining of their two bodies.

She collapsed on top of him, panting and struggling to catch her breath. Neph slid his big arms up her back, wrapping them around her and holding her. She had the vague sense of his body shrinking beneath her, his cock stretching her less and less, but still leaving her with a comfortable fullness.

His lips brushed the top of her head and she hummed in contentment. Suddenly his torso tensed beneath her.

"Fucking hell," he muttered.

Vrishti didn't have the strength to move. "What is it?" she asked.

"We screwed up the temporal drift."

Her brows twitched in confusion. "What do you mean? We didn't go anywhere yet."

"Yeah, we did. Just not where I mean to take us."

She lifted her head to look at him, but movement caught her eye from the direction of the bathroom doorway. A wide-eyed little girl stood there with black hair cut into a cute bob. Her shock turned to consternation as she crossed her arms over her chest.

The little girl took a deep breath and in a surprisingly strong voice yelled, "Papa! There's naked people in our *bathroom!*"

Heavy footsteps thumped down the hall, and a pajama-clad man took one look at them and immediately slapped a big hand over the little girl's eyes.

"Emma, shut your eyes." He reached in and grabbed the bathroom doorknob, yanking it shut with a solid bang.

CHAPTER 19

VRISHTI

"How far did we go?" Vrishti asked, glancing around the small room from her perch on the counter, marveling at the similarities along with the differences. The room looked new, the wood still clean and unblemished from years of use. The polished wood floor shone brighter, the fixtures gleamed; there was no corrosion apparent anywhere. The linens were different—the floor covered with a brightly woven rag rug and several plaid flannel robes had hung from the back of the door, two of which she and Neph now wore. A collection of bath toys cluttered the edge of the tub along with a bottle of baby shampoo.

"Not far enough. About two decades, and we didn't change locations. It's a good thing this cabin's been here all along."

"Emma … The man called her Emma, and that … Holy shit!" She'd only caught the briefest glance of the man before he'd hastily shut the door to protect the little girl's sensibilities. But now she was sure. He'd certainly looked a lot younger, with fewer lines around his eyes and no gray hair to speak of in his thick beard. "That was Eamon Stonetree!"

"The ursa queen's father?" Neph asked, his eyes widening. "I didn't get a look at him, but it would make sense. He and his brother built this house."

"Should we go out there?" she asked, staring at the closed door.

"Probably ought to at least explain our presence here."

"Including why we were naked on the floor in their bathroom?"

A soft knock sounded at the door and a deep voice said, "If you two are decent, I'd like to open the door now."

Neph reached out and twisted the knob, pulling the door open a crack. The opening widened and the same bearded face peeked in, eyeing them both for a second before pushing the door open all the way.

Behind him stood another man, equal in stature with slightly lighter colored hair and a clean-shaved face. They both stared grimly into the room.

"The kids are back in bed. You two care to explain why you were fucking on the floor of our bathroom? Where the hell did you come from?"

"It's kind of a long story …" Neph began.

"We time traveled!" Vrishti said perkily. Neph shot a withering glare at her. "What? It's the truth."

The two men shifted shocked expressions between Neph and Vrishti. Then Eamon shook his head and stepped back, opening the way for them. "Come on out. I guess I'll put on some coffee because I have a feeling this is going to take a good, long while to understand."

~

"ARE you sure you should tell us this?" Eamon asked after Neph and Vrishti finished explaining everything they knew about the future his daughter was destined for.

"Her fate is already set," Neph said. "Knowing the path you all have before you won't change the course of events. Emma will rule the Sanctuary during the most trying period in its history. You'll be there to guide her. I will leave it up to you how much you share with her."

The two other men stared at each other. Then Eamon's brother, Ted, sat forward in his chair pushing his empty coffee mug away from him across the smooth, polished surface of the table. Vrishti abstractly realized that it was the same spot she'd sat just after she'd sucked Neph off just a little while ago.

"We have your word that it's true? We'll get to be with them again … the Stonetree sisters?"

"Until the day they die," Neph said, ignoring Vrishti's sharp glance. They both knew Emma's mother would wind up sacrificing herself for the security of the Sanctuary. Vrishti supposed Eamon didn't need to know that—only that he would be with her before she gave her power up to her daughter.

Ted smiled brightly. "Good. I miss Mona like you wouldn't fucking believe. Our kids are everything to me. Thank you for this. Is there anything we can do for you?"

"We need a quiet, comfortable place to finish what we started," Neph said. "The location is immaterial, but it's probably best if it's secluded … where adventurous cubs won't accidentally stumble upon us."

Ted and Eamon both chuckled and shared an understanding glance. "Let me guess," Eamon said. "Somehow you're using fertility magic to time travel?"

"How'd you know?" Vrishti asked, grinning at them.

"We spent a few weeks inside the Sanctuary with the

sisters. They showed us some pretty amazing things. I suppose we shouldn't be surprised."

"It isn't commonly used this way," Neph said. "But the safety of our world depends on us."

Eamon nodded. "We have a place. An old hunting cabin a few miles from here. Remote, but comfortable. I imagine you won't need it for long, will you?"

"A few hours … a day, at most," Neph said, darting a glance at Vrishti that had her insides warming and fresh heat pooling between her thighs.

Eamon pushed back in his chair and smacked his hands against his thighs. "Well, let's get you two some clothes and I'll take you there."

CHAPTER 20

NEPH

The small cabin sported little more than a bed, a potbelly stove, a worn wooden table, and a pair of rickety chairs. But it was clean and weather-tight, the air gradually warming from the heat of the roaring fire Eamon had built for them shortly before departing into the snowy night.

Nothing but a single oil lamp lit the room, illuminating the quilt-covered bed where Vrishti sat, staring as though entranced by the flickering flame of the lamp. Neph's heart ached just looking at her profile, the warm glow gilding her skin. His fingertips itched to touch the smooth, dark silk of her collarbone that peeked out from the oversized flannel shirt Ted had loaned her.

He swallowed thickly and turned back to the stove, opening it to add another piece of firewood.

"Are you thinking of Aodh?" he asked, using the poker to adjust the stack of wood until the new piece caught flame. He heard her slow intake of breath but kept his eyes on his task, unwilling to see any sign of how much she wished for the dragon.

"I suppose," she said.

"That's good. The more focused you are on him, the easier it will be to travel to him. You are only a passenger, of course, but your desires can speed things in the right direction."

"Were we not focused enough that time? Is that why we didn't go very far?"

"I … got distracted. That was on me. Your orgasm began just as I lost balance. The only thing running through my mind just then was how close the floor was to my ass." He let out a soft chuckle and turned to her. She smiled at him and the knife in his heart twisted deeper.

"So next time we should do it lying down, is that what you're saying?" she asked. "And make sure we're both thinking of him. I get why you tried to look like him, but you don't need to do that for my sake. Just … tell me more about him. Tell me why you loved him."

He rose from his crouch and stepped to the table, grabbed one of the chairs and flipped it around facing her, then sat down.

"I still love him," he said softly. "Why don't you tell me why you chose him, even though you barely know him?"

She opened her mouth, then closed it again and tilted her head to look at the ceiling for a beat. Then she shrugged. "That's the thing, I never felt like I didn't know him. The first time I saw him … Well, he acted weird, to be honest. Like he had trouble looking at me, but that's how I felt too. Like if I let myself, I'd never want to *stop*. Then when he told me he was mine … it felt like the truest thing I'd ever heard. Like someone stating a simple law of physics. Like gravity. It just *is*."

Neph's lips curled in a soft smile as he listened to her. "That's how it was for us at first. I couldn't deny the draw to him. Even then we knew it had to be Fate who'd pushed us together, despite the fact that it never quite made sense. Our *world* didn't want us to be in love. I wonder sometimes if we simply found each other too soon, but now I know there was more at play."

She frowned. "You talk about Fate like it's a person."

"Oh, it is. The fucking bastard has toyed with our lives since the beginning of time. Some of us worse than others. Choice is an illusion. Just ask the turul how they feel about it."

"The … turul? You mean the air shifters who turn into birds and have an affinity for music?"

He'd forgotten she knew so little about the higher races. There were no turul in the Sanctuary, so she'd likely never have run across one in her life.

"Fate's cursed them to only have one true mate, who they recognize on sight once they find the person, but many of them go for centuries without setting eyes on their One. Fate no doubt knows the person's identity from birth, but isn't forthcoming about it. Dragons are just as bound by Fate as the turul when it comes to their mates, though they can breed with whomever they mark. At least with the nymphs and the ursa, there's some sense of control over the matter."

Her brows drew together. "Does that mean you and I are Fated too? I mean, if you and Aodh are, and I know he's meant to be mine. If we aren't, how does that work? Do we really just share him?"

A lump lodged in Neph's throat. He didn't want her to think she had no choice, even though she really didn't. None of them did. "Dragons often take multiple mates. Ursa females almost always choose bachelor pairs of males. I've even met a pair of turul brothers whose One is the same woman. What do you think, Vrishti?"

She stood up and closed the distance between them, slowly unbuttoning her shirt as she moved. When she reached him, the green and blue plaid hung open, displaying the inner swells of her breasts and her sternum, and her smooth chest all the way to her navel. She unbuckled the belt Ted had loaned her and the oversized jeans slipped halfway off her hips without even unbuttoning, showing the top fringe of her dark curls. Neph's cock roused at the gorgeous sight, his senses filled with her proximity.

"I think there's a reason I couldn't help but love you," she whispered, reaching up to brush her palm over his cheek. "You tried so hard to give me him, but it's you I want right now. I already have him. I think I had him from the start. Can I have you too?"

His chest burned with the overwhelming emotion that filled him. He couldn't speak over the flood of longing. Instead he only nodded, and when she bent her head to press a kiss to his lips, his restraint fled. He slipped his hands over her hips, shoving the baggy jeans down until they fell to the floor. He gripped her full, round backside and pulled her tight, then drifted his lips over her jaw and down her neck, using his nose to push the shirt aside and bare one luscious breast.

Vrishti tangled her fingers in his hair and arched with a moan when he latched onto her nipple and sucked. Her head fell back, the long, damp tendrils of her hair tickling his forearms where they crossed over her lower back. Gaia's tears, she was so sweet he could devour her, the fertile aroma of her sex flooding his senses as though she exuded magic from her very pores.

And he supposed she did—an ursa female in estrous carried the magic in every cell in her body, just waiting for the seed to be planted in her womb that would absorb all that power the Source had granted her to create new life.

He didn't want to ruin the moment by reminding her of their task. This time would be just for them.

She shifted in his arms as he nuzzled her other breast, teasing his tongue around her nipple. Bringing one knee up, she moved in to straddle his hips. The wooden joints of the chair protested beneath him and he tightened his grip on her backside, standing and moving the two steps to the bed where he laid her down on top of the quilt.

She lay panting and beautiful in the lantern light, propped up on her elbows with the shirt half off her shoulders and wearing nothing else. Neph stood back and tore off his own flannel shirt, then kicked off the borrowed boots and slid the jeans down his hips. They hadn't had women's sized boots for Vrishti, so she'd just shrugged it off and said she didn't mind going barefoot. The cold didn't bother her nearly as much, which was a good sign she was finally fully coming into her ursa nature.

She licked her lips as her gaze raked down his naked body, lingering at his erection. "Are you going to shift like before? Should we … pack or something?" she said uncertainly, glancing at the floor where their clothes lay.

Neph shook his head. "I'm going to make love to you. Right here, right now, in this bed. I'm saving my primal power for the drift, which we'll do next time *your* power surges. For now, it's just you and me and as many of those orgasms I owe you as we can make happen."

He crawled onto the bed, hovering on hands and knees above her bent legs. Dipping his head, he pressed a soft kiss to the inside of one knee, flicking his gaze to the dewy wetness that coated her core. He inhaled deeply, savoring the delicious scent that he'd soon be drowning in. As he peppered kisses down the inside of her thigh, she let her legs fall wide, her gorgeous swollen folds parting and unfurling like a dew-kissed flower.

She remained on her elbows, watching his slow exploration of her thigh, her panting growing more rapid the closer he got to her core. When he brushed his mouth over her outer lips, she spread her legs even wider. His mouth watered, the hunger for her almost a living thing. If he had shifted, the primal power would have had him already buried to the hilt in her, fucking her until the bed broke. As much as he sensed she would love that, he wanted to make it crystal clear to her what his answer to her question was: She could have him, body and soul, if that's what she wanted. So he would give her all of him tonight before their reunion with Aodh. Because he had no idea what might happen once he saw the dragon again in the flesh.

Her wetness met his lips and he darted his tongue out to trace her outer folds and savor the sweet flavor of her essence. The power that infused her juices buzzed on his tongue, sinking into his body like he'd just downed a shot of liquor, leaving him lightheaded for a second. He closed his eyes and hummed in pleasure at the euphoria. She most definitely was coming into her power now.

He'd had his tongue buried in her sweet pussy before, but this was the first time since her estrous began that he'd had the chance to taste her. Once the tingling sensation subsided, he braced himself, slipped his hands down her thighs, parted her with his fingertips, and licked. Dionysus save him, but she *was* ambrosia.

He sank his tongue into her, burying it between her wet folds and wrapping his lips around her entire sex in a hungry, languid kiss. He fixed his mouth against her, teasing the tip of his tongue up and down her slick channel before aiming at the center and licking up in one long, slow sweep to the swollen peak of her cleft.

Vrishti tangled her fingers in his hair, pulling him tighter as her moans of pleasure encouraged him. But there was no stopping him now; he'd had a taste of her addictive essence and wanted more.

He focused his tongue on her clit, drawing the tiny nub into his mouth and sucking gently, much to her apparent pleasure. She let out a shuddering cry, her entire body arching off the bed.

"Neph, oh, yes!"

The sound of his name sent a shiver of pleasure from his ears all the way to his cock. He would be inside her soon enough. Until then, he hoped to incite more similar cries from her.

He started by pushing two fingers into her tight opening, hooking them to seek out the soft, sensitive flesh of her inner wall, where the trigger to this delicious essence of her lay hidden. With his mouth still fixed on her clit and his tongue gently swirling and stroking, he pressed his other fingers to her backside, merely teasing there at first.

He massaged her inner muscles with gentle, thrusting strokes, pressing rhythmically at that sweet spot over and over until his hand was coated with the delicious, power-infused juices. Gaia's tears, there was enough magic in this alone to power a drift around the entire world. He had no doubt that during an estrous-fueled orgasm he could access any time in ancient history.

This bit of power would at least help him pinpoint Aodh's time and place, even if they waited to go there. He wanted this night to be theirs alone. It might be the only night he had.

She bucked harder against him, her fingers pulling painfully at his hair, but he was relentless. She'd earned every mind-blowing orgasm he could give her after all the ones she'd given him over the past two days. He wasn't about to stop until she lost control completely.

Sensing she was close by the flood of wetness that covered his chin, he went the final mile, pressing his finger against her ass and pushing deep. Her juices were so copious he sank into her easily and began fucking with almost no resistance, until her thighs clamped down on him and her hips jerked up. She pinned him between her legs, forcing his head tighter to her core, and he kept licking, relishing the breathy gasps and moans as her flesh throbbed and pulsed against his lips, and a full on flood of orgasmic fluid nearly drowned him in fertile power.

He rode out her spasms, gradually slowing his strokes, his licks, his thrusting fingers into both her tight holes. Finally he stopped and her legs relaxed, her thighs falling wide and her feet slipping down the blanket. Her hands fell away from his head and she let out an infinitely satisfied sigh.

Neph shifted up on his elbows, went to wipe his soaked face, but realized both his hands were covered in her juices too. Instead, he reached down and grabbed his discarded shirt to clean up.

Vrishti watched him with hooded eyes and a boneless look.

"That was worth waiting for," she said with a happy sigh.

CHAPTER 21

VRISHTI

Vrishti's gaze traveled over Neph's muscular, naked back as he added a fresh log to the small stove. His shoulders rippled like molten gold in the warm light, his dark hair brushing the very tops in a tangled mess. Her fingers still tingled slightly from the tight grip she'd had on his head while he tongued her into oblivion.

A warm pulse throbbed inside her womb, a small reminder that her estrous was still in full swing, even if she'd had a brief respite from the full force of the need. All she felt now was a pleasant ache of desire for the man who was teaching her how to embrace her nature.

Part of her still couldn't quite grasp the idea that she could choose him too, and that he was more than willing to share the honor of being her mate with the dragon they both sought.

The slightest pang of guilt flared in her chest at the thought of Aodh. She'd fantasized and dreamed so many times of making love to him alone, that it seemed strange to have fallen so thoroughly for someone else. But when Neph turned those hypnotic eyes on her, gazing down at her with such complete and utter adoration, she understood the rightness of it. Fate be damned—she believed she'd want both men even if she'd really *had* a choice.

And if she were being honest with herself, she really didn't mind having that decision made for her already. It made it easier to accept … easier to pull the covers back and shift over to let the big, lanky satyr climb in next to her and lean in for a soft kiss, and to know that somehow it would all work out. The pair of men would reunite and have the love they'd lost so long ago, and *she* would have *them*.

She shifted closer to the warm, hard body beside her, pressing her mouth harder against his, craving more of the desperate hunger he'd exhibited whenever he'd kissed her over the past few days. Neph murmured against her lips, pushing his tongue in deeper and tilting his hips against hers. His cock brushed against her belly, the hot, hard length teasing a shiver of pleasure that tingled between her thighs and reminded her that he hadn't found his own release yet.

He closed his hand around her hip, sliding it to her backside and tugging her tight against him. She recalled the unbelievably slow and patient make-out session they'd first shared and how painfully aware of his arousal she'd been the entire time they'd kissed. She'd wondered then how his cock would feel buried inside her, but knew better than to test that desire at the time … knew she needed to let him guide her through the process, to follow his lead. And she was glad she had, but now she could take what she wanted. The earlier fantasy surged through her mind full force—the image of her pushing him flat on his back, climbing astride his cock and fucking him.

Her involuntary whimper made him pull back with an amused look. "What are you thinking, kitten?"

His gaze drifted to her mouth where she worried her lower lip between her teeth, the words caught in her throat.

His thumb tapped her chin, then pulled her lip free and he dipped his head to suck her swollen lip between his own. He nipped it gently and pulled back again.

"Just say it. Nothing you could possibly think of would shock me."

She laughed. "I wasn't worried about shocking you. I'm still trying to wrap my mind around … well, *you*. It still feels weird for me to want you as much as I've wanted Aodh since we first met, but at the same time, it makes sense. But what I wonder even more is what you two are like together."

The fingertips drawing soft circles over the swell of her hip stilled abruptly and Neph pressed his lips together. His gaze dropped.

Vrishti lifted her hand to his cheek. "I thought nothing I could say would shock you," she said gently.

"Not shocked," he said, his voice catching. "I just need you to know I can't make any promises that he'll be happy to see me."

"But you love each other."

"If that's all we needed, we'd have stayed together, Vrishti. And I have to confess that this …" He waved a hand between the two of them. "… is likely to piss him off. At least at first."

"What? Why?"

He let out a sigh and rolled onto his back, swiping his hands over his face. Without looking at her again, he said, "You're not a virgin anymore. He's always had a bit of a thing for virgins, and I've cheated him out of it."

Vrishti's mouth fell open and she let out an involuntary laugh. "Seriously? Would he *actually* be pissed that some imaginary line has been crossed? After we went out of our fucking way to free him of his prison—that your *sister* put him in, I might add. He isn't *that* dense, is he?"

She stared down at him, indignant at his confused look.

"Are *you*?" she added, her ire rising. "I may be new to sex, but it seems to me you and I crossed all the lines on day one *without* you sticking your dick into me. As far as I'm concerned, my stupid virginity is *not* yours to cheat anyone out of." Her blood ran hotter the longer he stared at her without responding. In a huff, she sat up and threw her leg over his waist, smacking her hands down on his chest.

"This is my damn body, you got it? If he's going to be pissed about some … mythological state that I no longer inhabit, that is *not* on you. Let him be pissed at me, because I'm the one who gets to decide what I do with my own fucking vagina. If I want your cock inside me, I'm damn well going to have it!"

As she ranted, his gaze grew heated and a slow, wicked smile spread across his face. The very expression caused her core to pulse from the promise in those swirling eyes.

"Kitten, you are fierce when you get pissed."

"I'm fucking serious," she said, though her arousal sapped some of the determination from her tone.

"Show me, then," he challenged.

"Show you what?"

"How much you want my cock inside you."

A hot rush of excitement flooded her from her chest all the way to her core, but he was right. She narrowed her eyes.

"Fine," she said. She braced one hand on his broad chest and lifted her hips. Reaching between her thighs, she wrapped her fingers around the end of his shaft and aimed his tip between her soaked folds.

The mere contact made her already shaky control crumble further, and she clung to her anger like a lifeline. She needed to see him surrender to the pleasure she knew she could give, while still keeping the upper hand. She needed to prove her point, that she could—and would — control her own pleasure if she wanted to … and could control his as well.

Holding the end of his cock, she pressed him tight between her thighs and slid along his length, her slick juices coating the underside of his shaft. The wet friction shot jolts of pleasure through her core, but she held tight to her resolve, determined to see him crack.

"I could have just done this, couldn't I? Rubbed myself all over you without letting you in. Would that have worked? Could we accomplish what we need this way?"

Neph's brows twitched and he licked his lips. Swallowing, he shook his head. In a gruff voice, he said, "You needed to be penetrated."

"Did it have to be your cock, though?"

"No."

"You said the ursa use their fists on females … fuck them that way. I know my cousin talked about it before. She's never had a dick inside her, as far as I know, but she's far from chaste. Tell me, what fucking difference does it make what part of your body gets shoved into mine? Huh? I think you secretly wanted to have that imaginary honor of being the first dick inside me. Well, congratulations, but don't forget I'm the one who let you in, and I'm the one who gets to decide if you're allowed in again."

During her entire speech, she kept rubbing her pussy up and down his cock, teasing his cockhead at her entrance without ever taking him inside and repeatedly rubbing the very tip of him on her engorged clit. She was drunk on pleasure and power by the time he reached for her, wrapping his big hands around her thighs and squeezing.

"For fuck's sake, kitten, will you please just fuck me?"

"What if I want to come just like this?" she asked, letting the pleasure build in her core as she rubbed him harder against her clit.

Neph let out a desperate growl, tilting his hips up into her grip. She squeezed him, enjoying the way his eyelids fluttered closed and a breath escaped his lips.

"Do what you want. Please just take me with you. Let me come."

He looked so desperate, so worried, as though he genuinely feared she'd keep torturing him this way. But her desire had reached a fever pitch, her hot channel aching to be filled again. Not quite as desperately as when her estrous flared full force, but close.

She raised her hips and slid his tip down until the thick head pressed at her ready opening. Neph's features tightened with the strain of his need as she sank down little by little, her breathing quickening as he stretched her. He'd shoved into her so quickly the first time, she hadn't had time to enjoy it. This time she didn't care how badly he wanted in, she simply wanted to *feel* every inch of him sinking into her.

"That's right, kitten. Take me. Take all of me. I'm yours."

She closed her eyes, savoring the sensation accompanied by the raw, desperate need in his voice. In that moment, she knew he didn't lie, and that she indeed owned him.

That understanding made the pleasure exponentially more delicious when she began fucking him. Once fully seated on his huge cock, she twisted her hips, simply enjoying the completeness with which he filled her. He let out a rough groan, shifting his hands to her hips, but he didn't do more than squeeze, as though he restrained himself from forcing her to move. She braced her hands on his shoulders and lifted her hips, her eyes fluttering closed as the thick head of his cock brushed against the tender pleasure core inside her.

His swirling blue gaze was still fixed on her when she opened her eyes again, craving the look he gave her.

"You're so fucking beautiful," he rumbled. "Gaia's tears, I love you."

The sound of his words burned in her chest, and she bit her lip to keep the overwhelming emotion from bursting forth. The physical pleasure merged with that warmth, flooding her body with pure ecstasy. She gasped as it swelled in her core, then abated, only to swell even higher on her next downstroke on his cock.

He met her rising and falling motions with rhythmic pumps of his hips, pushing ever deeper and angling his hips just so, sending glorious currents of pleasure through her entire body. She'd never imagined being fucked could feel so good, and nearly lost track of the rhythm when the pleasure filled her nearly to bursting.

She let out a whimper and pressed her face into his neck. Neph chuckled into her ear.

"Don't worry, kitten. I got your point, but I need to fuck you hard now or I'm going to go fucking mad."

"Uh-huh," was all she could manage, and as he gripped her hips tighter and slammed his cock up into her, she bit down hard into the pliant flesh of his shoulder.

He let out a soft grunt followed by another low, gravelly laugh. "If you aim to mark me as yours, you might want to wait. Don't give him any more ammunition against me, all right, kitten?"

She let out a low groan and nodded, releasing her teeth from his skin and sinking them into her lower lip again instead. The steady, pounding slams of his cock into her tender core pushed her ever higher, his fingers digging into her hips and urging her down on top of him in matching rhythm.

She was at the edge already when he let out a growl, and with one hand cupped her face and angled her head so he could look her in the eyes. She got lost in those whirlpool depths, unable to look away despite the rush of dizziness that overtook her.

"I've got you. Come when I do, love. I want to fucking drown in you."

Her world spun in the maelstrom of his eyes, the ecstasy sucking her in until she could do nothing more than surrender to its pull. Staring into those depths, she cried out his name and leaned back, arching her head toward the ceiling as she let the need drive her movements, chasing that glorious climax as she met his violent thrusts with her own writhing hips.

Neph let out a rough, strangled yell, some strange, barely coherent combination of affirmations and endearments as his cock spasmed inside her, keeping time with her own pulsing climax. Her orgasm cascaded through her like a dam bursting and the noises of their fucking grew wetter and lewder, skin smacking with each movement. By the time she slowed and sank down onto his chest, her thighs were drenched with her fluids and his mixed together. She didn't care a bit about how big a mess they'd made when Neph slipped his arms around her and nuzzled at her ear.

"Anytime you need to prove yourself on my cock, you just go right ahead, kitten. I meant it when I said I'm yours."

She let out a happy sigh. "Couldn't let you get away with that. If he doesn't like that you've fucked me already, he can suck it."

Neph's chest vibrated with a deep laugh. "I'm going to tell him you said that, assuming he'll speak to me."

She frowned and pushed herself up on her hands, staring down at him in consternation. "Was it really that bad between you at the end?"

His face clouded, the swirling sea blue of his irises turning stormy. "I said some things I shouldn't have. Things that hurt him deeply. Things that weren't true, and he knew it. He was always the best at discerning a lie. He told me to take it back, but I knew it was the only way to make him go.

If I hadn't, my sister was prepared to take more drastic measures."

"Which is exactly what she's done now."

He nodded sadly. "Yeah. She promised she'd do this if he ever set foot back in the Haven. She's wanted to put him away for a long, long time, and now she has."

"What did you say to him?" she asked.

"I said I didn't love him. That I never would, and that he'd ruined any chance we might have had of being together."

CHAPTER 22

NEPH

"Oh. Wow." Vrishti slipped off him and grabbed the soiled shirt to clean up some of their mess. It was like every time she orgasmed, a dam quite literally burst inside her.

Now Neph watched a dam of a different type begin overflowing as an errant tear seeped from the corner of her eye.

"Kitten," he said in a rough voice. "Why the tears?"

She touched her cheek, rubbing at the wetness. "I don't … I can't imagine how that must have felt. If you'd said it to me, I'd be heartbroken. And you've really never seen him since?"

"Only once, but we didn't speak. The day is burned into my memory, but probably for the wrong reasons. It was his sister's wedding, which I should have paid more attention to, but all I could see was him and the utter hurt in his eyes. If either of us had been more aware, we'd have known *she* was there too, in the crowd."

"She …" Vrishti said, frowning. "She who?"

"Meri. The reason for all of this. She hadn't yet made her move, but not even a day later, everything changed."

The old regret surged forth like a dark, cloying cloud

inside his chest. His throat tightened around the words, and he shook his head when she touched his shoulder.

"What is it?"

Forcing air into his lungs, he gave her a plaintive look. "Vrishti, there's something I'd like to do with you ... I wanted to wait until the three of us were together, but I want you to understand what he and I have faced, and it's difficult for me to find the right words. It's better if I show you, but that means we must meld."

"Are you sure? Isn't that part of mating for your kind?"

"It is, and I'm not asking lightly. I *want* to meld with you permanently once we get to him. This would only be the first step. No different than the first time your claws tear my skin when you mark me. Ultimately, we'd have to do it three times ... and a fourth when we exchange blood. Now, I just need to be able to share my mind with you."

"All right. What do we need to do?"

"Nothing. We've exchanged essences enough that this should be easy." He smoothed his palm along the side of her face, savoring the way she sighed and leaned her cheek into him. Spreading his fingers out, he found the pressure points at her temple and just behind her ear.

The magic flowed through him swiftly, and the second it penetrated her mind, she let out a soft gasp, her eyes widening.

"Shh. Let it happen," he whispered.

Vrishti closed her eyes and sank back down against him, her head on his shoulder while his fingers maintained contact until the meld was complete. Within moments, the realm of her mind opened to him and he stared around in wonder at what he found.

A more beautiful mind he had never encountered. Vrishti's was meant to be Summer's home soon, but it was as if the immortal spirit that embodied that most fertile season had already claimed its place in her. He wandered through a verdant garden, filled with trickling streams and beds of wildflowers. Tall trees stood at the edges like sentinels, their deep green leaves rustling in a summer breeze. It was more beautiful than his own home, and he half-wished he could simply move in and never leave.

He wandered down a path lined with blankets of tiny blue flowers and found her, naked and reclining on a small, grassy hillock.

"There you are," she said, giving him a shy smile. "I admit I'm not used to having other people in here."

"You wouldn't be," he said. "You'd need a satyr's or a nymph's essence to trigger a meld. I am …" He paused, over-whelmed by the scenery, unable to adequately voice his feelings about being here to begin with. "… Honored that I get to be here."

His gaze drifted past her to the sparkling pool that lay adjacent to the green slope of the hill she reclined on. The water swirled in a familiar way that couldn't be a simple feature of her imagination. His mouth fell open and he stumbled down the hill to the pool's edge.

"What is it?" Vrishti asked, standing up to follow him.

"The water. This is all you too?"

"It hasn't always been, but yes, it is now. This garden seems to keep getting bigger every time I come here. I think of it as my secret place. When I started to practice using my power as an ursa, this is what I imagined. There was always a little brook, but this pool only just appeared today. Is there something weird about it? You have the strangest look."

He let out an involuntary laugh. "Kitten, it isn't strange at all. And I shouldn't be surprised. It just never occurred to me that you would quite literally have the Source inside you. That's what this is. It's a part of your soul."

"Oh … I guess that's good, right?"

He glanced back at her as he stood. Her uncertainty was endearing, and he stepped closer, pulling her into his arms. "It's just more evidence of how amazing you are. Now, I have something to show you. Hang on."

He pulled back, sliding his hands down her arms and tugging on her hands as he stepped backwards. With each step the mental scenery around them changed, melting away as though it were fog. Gradually, it was replaced by a different scene, one from his ancient memories.

What unfolded were his recollections of a particular summer day in Egypt around three thousand years earlier. The day Aodh's sister wed her lover, the man who would eventually hunt Neph's kind nearly to extinction before switching sides to become their general in the coming war against an even older enemy.

At the time, there had been no reason to worry. Meri had been banished from the Haven and their lives had gone back to normal, or what might have passed for normal. He and Nyx returned to leading the nymphaea, and despite the ache of loss from expelling Aodh as well, he'd found a way to rejoice on the day he visited in this memory. He had performed with his sister in a glorious dance for the new couple that celebrated the past and the future and bestowed a blessing on the groom. The power they gave him through their dance would prolong his life and grant him psychic power in keeping with the power the immortal blue dragon who was his bride already possessed.

But aside from the time spent performing that dance, his entire attention was on the white-haired dragon on the other side of the dais where the wedding itself took place. He could not keep his eyes off the pale, shirtless man, who was resplendently garbed in silver from head to toe, with silver bands around his upper arms, a hammered silver neckpiece that gleamed in the sun, and a loincloth woven from silver thread. Aodh was flanked by his sisters in gold and green, then by their brothers in black and red, each one the perfect embodiment of their own color while they witnessed their blue sister wed the love of her life. The five of them soon offered their own enchantments to accompany the ones all the higher races had agreed to bestow upon the groom to ensure he could survive as the partner of an immortal dragon.

Neph was fortunate that he had no such attachment to a human, but at that moment, he almost wished he'd fallen for one. There would have been no complicated questions about how to justify their relationship and still do their duties by their race—that of procreating and producing children.

But the problem was that humans and immortals didn't mix, at least not long-term. And the dragons had long held fast to their own laws that prohibited them from mating with each other. Except in very specifically prescribed cases, they were required to choose human mates, but the immortal dragons who led the race were too powerful for the average human mind to survive very long.

They generally chose loneliness over love, or learned to find joy in the ephemeral nature of the human life. No good thing lasted, but that made it all the sweeter for them.

Through his covert observations of Aodh that day, it was clear that the dragon had not chosen the path of joyful abandon his red brother and golden sister both obviously embraced during the revelries that occurred just after the ceremony. Aodh had sat with his dark brother and simply observed, his gaze pointedly avoiding Neph.

The wound was still raw, and the event itself drew attention to the fact that the dragons were willing to push boundaries for the sake of love and happiness, and that the other higher races would band together to assist. There was no precedent against bestowing such blessings on a human who had already been touched by dragon power before birth. Fate's hand was solidly in the mix for this particular human man, if a dragon had seen fit to grant him a blessing in the womb.

The thing that stood out strongest for Neph, however, was how rigid they were when it came to sticking to the laws they had made to govern how the races mixed.

They simply didn't breed with each other, and he knew that despite the way they all came together for this one glorious event, many of the younger members happily enjoying the opportunity to pair up for a day with one of their sister races, they would all part ways when dawn struck tomorrow and wouldn't look back.

So why the hell couldn't he stop himself from looking back? Even though this was merely a memory he chose to relive to show Vrishti the day in question, that thread still tugged at his heart whenever he looked at Aodh.

Vrishti squeezed his hand. "Are you all right?" she asked.

"Not really. I didn't even have the balls to talk to him that day. I was too afraid someone might see right through me and call me on it. They'd know I'd broken one of our oldest laws by loving a dragon."

"Seems like a pretty ridiculous law to me. If you guys make the rules, why have it?"

"Except we didn't make the rules to start with. We are all still children of creatures who never exactly coexisted peacefully. They all fell in love with the same entity. Technically, Aodh and I share a parent, but it's far more complicated than even that."

"He's your half-brother?"

"Not exactly. I know this won't make sense, but his father was my mother. Fate has thousands of faces, so you couldn't precisely call us siblings, or even half-siblings, because how Fate chose to present itself to our parents would have been different depending on Fate's goals. Knowing we were a product of Fate's machinations to begin with made us all work toward peace at the start. Our parents were at odds, and we made a pact to never wind up in such conflict.

"So we made the unwritten rule never to cross that line. A little fun once in a while wasn't frowned on, but actually seeking a mate among our own small group ... we'd never do that. Except it isn't so easy if you discover you've suddenly fallen in love with the one person you should never feel that way for, incestuous or not."

"I don't think he forgot," Vrishti said softly, drawing Neph's attention back to the party that surrounded them. She gestured across the grand hall to a moonlit alcove. Within it sat the silvery dragon with a goblet in his hand, his pale, burning gaze solidly fixed across the room, right on Neph.

Neph's heart pounded and a pain shot through his chest at the look of utter despair and betrayal on his lover's face. How had he not seen this that night? He had no recollection of this particular image of Aodh, but then he'd done his damnedest to avoid meeting the dragon's gaze, deliberately timing his observations when he knew Aodh wouldn't see him watching.

Curious, he repositioned himself and Vrishti farther from the revelry so they could have a better view, and when he did, he caught sight of a scene he'd entirely missed that night.

"What is it?" Vrishti asked.

"I've never shifted my vantage during this day before. It's never occurred to me to use my power to alter my recollection of the events. I avoided the memory more often than not, I admit. But this is interesting ..."

He tugged her back several more paces, then backward still until they sat upon the pair of thrones the happy married couple had vacated shortly before. From that vantage, he could see not only his past self, but the entire room filled with revelers.

One figure in particular stood out. She was clad in modest robes, slightly finer than the servants, but not as elaborate as the other nobles, and she made the rounds of the room in hedonistic abandon. As she moved, the energy of the room gradually shifted as though she were inciting the kind of debauched festivities he often saw in the Haven during one of the numerous holidays they observed.

The more he watched her behavior, the more certain he was that she must be a nymph, and yet she didn't have the dewy blue-green shimmer of the nymphs from the Haven. There were very few of the higher races in attendance outside a handful of dragons who were carefully disguised as humans, and several turul who would never pass up a chance to scope out a party for their potential Ones. But by this point, all the leaders had departed, leaving the lower-ranked attendees to their fun.

Nyx had been eager to return to Nereus that night, and Neph had had no particular desire to stay longer, so they'd both drifted back to the Haven, leaving the party to continue without them. Now Neph was beyond the scope of his own memory, having tapped into the actual flow of history as it had unfolded on this day. The participants in his own life were long gone, so for once he had a clear, unbiased view of the evening, and what he witnessed chilled him.

The unfamiliar woman continued to work the room, encouraging the others to fall into sensuous abandon, drinking more, eating more, and he wasn't the least bit surprised when the first couple climbed onto a table and started fucking to the rousing beat of the music that played.

She could have been a dragon, but he saw no signs of red smoke, and she didn't seem as interested in absorbing the orgasmic energy as she had in joining in on the fun herself.

She fell to her knees in front of the men, eagerly drawing them to orgasm, then burying her face between a woman's thighs and doing the same, with almost no diminishing of her energy.

It wasn't until he saw what she did after each tasting that he knew.

"Why is she touching their faces that way every time?" Vrishti asked, speaking for the first time in ages.

"She's melding them," he said. "But not out of love. She's after their secrets."

"She sure seems excited about something."

"I'm sure she is," Neph murmured almost to himself. "We just gave her the perfect puppet, and she must know it. She's preparing to take control."

Why he had never considered investigating Meri's history more closely, he didn't know. Perhaps this old memory was what had held him back. But now that he'd managed to see beyond the moments of his wallowing in regret over a lost lover, he intended to follow through and see where the rest led. He'd only heard snippets of secondhand stories about what had happened, how their enemy had come to be. Tonight, he would know the truth.

"Where are we going?" Vrishti asked when Neph grabbed her hand and led her away. "I thought you said that was Meri … Shouldn't we watch her?"

"We will. She'll be busy for a while, though. I need to see what happened with Nikhil before she got to him. He was just blessed with enough power to make him immortal and impervious to harm of any kind. At least, that's what we thought when we carried out the wedding ceremony. Meri shouldn't have been strong enough to control him."

"What about Aodh?" Vrishti asked. "Weren't you showing me what happened with him?"

"I already did. My point in all this was that I couldn't bear to even look at him. Neither of us stayed long enough to risk a meeting. I simply wanted the evening to be done, and I gather so did he, considering the speed with which he left. We were too distracted to see what was right under our noses."

He led her down a wide corridor, the sounds of the party receding behind them. Voices carried from behind a solid wood door—voices he recognized. Stopping, he drifted the two of them into the room.

Four figures stood on the wide balcony in the moonlight, each still clad in their colorful wedding garb—red, green, gold, and black. Neph's pulse raced. Was this where Aodh had gone? But there was no sign of the silver-clad man.

"That's Gavra, Numa, and Aurum," Vrishti whispered. "What are they doing? You would think they'd be back in that … room. With all the sex."

"They're on guard," Neph said, observing the quartet of dragons speaking in low voices.

Stealing closer, they paused just inside the door to listen.

"Nikhil's a sadist," Ked said. "I don't trust him."

Gavra let out a low chuckle. "Because he's too much like you, brother? You know better than anyone that makes him her perfect mate. Let them have their wedding night. We'll watch and intervene, if need be."

The night grew darker for a moment before Aurum spoke up. "They're in love and no doubt *making* love as we speak. How they choose to express that is really none of our business. I haven't seen Belah this happy since before Mother took Zorion away from her. Let her have this, even if it is temporary."

Ked's darkness blotted out even more light. Vrishti let out an alarmed gasp as the room disappeared, leaving them in a disorienting void that would have felt utterly complete if not for her hand squeezing Neph's.

"Who the hell is *he*?" Vrishti asked. "I don't think I like him."

"That's Ked, the Void. He's their brother too, and not a dragon you would ever want to cross, trust me."

He shushed her and pulled her closer as if he could protect her from the Void's shadows filling the room.

"Do not remind me of that day, sister. He was my son too. We should have been allowed to raise him."

"Ked, desist," a commanding female voice said into the darkness. He heard a rustling sound and the air was soon filled with a verdant aroma that reminded him of his home at springtime, all budding new life and sexual energy. The darkness faded, leaving behind a pleasant green glow, illuminating the four dragons once more. The other sister, Numa, had moved close to her dark brother and had his face braced in her hands.

"You knew a time would come for her to move on. This is that time. You may not trust the man she's chosen, but he is in part a product of your love for her. He carries your blessing twice over now. If she could handle being your sister, I have no doubt she can handle him. Trust her."

The hurt and betrayal didn't leave Ked's gaze, and Neph wished he could reassure the man that all would be well. Calder had told him all that had unfolded during the last few weeks as the Ultiori's prisoner, how the black dragon had rescued a pair of lovers who would become his mates shortly before returning to carry Calder and Nicholas out as well.

This was a man who would stop at nothing to protect the ones he loved and didn't react well to barriers. Neph supposed it was the nature of a Shadow as powerful as the Void.

They all turned at the sound of running footsteps coming down the hall outside the door. The door flew open and a breathless woman appeared, eyes wild.

"My mistress is in trouble! Please, help! He's gone mad. He's hurting her!"

The ensuing chaos was as much a sign as any that this was the moment Neph needed to pay attention to. He lifted his hands with one palm facing inward and made a slow, sweeping gesture, smacking his palm onto the fist he made with the other hand. The scene froze instantly.

"What happened?" Vrishti asked, clinging to his side.

"Nothing yet. This is when I think it all began, though. I need you to watch this woman and see where she goes next. I will follow the dragons."

"You stopped time. That's …"

"This has already happened. I'm merely adjusting to observe the events from different angles. It isn't possible to stop time."

"Oh, but we can travel backwards. Shouldn't we just *go* to when this all happened and change it? Whatever it is?"

"That is also impossible. Time and Fate are two immutable forces that we cannot fight any more than we can fight gravity. All we can do is learn from what occurred."

"But if the outcome is inevitable, why even try?" she asked in a defeated tone. "Why bother?"

"For love, kitten," he said with a soft smile. "Why do we do anything, if not for love? Now keep your eyes open. I'll meet you back here soon."

She glanced at the frozen figure of the girl—one of the servants who he'd seen at the sidelines of the festivities earlier. With a gesture, he reversed the motion he'd made before, and slowly the figures all began to move again.

"I told you we shouldn't trust him," Ked said. He exhaled a thick black cloud that swiftly snaked through the air to the girl, slipping around her eyes like a blindfold and into her nostrils. She stood, paralyzed and blinded long enough for the four dragons to shift and take to the air without human eyes to witness their transformation.

The smoke faded a few seconds later and the girl left the room with far less urgency than she'd arrived, a devious glimmer in her eyes.

Vrishti gave Neph an intrigued look, then kissed him on the cheek before following the girl through the door.

Neph stepped toward the balcony, summoned his own swift transformation into the shape of a large graceful egret, and took to the air in the direction the dragons had flown. Once he had them in his sights, he swiftly drifted ahead of them to the balcony they were flying toward.

Inside, he witnessed an alarming scene that reinforced Ked's assertion of the groom's sadistic nature. The bride was bound to a large wooden cross and hammered metal bowls were placed at strategic points near her hands and feet.

Blood flowed into each bowl, the fresh essence of life filling the room with the scent of the sky.

At first, he might have agreed that the groom was indeed a monster, that they'd made a mistake in granting him the gifts they had that day. But the look on Nikhil's face as he made love to Belah told a different story.

The dragon's blue eyes remained fixed on him with the utmost love and adoration, and his look mirrored hers. Despite the flowing blood, it was perhaps the *least* sadistic thing he'd ever seen. With a sudden, lurching thud in his chest, he recognized that look—that emotion that he kept buried for so long for the man he'd lost, and that had resurfaced again so recently when he made love to Vrishti.

The moment Belah's eyes closed and the blood flow ceased, he understood what had happened. He had no such proclivities toward pain and oblivion, but he knew all too well how alluring the fantasy of death was for creatures like them who could not die. He'd never known one to take it to that extreme, but he'd also never known one who had a lover willing to take them there.

As he observed Nikhil's worship of his bride in the moments that followed, he had new respect for the man. Nikhil carefully unbound Belah and carried her to a bath where he proceeded to gently wash the blood from her skin, then dress her in a fine, flowing sheer gown before laying her in the center of her bed. He then methodically disassembled the cross she'd been bound to, stacking the wood near the door. Finally he reverently picked up each bowl of her blood and set it on a nearby shelf, lighting candles and setting them on the shelf as well.

Every action spoke of love the likes of which Neph had longed for ever since that day he'd lied to Aodh and sent him away. How could something this perfect and beautiful have gone so wrong?

When the utter cold and darkness filled the room a moment later, he knew without a doubt what had happened.

"What have you done?!" the enraged black dragon snarled, then flew into the room and attacked.

Nikhil took several rough hits, but placed himself solidly between Ked and the bride, ever the protector. Gavra had been right—the pair of them were very much alike, and their love for this woman was likely to destroy them.

The human man lasted longer than he should have, which Neph realized he owed to the blessings he'd been granted during the wedding ceremony. The pair fought as humans at first, Nikhil easily putting Ked down, but it was a temporary victory. When he shifted back into his dragon form, Neph knew there was no hope for Nikhil winning this fight.

Black flames filled the room, and when they ceased, Nikhil was nothing but a charred shape crouching over the form of his bride as though to protect her.

Ked reached out a large claw and shoved the burned body aside. He scooped his sister into his claw and turned, launching himself into the darkness and the sky above.

Neph stood frozen in place, staring at what should have been the body of a dead man. Not even the blessings they'd granted could have protected Nikhil from Ked's fire. They weren't fools, after all. They may have agreed to give the man what passed for immortality in order to wed an immortal, but there were loopholes in those blessings. Any one of the immortals could kill him, if it came to that, and the blessings had also been somewhat mutable—they could be reversed to become curses if the givers decided the recipient was no longer worthy. Ultimately, that's what had happened, but Neph hadn't realized one of them had indeed tried to kill Nikhil that night.

Yet he had lived. How had he lived?

His gaze fell on the bowls of blood and he recalled the red that had stained Nikhil's lips when he'd arrived. The blood … How much of it had he drunk?

The door opening caught his eye and he reflexively shifted backward into the shadows despite knowing he couldn't be seen in this vision. The human woman he'd decided was actually Meri inhabiting a new body slipped silently in, with Vrishti following close behind.

Vrishti saw him a few steps into the room and her eyes lit with excitement. She started to rush to him until she saw the charred body on the bed and immediately halted. Her eyes widened and her hand flew to her mouth.

"Oh, my god! What happened? Where's Belah?"

"Taken away by her family."

"Was it true what the girl said? I could have sworn she was lying. I followed her like you said and she went straight to Meri, told her she'd done as asked. Then I followed Meri here."

"Misdirection," he growled. "I've never seen a pair more in love than those two were. She played off Ked's fears like a pro. Manipulative little bitch."

While they watched, Meri set to work, almost gleefully gathering the blood into one large stoneware bottle. In the process, she dipped a finger in and tasted it, her eyes rolling in ecstasy.

She climbed up onto the bed, straddling the charred form. "Let's see how well you bend to my will, puppet," she said.

She produced a knife from her belt and exposed the unburned side of Nikhil's throat, made a small cut and bent her head to it. Her actions might have been a sensual kiss if Neph didn't know better. Then she pulled back and made a small slice in her wrist and placed the cut to the mouth of what should have been a corpse.

"When her blood heals you and you wake up, you will be mine. Belah's gone. The dragons have betrayed you. It will be your life's mission to destroy them all."

"Oh, my god!" Vrishti whispered beside him. "Was he the enemy? But he's on our side now, right? Aodh said there was a man who could lead us all to victory."

Neph shook his head. "Meri was always the enemy. We didn't realize it at first, but after a while, everything Nikhil did began to have the distinct imprint of her. Nyx and I soon realized that she had to be behind it all somehow, but we weren't sure how. Now we know. But we also know her weakness."

"We do?"

"Her body is human. Watch…"

He made a spinning motion with his hand and the scene before them blurred for a moment, then halted again, displaying an armor-clad Nikhil standing at the window with blood on his hands and a giant, bloody dragon head at his feet. Beside him stood a gray-haired woman casting a disgusted look at the macabre trophy and offering praise to the man who had brought it to her.

Nikhil turned a blank gaze to her and merely nodded as though devoid of any feelings.

Neph sped the scene farther, and the next time they saw

Nikhil, still as young and fit as ever, an old crone stood beside him, her hand on the shoulder of a pretty young woman with a stare just as empty as Nikhil's.

"She can't live without a vessel," Neph said. "She no doubt blood melds her victims in order to mind control them, then transfers her spirit into their body when her old vessel dies. But her human vessels always die. Calder said that she'd been carrying out experiments, trying to create a hybrid creature. What if her goal was to create a new vessel for herself?"

"Would that even work? I mean, wouldn't whatever she created still age, even if it lives longer than humans do?"

"She had a taste of what it feels like to be immortal once, when she betrayed Aodh and inhabited his body. If she indeed captured Calder's father and the other Thiasoi soldiers, she's already a step closer to creating an immortal child. If she collects enough genetic material close to an immortal parent, she could breed a creature that is theoretically immortal.

"She already has immortal blood from Belah's wedding night. Calder learned that the Elites she controlled were created with immortal dragon blood as well, so somehow she acquired Aodh or his siblings' blood. That would be enough to begin with.

"Finding the right balance between the different elements might result in an immortal child. The trick would be finding parents who love each other enough to come together and conceive such a child, much less carry it to term. It would take immense power for a child like that to survive in the womb—more power than a mortal mother could provide for an extended period. The kind of power she could get from satyr blood. Or better yet, from the Source itself."

"But the Source is protected. Nyx made sure of that, and Assana's sticking to her guns about it too. I can't even get back into the Sanctuary until the Equinox. Oh …" Vrishti's brow creased. "Will you be able to come home with me then? Will Aodh? I promised my mother I'd return in time for the Equinox. That's when I inherit the Spirit of Summer."

"We still have plenty of time to figure things out. First, we need to free Aodh, then we should get to Nikhil and tell him what we learned."

"What are we waiting for?" Vrishti said, holding out her hands to him.

The visions of the past faded around them, leaving them back on the green hill in her flowery garden with the burbling brook nearby.

He glanced at the deep pool and nodded toward it. "Let me just do one more thing first."

She joined him at the water's edge and they both knelt. He placed both palms flat atop the water's surface, the mere contact confirming by the instant rush of power that this pool was indeed tapped directly into the Source.

"Follow my lead and think of Aodh," he said.

Vrishti nodded and touched her palms to the water. With a soft murmur of ancient words of power, Neph called the vision forth, asking the River to show him where is lover could be found and when.

The image that was reflected in the pool's surface was of the interior of a temple, with a sleeping behemoth lying beside another pool of water. Neph searched the scene, drawing backward until the he looked down from above onto a mountaintop, carefully obscured by dragon magic, but not to the degree where he couldn't recognize Aodh's mark of exquisite craftsmanship in the barely concealed cupola betraying the presence of the dragon temple beneath the earth.

Then Neph turned their view to the sky, scanning for signs of the era he needed to target.

"Nyx, you crazy bitch. You *really* wanted him as far away from the Haven and Meri as you could get him, didn't you?"

He chuckled as he pulled back and assisted Vrishti to her feet.

"What is it?" she asked. "Do you know where we're going? When … I guess?"

"Exactly," he said. "Let's do this."

CHAPTER 24

CALDER

Calder's consciousness floated in darkness, with no tether to reality beyond the raven's feather and the gold talon he held in each hand as though they were his lifelines.

A more complete and utter void he'd never experienced. If he didn't know Meri better, he'd think he'd simply died and this was the nothingness that truly existed in the afterlife. But he didn't trust Meri to have killed him. She'd wanted him too damn much for something so destructive.

A gray glimmer flickered at the corner of his eyesight and he turned, his pulse picking up. Only blackness met his gaze, however, and he returned to brooding and pondering what the hell she could have wanted him for to begin with.

Then he heard a rushing sound that couldn't have been imagined. Focusing his attention, he strained to hear it again. There it was … a low-pitched whoosh that grew in volume before receding again. At first he shook his head and wiggled his fingers in his ears, thinking it must be his own pulse, but he was so far removed from his actual body right now, that couldn't be the case. Could it?

He continued listening, stretching his attention as far as it could go into the blackness that surrounded him, hoping for more.

A flash of gray light again, and the rushing sound grew louder. Another flash he knew he couldn't mistake as actual light that practically seared his eyes. This time the silhouette of a man burned itself onto his eyes with searing clarity.

"Father?" he blurted before the image faded into darkness again

The gray light came again in a more even, rising glow rather than a quick flash. The silhouette came closer, still clouded in shadows, but clearer, with a familiar shape, from the tips of his massive horns down to his hoofed feet.

"Calder, it is you. That is unfortunate." His father emerged from the gray and the blackness receded, leaving them standing on the shores of a stormy sea, the ebb and flow of the waves rushing in his ears.

"I came to find you. I wouldn't call this unfortunate at all, because here you are," Calder said. "Gaia's grace, is it really you?" He rushed to the man, but stopped short when his father's grim face didn't match his elation.

"If you're in here, it is indeed unfortunate. We're trapped. Meri's hold on our minds is too great. I only managed to break through to you this time because I sensed your mother's blood nearby—your blood, in fact. The others weren't lucky enough to be blood-melded to a Dionarch. They're fully under Meri's thrall."

"Where the hell are we?" Calder asked. "She's got us in a mental prison as well as a physical one, it seems."

"I only catch glimmers when I manage to break through, but she's gotten better at keeping me under. She steals our blood, leaving us with only enough to stay alive. Our tie to the Source is thankfully not strong enough for her to exploit wholesale. It keeps us alive.

"We're in some kind of gelatin-filled tank, hooked to tubes that drain our blood over time. The creature she gives it to … is like nothing I have ever known. It has life, but no purpose yet. It feeds on our blood, but isn't yet strong enough to take sustenance for itself."

"She's trapped us to feed this creature? That's it?"

"Whatever it is, it is the most important thing to her. She's isolated us in here so well I can't even reach Nyx when I do manage to break away from her spell."

"But you have Mother's power. Can't you use it?"

"If I could stay awake long enough, I would try. Meri is careful …" He trailed off, frowning. "How do you know I have Nyx's power?"

"Uncle Neph visited me. I know you and mother blood-melded before I was born, and that you were the last of our kind to complete the ritual. At least legitimately. Well, you aren't the last anymore. Assana and I have both blood-melded our mates. Perhaps I can use their power."

"Do it," his father said without a moment's hesitation.

Calder moved to the water's edge, hoping the feel of the water would help strengthen his connection to the outside world. He drew on that still unfamiliar well he'd been infused with moments after blood melding with his mates.

"Help me, Father," he said, reaching out a hand to the man at his side. They clasped hands tightly and his father's mental energy infused his own, helping him push his consciousness out farther into the light beyond the water. He aimed for the sun he knew must exist up there somewhere, the embodiment in his mind of his golden dragon mate.

"Come for me, Aurum," he whispered. "Find me and bring Nikhil and the others when you do. We will end this bitch once and for all."

CHAPTER 25

AURUM

*A*urum felt the tickle at the back of her mind like a niggling forgotten memory. The sound repeated in a familiar rhythm that she recognized deep in her soul, but couldn't quite place, as if it were a single taste of a cake containing a hundred exotic flavors she itched to identify, and would if she could only have one more bite.

"Did you hear that?" Nicholas asked from beside her. They sat on the peak of Kilimanjaro, where they'd stopped to rest as they made their way north.

She gave him an excited look. "Yes! Do you think it's him?"

"It feels like him. Close your eyes." He turned to face her, crossing his legs and reaching for her hands. They twined fingers and opened their minds to each other, merging to one consciousness and focusing their shared power on the sound.

The noise was still a dull, incoherent murmur at first, but with enough focus, it soon coalesced into a voice. One she had longed for ever since the moment she'd lost it a few days earlier.

She let out an elated yelp and leapt to her feet, shifting swiftly to her true form. Without hesitating, Nicholas jumped onto her back.

"Let's go fucking get him!" he yelled.

Aurum launched herself into the sky, soaring for a few moments before banking hard in the direction Calder's call had come from. Atop her back, Nicholas let out a cry of elation and dug his knees in hard, urging her to fly as fast as she could.

They had found him again.

CHAPTER 26

NIKHIL

"Nikhil!" Belah yelled, rushing into the private chamber of the temple where Nikhil was questioning the Shadow they'd rescued. He looked up, alarmed by her excitement at first until he saw the wide grin on her face. "They found him! Aurum and Nicholas are on their way to Calder now."

"That's good news," he said. Without missing a beat, he turned back to the new addition to their team, who he'd been grilling for the past hour. "Tell me what we're walking into, Razik."

The wounded Shadow nodded. "Her base isn't easy to access. It's buried beneath the Giza pyramids, several meters underground with no exterior door. She drifts her men in herself two at a time. No one has ever actually left."

"We can deal with that limitation as long as we can get a layout. That's where Calder will come in. Anything else you learned when your team infiltrated the Ultiori camp?"

Razik flinched under the fresh gust of breath that blew from the pale-haired Guardian Nikhil had commanded to heal the Shadow. The seeping wound in his stomach slowly knit shut, and Razik let out a shaky breath, the furrows in his brow easing when the pain finally diminished. Nikhil didn't discount the man's exhaustion, but he was a soldier and knew the price of loyalty.

"They don't seem to care that none of their buddies are seen again once she takes them inside. Sounds like however she's rewarding them is worth it. I have a feeling it's with our blood. They passed around this drink one night that tasted like nothing I've ever had before. They actually called it dragon's blood, but it was more than that. It was this thick, sweet, fermented stuff. Turned my fucking stomach."

"How many of you were there?" Nikhil asked. "Did your squad make it out?"

The man's gaze sharpened. "They're alive. I was the decoy. When they discovered us, I gave the signal for my team to escape and led the Hunters in the other direction. I thought I'd wind up dead until I found the temple—hoped there might still be Guardian magic that would take care of those bastards if I led them there. Never counted on *you* showing up. Thank you."

"We'll get word to your team to join us when they can. Tell me more of what you learned about her base."

Razik let out a sharp grunt when the Guardian ripped his pants leg open to get at the knife wound there. Sweat beaded on his brow and he inhaled deeply, then exhaled through his mouth in a slow, even blow.

"Sorry, sir," the Guardian said.

Razik shook his head. "No worries, man. Just get it done."

The Guardian glanced up at him with raised brows. "This would go quicker if I gave you my Nirvana. It'd help you forget the pain, too."

Nikhil interrupted the Shadow's refusal. "I just have a few more questions. Afterward, I'll leave you two alone. We need you healed, Razik. However you're comfortable doing it."

The Guardian's lips quirked in a pleased smile and he went back to work, stitching up Razik's wounds with tiny, targeted breaths.

"Are you sure, sir? I should be fine after everything's healed."

"I nearly died from a battle wound once. If it hadn't been for a dragon's Nirvana, I wouldn't be standing here right now. Trust me, you need it. If you'd rather have a female attend you, that can be arranged."

Razik glanced at the Guardian, who had his big hands wrapped around his bloody thigh, lips poised within inches of his crotch as he slowly expelled a healing breath along the open wound.

"Ah, I don't think that'll be necessary, unless you have one to spare. Don't want to be greedy." He gave Nikhil an awkward smirk.

"You've earned it," Nikhil said. "So … the base?"

Razik nodded and dove into all the intel he'd discovered while undercover in the Ultiori camp. They'd just gotten orders to mobilize and make their way north. They didn't know specifics, but scuttlebutt was that the doctor had some kind of big target she intended to attack and wanted all the soldiers ready. Their destination was outside Cairo, a part of the world Nikhil knew well, but if Meri had a facility there, she'd succeeded in keeping it a secret from him all along. Meri was nothing if not devious.

The Shadow's energy clearly flagging, Nikhil finally ceased his questions and stood to leave. Finished with the superficial healing, the Guardian stood waiting near the door to the comfortable chamber.

"Any further orders, sir?" the Guardian asked.

"Find a female red, and the two of you see that his well is filled and he's fully healed by morning. I want him by my side when we're ready to move."

"Yes, sir," the Guardian said, an excited gleam in his eye.

Belah stood outside the room and fell into step beside him as they made their way back down to the throne room.

"Do Aurum and Nicholas have a bearing yet?"

"They've already drifted as far as they dare. Calder's somewhere near the pyramids."

Nikhil stopped in his tracks and looked at her, then nodded. "She's taken him to her base in Egypt. I can't believe I never saw any signs of her plans. After we left Alexandria, we never went back. Or at least, she never compelled me to return. I think she knew I'd grown weary of the familiarity of the place. Memories of you haunted me there, made me too difficult to control."

"Aurum and Nicholas are in Alexandria now. Should I send them somewhere else?"

The softer tone of her voice made him slow and press his hand to the small of her back. "Our time together in Alexandria gave me some of the best memories of my life, Belah. If Aurum and Nicholas can drift into her base from their current location, we'll meet them there. You know the palace didn't survive the Romans, though, don't you?"

She gave him a sad look. "I often wonder what would have happened had we been able to rule together after our wedding night. How different would the world be now?"

"Humanity filled in the gaps your kind left behind. They are nothing if not prodigious. Send word to your sister that we need Calder to learn what kind of opposition we'll face once we infiltrate the base. I need to know how many to send. As soon as we know that, we'll be there."

"Already done, Belah said.

Meri's rage spiked at the sight of the irregular peaks on the monitors connected to the tank. Brain activity had surged again in Subject Five, then briefly in Subject Six, before both had evened out to a disturbingly flat line. Flat was good. Flat was what she wanted. But the synchronicity of those two series of blips aroused her suspicion to an alarming level.

"Increase the dosage of the sedative on Five and Six," she said to the technician. "I want them effectively braindead when I get back."

"Yes, doctor," the tech said, immediately tapping a button to make the adjustment. "When will you return?"

They were all loyal pups, and their behavior toward her showed it. She was nothing if not a conscientious owner. Her dogs were given plenty of treats and suitably disciplined when they acted out. As a result, they performed happily with tails wagging.

She combed her fingers through the man's thick, pale blond hair. "I'll be back tomorrow, and I will have your favorite treat if you've behaved. Here's a little taste to tide you over."

She turned her barbed ring and nicked her wrist, then pressed it to his mouth, offering him a sample of her power-infused blood that had become a drug to her followers. It also gave her an unbroken connection to the network of their minds, allowing her access whenever she needed to check in on them, or to control them.

The technician's eyelids fluttered shut as he sucked at her wrist. A slow bulge swelled in his lap by the time he pulled back. "Thank you," he murmured.

"Good boy," she said, patting him on the head and giving the inside of his mind a similar stroke of appreciation while ensuring his complete submission to her will.

As she passed by her lab on the way out, she glanced in the direction of the hidden door, suppressing the urge to enter so she could look at the small, perfect treasure she kept secured inside that room. The satyrs' blood was doing its job, but just barely. Now that she had both Calder and Nereus, she hoped to find a way to get a message to Nyx. All she needed was enough power to send her ransom demands into the Haven. If the Dionarch were desperate enough, she'd open a portal for Meri, and when she did, Meri would have her army ready to strike.

The hunters were already mobilizing and making their way to Egypt. There was a certain pleasing symmetry to sending her message back in through the very Nile River portal where she'd first been expelled from the Haven. The Nile had been one of her favorite playgrounds as a young nymph, and ultimately where she'd begun her plan to take revenge on the Haven.

Except revenge seemed so petty now. She'd had a taste of true immortality once. If her plan worked, she would have it again, and an entire immortal army at her disposal. She just needed to get the baby to the Source and encourage it to grow. If Nyx wanted her mate and her son returned to her, she wouldn't say no.

If only there were a suitable womb with the power to keep the baby alive. During all her many experiments, the embryos were almost never viable. She'd finally discovered that human-based offspring were the most mutable, and could be compelled to drift from the womb where they were conceived if she gave them the right lure.

Her own womb was not an option—something she'd discovered early on. Her human vessels didn't possess enough innate power, and neither did most of the pure-blooded higher races she captured. Some worked better than others, but some crucial ingredient was always missing.

The baby needed far too much magic to sustain it. Finally she'd tried a test with an embryo conceived from two altered humans, rather than the pure-blooded specimens she captured from the higher races. Bless the dragons for their need to put their marks all over humankind. The female Elite had been blessed by Belah herself and had endured all the years of experimental transfusions, each one mutating her a little more. Add to her eggs the seed of none other than Nikhil himself, and Meri had the perfect offspring, or so she had hoped. She'd put all her dreams on that union, taking the embryo at the crucial moment and introducing it into the nymphaea blood-infused tank.

The baby had thrived in that environment, but at only a few scant months past conception, it was still far too small to be viable outside the tank. Immortality apparently wasn't yet part of its makeup, but it had the blood of immortals in its DNA: infusions from every last drop of the dragon brothers' blood that she no longer needed to power her Elites, blood from the ursa queen she'd captured who had escaped ages ago, blood from the turul princess she'd held captive for five decades, and now the freshest blood she could get, from the son of a Dionarch.

She only needed enough power for the immortal essences that flowed in the baby's blood to be triggered. That much power could only be found in one place—inside the Haven, at the Source.

The plan had to be perfect. By the time she got all the pieces in place, hopefully she would find a way to take the baby to the Source.

If only she could have kept that infuriating ursa queen.

None of the captives she'd managed to hold onto were powerful enough for the job. The turul princess might well have been if she hadn't escaped, though Meri would have probably murdered the bitch if she'd had the chance, after being forced out of her favorite puppet's head by the turul's infernal song.

She punched the button in the lift to take her to the chamber near the surface where she would depart from. The powerful dragon wards that filled the great pyramid above her sapped too much of her power when she attempted to drift through them, but they'd cloaked her base for ages. She had effectively hidden in plain sight, but had adapted by building a secret chamber far enough outside the zone of dragon magic that she could easily drift to the surface from there.

At least she finally had leverage against Nyx. That was one weight off her mind. If she could simply solve that one final problem, she would be ready to take over the Haven once and for all. The Source would be hers.

CHAPTER 28

VRISHTI

antern light played over Neph's face in warm, dancing flickers, setting fire to the intense, swirling depths of his eyes. Vrishti got lost in his gaze, her pulse racing in anticipation of the next step of their journey.

She couldn't quite believe she had only just set eyes on this man a few days ago. It seemed like a lifetime since they'd met and she'd promptly gotten sick from simply looking into these eyes. Seasick, she realized, smiling softly at the recognition that she no longer felt the same nausea gripping her belly. The vertigo this time was a very welcome sense of everything falling into place.

With a satisfied sigh, she lifted her palm to his cheek and stroked her fingertips over his stubble, noting the flecks of silver that appeared here and there illuminated by the lamplight.

"You're melded with me now," Neph rumbled, making idle caresses up and down her body. "That's why you can look into my eyes without getting dizzy."

She raised an eyebrow and involuntarily turned into his touch. "And you can read my mind, apparently."

His lips twisted in a sly smile. "I can. You are also wondering why I haven't started making love to you again so we can finally go to Aodh. You can look inside my mind for the answer, but I think you know it already."

She searched his eyes, considering the invitation, but he was right. "We have to wait for a surge in my power first. Which should occur before too long ... unless I'm pregnant, in which case it's over. You don't think ..."

"You aren't pregnant yet. We've melded once. You haven't even marked me. That has to happen at a bare minimum for my seed to take."

The brief surge of tension in her chest eased. "Good, because I don't want to get pregnant until I know the two of you have reconciled. Not to force an ultimatum on you. I want you *both*, but I want to know you've forgiven each other before we take that step. I would kind of like to wait and make it all official after I get back to the Sanctuary. Is it crazy that I want my mother to be there when I mark you? Maybe not *in* the room, but I want it to be a big deal. Like ..."

She paused, her cheeks warming at the confession she was about to make.

"Like a wedding," he said softly, saving her the trouble.

"Yeah, like that. Assuming he's still interested."

"Kitten, he may still have issues with me, but you've done nothing wrong. He's always been able to see to the heart of things. To understand the underlying truth. That's why I'm hoping he'll forgive me."

"I hope so too," she said, sighing and arching up into his exploring palm as it passed over the tip of her breast for the third time in his slow, constant caresses. After enduring two days of the same kind of sensuous torture, she knew his goal was more than simple pleasure. The slow, deliberate teasing was meant to push her desire to the edge, to urge her body into that almost painful state where she needed him so much it physically hurt.

She wasn't sure how long it had been since the first surge of power overtook her body like a wildfire, but she was due if the tiny, almost imperceptible ache inside her womb was any indication. She tilted her face up to his and he dipped his head, capturing her lips in an eager kiss while he slid his hand between her thighs and cupped her slick pussy in his palm.

The stroke of a single fingertip against her clit was enough to stoke that fire to another level, the ache growing to an ember. She let out a soft moan, tilting her hips up into his touch and spreading her thighs wider.

Neph shifted on his side, bending his head to take the tip of her breast in his mouth. She swept her fingers through his hair, reveling in the sensuous abandon he incited in her. Every touch he gave her sent her to a new height of pleasure, but the feel of his hard body, his soft skin, his silken hair under her own touch had the same effect.

The simple fact of his rigid shaft, its hot and silken hardness brushing against her hip, made her even hotter.

The thought of that thick length caused a sudden painful spasm in her core that made her gasp. Neph leaned back, his sharp gaze fixed on her face.

"That's right, kitten. Let it build until your body aches to be fucked."

"I want to see your other shape," she said, barely able to suppress another moan when he slipped two fingers into her tender depths.

"You need to be ready to get fucked when I change," he said. "That much primal power makes it tough to restrain myself."

"Please. I'll be ready when you do."

He licked his lips, leaving them glistening with saliva as

he swept his gaze down her body to her hips where they twisted and pushed against his gently fucking fingers.

A smile spread across his face. "Just one more thing, then you can have what you want."

He shifted around and placed one big palm on her thigh, pulling her leg against his chest before dipping his head between her thighs. Her abdomen tightened as his lips covered her wet folds and he swept his tongue deep, teasing it up the very center until he sucked her clit into his mouth. The pleasure of that contact sent a burst of acute desire through her and she cried out, tilting her hips against his expert licks. He took her almost to the edge, stopping abruptly as though he knew the exact point at which she would snap.

Then he slid off the bed and stood up, the full length of him visible in the amber light. His body was smooth and lean, muscles taut with pent-up need, the lantern light casting shadows that accentuated every hard plane of muscle down to the cords that arched over his hips leading to his glorious cock.

The sight of him like this made her sit up and slide to the edge of the bed, ready to reach for him again, but holding out for the answer to her request. She hadn't gotten to *see* him when he'd shifted, just before driving that massive satyr cock into her when her estrous had begun. Ever since that first night, she hadn't been able to banish that image from her mind of the huge, horned man with his fleece-covered legs and hoofed feet. And the spectacular erection he'd brandished like a weapon more than ready to conquer her body.

She pressed her thighs together in anticipation, digging her fists into the blankets at the edge of the bed. He stepped closer to her, his cock within reach of her mouth if she only leaned forward. He raised his hand to her head, cupping the back of her neck and tangling his fingers in her hair. He tugged until she had to arch her neck to look up at him.

"Would you take a full-sized satyr cock in that pretty mouth of yours, or would that be too much to ask? Because if you aren't ready for me, you might need to offer an alternative to your hot little snatch, kitten."

"I'll do whatever you need," she said. "I just want to see you for a minute before … before it starts." Despite the hold he had on her hair, her gaze slid down to his crotch again, lingering on the glistening pink tip of his cock where it peeked out from the foreskin. The tip was always visible like this when he was aroused, a feature that fascinated her.

"Is this what you want to see most?" he asked, gripping his cock in his free hand and stroking it lightly, the motion pulling on his foreskin so his pink tip was fully visible.

"I want to see all of you," she said, licking her lips and unable to tear her gaze away from him.

"Then all of me is what you'll get. Every last inch."

As he spoke his voice roughened, grew deeper, and seemed to vibrate straight to her core. His cock swelled perceptibly as did the hand that held it, growing proportionally second by second. At the base of his cock, his dark curls thickened and turned into luxuriant black fleece that only served to accent how much bigger his cock had become.

Vrishti swallowed, finding it difficult to keep up with the flood of saliva that inundated her mouth as much as the arousal now coated her thighs.

"Look at me, baby," he said, and the voice seemed to come from farther away, but was no less present and strong, its deep vibrations reaching her soul. He slid his hand under her chin, tipping her face up.

She blinked in wide-eyed wonder at the immense creature who now stood before her. The horns she remembered arched magnificently from his temples, nearly brushing the cabin's ceiling almost eight feet above. Those hypnotic sea-blue eyes still sent sparks of awe through her. His face was the same, only larger and somehow wilder, nostrils flaring and lips curled as though he were on the verge of a snarl. Everything about him was bigger, harder, and more *real* than he'd been before, filling up the cabin and all her senses as though there were nothing else in her world but him and her aching need to follow through on her quest to find the man they both loved.

"That's right, kitten. I want you to think of him when I take your mouth. Open up wide."

Vrishti parted her lips, her entire body alive with her need to taste him again. She lifted her hands and placed them on his hips, sinking her fingers into the soft, thick fur that covered him there. She stroked inward as she leaned closer, finally wrapping both hands around the base of his cock when her lips met his thick, shining tip.

He removed his hand from his shaft, resting it on her shoulder. Vrishti slipped one hand down beneath the base of his cock, found his heavy sack as silken smooth as the length she held in her other hand. He let out a low rumble of approval when she ran her palm around the heavy orbs.

Opening her mouth, she darted her tongue out and swept it in a smooth circle around his tip, her taste buds coming alive at the almost spicy flavor of him. Neph trailed his fingers up the back of her head and grasped her hair, on the verge of pulling but not quite. She sensed the barely restrained tension in him and lifted her gaze while she opened her mouth wider to take him in.

She teased the tip of her tongue tight against the under-side of his cock, watching his face as he stared raptly down at her. When she had his tip fully in her mouth as far as she could take him, she gave him a slight suck. Neph let out a low growl, his lips curling back again and his eyes flashing with need.

Caressing his balls with one hand, she stroked the other up his shaft, barely able to grasp his girth in her hand. She dragged her thumb up the underside while stroking her fingers along the top as she slipped her lips off his tip, then sucked him in again as deep as she could manage. He was so thick all over she could only manage a few inches before her jaw ached, but the rising ache in her core soon overtook that incidental discomfort. The awareness of his intense arousal seemed to infect her more by the second, the taste of his essence leaking onto her tongue driving her need ever higher.

She let out a soft whimper when the first spasm hit, but didn't release him, still determined to prove she could please him this way while he was in his wild, primal shape. But the ache didn't subside. It grew to an agony that gripped her womb and the muscles of her pussy until she was forced to pull back and let out a pained cry.

"Now. I need you now," she begged, but was unable to get any more words out or even move as she doubled over.

Abruptly, he swept a big arm around her back and another beneath one thigh, easily hoisting her up into his arms. She gasped at the sudden shift in perspective, reflexively wrapping her arms around his neck when he held her against him.

"Put your legs around me, kitten. Hold on tight, because we're going for a ride."

She did as he asked, hooking her ankles around his waist. He held her easily with one arm, slipping his other hand beneath her ass, his fingers probing her for readiness. When he thrust one finger easily into her slick heat, she moaned, tightening her hold on him.

Neph's eyes narrowed and his chest vibrated with a low

rumble. A second later, she felt him shift his cock, angling that thick head right at her ready opening.

She relaxed her hold on him slightly as he moved both hands to hold tight to her hips. With slow sureness, he pushed her down onto his massive girth, and she threw her head back in a cry of pure gratitude and ecstasy as the stretching fullness of him gradually eased that painful need to be fucked.

"Gaia's tears, you are Heaven," Neph murmured against her neck. He tightened his grip around her hips as he lifted her again, then lowered her, and she relented to his deliberate control over their fucking.

"Don't stop, please," she said, clinging to his shoulders.

"It's your turn, kitten." He turned and lowered them both to the bed, shifting backward until he was leaning against the wall at the head of the bed. "Think of him."

The shift in position granted her more control over the movements, and she braced her knees on either side of his hips, holding onto his shoulders while she fucked him. The rhythm became a compulsion, each stroke easing that unbearable need to be penetrated hard and have every muscle stretched to its limit.

And she pictured Aodh as she had that day after he'd confessed he was hers. The day he had kissed her and made his promise, then said farewell. After they'd parted, she'd watched from the mountainside path while he and his siblings shifted and took to the air. He'd been so magnificent she hadn't been able to get that image out of her mind since, but now she pictured that huge, winged creature in a different context—aroused and with an even bigger cock to fuck her with than the one she now rode like her life depended on it.

Neph let out a low chuckle and her eyes flew open, realizing he had to have glimpsed her filthy fantasy. He grinned wickedly at her. "You want to take a full-sized dragon cock, kitten? That can be arranged."

"I … don't know. It's just a fantasy."

He cupped her head in his hands and gave her a piercing look. "You are an ursa, baby. Your sweet cunt is meant for giant cocks. I have no doubt you can take it, and even less that he'll be willing to give it to you. Keep that image in your mind. I like it."

Now she couldn't avoid picturing that precise scene. She closed her eyes again, lifting her hips and slamming down on Neph's cock with renewed fervor. Her breathing became ragged as she worked herself ever closer to that peak she craved.

Neph shifted his hands up her sides, cupping her breasts and lifting them to his mouth. He pushed them together so he could easily toy with both nipples, teasing his tongue around and around one, then sucking each one in in and released it before switching to the other. She tangled her fingers in his hair, then grabbed onto his horns for leverage as she increased her tempo, aching for that final, delicious rush of her orgasm and the accompanying release of all that pressure that built inside her.

"I'm ready, baby," Neph said. "Hang on."

He released her breasts and slipped a hand between them, pressing two fingers between her thighs against her swollen clit. He pressed lightly at first, gradually stroking and adding pressure. She let out a gasp at the first hard rub, digging her nails into his shoulders. Then she crashed her mouth down onto his as he repeated the action, speeding up his strokes even as she sped up her relentless, almost frantic fucking, slamming down on his cock almost hard enough to hurt. But it didn't hurt—it was exquisite, every bruising stroke pushing her pleasure closer to the brink.

His tongue lashed hers and he gripped the back of her

head with his free hand, holding her tight to him while he continued to rub her clit. A harsh moan escaped her just as her body surrendered to sensation, a slave to his touch and the steady, driving thrusts of his cock meeting her writhing hips.

She released his mouth, desperate for breath as the pleasure overtook her. Pressing her forehead to his, she opened her eyes and was met with the wild swirling depths of his. In a sudden, overwhelming rush, the swelling ache of built-up power inside her burst free and she cried out, tightening her grip on his horns. He kept his hand between her thighs, his rubbing fingers growing slick and wet from the sudden flood of power-infused fluid that surged from inside her.

Around them, vines and moss grew over the walls of the cabin, the growth seemingly oblivious to the fact that it was the middle of winter outside. Fragrant flowers bloomed as the waves of Vrishti's climax took them both even higher as she stared into his eyes. The vortex in his depths sucked her in and they were flying, the peak of her orgasm seeming to launch them straight into the current of some kind of mystical river she'd only ever read about in her mother's library.

CHAPTER 29

AODH

$\mathcal{A}$odh slept like a stone, but despite triggering a hibernation state that dulled his senses enough to allow him to slumber undisturbed, something had broken through that barrier. He'd spent the last vestiges of his power to close his chamber and put himself in this state, infusing the heated pool with the drugging smoke that he rarely ever used on himself. He could still smell the pleasant, wintergreen scent of his power in the room, but now there was more. Something more potent, more *alive* than even his perpetual dreams of his mates.

The scent roused him only a little at first, but then he heard the voices. One a surprising and pleasing sound that matched his dreams of Vrishti moaning his name in pleasure while he fucked her. But she wasn't moaning his name.

"Neph! Oh, god, please don't stop! I need more."

The other voice clarified in his mind, and along with it, all the tangled mess of old hurts surged forth.

"Almost there, kitten. Just hold on."

Neph. The man's scent filled Aodh's head so potently he had to be real. Within this hibernation prison he'd made for himself, he couldn't open his eyes to be sure, but the numbness of this form had faded and he was almost positive he felt skin pressed against his scaled side.

The sensation warmed as the sounds grew louder, and there was no mistaking the rise in volume of a pair of voices mixed in sensuous abandon and the smack of flesh on flesh.

Excitement and arousal flooded him, but all he could do was wait. They had come. They were *here*, if his senses could be believed. In all the centuries of perpetual dreams he'd endured, nothing had had this level of intense clarity.

The voices rose in tempo, the sounds growing louder as his senses awakened fully. Hot skin pressed against his side. A pair of breasts, a cheek, a pair of hands with fingernails dug in as though grasping for purchase against an onslaught of pounding thrusts. He recognized those impassioned grunts all too well, his entire body thrilling at the ancient memory of the cock that accompanied those sounds burying itself into him long ago.

But at the same time a contradictory surge of rage filled him as the understanding of this tableau clarified in his mind.

Neph had come for him, and Vrishti too, but by some cruel twist Neph had chosen to wake him by defiling the perfect, innocent Vrishti right in this very chamber. Despite his recurring dreams of forgiving the satyr, Aodh was forced to endure the sounds of their heated tryst, yet another sign of the Dionarch's need to control what Aodh held most dear.

The sounds of Vrishti's passionate cries distracted him briefly from his anger and he couldn't help but dwell on the breathy, desperate moans she made while being fucked, and the way her small hands clung to his scales like her life depended on it. He could picture the satyr easily in his primal magnificence, overcome with a satyr's essential need to take pleasure sometimes in the most deliciously brutal way possible. Yet despite that rough, barely controlled surrender to his lust, Neph's sensibilities required that he see to his partner's pleasure too, and the texture of Vrishti's aura was unmistakably potent with the built-up pleasure he drew from her.

Aodh hated him for it, but was enraptured by it at the same time. For the first time in nearly four centuries, he itched to wake up and take control of his life again.

"Come for me, Vrishti," he thought. *"Wake me with all that beautiful power I feel."*

Her sounds of ecstasy made his petrified cock ache, and Neph's rutting grunts were both enraging and arousing. He wasn't sure if he wanted to fuck the man or set him on fire once he awoke.

At that second, Vrishti's voice rang out with an impassioned "Yes!" and Neph matched her with one of his own, less coherent cries. The power of their auras merged, seeping in through Aodh's petrified scales and enveloping his sleeping dragon form completely.

Aodh's self-inflicted prison melted away, the warmth of Vrishti's panting body becoming more evident as he regained his full capacity to sense the outside world.

The second he opened his eyes and saw the huge satyr still buried inside the pretty dark-haired girl, he let out a roar of displeasure and swiped at Neph with one huge claw, hitting him squarely across his broad chest with a solid smack.

Neph had no time to react, his eyes flying open as he went sailing through the air, landing with a splash in the nearby pool. He came up spluttering, but Aodh had already coiled his huge body protectively around Vrishti's dazed form, stretching one wing up like a canopy to cover the hollow he'd created for her between his belly and his rear legs, his tail wrapping around them both.

He peered down at her, inhaling her fertile scent like he'd just been released from prison and she was his first breath of freedom. And he supposed she was, in a sense.

She stared up at him, her lips parted and soft breaths gusting from her where she lay half-seated on his bent rear leg.

"I came for you," she said, finally finding breath to speak. "I promised I would."

The scent of her arousal and the remnants of her recent orgasm still inundated his senses, and he almost misunderstood her meaning. What he scented on her was more than just her own essence, though. She was covered in Neph, a scent he discovered could still drive his lust into a frenzy of need.

"You did," he rumbled. "And I'm going to make you come again, just for me."

He flicked out his long tongue, teasing it over her full, brown breasts. She arched into him, utterly devoid of the kind of fear he might have expected her to show once faced with him in his true form. She relaxed back against him and spread her thighs eagerly, yet another incongruous action compared to the image he had of her from memory. The woman who now reclined in lust-filled abandon on his tail and rear leg was closer to the Vrishti who visited him in dreams. The visions he'd long had of he and Neph sharing this girl often featured her eagerly entertaining both their lascivious fantasies with her body.

"Please," she said, tilting her hips up as he teased his tongue over her glistening skin, working his way down her body to that well of pure ambrosia he knew awaited him between her thighs. Then the reason for this desperate need of hers hit him, along with the almost overpowering swell of magic that brightened her aura to a near blinding green light.

"You are in your estrous," he rumbled, his interest abruptly piqued. While a guest in the Sanctuary, he knew his siblings had sustained themselves by servicing the local females through estrous, but Aodh had instead accepted the invitation of the Queen to occasionally play with her mates. He couldn't bring himself to be intimate with another ursa female, because he knew he could never do her justice when his thoughts would be on Vrishti. She'd been within easy access then, yet he didn't dare distract her from discovering her true nature.

"I need you, Aodh. Please help me." She reached up and gripped at his big snout, aiming him between her thighs. This forced him to drift his tongue lower and taste that intoxicating mixture of her essence and Neph's, the two things he could not resist.

With a rumble of desire, he slicked is big tongue down through her cream-coated folds and pushed it deep into her. She dug her nails into his scales and wrapped her legs around his snout, rocking her hips against his lips as he drove his tongue deep into her. She took the thick appendage easily, the tight flex of her sweet cunt gripping him in a way that made his cock pulse with the desire to fill her up in other ways. But he wouldn't trade this for the world.

He fucked her eagerly with his tongue, savoring the remnants of her other lover that he hadn't had a taste of in more than three thousand years. Sweet Mother, he'd missed Neph's taste on his tongue, but he'd only imagined how Vrishti would taste. The combination of the two was more intoxicating than he was prepared for.

Vrishti writhed, grinding hard and moaning her pleasure with each of his deep thrusts into her. He gusted out a brief cloud of white smoke to help ease her frenzy and let her feel the pleasure without the distraction of the desperate need. She relaxed a little, her tense grimace turning into a euphoric smile.

She opened her eyes and stared up at him with somewhat glazed though lucid eyes. With her gaze fixed on him, she arched her back and let out a long, shuddering moan as her body convulsed and her orgasm rippled through her. A torrent of power filled him, more potent than he'd ever had, even from the orgasm Neph had given her that woke him up. The power wasn't just in her aura—it came from the surge of sweet nectar that gushed over his tongue as well, and he swallowed every delicious drop.

When the spasms subsided, he gently withdrew his tongue from her and nuzzled her with his snout.

"Are you all right?" he asked. "Did Neph hurt you?"

She let out a sated breath and nodded. "I will be soon. Is *he* all right? I thought I saw you attack him. You wouldn't believe what we had to do to get to you."

She crouched down and crawled on hands and knees to peek beneath the membrane of his wing out into the room beyond. Aodh knew from the sounds Neph was making that he was fine … He'd climbed out of the pool and was now simply sitting on the edge, waiting. But with a naked Vrishti cocooned within his embrace, Aodh had far more enticing things to pay attention to. Her round, caramel backside was aimed right at his nose, her delicious pink petals wet and open to him again.

He couldn't resist a nuzzle of her there, and a delicate lick from her clit all the way back to tease around the tight rosette of her anus.

Vrishti let out a gasp and stopped moving, resting her forehead against the pliant membrane of his wing where it stretched before her like a curtain. She shifted her knees wider, giving him a perfect view of the tight, spasming clench of her core as though it were crying out to be filled again already.

"Your estrous waves are hitting quicker now," he said. "You're at the peak. How long since it started?"

"I don't know," she said, her voice tight with near-painful restraint. "It's all happened so fast since then. But I need you." She gave a desperate, pleading look over her shoulder, but then her gaze shifted in a different direction. Following her stare, he realized she was staring at his engorged cock where it lay tucked between his thigh and his belly. "I need you to fuck me."

"Vrishti … not like this. I will shift."

"No! I need you big. Please! I'm an ursa, I know I can take it."

"You were a virgin before Neph. And he's big, but not this big."

Despite his protests, his cock pulsed with the very idea of pushing into that tight pink heat he'd had his tongue inside moments earlier. And if she really was at the peak of her estrous, she was right—she needed the fullest penetration she could get, and her pussy would easily accommodate something as huge as his massive erection.

"Don't you want me?" she whimpered, sending a jolt of shame through him. How could he possibly deny her anything she asked of him?

"I want you more than life," he rumbled. "Stay just like that, love, with your pretty cunt open wide for me.

He folded his wing and uncoiled his tail, shifting his bulk to reposition so he could give her what she asked. It opened their private cocoon up to the room where he was forced to acknowledge—even just to himself—that Neph was exactly where he'd thought, and hadn't made any overt move to approach him. The satyr must understand what Vrishti needed, but why hadn't he come to help her? Aodh could have been feral after all these years—he might have actually hurt her.

"You forget you have a drop of my blood in you, Aodh. The second I arrived, I knew your mind was still intact."

"Fair enough. Now get out. Leave me with my mate and go back to your own time. You banished me once. I can banish you now, if I want."

"I'm not leaving her. She needs us both, and you know it."

"Please, Aodh," Vrishti said, her desperation cutting into his belligerent exchange with the satyr.

Choosing to ignore Neph in favor of Vrishti's more pressing need, he redirected his attention to her. He dipped his head to her cheek and nuzzled softly, blowing out more calming breath and flicking his tongue along her jaw and neck. He darted it out again at her breasts, toying with each one and cupping the heavy globes in the forks of his tongue. They felt like plump, ripe fruit, and he would have loved to lick them forever, but her aura had reached that blinding power again so he couldn't delay. She needed to be penetrated by something far more punishing than his soft tongue had been.

When he slipped is tongue between her thighs again, he found her utterly soaked and dripping magic-infused wetness—more than enough to ease his passage into her. Experimentally he teased his forked tips around her anus again and was pleased at the eager response she gave him.

He glanced at Neph with an arched, scaled brow. The satyr only gave him a wary look and said, "Don't tease her any more than you have to. She's been ready for you for days."

Still skeptical that she was really ready for him at full size, he tested her opening with his tongue again, this time deliberately pushing and stretching her until he was confident she could at least accommodate his tapered tip, if not the full length of him.

He crawled closer until his entire body hovered over hers.

His cock brushed along her ass, the silken warmth of her skin sending pleasurable shocks through his entire body. He gently brushed a talon against her cheek, hooking her tangled, damp hair and pushing it over her shoulder so he could taste the glistening skin at the side of her throat. She moaned and pushed her backside up into him.

His entire body was big enough to cover her completely and he almost wanted to wrap his wings around them both and hide their coupling from Neph's view, but something kept him from doing that. He wanted the satyr to see her come just for him. He'd never fucked the other females they'd shared in his dragon form, so this would be a first.

He tilted his hips back until his cock grazed the cleft of her bottom, his tip easily drifting down between her cheeks along that perfect path that led to heaven. When he encountered the core of her wet heat, he dug his claws into the stone beneath him and pushed forward just enough to feel the sweet, hot give of her entrance as it opened for him.

Vrishti let out a low moan, turning her head until her lips brushed his snout.

"Yes," she whispered. "Deeper, please."

He pushed harder, his head already buzzing with the acute pleasure of only his tip being encompassed by the perfect, tight hold she had on him.

She pushed back with a pleading whimper of *more* and he sank even deeper. Nearly halfway to the hilt and he was already uncertain whether he could even last long enough for the first stroke. His cock pulsed inside the exquisite tightness of her sheath.

"*Fuck me,*" she gritted.

With a half-groaned apology for his failure at restraint, he bucked his hips hard, shoving his entire length deep into her.

Vrishti screamed, and for a second he panicked, pulling out swiftly to be sure he hadn't hurt her, but just as he was about to remove the tip of his cock, she pushed back onto him hard, her channel taking him fully and easily again.

"Yes!" she yelled. "Don't stop! Oh, please, don't stop."

Aodh dug his claws in and unfurled his wings for balance so he could take her the way she begged for it. He lifted one big talon and clutched at her shoulder, holding her tight so he could drive into her deeper, harder.

With each solid, piercing thrust she cried out, her ecstasy building higher until he saw nothing beyond the brilliant fertile green of her powerful aura. Her muscles tightened around him like a vise, and that was the end of his restraint. He roared, secretly elated at the look of envy he saw on Neph's face across the pool as he spilled his orgasm into her in a hot flood. Vrishti let out a strangled cry and another flood of her own power gushed from inside her, coating his cock with both their juices and filling his well to the brim with potent magic.

She panted and moaned weakly under him, but protested when he started to pull out of her.

"Please, not yet. I feel it coming on again already. I need more. Fuck me harder. Deeper!"

With a groan, Aodh pushed deep again, happy to accommodate her but sensing her flagging energy. She was a slave to her need now, but he would happily stay buried inside her until the waves of her estrous finally subsided.

"Let us mark each other, Vrishti. Let me put a baby in you to make it stop."

"No, please don't. You and Neph ... Need you both together. Happy. Please." Her words came in between halting, breathless pauses as her core constricted around his cock. He glanced at the satyr, who still waited, though not entirely patient. Neph's fingers clutched the edge of the pool, knuckles white with tension that was evident in the tight flex of his forearms and chest. His magnificent cock was hard and weeping from the tip.

She needed more ... needed them both. He knew what he needed to do, but hated the idea of appearing too eager for a reconciliation. Finally, he told himself this was all for her. He still had unfinished business with the satyr, but that could wait.

Hooking one big claw beneath her, Aodh gently lifted her and tilted back onto his haunches at the same time.

"Lean back into me, love," he rumbled as he pulled her up and onto his still stiff and throbbing cock. She was almost boneless from fatigue, but her core still tightened deliciously around him, and she let her thighs splay wide across his bent legs as she slipped her arms up and around his big neck to hold on. He bent his head over her shoulder, easily reaching between her thighs with his long tongue for an indulgent taste of her where they were still joined. This was the best part of sex in dragon form—he didn't have nearly as much flexibility or reach as a man.

He held one forearm across her midsection for stability and hooked the other beneath one of her knees for leverage as he began pumping his hips up into her again. She moaned out a pleasured *"yes, oh, Aodh, yes"* as she let him fuck her.

Then he darted his gaze across the pool and shot Neph a quick message. *"She needs us both to bring her down from this. Come do your part. For her."*

Neph's gaze instantly heated, the look sparking an almost painfully enticing memory of how they'd once been together. Aodh forced himself to tamp that down and refocus on Vrishti's pleasure. In his periphery, he was aware of Neph swimming across the wide pool and hopping out on the near side. His big satyr body dripped with steaming water as his hooved footsteps reverberated across the stone floor. He was nearly as tall as Aodh in his primal form, his cock almost as big. When he stepped between the dragon's thighs, he was careful not to touch Aodh's skin. Instead he cupped Vrishti's cheek reverently in one palm.

"I'm here, kitten. Do you want me inside you, too?"

"Oh, Neph. Please, yes, I need you so much."

Their exchange sent a sharp spike through Aodh's heart. What had he missed between these two? Could he even compete with the level of love clearly present in those few words? With an ache in his chest, he pressed his snout to her neck and closed his eyes, choosing to drown himself in the scent and feel of her that surrounded him. She was here. That she had come for him—no matter how she'd done it— had to count for something.

A moment later she let out a hitching moan and the sensation of hard, hot flesh pressed against the base of his cock. Keeping his eyes tightly shut, he leveraged her up along his length to position her for the next part. His entire body came alive when Neph pressed his hard length against Aodh's erection and wrapped his hand around their bases. In another lifetime this would have been a prelude to Neph stroking them both off, but he didn't move his hand. He only held them tight together while Aodh slowly settled Vrishti back down onto both their hard cocks.

"Tell me if you can't take us, kitten," Neph said. "We'll stop the second you say so."

"Oh, god, please don't stop," she moaned as her tight, ready flesh encompassed both their cockheads, squeezing Neph impossibly close to him.

Aodh eased her down onto them with tortuous slowness, each increment forcing his cock tighter and tighter against Neph's, every second throwing him back to a time when he had let himself get lost to the love and pleasure they had shared. They were both so big, he didn't know how she managed to not scream from the agony of how fully they stretched her, but her aura swelled again not from pain, but from pleasure every bit as exquisite as the shivers that raced down his scales all the way to the tip of his tail.

When she encompassed them both fully, Aodh's reflexes took over and the old rhythm he and Neph once had seemed to come naturally again. They fucked her together in perfectly synchronized motions as though they were one being.

Vrishti kept one arm hooked around Aodh's head, but removed the other. When he opened his eyes, she had her hand tightly gripping one of Neph's horns and holding on while the satyr tongued her perfect breasts, the full orbs bouncing with the force of their unified thrusts.

Her aura swelled again to a bright green glow, and within moments she let out a hoarse cry of ecstasy, her core tightening around them so completely he couldn't help but feel the sudden rush of Neph's orgasm shooting up the length of his cock. The sensation pushed him to his own Nirvana, and he shot his essence deep inside her to mix with his old lover's.

At the last second, he raised his head and his eyes locked with Neph's. What he saw was cautious hope, and perhaps even a question that hovered at the edge of the barely existent barrier between their minds.

But Aodh didn't have an answer. Not yet.

"I don't know if I can forgive you," he said and he pulled out of Vrishti and slipped away, leaving her wrapped in Neph's embrace.

CHAPTER 30

VRISHTI

odh's abrupt departure left Vrishti cold and empty. She clung to Neph, whose shape diminished in her arms, the shrinking of his form back to human size reflecting the sense of defeat that flooded the room as potently as the scent of their lovemaking had only a moment earlier.

Still struggling to regain her senses, she couldn't help but notice the pain that crossed Neph's face in a sharp grimace as he watched Aodh leave. The desperate longing and loss was so palpable through their shared mental link that Vrishti felt almost as if it were her own. Tears sprang to her eyes and she wrapped her arms around his neck and held tight.

"We just got here. Don't give up on him yet," she whispered.

Neph tightened his hold on her almost desperately, burying his face against her shoulder, his emotion barely contained in soft, hitching breaths that she knew were not remnants of their strenuous fucking, but something far deeper at work. He finally inhaled and shifted his hips, his flaccid cock slipping out of her allowing the remaining flood of their shared essences to course down her thighs.

He cupped her face in his hands and gazed into her eyes. "You both are my life now. I will endure whatever I must to make things right."

His gaze shifted over her shoulder and she turned her head to see Aodh, now also back in his human form, pacing on the far side of the room beyond the detailed statues of herself and Neph. She swallowed the shock at the imagery of those two likenesses, which perfectly embodied how she pictured herself when he was aroused and ready to fuck. But it was a far cry from how she felt now, and the monuments to their fertility only irritated her.

"Stay here," she said, giving Neph's hand a squeeze. He returned her comforting glance with a tight nod before she dove into the pool in a smooth arc and swam across to the other side.

The air in the cavernous room was cool and slightly damp farther away from the pool, but smelled distinctly of Aodh. She was struck with the realization that Neph really had gotten all the details just right when he'd assumed his former lover's shape for her sake. That had to count for something, but she wasn't sure how she could convey that to the man she walked toward now.

Everything about Aodh was exactly as Neph had shown her, and the sight of him naked and in the flesh took her breath away. He didn't seem to hear her as she approached. His fists continued clenching and unclenching, tightening the muscles of his arms and shoulders as he walked. He was naked, his otherworldly pale skin glowing in the ambient light of the room, his flexing buttocks a mesmerizing sight as he stalked in the opposite direction. When he turned and saw her, he stopped and stared, his eyes widening in surprise, then horror.

"Sweet Mother, Vrishti. I'm sorry. I didn't want our first time to be like that."

She shook her head, causing the wet tendrils of her hair to stream more water down her back. She grabbed the sodden tangle and wrung it out as she walked closer to him with a tentative smile.

"We needed each other. It's all right. You're awake, and I'm ... sated, for the time being. That was ..." She tucked her lower lip between her teeth and glanced back across the pool where Neph patiently waited, yet again relegated to his own corner, it seemed. She didn't finish her sentence. Instead, she sighed. "It doesn't matter how amazing it was to me. It clearly wasn't what I'd hoped it would be for the two of you."

Aodh pressed his lips into a tight line. "It isn't that. Making love with both of you could never be unpleasant. I just had a different idea of how making love with you the first time would go ... and it was nothing like that." His face twisted in a half-grimace and he shook his head as though trying to dispel the image.

Vrishti frowned, reminded of the conversation she and Neph had had about the relative significance of her sexual status to the dragon. "What? Did you think I'd be chastely saving myself for you all this time? My estrous could have happened at any point during the last month in the Sanctuary. It could've been your brother who took care of me, do you realize that? At least he was available."

Aodh's mouth fell open and he shut it again, his jaw clenching. "A month. That's all it's been for you." His eyes flashed with white fire and he shook his head. "I've been waiting here for *four hundred years* since Nyx banished me from the Haven and stuck me in this fucking prison. All I could think of was you—thoughts of you kept me sane here.

"I don't care who touched you before me. If Gavra had been there for you when you needed it, I'd thank him. Hell, I'm grateful Neph was there for you. What I can't fucking deal with is his goddamn 'woe is me' attitude now that he's here. He fucking *owes* me for what happened. He left me hanging after the shit went down with Meri, and then his sister pulls *this* bullshit. If he wants anything from me, he needs to fucking man up."

His voice gradually rose in volume as he ranted until finally he put his hands on his hips and turned to yell across the room. "Do you hear me, you son of a bitch? Grow a fucking pair and finish what you fucking started!"

Vrishti blanched at the sudden outburst of rage. "I'm sorry," she said meekly.

Aodh sighed and closed the distance between them. He lifted his hands to cup her face, stroking her cheeks reverently. "You being here is more than I hoped for. I knew he had the power to come, but I had no idea he would bring you with him. You've done nothing wrong. He and I just have old bullshit to deal with, and I didn't expect you'd wind up stuck in the middle of it. I'm the one who should be sorry."

"He still loves you," she whispered, staring up into his eyes, her entire body thrumming from the warmth of his touch, now that they were face to face and she was self-possessed enough to be aware of more than her own needs.

"It's true," Neph said, his voice coming from behind her now. Close behind her like he'd simply appeared out of thin air. Her heart pounded at the proximity of them both, and she silently hoped her body wouldn't distract her from this conversation with another wave of her fucking hormones. Arousal was inevitable, though, she supposed.

Aodh's jaw clenched and his nostrils flared. He ignored Neph at first, his fingertips tightening at the base of her skull. "You say something if you need us again, all right? Your needs are more important than this." Then he shot a glare over her shoulder that could start fires.

CHAPTER 31

NEPH

If looks could kill, Neph was distinctly grateful he was immortal. He inhaled slowly, bracing himself for the long overdue conversation. As the air passed through his nostrils, he caught the distinct and unmistakable scent of Vrishti's fresh arousal. By Gaia's grace, she was the perfect match for them both if she responded to their mere presence this way.

But as she stepped to the side to let Aodh pass, Neph couldn't miss the worried crease of her brow. He'd heard her whispered plea to the dragon from across the room and loved her for it, even though he knew it wouldn't be enough.

"We're doing this now," Aodh said. "I'm ready to get the fuck out of here, but I need to know we have an understanding first."

"Anything you need," Neph said with a nod.

"What I fucking *need* is for you to admit the truth. Tell me you were wrong."

"I lied to you. I never stopped loving you, but I wasn't wrong to send you away and I think you know that."

Aodh's eyes flashed and he bared his teeth, taking another

step forward to stick his finger in Neph's face. "Bullshit. That's your sister talking. *She* was the one who couldn't stand the sight of me. She thought I'd corrupted her precious twin and would do the same to her son. I guess the joke was on her when Fate sent my sister to be your nephew's mate."

"I wanted to keep you there, believe me," Neph said. "I didn't give a fuck about what she thought, because I think part of me knew even then that we belonged together, despite our fucking laws. That's why I was willing to entertain the idea of a third … so we could …"

"Bullshit!" Aodh roared. "You were stalling! Keeping me distracted with false hope. Meri was never right for us, but at least she showed me what a fucking coward you were. If you loved me half as much as you say you do, we'd have blood-melded without her and none of this would have happened."

Neph jerked back as though struck, his ready response dying in his throat and leaving him mute with the weight of Aodh's words crushing him.

"That's what you wanted?" he rasped. A rush of heat flooded him when the clarity dawned. How had he never seen it? The pair of them had been Nyx's and Nereus's only witnesses to their blood melding, so there could be no argument from any of the other immortal leaders whether the female Dionarch's union to her beloved satyr was legitimate.

Aodh's wild anger diminished, his eyes now filled with hurt. "Instead you left me half-marked. My soul tainted by my mistake with Meri, and your blood a reminder of what I'd done wrong. Damn you for that."

Neph snapped his hand to the back of Aodh's neck and yanked him close, crushing the dragon's mouth with his own. Aodh growled a protest, digging his fingertips into Neph's shoulders. His teeth remained clenched at first until Neph swept his tongue against his lower lip. Aodh let out a groan and opened, but didn't wholly surrender the way he once would have. He fought for dominance as though to prove a point, though Neph had no idea what it was.

In that kiss, he was reminded of the desperation of their old love, how filled with craving for a thing they didn't believe they could ever have, and didn't dare take it for themselves lest risk the wrath of the very gods.

Aodh gripped Neph's shoulder, slid his hand to the back of his neck, and held them tight together while he returned the assault with nips and tugs of his teeth against Neph's mouth. Their tongues plunged past each other, tangling deep. The unspent anger was reflected in the way he tightened the grip of his other hand on Neph's hip and pulled them flush, their cocks stiffening against each other as they kissed.

When the bite of the dragon's teeth turned vicious, Neph didn't stop, instead returning the onslaught more ferociously himself, and when Aodh's teeth drew blood, Neph relished the pain, letting out an exultant chuckle and squeezing his fingers tighter at the base of Aodh's skull.

He summoned his primal power to return the favor, his body aching for it now that his own blood had been spilled for the second time into his lover's mouth. He bit down on Aodh's lower lip, simply sucking at first and enjoying the erotic groan the dragon emitted and the way his hot erection surged against his hip. Then he bit down hard, forcing all his magic into the need he had for this to work, for his teeth to pierce Aodh's impenetrable skin so he could grant the dragon that one wish—something he'd wanted himself since the very start.

The flesh of Aodh's lip held taut, the dragon's fevered touch giving no sign that he caught onto Neph's efforts, though he responded with increased passion at the bite. Then the tender flesh of Aodh's lip suddenly gave and a flood of pure heat washed over Neph's tongue, carrying power the likes of which he'd never tasted.

In a blast of awareness, their minds were one, and every single old hurt rushed through him, slicing his soul like they were fresh. But they weren't his hurts, he realized, and his heart broke at the understanding of what his actions had cost this man for so long.

As swiftly as the awareness filled him, it was ripped away. Aodh let out a curse and jerked back, but he seemed unaware of the degree of Neph's assault. All Neph sensed now was the red haze of lust mixed with anger and hurt that his stunt somehow hadn't put a dent in—it had only made it clearer to him what Aodh suffered from.

Before he could lean back in to renew their passionate embrace, Aodh spun him around and shoved him hard against the huge stone statue of Vrishti that cast a shadow on their volatile reconciliation.

With his face pressed into the carved stone belly of the woman he loved, he felt Aodh's hands tight at his hips.

"I know what you did, but it isn't enough," Aodh growled. The dragon's fingers slipped between his ass cheeks and prodded. Neph grunted when one thick digit breached the barrier of his anus and twisted around.

To the side, Neph heard a soft little squeak of surprise and Vrishti said, "Aodh! What are you doing?"

"Taking what's owed me," he said.

"It's all right, Vrishti," Neph said, twisting his face where Aodh had it held tight against the stone statue. His bloody lip left a smear across the pale, polished marble and he reached out for the flesh-and-blood woman. She stepped close, gripping his hand and brushing her fingers through his hair.

"Don't hurt him," she said to Aodh.

"Let him do what he needs to do, kitten. If you can take us both at full size, this is nothing."

Aodh chuckled behind him. "You say that now, but unless you've found another cock you like better than mine, I know you've never been on the receiving end before."

Vrishti gave him a puzzled look. "Is that true? I thought you said you liked that."

"I told you *he* liked it, kitten. He isn't lying, and it will hurt, but if it means earning his forgiveness, it's worth it."

She pursed her lips, her dark brows tilting together in consternation. "No. If he makes love to you, it shouldn't hurt. I won't let it."

"I'm afraid you don't have a choice. If he wants to hurt me, he will." He grunted at the sudden harsh invasion of Aodh's thumb into his ass. The stretch didn't hurt, but sent a surprisingly pleasurable shiver through his body. His ass clenched around the digit and his cock pulsed with fresh arousal.

"Stop," Vrishti said, moving up beside Neph's hip and pushing at Aodh's hand. The invading finger disappeared and Neph closed his eyes with relief, but his shock returned at the sensation of another hand on his ass—a smaller one this time.

Her soft fingertips feathered over his puckered opening, so light he might have mistaken her touch for a breeze. She caressed down, teasing the underside of his cock before cupping and squeezing his balls gently. He spread his legs reflexively, letting out an involuntary groan of pleasure. He'd never pictured himself so fully at the mercy of both his lovers, yet he was now, and it terrified him.

He remained bent over against the statue, gripping the spread ankles of the larger version of Vrishti where she sat on the wide pedestal. He briefly thought of how precise the likeness was to her true features—the delicate folds of her snatch so adoringly carved from the stone. He could fix his attention on that and lose himself to the sensations, but fascination overtook him. He had to know what she intended. He craned his head around to see just as she gripped his nearest cheek and crouched at his side.

Keeping the fingertips of one hand gently resting against his anus, she reached beneath him and gripped his shaft. She squeezed and stroked with the perfect amount of pressure, speeding up to the ideal tempo to make him moan her name. At the same time, she teased her fingertips lightly around his opening, never once attempting to push inside the way she had once before. But that lack of penetration didn't matter. The position she had him in—*they* had him in, he was reminded when one big hand descended on his other ass cheek with a resounding slap—was enough to push his sense of personal boundaries to its limit.

His cock kicked in her hand when Aodh's palm hit his ass, a measure of pre-ejaculate seeping from the tip and catching beneath her grip. She let out a surprised gasp.

"Do you like it when he spanks you?"

Neph pressed his forehead to the cold stone in front of him. "I hate it."

"He's lying," Aodh said, landing another hard, stinging smack to his ass.

His balls tightened and he groaned.

"Neph, you're even harder than you were a second ago. I think you do like it."

"Please," he said. "Just let him fuck me."

The dragon's big hand whistled through the air, landing on the same tender cheek again with a sharp sting. This time Aodh left it there, squeezing hard. "You want my forgiveness so much you'll take my punishment and love it, is that it? I want inside you so much now you're lucky she's making me wait for whatever scheme she has to make it easier. Making sure you're drunk with need to come already makes sense, but seeing her tease you like this is making it hard to wait."

Neph didn't bother responding, his breath coming in ragged gasps as Vrishti's fist pumped him quicker now. Desperate for some clue what he was in for, he opened his mind to them both, mentally falling to his knees and begging for some hint.

But at that moment, she pushed a finger past his anus and his entire world exploded. His cock bucked in her hand and her palm swept up to his tip, holding it while his orgasm spilled into her cupped hand. She continued pumping her delicate finger into his ass for another few seconds until his seed was fully spent in her hand.

He remained there, dazed and clinging to the statue's ankles, eyes clenched shut, waiting for whatever they chose to do next. Her breasts brushed against his thigh and hip as she rose again. Then her finger disappeared from his ass and hot wetness fell against the sensitive flesh in slow drips. Dion's balls, she was using his own spend as lubricant. Would that even work?

Of course it would … He knew as much after doing the same thing to Aodh on numerous occasions, teasing the dragon by bringing himself off against his ass before violently burying himself in the other man using only his own semen to ease the passage. She couldn't have known that, but the idea made him strangely proud of her for thinking of it.

All thought departed his mind and he let out an involuntary gasp when her slick finger sank into him again.

"That's right, get his ass ready for me. Sweet Mother, you look like you know what you're doing." Aodh's deep, lust-filled voice roused Neph's cock to full hardness again almost instantly. He peeked over his shoulder and saw a warm flush color Vrishti's cheeks, but she didn't pause in her ministrations to his ass.

"Tell him, kitten," Neph said, hoping she'd share her

secret because he longed to hear her admit it as the very idea turned him on too.

Her bright gaze flashed to his for a second, her steady thrusts slowing. "This is how I'd want to be prepared for it," she said.

"You wouldn't have to worry, baby," Aodh said. "I'd prep you with my tongue. You'd be more than ready after that."

"Then why don't you do that for him?" she asked.

Aodh laughed, the deep sound rumbling up from his chest. "I didn't intend to make it easy for him. Watching you do it is much more fun."

"Are you all right, Neph?" she asked. She brushed her free hand down his spine, sending a shiver of exquisite pleasure through him.

The big hand on his other ass cheek squeezed. "Answer her," Aodh warned, rubbing lightly on the tender mound of flesh.

"Don't stop," Neph rumbled.

She slid her finger out and pressed two at his opening, stretching him farther with several slow, tortuous strokes, then added a third. Even tripled, her fingers were nothing compared to the thickness of the dragon cock that awaited him.

"My turn," Aodh said and Neph caught a glimmer of triumph both in his voice and through their shared mental connection. The dragon's craving for dominance was even stronger now, and entirely out of character—at least where Neph was concerned. He'd always been the dominant party when they made love before, with the dragon eagerly giving up his ass to be fucked every time.

When Vrishti's fingers slipped out of him and slid wetly down to cup his balls, they were swiftly replaced by three even larger fingers. Aodh pushed his in slowly, shifting close to Neph's side so that their thighs rubbed together and

Aodh's massive erection brushed over the tender cheek he'd just spanked. The dragon bent over and placed his mouth at Neph's ear.

"You're lucky she loves you. But that just means I get to torture you with pleasure instead of pain," Aodh said, then darted out his tongue and swept it teasingly along the outer crest of Neph's ear. He pushed his fingers into Neph's ass slowly, hooking them ever so slightly so that they rubbed against some hidden bundle of pure, agonizing pleasure inside him.

Neph let out strangled cry at the nearly orgasmic shock that blasted through him. His cock surged with fresh heat and aching need just from that touch, so perfectly designed to make him beg.

"Please." His ass clenched then relaxed as the pleasure dissipated. The sudden rush of air before the sting of a fresh smack barely registered. Aodh shoved his fingers in hard and deep as his palm connected with Neph's other ass cheek this time, harder than before.

"Keep begging," Aodh said, spanking him again. "Tell me how much you deserve this for what you did to me."

"It isn't enough," Neph said, hyperaware of the depths of Aodh's sense of betrayal now that they were fully melded. "Nothing I do will be enough."

"I'm not here to ease your fucking conscience," Aodh said, landing another hard smack to his ass cheek. It burned with fresh fire, but Vrishti's steadily stroking hand on his cock and balls was a strangely perfect counterpoint to the brutal treatment the dragon inflicted upon him.

Suddenly it hit him what was different. Aodh's typically gentle nature was contrary to this brutal creature so eager for a fuck. Neph had always been the one with that particular goal. Aodh merely took his own pleasure from receiving whatever Neph chose to dole out. Either he'd changed more than Neph over their years apart, or the blood meld had transferred some of those needs.

But did it matter? All he cared about now was getting fucked. Getting Aodh past this so they could move on.

"Please fuck me," he begged, pushing back into Aodh's thrusting fingers, each movement driving him closer and closer to another ground-shaking orgasm. *"Please,"* he said again in his mind, once again mentally begging and putting himself completely at the dragon's mercy.

"I will if you do one thing," Aodh said, his voice reverberating inside Neph's mind rather than spoken aloud.

"Anything," Neph gasped out loud.

"Show me every detail of your time with her. Leave nothing out."

"It's up to her," Neph said, shooting a desperate glance at Vrishti. She stopped stroking him and frowned.

"I want to do it together. We can meld just enough to share our minds—the three of us—right? I don't want to go as far as mating yet. We need the power of my estrous still to get back home."

"You have to take his essence for that, kitten. Taste him."

She darted a look between the two men. Then her gaze drifted to Aodh's cock.

The big dragon's thrusting digits left his ass suddenly, and Neph suppressed a sigh as he relaxed, finally able to regain his sanity for a second.

"You're already filled with me, sweetness," the big dragon rumbled. He slid one hand down Vrishti's side to her hip and dipped the other between her thighs. She let out a soft gasp, then a moan as Neph saw Aodh push two fingers up into the lovely young ursa.

Aodh withdrew the shining digits and lifted them to her lips. "Everything you need is right here. Him and me. Take us so you can both show me everything."

She parted her luscious lips, and Neph watched enraptured as her eyelids fluttered closed and she sucked the dragon's fingers clean of their juices.

He started to stand up to complete the meld, but Aodh pressed his hand against his shoulder, holding him down. He shook his head.

"I've got this," Aodh said.

Neph nodded. He'd almost forgotten how completely their souls could be merged after a blood meld, but then this was the first time he'd ever tried it. Aodh must have been aware of the power he could have had all this time, but was only able to access a small fraction of it. Now he had it all. Experimentally, Neph reached within for his own power and found the new energy coalescing in his lungs. He exhaled white smoke that gusted against the Vrishti statue's spread pussy, making it glow.

Then they were both inside him, their mental presences as natural as his own thoughts.

"Show me," Aodh said.

"Finish what you started," Neph challenged. "Then we'll show you." The request was contrary to anything he'd ever asked of the dragon before, but with the three of them connected this way, it seemed only fitting to have the dragon inside him in another way.

As though sensing that need for the physical as well as mental contact, Vrishti moved to his head and caressed his cheek. At his rear, the dragon gripped both his ass cheeks, released them, then gave them both solid, resounding smacks with both hands. Then he held Neph wide and positioned his cock at his tight opening.

Neph forced himself to relax and was dimly grateful for the tapered shape of Aodh's cock. His tip breached him, and he let out groan of anticipation. He released the statue in favor of the real woman, hooking one arm around

Vrishti's waist and pulling her tight while the dragon pushed deeper.

"Now," Vrishti whispered in his ear, and the images flooded her mind, filling his own with the memories of the past two days. In his mind's eye he was keenly aware of everything *she* had seen and felt from the first moment she'd set eyes on him.

When they got to her solitary moments in the shower that first night, Aodh paused his slow fucking. At the same moment, the scent of Vrishti's arousal spiked and he opened his eyes to look up into hers. Her lips were parted, and that look of barely contained need that had been a fixture on her pretty face for two days straight looked back at him.

"Let me taste you again," he rumbled, sliding his hand over her hip and pushing her against the statue. She eyed the ledge of polished marble between the bigger likeness's ankles. With a nod, she gripped the marble knee and Neph wrapped his arm around her waist, helping her up. His slight shift in position caused Aodh's cock to push deeper, and the other man gripped his hips, squeezing.

"Better than my fucking dreams," Aodh said as Vrishti settled herself against the statue's belly and pulled her knees up to her chest, holding her ankles wide. Neph's mouth watered at the sight of her dewy folds, parted and pink and juicy before him, even more enticing than the larger version he'd been staring at all along.

"Taste her," Aodh said, and his deep voice resonated through the air and inside Neph's mind, the dragon's mental presence even stronger now as he drove his cock in deep once again.

Before indulging in Vrishti's ambrosia, he refocused his mind on those first two days, silently prompting her to resume that singularly beautiful memory of her carrying out his first command to pleasure herself.

CHAPTER 32

VRISHTI

Reliving that particular memory was far more amazing than it had been the first time, though this time Vrishti had layer upon layer of new understanding to add to it. They were both inside her head now as she went back to that night, the two men quite literally joining her there as actual presence and not just fantasies.

Could they see her fantasies? Those were still vivid in her mind as she climbed out of the shower and sat on the toilet lid with the mirror, watching as she touched herself.

It was as though they were in the room with her, watching her tease herself with her fingers delving into her wet pussy, toying with her swollen clit, and then adventuring lower. She'd already reenacted the moment for Neph, but even this time around was more deliciously potent with pleasure. In her mind, she pressed her finger to her anus, but in reality it was Neph's tongue, then his thicker fingertip pushing into her.

She let out a soft gasp that was reflected in the sounds each of the men made as their own pleasure surged higher. Neph hooked his arms around her thighs, pulling her closer to his shoulders while dipping his hands back to part her folds so he could get to the swollen, aching bundle of nerves that so desperately needed his mouth. He sucked her clit as he penetrated her ass with one finger, still partially mimicking the things she had done to herself, if only for a moment.

"Not yet, sweetness," Aodh rumbled just as she thought she could be free to fly over that edge she'd barely managed to resist the first time. Her eyes flew open and she stared at him, then down at Neph, who had removed his mouth from her, though he still trailed his fingers up and down the soaked folds of her pussy, keeping her spread open, but not providing enough contact to make her come.

"Wh-why?" she asked.

"Because he wants to be in contact with you when you lose your mind under my tongue, kitten. Save it a little longer."

She let out a frustrated groan, but nodded. This she knew she could do, even if she wasn't exactly pleased about it.

She closed her eyes and drifted back to that night, then the following morning and the enforced nudity, and how very *aware* of her own body she'd been while Neph stripped and had breakfast with her.

The ensuing activities came back into focus with crystal clarity, from the moment he'd first touched her as Aodh and they'd each observed each other without touching at all, merely pleasing themselves.

Vrishti opened her eyes at the low growl that emanated from Aodh's throat and met his piercing, silvery gaze.

"He let you see me, and that pleased you." His gaze fell to Neph's back, and Vrishti glanced down to see the satyr's brows draw together, but he kept his focus entirely on her tender flesh.

"Of course it did. The first time he kissed me, I was

kissing you. I was with only you for an entire day. He even tasted like you."

Her voice softened at the memory of the first taste she'd had of Neph when he'd shared his true essence and not a fabricated version of Aodh's. She gripped his head in her hands and pulled back until he paused his licks and looked up at her. The lower half of his face shone with her juices and he cast his eyes down as though he couldn't bear to let her see what lay inside. Yet every emotion was bare for her inside their minds—the rawness of what he'd felt when taking on that beloved shape for her benefit. How much it had cost him to ease the process for her.

"You did that for me ... became him, even though you were ashamed to ... to use his likeness that way, without his consent."

Neph's throat rippled as he swallowed and nodded. "It was a sacrifice I had to make to reach him, not just to please you."

"Show it to me again," Aodh said, his gaze filled with a strange desperation as he thrust harder into Neph's ass, one hand now gently stroking up and down the other man's side.

Inside Vrishti's mind, the scene unfolded again, this time from Neph's point of view—a vision she hadn't seen before of one moment just before breakfast the first day when he'd looked in the mirror. *Forgive me for being glad I get to have her first. You broke all the others in, but this one I want to myself for a little while, even if I have to look like you to have her."*

Vrishti watched, enraptured, while Neph's memory unfolded, showing her every moment of the rest of that first afternoon up until their shower after lunch, and then them falling asleep entwined beneath the covers. When they reached the darkest part that featured his dreams of fearful rejections that left him chilled in the winter cold, she knew they'd reached the moment when she understood the most important thing about the entire experience.

She closed her eyes and overlaid the events of that evening as she recalled them, from her eager attention to him in the shower to her awareness of his slip when he'd fallen asleep, and then her study of Neph's sleeping shape afterward.

Aodh let out a long, rough groan and she looked at him again, saw the pain of realization in his eyes. Then he pulled back, removing himself from Neph's ass. The satyr turned an apprehensive gaze to the dragon.

"We're not going to keep doing this," Aodh said. "I fucking love you. Both of you. I hate how we left things, and it's going to take me more time to get past, but she deserves our honesty at least." He raked his big hands through his hair, his gaze resting on her. "About how many orgasms does he owe you?"

"I … I'm not sure."

"Move over," he said to Neph, patting the satyr on his rump. He stepped forward and knelt before the pedestal Vrishti rested on with her legs still spread. Her tailbone ached from the hard stone, but every discomfort disappeared after he emitted a fresh cloud of white smoke and pure euphoria set in. Then Aodh's mouth was on her, tongue dipping between her folds and licking upward until he sucked her clit between his lips. Her breath came in sharp gasps as he concentrated on her pleasure, teasing it to a crescendo while Neph dropped to his knees and watched. The satyr rested his hand on Aodh's pale, silken hair and urged him on.

"Don't forget her favorite thing," he said, curling his fingers around her ass and teasing his thumb at her rear opening. Aodh let out a grunt of acknowledgment and pressed his own finger at her slick rosebud. He pushed inside and her world flew apart. Her hands flew out and gripped for purchase at the smooth stone on either side of her while the spasms shook her.

Just as she was coming down with shaky breaths, Neph descended on her, taking over. Aodh sat back on his haunches, smiling and wiping his lips with the back of his hand. "We're not stopping until you beg us to, baby."

She didn't have the presence of mind to respond under the diligent ministrations of Neph's tongue. He pushed two fingers into her slick channel and slid another into her ass, sending her ecstasy into the heavens once more. Then Aodh took his turn again. With each successive orgasm, the world grew hazier, and she was nearly certain the pair of them had taken on dimly pulsing auras.

She could barely even move when Neph asked her something she thought involved fucking. She nodded, simply thinking that yes, she liked it when he fucked her. The next thing she knew, his thick, curved cock was sliding into her, and the slick friction made her moan with pleasure. His swirling gaze fixed on her from above as he plunged deep, and when Aodh took up position just behind him, Neph froze.

"You ready for me, lover?" Aodh asked.

"More than ever. Fuck me," Neph responded. Then he gripped Vrishti by the back of the head and his mouth found hers, tongue plunging deep as he groaned in pleasure.

Aodh wrapped his thick arms around him, his strong, intense gaze fixing on Virshti past Neph's shoulder. His eyes fluttered closed as he began to move his hips, pushing Neph's cock deeper into Vrishti as he fucked him.

All she could do was hold on, and as she arched her back and reached out, she found two hands—one pale and huge, the other darker and more graceful, each taking a strong grip of her small brown hands. She kept her eyes open despite the rising swell of pure pleasure. It wasn't just one man pretending this time. They were both with her now, both making love to each other, to her, and both their pleasure seemed magnified inside their minds as she lent her own to the mix.

While she watched, their features rippled and shifted, the shape of the cock inside her changed, became thicker at the base, more tapered at the tip, and the lips that crashed down on hers were the dragon's while the satyr looked on from his vantage point at the dragon's backside, where he steadily pierced Aodh's ass with his cock.

The orgasm tore through her in a torrent of confusion mixed with utter completeness in that moment. They were two, yet one. And soon they would both be hers forever.

$\mathcal{V}$rishti wasn't sure who carried her into the pool a few moments later. She couldn't tell them apart now, and she'd sensed some strange juxtaposition of them in her mind as well. Like they hadn't just swapped places, but merged entirely into one being—one creature—whose purpose was intent on proving its love to her and itself.

When the heated water enveloped her, she let out a deep breath and looked up into a pair of piercing silver eyes.

"Is it really you now?" she asked, reaching up to trace a wet line down the side of Aodh's jaw. She glanced behind his shoulder and saw Neph—at least she believed it was Neph—coming closer and slipping into the pool beside them.

"Does it matter?" Aodh said, a slight smile playing at his lips. His eyes were deep with weariness, but he looked content as he cradled her against him and stroked his fingertips along the edge of her jaw.

"You saw the rest," she said. "You know it matters to me."

Neph settled himself in the water beside them and stroked a wet line over the top of her shoulder, then bent to kiss it. "It shouldn't, but only because things are different now, kitten. Blood meld with us and you'll understand. We share a soul now, Aodh and I."

"We can literally be the same person if we choose to be," Aodh said. "When you saw me making love to you, it was me in almost every sense. All except some very basic physical details."

"You mean, like at a cellular level, you were still different?"

He lifted an eyebrow and looked at Neph. The satyr chuckled. "Yes, if you want to be precise. The physical appearance was a very detailed illusion, but our senses and minds switched places too. I could feel everything as though I was making love to him …"

"And I was making love to you," Aodh finished.

She frowned, not quite satisfied with their explanation. It wasn't enough, for some reason. Aodh cupped her chin, forcing her to look into his eyes. "What is it you need, sweetness? Whatever it is, we will give it to you."

"I get it. Assana told me about blood melding. I've had conversations with all three of them at once when only one of them was standing beside me. And I want that too, when it makes sense for me. But I want to have *you*, Aodh. Just once. Just you." She glanced at Neph, worry for him pulling her brows together. "You understand, don't you? You had me first …"

Neph held up his hands and nodded. "I understand perfectly, kitten. Pretend I'm not even here." Before her eyes his skin shimmered and grew translucent, colorless, and he seemed to fade into the steam until nothing but a vague, smoky outline remained, one that dissipated quickly.

Vrishti gasped. "Neph? Where did you go?"

Aodh chuckled. "He's here," he said, lifting a cupped palm from the pool and letting the water trickle out of it. "Nymphaea are water shifters."

"I know but … I didn't know he was literally water."

"He is at the moment, but we need to address what you asked for. You have me now, sweetness. Just me."

She stared into his eyes, suddenly at a loss.

"I missed you," she finally said, feeling supremely lame once the words were out and the last couple hours came back to her in a rush.

Aodh laughed and gave her an indulgent smile. "I missed you like you wouldn't believe. I even built a statue, if that shows you anything." He nodded toward the impressively accurate likeness they'd fucked her against moments earlier.

She studied the statue of herself, half-reclined with knees bent and thighs spread, exposing herself to the satyr on the opposite side. "Is that how you picture me? And him?"

"In my dreams, you were both more or less like that, yes. That was all I had to go by for you. I never did get to see you naked until today."

"You could have, you know. There was time."

Aodh shook his head. "Your mother wouldn't have allowed it so soon. Now, perhaps …" He traced a pattern into her chest just beneath the dip of her collarbone, and her entire body warmed a few degrees as though exposed to bright summer sun. Vrishti glanced down to see the tiny sunburst at the top of her breasts glow with golden light.

"What is it?" she asked. "Mother wasn't exactly clear, and I didn't have time to untangle her riddles."

"Insurance," he said, the little pulsing pattern reflected in his eyes. He looked like he was reading something, so intense was his focus was on her chest. She raised her hand to her chest and covered it up.

Aodh lifted his gaze, the crinkle in his brow easing and his eyebrows lifting. "She must have been worried you wouldn't come home in time. How close were you to the Equinox when you came for me?"

"Equinox wasn't for another month … more. It was the middle of February." She brightened when she did the math and realized what day it had actually been when they left. "Perfect timing," she said, shifting on his lap so she was straddling him, still intent on having the one thing she'd wanted all this time—ever since their first kiss.

"For what?" he asked.

"It's Valentine's Day," she said. "It's romantic that today's the day you make up with Neph and I get to make love to you for the first time."

"We've already made love several times."

"That was with both of you. Now it's just you."

His frown betrayed an incongruous uncertainty that made Vrishti's chest constrict.

"Don't do that," she said softly, resisting the urge to slide off his lap and call Neph back.

"Don't do what?"

"Look at me like you aren't even sure you want me."

Aodh's nostrils flared. "Vrishti, my wanting you is *never* going to change. That mark of yours that your mother gave you worries me, though. Whatever is happening in the present … the *real* present … must be dire enough that your mother gave you this link to the Summer Spirit before you left her. She was Queen of the ursa once, so she knows how important it is that you make it back there alive."

"We have time, though. We have all the time in the world right now. Can we just have this moment to not worry about the fate of the world?"

Aodh tightened his grip on her hips beneath the water and some of the weariness left his eyes. Letting out a soft sigh, he nodded.

"Having you here to wake me was more than I could have asked for. I don't even know how Neph knew it was you." He slid his big hands up her sides, pausing when his thumbs edged beneath her breasts and caressed the round swells of their undersides.

Vrishti shifted closer on his lap, sliding her hands up his thick shoulders and hooking her fingers at the back of his neck. She avoided looking down between them, though she desperately wanted to see his magnificent cock again. The base of it nudged up against her core, hard and hot, making her wonder whether he'd been this aroused all along, even with those serious thoughts going through his head.

His mouth twitched. "You have to know I get hard just looking at you, sweetness. Of course I'm aroused when you're naked in my lap."

She scowled. "Stop reading my mind. I want to feel you make love to me without any magic. Just you and me and our bodies."

"I can do that," he said, his voice lowering in pitch. He shifted his hands higher until they cupped her heavy breasts, his thumbs gliding back and forth over her nipples. Warmth flooded her and she sighed under his touch. His heated gaze fixed on her face, the steam from the bath condensing on his pale cheeks. His lips, however, were flushed and pink, sending her back in a rush to the sight of him sucking and lapping at her core, bringing her to repeated heights of ecstasy.

Impulsively she bent her head and darted out her tongue, sliding the tip along his lower lip, then the upper one. He closed the distance with a slight shift of his head, surprising her with the hungry way he captured her mouth with his. She moaned and tightened her hold on him, tilting her head and shifting tight against him. She rose so that her spread folds glided along the length of his cock until his tip was pressed between.

His hands slipped around her, sliding up her back to support her as she sank down on top of him. His rough groan when she was seated fully sent a pleasant vibration straight through her, causing her muscles to clench around him.

"Sweet Mother, this is more perfect than I could have imagined," he murmured. "Thank you."

"Uh-huh," she said, pressing her forehead to his and peering into his eyes as she began to move on top of him. This *was* perfect. Every bit as perfect as the way Neph had made love to her the night before they'd left. Which had only been a little while ago but it seemed like forever. She missed the big satyr, but she was grateful for this private moment with her dragon. Every single moment with either of them was worth savoring.

CHAPTER 34

Neph easily merged with the water itself, his magic making him indistinguishable from its molecules. He could have stayed to bear witness to the love-making of the pair of people who meant more to him than his own immortal life, but he intended to honor Vrishti's wish to be alone with the dragon. He understood it all too well. They would be three-in-one when she decided she was ready for a blood meld to complete their trio, and there was no going back after that. She would need these last hours or days to enjoy her autonomy before that happened. He could still easily sense Aodh through their newly forged blood bond, but opted to keep a mental wall in place to let the dragon have his space as well, which Aodh needed for other reasons.

Before he erected the wall, Neph had caught a snippet of their conversation and frowned. The time shift of their journey was something neither Vrishti nor Aodh could have been aware of. It wasn't as precise as she made it sound. While it may have been February fourteenth in their present when they left, a journey as far into the past as they'd made still took *time.* Not three thousand years, but they'd likely lost days, and would lose more on the journey back. By his calculations, they'd still arrive before the Equinox, but he wasn't sure how long before.

There was very little he could do to control that shift, so he saw no point in bringing it up now. They would have to deal with it when they got home.

With his mind carefully separated from theirs, he let the air current and the heat carry him in vapor form into the air above the pool. Then with a slight effort of his will, he pushed toward what appeared to be the most likely spot for an exit to the huge, hemispherical room. He needed to see the sky to get his bearings on both where and when they were ... to confirm what the first glimpse of the architecture of the room suggested as well as his suspicions of how much time they might have lost in getting here.

A barely perceptible current pushed at his vaporous body and he knew he'd found what he sought. In an instant he drifted beyond the door, reassuming his human shape on the other side. He found himself in a dimly lit stairwell with recessed glowing lights placed at wide intervals all the way up a narrow spiral.

He climbed for several minutes, until he came out in the back of a dark room in a hidden alcove behind a shining, jade bed covered in luxurious bedding spun from dragon magic.

Aodh had hidden his cave well. Either he intended to never be awakened, or he had counted on Neph eventually finding him and being able to drift directly to him.

As Neph moved through the rooms, however, something struck him about this place. It was clearly a dragon temple, yet it showed no signs of ever having been used. Over the past centuries, he'd taken time to conjure visions of the dragons, curious if he would catch a glimpse of Aodh. He'd held out hope that the dragon would find a true mate out in the world and would eventually forget about him, but the utter absence of the big white dragon in any of his visions left him more and more dispirited and filled with regret.

But in the process, he had seen this place filled with young dragons, both frightened and apprehensive, yet excited about the new world that would await them on the other side of a five-hundred-year hibernation.

This was the first temple.

All he'd known about where to find Aodh was the time and geographic locale. This temple was a surprise, but now it made perfect sense. It also made the next step of their journey a hell of a lot easier.

They were already exactly where they needed to be. All he needed to do was leap forward in time about three thousand years and hope that the drift itself didn't devour too many of the precious days they had left.

He found another stairwell at the far end of the throne room and climbed, his skin tingling with the fresh tropical air that blew in periodically. He knew this island well, had very likely used the portals here while Aodh was in residence —in captivity.

If he had only known.

When he reached the huge cupola covering the entrance to the temple, he inhaled deeply, savoring the sweetness of the air. The world back then had been so pristine, the elements uncorrupted. They could stay and pretend the future hadn't occurred, simply hide away and come out only when they needed food.

The thought was tempting, but he knew better. The shimmering barrier that surrounded the entire island was evidence enough of what he needed to get back to. His sister's sanity was at stake. His home's safety. And the integrity of his own soul and his love for the two people who awaited him down below.

When it was done and Meri was destroyed once and for all, they could revisit the idea of hiding away together, but that wasn't to be. They were leaders of their respective races—Vrishti would be the next ursa Queen once the seasons in the Sanctuary shifted. She needed to be there when that happened.

Aodh had never had a significant role leading the dragons, but the Council's status had changed drastically over the last few months. They needed each other more than ever to weather all the changes.

And his role … yet another vision that eluded him, but his sister would need him if they were unable to rescue Nereus, and if they succeeded, he would want to be there to reunite with his best friend.

Nothing good ever came easy, but he'd always known that. Confident in his chosen trajectory for their next trip, he descended again, taking his time and exploring the temple as he went. When he made it back to Aodh's cavern, they needed to be ready to go.

CHAPTER 35

AODH

Stone ground against stone, the sound echoing through the cavern above. Aodh didn't dare move from where he lay flat on the cool ground beside the bath, the sleeping Vrishti using his big body for a bed. They'd made love, both faithfully refraining from opening too much of their minds to each other. It had been close to how Aodh had always imagined his first time with her might feel. Better for the fact that he had none of the expected worry for her physical comfort. She took her pleasure from him eagerly and openly, the way he'd hoped she would once fully attuned to her power as an ursa princess—the future vessel of Summer.

She was clearly exhausted now, her breathing slow and even as he continued to softly caress her bare back. He hazarded a slight turn of his head to see Neph slip through the big stone door and close it tightly behind him. The big satyr looked at ease. He'd always been the most self-possessed man Aodh had ever known, but he looked more relaxed, less burdened than he'd ever seen him.

"What did you find?" Aodh asked silently, focusing his

mental power on Neph and avoiding opening a door to Vrishti's mind so she wouldn't be disturbed.

Neph gave Vrishti a warm glance, his love for her evident in the way his gaze lingered on Aodh's hand and the satisfaction that flooded their mental link. He came around the pool and sat at Aodh's head, then cupped the dragon's skull and shifted beneath so that Aodh was cushioned against the satyr's thigh.

Without speaking, Neph began gently petting Aodh's head, combing his fingers through the damp hair. The touch was hypnotic, comforting, and filled with a love that made Aodh's eyes burn with tears at how much he had missed this man's touch.

"Nikhil is commanding the army from this very temple in the present. It will be an easy trip once she wakes up."

"Does he know where Meri is?"

Neph didn't answer for a moment, and Aodh sensed him carefully considering his reply.

"I admit I'm not as up to date as I should be. The last contact I made was the day before Vrishti arrived. Calder had succeeded in letting the enemy capture him again and was being transported north from Madagascar. They were waiting to find out if she took him to her base. When Vrishti showed up, my priorities changed ..." He reached a hand out and brushed a light touch over the sleeping ursa's smooth forehead.

Vrishti let out a soft sigh, her hips twitching slightly against Aodh's belly.

"She's close again," Aodh said. *"Her aura fills with energy at a rate I've never seen for someone sound asleep. She's right not to mate us yet, but the idea of putting a baby in her is so tough to resist."*

"We won't waste time when we get you out of here. If we're blood-melded with her, we can take her straight home as soon as

the Equinox begins. She needs to be there, not off chasing after our old mistakes."

"I won't leave everyone else to fix it for us," Aodh said.

"Everyone's been wronged by the Ultiori in some way. It isn't as though we have to talk anyone into going after Meri. Least of all Nikhil. She destroyed his life. You and I could have managed."

"That may be true, but you and I both know how unpredictable she is. They will need us. Blood-melded, with Vrishti safe in the Sanctuary. This isn't her fight."

"She'd feel differently if you asked her, you know."

"I don't care. We protect her at all costs. You of all people should know why."

Neph nodded, his gaze darkening as he looked at Vrishti again. *"She is a direct link to the Source. I've seen it inside her. Felt it. She has enough power to get us all back into the Haven now, if we can get to a functioning portal."*

"Our mission is to keep Meri out, though. Nyx seemed to think Meri would be drawn by my old link to her. She inhabited my body long enough to leave a mark, even without a full blood exchange— if I can draw her out and distract her, perhaps the others can neutralize her base. Rescue whatever captives she still has ..."

"Nereus and the other Thiasoi are the priority. Their power will be key to defending the Haven."

"If we destroy her, that won't be necessary." Frustration rose in Aodh's chest. Getting to the bitch and making her pay for what she'd done to him would solve all their problems.

"We can't take any chances. The Haven is vulnerable as long as Nyx is out of commission and I'm not there to protect it."

Aodh took a deep breath, the rise of his chest causing Vrishti's head to brush against his lips. He pressed them to her crown and inhaled deeply, finding strength in their contact. The Haven was the core of half their world's power and survival. It even supplied some power to the Dragon Glade and

Aodh had no idea of the consequences were Meri allowed to breach the Haven and reach the Source. At the very least, she could abuse control of it the way Nyx had in order to leverage his capture. And Meri had a far bigger vendetta against them all, he was sure she wouldn't simply use the Source as leverage.

With a deep sigh, he nodded and spoke aloud in a low whisper. "You're right. Once Vrishti's safe, we focus on defending the Haven first. Then we go after her. I want her dead."

Atop him, Vrishti emitted a low moan, her aura brightening perceptibly around her. The energy of it crackled against his skin like static. He brushed his hand down her back, resting it at her hips. A warm pulse throbbed inside her beneath his palm, growing stronger with each second until her entire body twitched with each surge.

"Aodh," she whimpered, clutching at his shoulders. She buried her face against his neck and cried out when another spasm hit.

Neph rested a hand on her shoulder from above.

"It's time, kitten. We've got you."

"Need you ... please ..." she murmured, curling into herself on Aodh's chest. He wrapped his arms around her and rose, cradling her against him as he slipped back into the warm water, hoping the heat would at least ease her discomfort until they could take care of her.

She clung to his neck, her thighs flexing and rubbing together against the forearm that cradled them.

The water surged behind him with Neph's entry, sending big swells across to the other side. When Neph came around him, he was already fully shifted, his massive primal shape a head taller than Aodh. He lifted an eyebrow at the other man.

"I have to be in this form to access my power. You should stay in your human shape—it'll be easier for me to drift the three of us if you're both smaller than me."

Aodh nodded and followed Neph to the center of the pool, hyperaware of the pulsing energy of Vrishti's aura surrounding him and the growing potency of the fertile fluid flooding from between her thighs, easily scented despite her lower half now being submerged in the water. His cock ached, but it was Neph who needed contact with her magic to transport them where they needed to go. He would bide his time until they arrived.

When he met Neph in the center of the pool, the satyr hooked one arm beneath Vrishti's back alongside Aodh's, the pair of them supporting her.

"Are you ready for us, kitten? We're going to make you feel better now." Neph spread his fingers and drifted them down her chest, easily spanning the width of her torso with one hand. He paused at her breasts, teasing both nipples into hard peaks. Vrishti arched into his touch and moaned, her feverish gaze on Aodh's face.

"Kiss me," she said

Aodh bent his head, eagerly capturing her lips and savoring the potency of her need in that kiss. She moaned into his mouth, her hips bucking up. He opened his eyes and released her, glancing down to see Neph's hand between her thighs, several fingers buried deep inside her and his thumb rubbing at her clit. Her head fell back, her dark hair trailing in the water. Unable to resist the warm, brown column of her throat, Aodh bent his head and pressed his lips to the base of it, drawing his forked tongue up along the length as she spasmed in the first of several orgasms that would ease the latest surge of her estrous.

Her energy flooded him, leaving his vision hazy with bright green power and his cock aching painfully with the need to be inside her.

"Fuck, we need to do this," he said. "I need to be inside her."

"We'll both be inside her for this, lover," Neph said. "She's ready for you after the way we worked her ass over earlier with our mouths and fingers. Aren't you, kitten?"

Her eyes flashed with pure desire. "Ohh, yes. I want that. I want you both."

Aodh looked down at her, nostrils flaring. "It's been a little while. Forgive me if I want to make extra sure."

She swallowed and nodded, then glanced up at Neph. "Shouldn't we be … you know … lying down?"

He chuckled. "We're in water. Nothing's going to break, and if we fall over, we'll just float. Come here … I'll hold you for him."

Aodh relinquished Vrishti into the satyr's arms. She went, wrapping her arms around Neph's big neck. Neph hooked his arms beneath her knees helping her wrap her legs around him. He glided his hands to her ass, where he cupped her cheeks and spread her open, venturing one finger along the seam of her pussy as though he were incapable of not touching her.

She glanced over her shoulder at Aodh, then lifted herself a little higher, resting her elbows on Neph's huge shoulders.

"Is that good?" she asked, a little breathless. Her lips remained parted and she licked her lips as she stared back at him.

Aodh's desire nearly overwhelmed him at the sight. In Neph's big arms, her ass hovered above the surface of the water, and she was fully on display for him, her glistening folds wet and swollen like ripe fruit, her little puckered anus beckoning for him to keep his promise to make sure she was ready.

"Dragon tongue?" she asked expectantly.

Sweet Mother, yes. He concentrated his power into his natural shape, sending water sloshing over the sides of the pool as he grew in size. There was barely enough room for him at full length, but all he needed was to reach her ass with his full-sized dragon tongue.

"Don't let her come," Neph warned. "We need all that power."

Aodh made an incoherent sound of acknowledgment as he dipped his big head and slipped his tongue out to tease between her thighs. Her wetness hit his taste buds in an explosion of fertile flavor, and she let out a gasp. He toyed with her juicy core for a moment, sliding his forked tips back and forth between her folds and then pushing deep into her slick channel to immerse his entire tongue in her.

She clenched around him, the sensation causing his cock to protest at being denied the pleasure, but he would be buried in her soon enough. He slipped out of her, moving back and gliding his tongue higher until he sensed the puckered texture of the place he would own in moments.

"Oh, yes!" she cried, followed by a shaky moan when he pushed his tongue beyond her tight barrier. She trembled in Neph's arms, her tight opening clenching, then relaxing as he pushed deeper, flaring his big tongue to stretch her. He twisted and swirled, encouraged by the ease with which she took him, but his tongue's flexible flesh was a far cry from the rigid thickness of his cock. He needed to be sure she was ready.

"Enough," Neph said. "If she isn't ready after that, she'll never be. Go slow."

Aodh grunted in assent, nearly incoherent with the buzzing need to feel that tight haven wrapped around his cock and taking him fully. He swiftly shifted back to his human shape and stepped in close again, gripping her hip with one hand while he held his cock in the other.

Vrishti pressed her face into Neph's neck while the satyr lowered her and Aodh pressed his tip at her tight rear opening.

His flared cockhead breached her barrier with only a slight push, and he paused, partly to clear his head so he could focus and partly to allow her to acclimate to the hard thickness of him.

"More," she gasped. "Don't stop."

He tucked himself tight against her back and wrapped his arms around her torso beneath her breasts, burying his face in her hair. She released Neph and hooked both arms behind Aodh's neck, leaning back against him while Neph supported her lower half, holding her steady while Aodh slowly eased his full length into her.

She spasmed once and let out a little cry of pain, but relaxed again when Neph slid his fingers between her thighs and began to rub her clit in slow circles.

"Sweet Mother, you are perfect," Aodh rumbled against her ear.

"S-so are you," she panted, and let out a low moan, her aura brightening with a red glow around the green now that he was inside her, starting to thrust as slowly as he could and still maintain his sanity.

Neph closed in. He held her thighs with both big hands and widened his stance to lower his hips to their height, aiming the tip of his huge cock at her spread folds. Aodh and Vrishti both watched, feverish with need as the satyr teased his tip in circles around and around until Vrishti's aura flared bright enough to blind him.

"Fuck her already," Aodh growled.

When Neph pushed into her, the increased tightness traveling up the length of Aodh's cock sent a swift surge of pleasure all the way through his body. He grunted and clung tighter to her, sinking his teeth into the flesh of her shoulder in an effort to hold back his orgasm.

"Please," Vrishti begged. "Don't make me hold it in. Need to let go."

"Just a little longer, kitten," Neph said, his voice strained. He hauled her legs around his waist and pressed into her, sinking to the hilt in a long stroke that made Aodh's eyes go hazy. The satyr rested one hand at Aodh's hip, fingertips digging in hard. He slid the other to the back of Vrishti's neck and leaned down to kiss her while picking up the tempo of his thrusts.

Aodh closed his eyes and opened his mind, gratified to find the satyr awaiting him alongside Vrishti in the most beautiful flower-filled garden beside a shining pool. In their minds they joined again, the ecstasy doubling for all three. As they moved inside her, the waters of the pool began to ripple toward the shore, like some unseen force had triggered a tidal surge. The waves lapped at the banks, growing higher with each deep, delicious thrust of their cocks into her tight, hot depths.

"That's right, kitten. Wait for the power," Neph said between harsh grunts.

Aodh was nearly at his limit, his built-up ecstasy ready to overflow any second. When the first violent wave crashed into their bodies, drenching them with its potent power, Neph cried out, "Now!"

With a resonant roar, Aodh let go, his cock pushing deep and his balls tightening as he shot a flood of hot essence into her. Vrishti stiffened and cried out, her nails digging into the back of Aodh's neck, her head flying back against his shoulder as she arched with the force of her climax.

A hot flood coursed between them, drenching his balls and upper thighs. Just as he felt the violent spasm of Neph's cock alongside his own on the other side of the membrane that separated them, the bottom of the world fell out from beneath them.

There was a strange synchronicity to the locale Meri had chosen to complete her plan. She'd been expelled through one of the Nile River portals, at the very spot where she now stood among the reeds, staring down at her own reflection.

Only it wasn't *her* reflection. It was yet another of the many vessels she'd been forced to use over the centuries to stay alive. This vessel couldn't shift, nor could any of the others, and she wondered if she could even remember how once she finally had an immortal vessel once again. The child she'd left behind, safe in its secret chamber beneath the pyramid, was only the first step in her long-term plan to command an army of immortals. Reclaiming the Haven was the second. That immortal baby would be the key to Meri's victory.

"She isn't immortal yet," she reminded herself. The Source would fix that, but she needed this vessel to last at least another two decades until she could breed a new one from what would hopefully be the first immortal hybrid in existence. The Source would allow the child to mature enough

for Meri to speed the entire process along. When she had the Haven conquered, the Sanctuary would soon follow, and she'd have all the Source's power at her disposal to build that army, and in the process to create the perfect immortal vessel for herself.

She felt a pang of longing at the thought of the tiny creature she'd left behind in the tank of gel-like fluid, flooded with the powerful blood of the satyrs who sustained it.

Catching herself, she chuckled softly. Was she actually acquiring maternal feelings for the child? How preposterous. It was a tool, the culmination of all her hard work attempting to create a creature that possessed all the powers she would need bred right into its DNA, allowing her to finally be done with her reliance on the human race for her survival.

On that note, she turned away from the river, and directed her mental focus outward into the villages nearby. Only one day left until the Equinox, and her entire army was in place. They were spread out, disguised as locals so as not to draw suspicion, but ready at a moment's notice to drift to her location when the time came.

For the first time in ages, she was in the mood to celebrate. Filtering through the minds of the nearest men, she found three who were due a reward for their service and commanded them to meet her at the rooms she kept at a local hotel.

She missed having the stamina of a nymph, but this new body she'd taken was young, athletic, and beautiful, and could easily keep up with the appetites of a trio of horny soldiers. And now that the prospect of an afternoon of her favorite game was fixed in her mind, she couldn't wait for it.

Tomorrow, she was going home.

CHAPTER 37

CALDER

Calder opened his eyes to slits, carefully maintaining his limp shape in the tank Meri had him and the other Thiasoi suspended in. He didn't want to draw the attention of any guards who might be in the room. But all he saw was a sole technician seated at a control panel behind a glass wall, his attention fixed on a pair of monitors that blocked most of his face from view.

Calder took quick stock of the surrounding area without turning his head. The tank seemed to be in its own room, surrounded on three sides by solid concrete walls, and on the fourth by a plate glass window that looked into the technician's booth. Within the tank's room were cameras positioned at each corner, rotating at intervals. He could only see two of the corners, but had to assume the entire room was similarly equipped.

There were no blind spots convenient to the exit that he could see. Even the door between the booth and the room was a clear glass sliding door similar to the prison cell doors where he'd been held most recently before the dragons rescued him and Nicholas.

"Those doors wouldn't be able to keep you in now," Nicholas whispered in his mind.

"All the more reason to be extra cautious. She finds out, she could neuter me like before. Cut me off from you ... from my power. I still don't know how she did that."

"That kind of mental blocking sounds like my brother," Aurum said, her voice sending a pleasant warmth through his limbs he hoped didn't show up on his vital signs.

"She had access to Ked's blood. It would have taken a toll on her vessel to use it, but she clearly found a new vessel not long after."

The technician began fidgeting then, glancing at his wrist every few minutes. Calder watched intently, waiting for his moment.

The second the technician stood up from his chair, Calder moved. He drifted out of the tank, instantly landing behind the man. He clutched the technician's head in both hands and snapped his neck with a swift jerk. He shifted to assume the shape of the dead man in the split second he took to drag the body around the side of the desk, exhaling a cloud of dragon smoke to conjure a replica of the technician's dark blue cotton scrubs to cover his naked body.

The security panel by the exit beeped just as Calder snatched the dead man's ID badge off his pocket and stood up. The door opened as he blew out another cloud of smoke to camouflage the body in its little corner.

"Couldn't fucking hold it until the end of your shift, man?" the new technician grumbled on his way through the door.

"Sorry," Calder said, grabbing the empty water bottle on the desk and shaking it. "Needed to hydrate."

The other man chuckled, his demeanor brightening. "She was in a *good* mood when she left, wasn't she? That always means a nice, long bonus session. Hey, toss me a fresh bottle."

He gestured to the opposite end of the booth. Turning,

Calder saw a mini-fridge and stooped to open it and retrieve one of the many bottles of water that were chilling inside. His foot bumped the now invisible leg of the dead man and he surreptitiously scooted it back out of the path.

"Here you go, man," he said. As he handed the bottle to his new coworker he met the man's gaze, immediately triggering the hypnotic swirl in his eyes and expelling more dragon breath. "Gotta love a well-earned bonus."

The man stood transfixed for a second, his hand holding the other end of the bottle, but making no further move to take it. While Calder's gaze stunned him, the dragon breath did its work, filling the man with a sense of rightness and utter well-being.

"Everything's kosher here. Nothing out of place," Calder said, enunciating the words slowly so that the suggestion sunk in deep. He had no guarantee that Meri wouldn't take a peek into the man's mind at any point, but his own temporary hypnosis should prevent the sounding of an alarm for several hours without her influence.

"Yeah, man. Why wouldn't it be? She'd fucking kill us if it wasn't."

With a terse nod, Calder swiped his badge at the panel by the door and left, picking up his pace as he scanned the corridor, readying his power for more hypnosis in the event he came across more of Meri's minions.

He came around a corner and spied a pair of doors across from each other. By his navigation, one of the doors must lead back into the big room with the tank. He made a note of it, then tested the handle of the other door. It opened without issue, giving access to an elaborately equipped laboratory with a huge chair-like contraption in the center. Above the chair were several lights suspended on long, articulating arms.

The place was devoid of life, utterly sterile and still. It gave him a chill that he sensed must be Aurum's gut reaction to the room.

"Depressing," she said.

"We're no stranger to rooms like that," Nicholas said.

Calder silently acknowledged his mate's comment. He'd rather not dwell on those old memories, but Nicholas was right. The pair of them had spent countless hours in labs such as this, undergoing Meri's tests, having their blood stolen, their semen extracted, and then later in their captivity, being forced to couple with equally unwilling females of various races. They'd found solace in each other at least, which was more than he could have said for most of the other victims of the vicious bitch's schemes.

Just as he was about to retreat from the room, Aurum stopped him.

"There's something alive here. I can see an aura. That glow through the steel door there."

Calder turned in the direction she'd indicated. He walked toward the steel door and reached out for the levered handle. Opening it blasted him with ice-cold air.

"Fuck. It's just the cooler," he muttered, eyeing the frosted bags and containers that occupied the floor-to-ceiling shelves that lined both sides of the enclosure, leaving a narrow walkway between. But with the door open, the glow was stronger, coming from the other end of the compartment.

Bracing himself for the unpleasantness, he moved into the cooler, goosebumps immediately rising up on his skin. There was certainly something odd about that glow, and conspicuous about the emptiness at the far end of the cooler.

He ignored the outer door latching behind him. Studying the room closely, he walked forward. Halfway into the room, something on the shelf caught his eye and he turned to see a series of glowing chambers within a grid of glass. In each one was a tiny creature held suspended. Typewritten labels on each one numbered them in sequence with what looked like a kind of code: *D+U=Unviable; N+D=Unviable; D+T=Unviable; U+T=Unviable; N+U=Unviable*. There were countless others with increasingly complex codes and dates arranged in ascending order. Embryos, he realized with a horrific sickening feeling.

"How many were yours?" Aurum asked in a solemn tone.

"Anything with an N on the label might be. She never captured a female nymph, as far as I know, but she destroyed every single male she kept but me and my Thiasoi brothers. We were too powerful to waste that way. I guess she kept me as her breeding stock, but had a different use for them."

Chilled from the sight more than the temperature, he forced his gaze back to the wall. "There are footprints in the frost. One set … a woman's. There must be something on the other side of the wall."

"Be careful," his mates said in unison as he took a chance and drifted three feet forward.

The temperature increased dramatically, the sudden change shocking. But the most shocking thing of all was the sight before him.

The room was devoid of an exit, and was only big enough for the tank in front of him and a path around it wide enough for one person to walk, with a wider space before an angled control panel that had a steady readout of stats on the resident of the tank.

It was a smaller scale replica of the tank he and his Thiasoi brothers had been held in. Above the tank was a cylindrical contraption filled with red fluid, white lines on the side demarcating volume. It was full, but a long, red tube steadily fed the contents into the tank where the fluid… the *blood* swirled in smoky, marbled whorls around the object inside, gradually being absorbed through its outer shell.

Its skin.

Which was pale pink and translucent enough for the tiny beating heart to show inside its chest. Its aura glowed a faint pink, pulsing with each beat.

"Sweet Mother. A baby?" Aurum asked.

"It isn't human, whatever it is," Calder said. "But it isn't one of us, either. What is it?"

He stepped closer to the control panel and observed the readout. Beside the panel was a thick, leather-bound book with intricate patterns tooled into the cover.

The leather binding creaked when he opened it, revealing yellowed pages covered in delicately written script in the ancient nymphaea language.

"A grimoire?" Aurum asked.

"Or a journal …" Nicholas supplied. *"It looks like the one my mother left me."*

Calder flipped the pages, swiftly skimming the text. It began as a series of entries of mere speculation. About a century after being expelled from the Haven, Meri had begun making an effort to see if she could improve her situation. By the dates in the top corner of each page, he placed the first few entries at a few decades prior to the first series of abductions and the subsequent rise in attacks on the higher races.

The entries didn't begin to look like true lab notes until shortly after that date, roughly three thousand years ago. From that date on, she methodically tracked her various tests, detailing the results, the grid-like notes interspersed with more detailed narratives of her conclusions.

Nikhil would be a worthy vessel, but for his one weakness. Aodh had the same weakness—their cocks are good for pleasure and procreation, and not much else but a distraction. I need a female vessel suitable for the spirit of a nymph ...

... A cocktail of dragon blood works on humans, but only if it is not Immortal blood. Immortal blood kills them within moments, shortly after they go mad. Why has Nikhil survived? He was human before the wedding ...

... Unable to crossbreed the races in captivity. Are we truly incompatible? How are we able to breed with humans? Missing something crucial ...

... The blood mutates each test subject after the transfusion. Somehow Nikhil and his twin pups are the only ones yet who have been mutated by Immortal blood. Still don't understand this. He claims they were all dragon blessed. He isn't clear on how this works ...

... There is some mix of mutation plus affection that works. Subjects DBM-599 + UF-276 conceived after only two weeks sharing a cell, the first time testing enforced proximity for an extended period. UF estrous may be a factor, but inconsistent. Cannot discount the possibility that an imprinted pair may be required, but conception still does not guarantee viability ...

... Nikhil has taken a liking to the ursa cub. His interest in the fertility experiments is flagging. Perhaps it's time to let him have his son ...

... not just affection as previously believed. Love between the turul princess and her guards has produced several specimens of near perfect viability. Something is still missing. The embryos still don't survive in the artificial womb. It's as though they starve despite adequate nutrient solutions being provided. All in vitro experiments with similar human embryos prove viable with almost no issues. What is so difficult about the higher races? Perhaps revisit human DNA for clues ...

... Nikhil is testing me. His mind has been inaccessible at times. Something has shifted in the River, I'm sure of it. If only I had my own connection still. Need to bring my dog to heel before he gets

out of hand. He is the only Immortal mutant left untried in the experiments. It's his turn. Will attempt to cross-breed a pair of mutated humans for the first time ...

... Human DNA is the key to viability. They are a tenacious race which does not need love to proliferate. Odd that the higher races do. But that bears the question whether Nikhil and the female pup I compelled him to breed with shared something I was unaware of. Did their mutations add love to the equation? ...

... It doesn't matter now. She is alive. And she is beautiful. The satyrs will finally serve their purpose. If I had access to the true Source, this would be so much easier...

"Fuck," Calder said out loud. "She stops there. No suggestion what she plans to do with this embryo. The woman's not exactly the maternal type."

"What are we going to do with her?" Aurum asked.

Calder stared at the tiny floating creature. The tank that held it was big enough to house a full-sized infant, but this little creature was still incredibly tiny. It had arms and legs, fingers and toes. It could have been human except for the strange aura that surrounded it and the distinct pair of tiny protrusions on its head suggesting it might soon have horns, as well as the faint webbed outline of wings along its back. Its feet ended in tiny claws.

The notations in Meri's book suggested it could not live without the infusion of Source-imbued satyr blood. A quick glance at the container above the tank suggested it had a supply that could last a few days. Perhaps a week. He needed to get his Thiasoi brothers and his father out of their damn tank. Once they completed their mission, he would volunteer his own damn blood for this baby if he had to.

"We leave her for now. When we've dealt with Meri, we can come back. This room is on its own power grid. It's completely secure. She'll be safe."

Aurum's mental presence inside his mind hummed with uncertainty. *"I don't trust what Meri has planned for her."*

"Then we'll just have to make sure we get to Meri before she can complete this abhorrent experiment. Whatever the fuck it is. We need to finish scouting this place for the others."

CHAPTER 38

NIKHIL

"Can we move this many in so short a time?"

Nikhil surveyed the throng of dragons and turul who were awaiting his next command. Belah's question nagged at him. More than five thousand filled the throne room and the vast halls and chambers of the temple beyond. He could set eyes on maybe a fifth from his vantage atop the stone table-map that had once been this temple's throne. Belah stood beside him, ever the queen of her domain.

"It will take too long," he finally said, "even with Aurum and Nicholas helping. We can only drift a few at a time. Starting from the Madagascar temple will shorten the time a bit, but drifting still isn't instantaneous. The farther we have to travel, the more time it takes."

"And none of the glyphs around the portal send us straight there."

"There was never a hibernation temple in Egypt. Dragons haven't lived there since … since the start."

Dark shame twisted inside him. His vendetta was the reason for that. He'd killed any dragon he came across once he'd had the power to wield a blade again. His newfound magic had aided the slaughter. Any dragon he hadn't hunted down in those first years after he lost Belah swiftly fled. Eventually Meri reined in his bloodlust and he only captured them, her control over his mind redirecting his need to breeding rather than killing, which was no less brutal.

Belah rested a hand on his arm, squeezing lightly.

"Aurum and Nicholas are ready," she said, her touch the only acknowledgment of his silent struggle. "We should get started."

"Aye." Raising an arm and pointing at the narrow, nearly concealed entry to the underground cavern where the portals lay, he called out to his army. "The Equinox is the day the enemy is likely to be strongest, and our homes the most vulnerable. Now that we know where the darkest heart of our enemy lies, we can strike. Follow me to the portals below. Travel in quads to the Madagascar temple and wait there for my next command."

Bodies parted for him and Belah as they hopped off the table. Lukas and Iszak fell into step just behind them, the rest forming orderly ranks behind their respective commanders. With their bond, Nikhil trusted no others more than the pair of turul brothers to be his commanders. When asked, both had eagerly agreed, and Nikhil had seen the familiar glimmer of bloodlust in their eyes. They still had as much of a stake in seeing the enemy fall as any of the rest.

He and Belah stood beside the portal as the North brothers took the lead, stepping into the center and triggering the magic to send them halfway around the world. The first quad went after, then another until a steady flow of bodies stepped in, lit up the marks, and then disappeared.

"I wish you would stay here," Nikhil said. "I don't want you and the baby anywhere near Meri when it comes down to the wire."

"You know better than to order me to stay in the Enclave

with the other expectant mothers. Evie is here. Erika is here, and she is human. Only the mates close to delivery are staying behind."

Nikhil's skin prickled. "If she captures you …"

"She won't."

"You know she steals babies straight from their mothers' wombs. She doesn't eat them like the legends say, but they rarely survive. She is the Lamia."

"I have just as much a right to see her ended as you do, Nikhil. She took you from me. Getting you back was the hardest trial I have ever endured. Second only to living without you. I will *not* leave your side again."

Nikhil's nostrils flared in response to her vehemence, but some of the heaviness in his chest eased, and for the first time, he thought he understood why she loved relinquishing control to him so much. Having the decision of whether to make her stay taken from him made it easier. She was coming, and that was that. The truth was he wanted her beside him every bit as much as she wanted to be there, despite the risks. If all went well, they would never have reason to be parted again.

The room seemed to grow warmer with the steady flow of bodies filtering in from above. The cavern itself was large enough to comfortably hold a hundred or so. More if the adventurous ones chose to dive into the big pool in the center, but they weren't in a playful mood today.

When the sounds of splashing hit his ears followed by exclamations and laughter, he clenched his teeth, preparing to discipline whoever it was that had chosen to ignore his commands. He'd been so pleased with the level of discipline among the troops, many of whom had no military backgrounds whatsoever, even though almost all had endured some level of training in their lives to help them guard against capture by the Ultiori hunters.

He held up his hand, halting the next quad ready to travel. The four turul nodded, giving into their own curiosity to peer over the heads of the others who blocked the view of the pool.

"What the hell is going on?!" Nikhil yelled. He stepped around the huge statue of a satyr in full primal shift, ready to rut, then pushed his way through the crowd.

The closer he got to the pool, the thicker the air became with the potent scent of strong pheromones and fecund magical essence. His cock stiffened and his skull buzzed with acute arousal, an almost overwhelming need to breed.

Just as he reached the water's edge, a female voice rang out, echoing through the cavernous room in an incoherent, orgasmic cry to the heavens. And as though that power had mass, it flooded outward in waves, pushing the water into ripples over the edge of the pool and hitting him square in the chest with a blazing rush of pure ecstasy. Almost as a single being, every other person in the room seemed to shudder and gasp. Bodies stiffened, heads flew back, and cries rang out.

It gripped him unexpectedly like a sensuous caress pulling the pleasure from his soul outward until he couldn't bear it. His legs trembled, his balls tightened, and before he could grip his cock to stave off the sudden onrush, his orgasm erupted from him in a blast of tingling release.

As the wetness coated the inside of his pants, he finally registered the tangle of limbs and bodies that had materialized out of thin air in the center of the pool.

"Oh, it's Aodh," Belah said, her voice breathless and husky as though she'd just been well fucked.

Not just Aodh, whose pale hair and sturdy build Nikhil recognized. Towering over the already huge dragon was a horned man with hypnotic whirlpool eyes. And between the pair, locked to them in a torrid embrace with both her holes filled by their cocks, was a dark-skinned female whose voice he'd heard echo through the room, and whose power he was certain was what had caused the mass climax everyone had just experienced.

The trio stilled as everyone around seemed to gather themselves for a second. Then a slow patter of applause began, growing in volume as more took up clapping and cheering until the entire cavern and the temple above seemed to shake with the roar of their approval.

The female's eyes widened to the size of saucers as she peered past the arm of the big satyr. Her lower lip whitened in the grip of her teeth. Nikhil could swear he saw her curse just before she buried her face in the satyr's chest and the pair of men closed in, protecting her from the sight of the crowd.

"I recognize your brother and the Dionarch, but who is the girl?" Nikhil asked.

"She's the ursa they are Fated for. Aurum said he'd found her. It seems Neph was right not to join us after all."

"Unfortunate that it took them so long to get here," Nikhil said. "We will have to get them up to speed quickly."

Before his eyes the big satyr shimmered and shrank, his horns disappearing in a foggy wisp. He carefully lowered the girl into the water and she turned into Aodh's embrace, letting the big dragon shield her with his wings. Neph approached them, the water making waves as he made his way through it and vaulted up onto the edge.

"What day is it?" he asked without preamble.

"Two days until the Equinox. We're mobilizing to hit the Ultiori's secret base. One not even I was aware existed," Nikhil said.

Neph cursed, shooting a quick glance over his shoulder at the other two who approached more slowly.

"We need to get her back to the Sanctuary. She must be there on the Equinox."

"It will have to wait. We are pressed for time as it is. Your presence will speed things up—give us the advantage we were already lacking. Are you blood-melded? If there are three of you who can drift, even better."

Neph frowned. "Just Aodh and I are. Your plan is to reach the enemy's base before the Equinox?"

"We don't dare wait longer. She's been moving her army north. Aurum and Nicholas have tracked down Calder. He's infiltrated their base while Meri is gone. We expect she's organizing for something but she needs to wait until the Equinox to have the power to achieve whatever it is. All we know from the intel we've gathered is that's when she's carrying out her plans, somewhere on the banks of the Nile, near Cairo."

Neph nodded and lifted his gaze to survey the big room. "How many total?"

"Five thousand. A few hundred have ported to the Madagascar temple. Drifting from there will save time."

"Bring them back," Neph said. "We're taking everyone in one shot."

"All at once? How?" Belah asked. "I thought they had to be in contact with you."

"They will be," he said, and grinned.

Aodh lifted Vrishti out of the pool, expelling a thick cloud of white smoke that settled over her body, condensing into a white silk robe that provided just enough coverage for her blazing flush to return to her normal deep caramel tone.

"Do we know how long it took?" Vrishti asked.

"Too long," Neph said. "We'll get you home on time, I promise, but we have to take a detour first."

The young woman's eyes brightened, giving Nikhil the

sense that she wouldn't have gone home if they'd been able to. She'd fit in perfectly.

"Where are we going?" she asked.

Neph gave Nikhil an expectant look.

"Egypt," he said. "Meri's base is buried beneath the pyramids. The palace in Alexandria is a tourist attraction now, but the secret catacombs beneath are still intact. All the chambers I built are still sealed. The plan is to drift the army in, take over her base, then attack her at the water's edge. Every Equinox she performs the same ritual at the same location on the banks of the Nile River, so we know where she will be. She'll be heavily guarded, which is why we need the bulk of the troops to converge on her there. Most can take to the air. At least the Ultiori can't fly. They can drift, but only short distances."

"Every Equinox," Neph said, then emitted a deep chuckle. "Never knew you to be so predictable, Meri," he muttered.

"Do you know something I should be aware of?" Nikhil asked.

"She was expelled from the Haven through a portal on the banks of the Nile. We locked that one permanently after we kicked her out, but enough power at the right time could pry it open a tiny bit. Not enough for her to actually get back inside—only enough for us to know she tried."

"Neph and I should lead the attack," Aodh said. "Being forced to confront us will weaken her ... distract her."

"I want to face the bitch when I kill her for good," Nikhil said.

"A sword through her heart won't work," Neph said. "She's the worst abomination known to our kind. A Lamia who takes the blood of others so she can steal their bodies when it suits her. She'll have blood-melded everyone in her army, so if you simply kill the vessel she's in, her spirit will seek out the next closest one she's melded with. We can't kill her until we can be sure we've isolated her from all her victims. A prison like the one Aodh was in will work, but takes time to build. Several hours of preparation, at least. Let us survey the area first. Perhaps we can set a trap to capture her before we destroy her army."

"We need to get everyone there for this to work. Care to share your thoughts on that?"

"I will take the entire temple," Neph said.

Nikhil laughed. "You're fucking shitting me." Neph's face remained completely unperturbed and Nikhil's laughter died. "You're serious, aren't you?"

The satyr glanced over Vrishti's head at Aodh. The dragon lifted one shoulder. "Our powers are merged, now that we're blood-melded. And I built this temple from the ground up. Every stone is infused with my magic. It's as much a part of me as any artist's creation is a part of them. I see no reason we can't move the entire place."

Nikhil's mouth fell open and he spent several beats simply staring between the two men.

"We'll put it back when we're done," Neph offered.

Nikhil dropped his gaze to the wet-haired young woman between them. "Is your power part of this? I'd rather my army not be distracted by your particular—ah—*magic* when we move them. I need them focused."

Vrishti blinked and twisted her lips in an embarrassed smirk. "I'm sorry about that. But as far as I know, this kind of drift doesn't need my power. Does it?"

Neph shook his head. "We only have to transport matter across a distance, not through time. Between Aodh and I, we have more than enough power after servicing you to do it several times over."

Vrishti bit her lip and blinked up at the big satyr. On her other side, Aodh shifted closer and brushed his lips over her temple. When the girl shuddered in pleasure, Nikhil had to resist taking a wary step backward. He'd need Belah to conjure him fresh pants as it was. Fertile power as potent as hers was dangerous.

"Vrishti hasn't been blood-melded yet," Neph said. "When this is done, we're taking her home to the Rainsong Clan where we can mate her with her mother's blessing. Let's get on with it, yeah?"

Nikhil continued scrutinizing the young ursa, his gaze dropping to the small, glowing sunburst that adorned her chest, just visible in the opening of her robe. "You're the Summer princess. Your mother was at my wedding to Belah. Do you have the same powers she had?"

"I—I think so. I don't know what powers of hers you witnessed, but I am mid-estrous so …"

"Sweet Mother, child, you're in your estrous?" Belah blurted. "Do you know how dangerous that can be?" She looked between Aodh and Neph. "You can't leave her alone until you've mated her. Not unless you have a surrogate in mind to service her while you're gone. I wouldn't trust any dragon here not to mark her, and the turul aren't equipped to absorb that much power. We *all* felt it. I didn't even have to *touch* her and my well was filled when you three arrived."

"It's all right!" Vrishti said. "I usually have a few hours between waves now. And I want to stay with them anyway. I can help."

Nikhil's eyes narrowed. "That much power may be more danger than it's worth if it's as unharnessed as it seems. Show me you can control it. If you can't, Neph is right—you need to go home."

CHAPTER 39

VRISHTI

Vrishti took a deep breath. This was the man Aodh had told her about who would lead them to victory, and despite how intimidating he was with the vividly glowing tattoos around his wrists and neck, and the piercing gaze he'd settled on her, she forced herself to face him.

Pushing her shoulders back, she held his gaze, determined to prove herself. This was her chance to show them that she was indeed the daughter of Summer, and had learned to use the power that was her birthright.

"I've learned how to channel the excess energy. Watch." She turned around and bent at the edge of the pool, placing her hand in the water. Closing her eyes, she drew from memory the words she'd read in one of the many tomes in her mother's library. The growing mass of power in her core ceased its pulsing and flowed through her veins, up her arm, and into the water. In her mind's eye, she pictured what she desired, letting the magic flood from her fingertips.

Around her she heard the collective gasps of the room, and when she opened her eyes was gratified to see her vision made real. The pool was now covered entirely in a blanket of blooming lotus blossoms ranging from pale, pristine white to pink and deep lavender.

She stood and turned, smiling up at Nikhil, but her face fell at his stern expression.

"If I could have fought my enemies by conjuring flowers, my life would have been a lot easier. This is not enough." He lifted a palm and Vrishti watched as the hollow of it glowed green for a second, and a smaller replica of her own efforts grew out of the center of the magic.

Vrishti gritted her teeth and squatted down again, smacking her palms against the stone floor. Glaring up at him, she spat, "Well then maybe *this* will be!"

She chanted different words, angrily channeling more power from the seemingly endless well of energy that kept churning deep in her belly.

The ground beneath them shook. Stone ground against stone, cracks echoing through the cavernous room as the floor split beneath them and thick vines burst forth, snaking around the room and finding purchase around the ankles of the hundred or so individuals who stood waiting for their commander's orders.

Nikhil jumped back and nearly fell when one of the vines snagged his leg, swiftly coiling upward past his knee.

"Vrishti!" Neph yelled. "You made your point!"

She stood up, dazed by the rush of power, her vision clouding. She shook her head but lost her balance, grabbing hold of Neph's and Aodh's arms when they reached to catch her.

"Make it stop!" Nikhil yelled.

"I—I don't know how to put it back," she said, eyes widening in shock as the vines continued to writhe from the floor, tangling around the struggling people in the room.

"Burn them!" Nikhil yelled, gesturing to Belah as flames erupted from his hands. He reached down to grip the base of the vine that had coiled itself around his leg. He gritted his teeth and held on.

Around them, some of the crowd had jumped into the pool, only to find themselves still assaulted by writhing vegetation. Many shifted and took to the air, the dragons expelling gouts of flame downward at the onslaught. The cavern filled with smoke, but within a few minutes, the ruckus subsided.

Nikhil regarded her with his intense, dark-eyed stare as he bent to brush the charred segments of vine from his leg.

Vrishti chewed on her lip, not quite sure what to expect, but refusing to look behind her at Aodh or Neph for support.

Finally, Nikhil laughed and her tension eased a bit. "Undisciplined, but fierce and strong. Next time use it against the enemy, please."

"I will, I promise," she said with a hesitant smile. She shot a glance behind her and relaxed at the beaming smiles Aodh and Neph met her with.

"We have no more time to waste," Nikhil said, forcing everyone's attention back to him. "Do what you need to do to prepare the temple for transport. The closer we can get to the river, the better, but naturally we don't want to raise any kind of alarm from the human population. Come upstairs and let's look at the map to find a suitable landing spot."

Chastened by her near disastrous spell, Vrishti hung back when Nikhil led Neph and Aodh up the stairs. She avoided the curious looks of several of the males in the room, shrinking back to the relative safety she felt beside the statue of herself. Gradually the others began to filter up the stairs as well, leaving her in near solitude to survey the charred remains of what she'd caused.

Many of the beautiful lotus blossoms remained on top of the pool, but they were now surrounded by floating chunks of charred vines. She let out a shaky sigh and covered her face with her hands.

"You'll learn to control it," a feminine voice said nearby. Vrishti lowered her hands as a soft touch rested on her arm. She looked up to see a striking red-haired woman looking back at her. The woman's eyes were even redder than her hair, but her skin was a smooth alabaster so perfect she nearly glowed.

"I've only had access to it for a couple days. My practice spells were limited to magic only a fraction as powerful. I want to help, though, and I know I can. I've studied, at least … I just … haven't had much practice."

"You're lucky that you had time to acclimate. I kind of got thrown in cold. It's a shock to discover the world you always knew isn't really the world you belong in. I'm Rowan, by the way."

The pretty redhead reached out a hand and Vrishti took it. When she squeezed, a spark of familiar fertile energy shot through her and the woman's eyes widened and she dropped her free hand to her belly.

"Sorry," Vrishti said. "I didn't know you were pregnant. I read that the power has a special affinity for unborn babies. In a good way, I mean … it's attracted to new life. As though its entire reason for being is to make things grow."

"I believe you," Rowan said, smiling warmly as she held onto the slight swell in her abdomen. "But I do recommend working on your restraint a bit. At least when you're in mixed company. Come, let's go up and see where we're going next."

She held out her hand and Vrishti reached for it, paused, and closed her fist.

Rowan kept her hand outstretched. "You can do it," she said.

Taking a deep breath, Vrishti focused on tamping down

the churning well of potent magic inside her, then took Rowan's hand. She let her breath out when nothing sparked and let the woman lead her across the room to the exit.

"Would you like something more substantial to wear?" Rowan asked, glancing back at her as they ascended a narrow spiral staircase. Vrishti glanced down at the sheer white thing Aodh had covered her with and mulled over the offer.

"It would make it easier on the rest of us," Rowan offered. "You're beautiful, and fertile. The statue down there barely did you justice. You also aren't marked, and there are several hundred unattached male dragons up there who don't have a clue you belong to Aodh. It doesn't matter that you materialized with his dick inside you. Dragons are all about the prize, you know. You'll look like another shiny thing for them to possess."

"If you think it'll help. I just need to be able to… ah …"

"You want easy access, I get it," Rowan said with a sly grin. As they walked, Vrishti heard her let out a long breath and the narrow stairwell filled with red smoke for a moment before it condensed, clinging to Vrishti's skin. It seemed to absorb the white robe and flow downward, the basic pattern remaining unchanged, but tightening around her midsection and her breasts, a soft skirt flowing farther down her legs to cover her thighs by a few more inches. Around her lower legs, the smoke clung, condensing into soft red suede boots that covered her from the knee down, ending in comfortable, moccasin-like feet.

When they reached the throne room, the crowd parted for them both and Vrishti's neck prickled from the appraisal of all the eyes on her. Rowan stuck close, keeping her hand twined with Vrishti's.

Vrishti leaned into her new companion. Under her breath, she asked, "If I were marked, would they be looking at me that way?"

"Very likely still, yes. It isn't just that you aren't marked yet, but your aura is lit up like a Christmas tree to them. They can scent the men on you at least, so they won't cross any lines."

"Good, because I'm an ursa, so I'm the one who gets to do the marking. I plan to do it on my terms, on the Equinox after we've taken care of this."

"Sounds like a good plan," Rowan said, smiling at her. "But dragons are all about marking their mates, so be prepared to get one of your own."

Neph and Aodh were standing to the side of a huge topographic map of the world that seemed to be carved into the giant stone tabletop. Aodh jabbed a fingertip down in one spot.

"This is where we land. It's remote enough to avoid drawing attention, but close enough to drift in moments. Anywhere within a hundred miles is ideal, so this is as far as we dare go from the portal, which is Meri's likely target."

Vrishti moved around the table to stand between Aodh and Neph. The big dragon made room and slipped his arm around her waist, pulling her tight to him and pressing a kiss to her temple. Her chest warmed with the contact in the same way it had the night she'd woken to see Neph sound asleep in his human shape after spending all day pretending to be Aodh.

She reached for the satyr and he took her hand, smiling down at her. In only a couple days, their union would be official, with her mother's blessing and her full power realized when she took over as the vessel of the Summer Spirit.

"Very well," Nikhil said, tapping the map gently with his knuckles. "What do you need to do to prepare?"

"Make sure every individual in the temple is linked to another physically in some way. The closer, the better, but holding hands should be sufficient. Aodh and I will handle it from there." Glancing at Vrishti, he said, "Do you mind waiting for us here? Since we aren't fully melded yet, it's best if you're linked to the others when we begin."

Vrishti nodded, her heart pounding. Then they both kissed her before disappearing in a shimmering cloud. Rowan stepped in to resume her spot by Vrishti's side, gripping one hand.

"We've got you," she said. A tall, dark-haired man joined Rowan, linking their hands together, and then a younger man stepped in on Vrishti's other side and slipped his hand into hers.

"I'm Trevor," he said in a low voice. "Her better third." He gestured to Rowan, his gaze sparking with affection and humor. Around them, all the other residents began to join hands, first forming a circle around the big table, then spiraling outward until she saw them linking in a line out the doorways that bordered the room, the branches sometimes linking three hands together where they split off to continue in an unending line of linked bodies.

Vrishti closed her eyes, hoping she still had her melding link to Neph and Aodh. She found herself in the lush garden she'd begun to consider her sanctuary within the Sanctuary before she'd left, only now the small pool had grown to a large pond that rippled in the sunlight, its surface glowing with the power it held.

"Here," Neph called and she turned, spying a waterfall upstream from the pond that formed a wide, shimmering curtain she could just make out the shapes of her two lovers beyond. She went to them, passing through the veil of water and found herself again in the cavern beneath the temple. The pair of them dove into the pool together and swam to the center where they stood face to face, hands cupping each other's cheeks.

Aodh appeared tense at first, his gaze wary as he met

Neph's more desperate look. "Will you give me time to make amends?" Neph asked.

"I have no choice, but don't expect it to be easy for me. Torturing you isn't my purpose, at any rate. Vrishti's happiness is what matters most to me now. Not yours. Understand that and I think we can at least coexist. Now, shall we get this done?"

"Yes. Give me your breath first and help me see the temple as you have built it."

They bent their heads, tilting slightly as their mouths came together. Aodh's chest moved as he exhaled long and slow into Neph's lungs. The sight was far more intimate to Vrishti than even seeing the pair of them buried inside one another in their swiftly shifting lovemaking before they'd drifted across time.

This time they merged in a different way, their intimacy focused on each other instead of on her. Aodh's hurt was apparent in his cautious acceptance of Neph's touch when the satyr pulled him into a deeper kiss, enveloping the dragon in his arms as he grew in size to his fully horned, massive height.

Aodh didn't shift, but seemed to surrender to Neph's touch, allowing the bigger man to grip one thigh and lift it high over his hip.

Vrishti's mouth went dry when their kiss broke and Aodh rasped, "Do it now."

With a half-sneer and growl she knew was a prelude to fucking, Neph spun Aodh around and pushed him against the side of the pool. His big hand on the dragon's shoulder, he held him down, whirlpool eyes raking over the sturdy, broad back beneath him. With his free hand, Neph stroked his massive erection, squeezing until clear fluid leaked from the tip. He pressed it between Aodh's cheeks and the dragon groaned.

"Don't you fucking dare be nice about it, you bastard," Aodh spat over his shoulder. "I'm not in the mood to like you again so soon."

Neph chuckled. "My pleasure," he said, then in one swift, punishing thrust, shoved deep inside the dragon's ass.

Vrishti let out a sharp cry of surprise, her own backside clenching tight at the memory of how it felt to have something as big as Aodh buried in it. She couldn't even imagine Neph's huge satyr cock fitting in her there, but when Aodh's pale eyes met hers, they flashed with pure ecstasy and she knew he loved it.

"Come," he said in a rough voice and reached out to her with one hand. She went, her mental shape moving swiftly and kneeling before him. She gripped both his hands in hers and simply held him while Neph pounded into him from behind.

Through their joined minds, she could sense the ever rising pleasure the pair both experienced, and along with it the distinctly conflicted feelings. Neph's desperation to remind the dragon how deep his love endured was at odds with Aodh's lingering sense of betrayal that would need far more than a good fuck to be mended. But she was heartened to see them agreeing to work together. That they had blood-melded suggested their commitment to each other, if not an easy willingness to let bygones be bygones.

Within moments the pair of them shuddered as one, and she realized that despite her presence in their minds, they had a deeper bond she couldn't be part of yet. And when their heads tilted back, their voices rose together in their climax, and their bodies rippled with more than mere ecstasy. They became liquid, skin fading swiftly to translucence until they were both nothing more than water flowing back into the pool. A moment later the water before her churned and bubbled as though boiling and a massive cloud of white steam flowed forth, covering the entire floor of the big room, snaking around her in a tickling cocoon before rising higher and making its way toward the doorway.

Vrishti opened her eyes in the throne room just as the steamy cloud of her lovers flooded it, and she breathed them in with everyone else. The power filled her up in a way their cocks never had, and she closed her eyes, savoring the sensation of them inside her lungs, infusing her body.

Around her everyone let out a collective sigh. Then the ground beneath them began to shake. At first it was only a slight vibration, but then it took over her entire body, every cell seeming to light up, first with a tingling sense of pure, euphoric contentment. Then a rush of movement took over and she knew they'd entered the drift.

The sensation was nothing like the other times she'd drifted with Neph. This time she was one with all the other creatures in the temple, their cells flowing together in a tidal wave of motion, intent on a single target that Neph and Aodh pushed into her mind through their meld, allowing her to picture the expanse of desert to the west of the Nile where they intended to place the monolithic temple.

Within moments she was nothing more than particles of sensation, her entire purpose to move through space and surrender to the flow of the universe around her. In the midst of it, she understood the inner workings of Neph's magic. His connection to this constant flow of magic through the world, the thing he referred to as "The River" that connected everything, and the essence of the Source that he possessed which fueled his power. It didn't take much of the Source to do this immense magical feat, and within her, she had access to an infinite supply. She knew if she practiced she could do as much, if not more, with that much power. When she made it back to the Sanctuary and their lives were calm once more, she resolved to practice so she could master it herself to this degree.

The rush of kinetic power subsided slowly and then stopped, her body becoming hers again as though she were a cooling mist condensing into a crystalline shape that was unique among all the others also reforming around her. Together, they sank down to the ground like so many perfect snowflakes falling in the Appalachian forest that winter night when she'd first known she loved Neph.

When she opened her eyes they were there with her, her body somehow having moved itself down to the empty cavern where they had done their magic. They were both standing at the edge of the pool, clothed now in the same military-style cargo pants and drab t-shirts Nikhil's other soldiers wore.

Her heart shot into her throat at the realization of what this meant for all of them. Their enemy had an army, and so did they. They were literally about to go to war today.

Neph stepped close and rested his hands on her upper arms, squeezing gently, the warmth of his palms sinking through the conjured dress Rowan had given her. "Yes, we are at war, but if today goes well, this will be the only battle we must fight. Are you up for it? We'd be more comfortable if you remained here, safely guarded."

She took a deep, shaky breath in an effort to steady herself and shook her head. "I'm not leaving the two of you if I can help it. We're stronger together."

"If we were blood-melded and fully mated, we would be even stronger."

"No. You know I'd risk losing full access to the Source if we did that. We need my power even more now. If there's even a chance of pregnancy before this is done, I want to wait."

"It's all right," Aodh said. "Just promise us you'll never leave our sight."

She shot him a grateful smile. "No way in hell, as long as you make the same promise. We're together for the long haul now."

Neph chuckled, his smile warming her insides with its slightly flirty tilt. "By the time this is done, there *will* be a baby in you, I promise."

Her breath caught in her throat at the utter seriousness in his tone, giving her the sense that he'd like to do that very thing right now. Shaking her head, she reached out for their hands. "Later. Now we go take care of this bitch who hurt you both."

NEPH

a cold blade seemed to slice down Neph's spine after blurting out the unexpected words that had popped into his head. Sure, he ached to fill Vrishti with his seed until her belly swelled with their child, but the words hadn't come from his own desire to breed. It was as though they'd been spoken through him by some outside source—the power that fed him the visions, yet refused to show him any hints of his own future. Despite his desire for that exact thing to happen, something about it felt wrong, as though this was not a thing he should want despite knowing this was one of the very reasons he and Aodh had longed for a female to complete their triad.

Shaking off the strange sense of foreboding, he bit his tongue when the urge rose to lock her up inside this cavern. They'd made their vows to each other to stay together and he intended to stick to that until they were properly mated, marked, bonded, and blood-melded every which way.

"You should mark her," he said to Aodh silently via their mental link.

The white-haired man shot him a surprised look, his

eyebrows raised. *"Even if she agreed, to what end? It's her marks on us that matter to the ursa."*

"Protection. Something doesn't feel right, but I'll be damned if I can see it."

"What can you see?" Aodh asked, maintaining a steady pace with his gaze now fixed ahead of him on Vrishti's back as they climbed the narrow spiral staircase back up to the main hall.

"Death, but that is no surprise. We will be slaughtering our enemy soon. Beyond that, I see more blood. A river of it, but no sense of who it belongs to."

"She has her mother's mark as a safeguard. Even if we fail—which we won't—she will be all right."

Neph still couldn't shake the prickle at the back of his skull, but hoped he'd have a better sense of where things stood once they got underway.

The din of the massive crowd met them before they reached the main hall, and when they emerged through the secluded doorway at the top of the steps, the bodies were packed in nearly too tight to move through. Peering over everyone's heads, Neph saw Nikhil standing atop the table in the center of the room. He wore drab, loose-fitting robes, his head wrapped in a patterned turban. Beside him, Belah stood, blue smoke twining slowly around her, condensing into a black robe that covered her from head to toe until only her brilliant blue eyes were visible through a small opening.

"The enemy will be hiding in plain sight, as we should as well," Nikhil said. "The temple's protective cloak remains around it, so it blends in with the desert, appearing as a sand dune to the casual observer. We are close to the Pyramid Gardens, so it is safe to filter out of the temple and pretend to be tourists before making your way into the city. Do whatever you need to blend in with the locals until you receive my command. Travel in small groups, no fewer than two, no more than four, with at least one dragon and turul per group. Watch and listen for the enemy and neutralize any you come across as swiftly and silently as possible, ideally without their knowledge. We don't want their leader alerted to the danger until it's too late. Go now. Alpha team, you are with me."

The dragons and turul funneled toward the end of the room and through the huge doorway, heading up the stairs to the rooftop exit that Neph had ensured was the only part of the temple not submerged beneath the sand. Within half an hour, only a group of about two dozen remained behind, all now clad in garb similar to what Nikhil and Belah wore.

"Time to get dressed," Aodh said, and with a breath Neph felt his body being covered by a soft, comfortable robe that fell to his feet and was topped off by a snug turban. Vrishti's pretty red dress transformed into a black garment identical to the one Belah wore. When the costuming was complete, she blinked up at him, her long, dark lashes even more pronounced now that only her light brown eyes were visible through the little window of her head covering.

"You need to fix your eyes," she said, the corners of her own crinkling the way they did when she smiled.

Neph calmed himself with some effort, forcing the swirling in his irises to cease and display a uniform color. "How is this?" he asked, smiling back at her.

"Very pretty," she said. "Aqua is a good color for you."

Joining the others beside the table map again, he resisted the urge to hold her hand, but was relieved to see Aodh slip his arm around her waist and tuck her close.

"Can you create an accurate local map for us, Aodh?" Nikhil asked.

The dragon nodded and exhaled a lungful of white smoke, which descended onto the table like a heavy mist falling over the surface of the world. Beneath it, the stone shifted, became liquid, then bubbled up and reformed into the strangely angular modern landscape Neph had only spied in visions.

When the fog lifted, the table displayed the familiar snaking banks of the Nile River and the villages that dotted the shores on either side. A complex web of crisscrossing lines denoted the streets of Cairo that extended north, covering the landscape in a net of human thoroughfares all the way to the sea.

"Show me where this portal is that you believe is Meri's target," Nikhil said.

Neph studied the length of the river to get his bearings. "There is no portal any longer, but it was once here." He tapped an upraised island that floated in the center of a wider portion of the Nile south of Cairo. "We used it frequently and even had a temple built there that we shared with the dragons before. The portal is inaccessible now. The bigger ones were blocked entirely when she was banished. The smaller ones only locked. None can be opened from the outside now, either way."

"Meri wouldn't know this," Nikhil said, looking at Neph for confirmation.

"Unlikely. Nyx only took that final step since the last dragon ascension. She didn't dare before that, as long as she held out hope of Nereus and Calder returning. When Calder came home, she'd given up on Nereus—when she believed her son couldn't find his father, she lost hope and shifted her focus to protecting the Haven."

"The three of you will go there to wait for her. Set a trap if you can. My team will secure her base along with Calder's team."

As if on cue, a pair of figures materialized behind Nikhil. Vrishti let out a pleased squeak, then rushed around the table to envelop Nicholas and Aurum in a big hug.

The dragon and ursa accepted her embrace in bewildered surprise at first. Vrishti tore off her covering and said, "It's me, Vrishti!" The revelation incited a round of more enthusiastic hugs, which involved the big black-haired ursa hoisting her up and spinning her around.

Neph prickled at the sight, even though he knew Nicholas was very happily mated to his nephew and the gold dragon. Seeing Aodh's happy smile put him at ease, however, and he moved up to greet the newcomers, too.

He assured himself of their good health and some of his tension eased when Aurum confirmed Calder was alive and that he'd succeeded in releasing Nereus and the other Thiasoi soldiers. Everything was going their way. Hopefully it would continue to, but there was still one issue to resolve.

"We still don't have a way back into the Haven."

Nicholas set Vrishti back down and rubbed his hands together. "On the Equinox, my mates and I will be able to enter the Sanctuary with no issues, now that we're blood-melded. We'll head straight to the Haven. Hopefully the prospect of being reunited with Nereus will convince Nyx to reopen the way into the Haven, at least long enough to allow her mate to return home. If you three are still out here then, you should be able to go home then as well. If our attack on Meri must continue beyond tomorrow, we'll need the way open for the ursa and nymphs to exit so they can assist us in defeating her."

Belah nodded in agreement. "Then with the enemy defeated, we can relax the security and allow the higher races freer access to each other's realms. It can be like it once was."

Neph regarded Belah's blue eyes as they glanced around with hope at the remaining dragons and turul who had volunteered to join Nikhil's army. The veil she now wore was a human construct, but was the perfect parallel for the barriers they had erected between their races all along.

Taking them down would not be so easy. There were many members of each race who still believed in sticking to their own kind, but one thing he was sure of was that Fate might have other ideas. If he and his mates were any indication, their four races would soon be more integrated and far stronger for it.

He met Nikhil's gaze over the head of the commander's mate. In his mind's eye, he saw the former human's past as clearly as he had when visiting it with Vrishti earlier, but he could see a future for the man, too, one that was no longer driven by blood or vengeance, but by love and family. They *would* win, but what would be the cost? And why the hell did he still feel as nauseous as if he'd fallen under his own hypnotic spell?

"Are you ready?" Nikhil asked in a low, even voice.

Neph nodded. "Keep in contact with us and let us know your progress. If anything goes wrong—or right—we will let you know as well."

"We will do the same. Be safe," Nikhil said with a nod, and he, Belah, Aurum, and Nicholas moved to the crowd of waiting soldiers. They split into groups of eight, linking hands with the other dragons and turul. As a group they shimmered as though they were merely a desert mirage before they faded out of sight.

A small hand slipped into his on one side and he glanced down to see Vrishti smiling up at him, her veil pulled down so he could see her face. Impulsively he bent and kissed her, unable to suppress a desperate moan at the overwhelming emotions that bombarded him.

"You stay within sight of one of us always," he said.

"Please don't worry about me," she said, giving him an earnest look as she pressed a palm to his cheek. Aodh came up behind her and rested both hands on her shoulders.

"Until we're completely bound, you have to understand

we will worry," Neph said, speaking the words that Aodh's serious look told him he agreed with.

Vrishti pressed her lips together. "All right, I will compromise, but not yet. We need to be blood-melded to get you into the Sanctuary on the Equinox anyway, but I don't want to chance getting pregnant at all before I go home. I know what the barrier can do to an unborn child, and it would kill me if that happened to our baby. Just before we go. No sooner, all right?"

Aodh inhaled slowly and nodded. "I can accept that. Shall we go take care of this bitch once and for all, then?"

Aodh linked hands with Vrishti, and Neph completed their circle, wrapping his hand around the dragon's. A spark of hope shot through him at the gentle squeeze Aodh gave him just as their bodies dematerialized with the force of the drift.

CHAPTER 41

VRISHTI

They landed in a lush temple garden that might have belonged in another era. The only evidence of the wear of time was the ruined, broken state of what had once been several stately columns decorated with carvings of papyrus fronds. The morning sun shone bright above them, warming Vrishti instantly through the dark fabric of her robes. She gritted her teeth against the growing ache in her lower abdomen. Now that she knew it signaled the swell of fresh power from the Source, she didn't want to beg for release. She might need that magic to cast a spell soon.

Her skin tingled with excitement when her senses told her the ruined temple gardens they'd arrived in were empty.

"We're alone, aren't we?" she asked softly.

"For now," Aodh said, pulling her into the shadows of a fallen sandstone column and peering past a stand of palms toward the reeds at the edge of the water. Neph crouched, his body shrinking into itself, and a moment later, a slender-legged egret had taken his place, shaking off the conjured robes into a pile around its feet before stretching its wings and taking to the air.

Vrishti followed Neph's path as he soared above them in a wide arc that stretched out over the shoreline of the river before sailing back down to land in the shadows beside them.

He shifted again, appearing naked and shaking off feathers for a second. "No sign of her. She'll drift in, but it's unlikely she intends to do anything until midnight, which gives us the rest of the day to prepare a trap and wait."

"A snare, perhaps?" Aodh asked.

Neph nodded. "Simple, easy to conceal."

Vrishti frowned. "Wait, you're going to catch her with *that* kind of trap? Will that work? I thought she was some kind of super-powered villain."

Aodh chuckled. "Not a snare made of rope, sweetness. One made of magic. You can help. Come, we'll show you."

She followed them to the water's edge where they stripped and followed a naked Neph through the reeds into the river. The coolness of it eased some of the ache inside and she followed the two men as they dove beneath the surface. They were in a small cove where the water was relatively calm. Something about the way the light filtered in made the deep pool as magical as one of the many pools she'd bathed in during those brief weeks first living in the Sanctuary. But this pool had a sense of abandonment. She held her breath and followed Neph down to the bottom where he yanked at reeds until he'd revealed a stone circle of glyphs set in the ground, nearly concealed by river silt.

"This is where we set it," Neph said, surprising her with the clarity of his voice inside her mind. *"The portal opening was here. When she tries to activate it, she'll be trapped and we can deal with her after dispatching her army."*

Vrishti nodded. *"What can I do?"*

"Show us your stuff," Aodh said with a grin made sinister by the streams of small bubbles flowing from his nose and the corners of his mouth.

Neph gave him a playful shove. *"Aodh and I will set the trap for her. What you can do is work on other hidden traps for any undesired visitors—other Ultiori who come to her aid once we trap her. Those vines of yours ... can you prepare them to trigger when intruders step into the zone?"*

"I think so," she said. *"Let me just catch my breath."* She started to swim to the surface when a big hand wrapped around her thigh. Glancing down, she saw Aodh shaking his head, his hair swirling around his face like seaweed. He pulled her back down into his arms, enveloping her and holding her close. She thought he was only going in for a kiss, and pushed to protest, her lungs already aching from lack of oxygen. His mouth covered hers, his tongue dipping between her teeth to urge her to open. Just as she started to panic, a cold current flooded her mouth and she inhaled reflexively. Her eyes flew open at the infusion of power he'd given her, suddenly no longer in need of breath.

When he pulled away, he regarded her with a heated stare for a second. *"Stay close,"* he reminded her before turning to join Neph at the edge of the circle of glyphs.

She swam several yards away and settled down among the reeds, keeping her eyes focused on them while she pressed her hands to the soft, silty floor of the pool. It took some effort, but she was able to harness the churning knot of power in her womb. Uncertain whether the chant would work if she only said it silently, she spoke the words, which came out in fat, glowing bubbles that sank as though filled with stones, rather than floating to the surface.

Beneath her hands, the earth shifted, writhing as though a colony of serpentine shapes had awakened to her touch. She settled the mass of vines with her chanting, focusing the energy on the command to attack when their enemy came. Having never encountered one of the Ultiori herself, she altered the spell to universally trigger upon the proximity of any other creature who meant them ill will.

By the time she was finished, her lungs ached again, but the ache in her core had diminished to a dim throb. She swam back to the ring where Neph and Aodh had encircled the dormant portal with their own hidden magic. The glyphs glowed for several seconds until they each brushed their palms across the surface, replacing the layer of silt and returning them to their unused appearance.

She reached Neph first, touching his shoulder gently, then pointing to the surface with raised brows. He shook his head, pointed at Aodh, then himself, then touched her lips with his fingertips. He gripped her hand and she floated close, surrendering to him as he tilted her head back with one big hand and pressed his mouth to hers. She inhaled deeply when he breathed for her, marveling at the difference in the breath he gave her compared to what Aodh had provided earlier.

The water pushed against her back, and a second later, warm skin slid against her naked backside as Aodh joined them. He made no pretense of offering her air when he took over, his mouth covering hers and his tongue plunging deep in a passionate kiss instead. She wrapped her legs around Neph's waist to keep him close while she returned Aodh's kiss. The ache in her core returned with a vengeance when Neph's fingertips brushed along her outer folds before teasing deeper.

Vrishti moaned into Aodh's mouth when he slipped his hand down her back, meeting Neph's between her thighs. They both filled her with their fingers, working her until she couldn't help but inhale sharply. Aodh was prepared, his mouth still sealed over hers and his lungs ready to feed her precious air infused with his euphoria-inducing magic.

Neph moved his thumb to her clit, gliding through her

wet heat to press at the little nub while they continued to stretch her opening as though preparing her for something. She didn't care much between the constant thrum of pleasure pulsing through her body from both sets of hands driving her higher and higher. Their mouths went to her breasts, and she couldn't help but expel a sudden cry that came out oddly muffled and strange beneath the water.

When Aodh moved behind her, Neph cupped the back of her head and pulled her into another breath exchange that became a deep kiss. Aodh closed his hands around her hips, lifting her up, and she went easily, floating gently under his control. Neph kept hold of her lower legs, ensuring she remained hooked to him while the dragon moved in close, brushing his lips down the side of her neck.

The thick, doubled-tips of both their cocks pushed at her aching opening and her need soared. She bit her lower lip hard to keep from releasing any more precious air while they guided her back down onto their cocks, the delicious stretch of them something she was certain she would never get enough of, regardless of whether they were full-sized or not. They were still huge, their collective girth enough to remind her how much attention her previously virgin pussy had received in only a short time, but the pleasure was more than enough to compensate for the pain.

The buoyancy of their bodies made their movements even smoother than before, and they moved her up and down their cocks with languid ease, in no rush to race to climax. She arched her back, hooking both hands behind her to hold onto Aodh's neck while still clinging hard to Neph with her legs. There was nowhere she could go, as solidly buried in her as they were, and Vrishti thought that this moment, in this place, with the world blotted out by the water above them, she could forget that they may have to fight a war in only a few hours.

But they would win, and then she would blood meld these two men she loved and take them home, make them both her mates. And when she and her mother completed the ritual to grant her Summer's Spirit, nothing would ever part the three of them again.

With that thought, she let go, eagerly accepting Neph's mouth so he could breathe in her orgasm as her climax overtook her. In the middle of her series of delicious tremors, the pair of them drew even closer, their cocks shoving deeper in perfect synchronicity as they both came. Their essence filled her as the flood of excess magic flooded out of her and into them.

When she opened her eyes, they both glowed with subtle, shimmering blue-green light.

Aodh slipped out of her first, pressed one last kiss to her shoulder and smiled down at her. *"Let's go,"* he mouthed to them both, pointing toward the surface.

She and Neph both nodded, but the satyr didn't release her right away. As Aodh swam off, Neph's grip tightened and she gave him a questioning look. Something in his eyes startled her—a subtle fear that made no sense. She slipped her fingers through his hair and pulled him into a kiss, hoping to impart some comfort. When they parted, he smiled at her and finally released her. She kept hold of his hand as they swam side-by-side to the shore.

CHAPTER 42

MERI

The solution to Meri's problem eluded her. Even after a dozen very satisfying orgasms, she would have hoped for some spark of inspiration, but none had come.

She pivoted her hips, grinding her pussy into the mouth of the hunter who lay flat beneath her. With her hands splayed on his chest, she ground her pelvis harder against his lips. He let out a muffled groan, tightening his grip around her thighs, but he was a good boy who knew to lick harder and faster, even if he was smothering.

Her other two hunters were at the foot of the bed, one bent over with his hands braced on either side of the hips of the hunter whose tongue was buried inside her snatch. The other hunter nailed him from behind for her entertainment.

They'd been uncertain about her commands at first—no doubt their brothers who'd had the pleasure of a night with her had left out the part about how much she enjoyed ordering them to play these kinds of games. She deliberately chose men at the far left end of the Kinsey scale to serve her, just so she could indulge her own secret fetish of making them act outside their comfort zone.

By now they didn't care anymore; their libidos had taken over, and all they were after was yet another climax, but she still loved it when she caught a glimmer of disgust in one man's eyes when he remembered he had his dick buried in another man's ass. They wouldn't be able to look at each other for weeks afterward, but they'd still get hard and secretly jerk off to the memory every night, thanks to the steady flood of praise she fed their malleable minds during the process.

She let her mind wander as her climax drew near and could almost picture two different men before her. The blond who was bent over before her wasn't as big, but he had similar fine features to a dragon's and was just as bulky in the shoulders and thighs. The dark-haired man behind him was almost a dead ringer for her other old lover, aside from his static brown eyes. And he didn't like what he was doing any more than the man he was doing it to, which was exactly how she wanted it.

"Fuck him harder. Don't fucking close your eyes. Look at me."

Both men obediently lifted their faces. The blond soldier's eyes pleaded with her as he clung to the bed in front of him, pointedly avoiding glancing down to the erect cock that bobbed mere inches below his face. He had to have guessed what was coming next.

"Take that dick in your mouth, you fucking dragon whore. You'd better make him come if you want your own prize after. You're getting filled from both ends before you're done here."

The man beneath her slowed his licking for only a second, but he wasn't new to this scenario. She always rewarded the men who endured her demented fantasies with the coveted role as her personal toy for a month after playing out this particular one well. The fact that his cock was stiff as a fucking obelisk was proof enough that he at least enjoyed being her favorite for the day.

Meri was nothing if not appreciative of a good performance. All three would get to have their way with her when she had satisfied her need for petty imaginary vengeance.

"That's right, you little slut. Suck him all the way in. Work his cock like a lollipop. I want to see both cocks shoot their sticky spunk into you at the same time, so get busy."

The blond gritted his teeth at first, then opened his mouth, gingerly darting his tongue out to swipe it around the purple mushroom head of the cock in front of him. He looked like he was about to take the most vile medicine, but they always looked that way at first. True to her expectations, once he wrapped his lips around it and started sucking, it was like he was born for it. Hell, he even looked like he *enjoyed* it.

To top it off, he lifted his gaze to her while he pumped the cock with his mouth and fist, his wide blue eyes begging for her approval.

"Oh, fuck yes, baby. Just like that." She leaned over to give him an approving pat on the head, which spurred more enthusiastic pumping and sucking. The man beneath her groaned, his hips surging up forcing his cock deeper.

They were close, their impressionable human brains no longer caring a bit that they were all straight men engaging in the most depraved scenario they could have ever imagined. And the closer they got, the more she enjoyed herself. The hands gripping her thighs slid around to her ass, fingers prying her farther open for the talented mouth to devour her more fully. The added contact sent a spark of fresh ecstasy through her, and she gasped as her core tightened and heated.

Her eager attendant seemed to sense her impending climax and buried two fingers into her channel while his tongue picked up the pace on her clit. A steady, rising growl rose from his throat, his hips now thrusting wildly up into the blond's mouth.

Meri rode his mouth harder, clutching at her breasts and tweaking her nipples to push herself all the way over. It came in a rush like it always did when the scenario had played out that perfectly. She threw her head back and yelled into the air, her voice soon joined by a clear male voice as the dark haired stand-in for one old lover spilled his seed into the blond's ass. The man beneath her followed shortly, his groans of release muffled by her soaked snatch where she still slowly ground into him as she came down from the heights of orgasm.

This had to be it. Of all the orgasm's she'd had, this one had to be the one to inspire her to find the answer. Her mind had always worked best when flooded to the gills with dopamine—that funny little chemical humans had only just discovered within the last century.

She eased off her attendant's face and leaned back against the pillows behind her. Nothing came to her but the same circular thought pattern she'd had all day. She had to take the baby with her to the Haven, but it wouldn't survive outside the tank. But the baby was her entire reason for getting back into the Haven to begin with.

"What the fuck do you want?" she snapped when she realized her three hunters were watching her expectantly. The man who'd been beneath her dipped his head in deference.

"Mistress, Ryan performed well. His reward ..."

"Fuck his reward. You think he deserves it, you take care of him yourself. In fact, *both* of you take care of him. I have more important things to do, but when I get back, you'd better have gotten him off at least five times."

He blinked at her, then nodded. "As you wish," he said, then shifted around on the bed to make room for a bewildered Ryan to climb farther on and lie down.

Their third partner, the Neph lookalike whose name escaped her, shot her a withering look that he tried to cover up, but wasn't quick enough.

In a flash of pure rage, she narrowed her mental focus to a pinpoint and burrowed into his mind, easily taking control as though his body were her own. His consciousness was forced to the sidelines as she moved him onto the bed between Ryan's thighs and used his hands to push Ryan's knees to his chest. Then she bent with demented glee until his face was mere inches from Ryan's reddened opening, remnants of his own semen still coating the other man.

"I can make you tongue his ass while Carter gets the much more savory job of simply sucking his cock. You want to taste your own cum coming out of him, or are you going to behave?"

"Behave! I'll behave!"

"Good," she said and released Ryan's legs, along with her hold on the Neph lookalike's mind, her consciousness shifting back into her own head. She was gratified to see the hunter eagerly go down on the other man.

They were still taking turns when she drifted out after dressing again. The image of the dark-haired Neph lookalike going down on the man she'd chosen as the dragon's stand-in left her oddly unsatisfied despite the pleasant tingle still present between her thighs. She normally left those scenarios in a much better mood, but she was too antsy about her dilemma for her enjoyment to last.

She pictured the temple ruins in her mind, one of her favorite places to go to think when she was home. The hope of what she would soon accomplish there somehow helped calm her mind. At the very least, she could time her drifts between the Haven's locked portal and her lab, and maybe the passage back and forth would help knock some idea loose. It was her version of pacing when stressed, she supposed, but she needed to do *something*, and clearly sex hadn't been the answer.

~

MERI OPTED to begin on the island where the ancient temple ruins were nearly overrun with lush vegetation. The Nile flowed north on either side, the current's power as discernible as a strong breeze to her nymphaea spirit. She remembered the temple when it was still a whole structure. The gardens here had once been a favorite meeting place for her old lovers, when they'd still entertained thoughts of making her their third. And when she'd been expelled from the Haven, one of the resident priestesses had pulled her half-drowned body from the waters of the river. The river had been her enemy that day, following the Dionarchs' twin commands to bar her passage and never allow her to travel within its waters again.

Decades had passed before she reclaimed her power, but her nymphaea body had not lasted. Deprived of her connection to the life-sustaining magic of the Source, she'd withered and would have died if she hadn't discovered that the life's blood of every other living creature on Earth could serve as a substitute to the Source, if only temporarily. As long as the creature whose blood she drank still lived, she could be sustained. It had only taken a few tests for her to determine that once blood-melded with another creature, she could easily assume control of their weak minds, allowing her transient spirit to take up residence for as long as the new body lasted.

This was how her child was being kept alive—with regular, constant infusions of the satyr blood. Theirs was still imbued with power from the Source itself, so was the closest she could get without being inside the Haven. But the satyrs were not immortal, and the irregular brain activity she'd seen in Nereus's readouts meant she could not rely on them forever. If one died she'd lose that supply; or—Gaia forbid—if one awoke, she would have no choice but to kill him.

Now she was so close to succeeding in regaining access to the Haven. At midnight tonight, she would begin the ritual to force open the portal and send Nyx her message. If only she'd known who she had all those years before she let Calder escape the first time. He'd only been a child when she left the Haven. So when she'd captured him centuries later, he had feigned unimportance, claiming she may as well kill him for all the use he was to her. And in truth, he'd *looked* like one of the less notable satyrs she'd known—the bastard had disguised his resemblance to his parents, or else she'd have known him instantly.

The second time around, she'd had the power to force his true face and had known who he was. Thanks to his blood, her child was now even more powerful.

She could repurpose one of the satyrs as a surrogate womb for her baby. Once again she wished she still had her own nymph body with its life-sustaining blood. Her current mutant human vessel with its cocktail of blood from the higher races was powerful, but still couldn't sustain a life within its womb. Even a satyr's body cavity would be preferable—and more likely to work.

Unfortunately, they'd be a burden to carry unconscious, and she didn't trust them enough to allow them any shred of consciousness, even with her melding controlling their minds.

Frustrated by her lack of an ideal solution, Meri wandered toward the water, aiming to revisit the portal gateway before drifting back to her lab to make preparations for her last resort. The satyr only needed a heartbeat for a few hours—she could remove any part of him that made transport unwieldy. Calder would be the ideal subject with his half-immortal blood. She might even let him keep his cock.

The sun was too low in the sky for her to waste more time agonizing over a better solution. That would simply have to work.

She'd reached the sandy beach at the edge of the gardens and stopped, frowning down at the set of footprints in the sand. Her hunters knew the spot, but she hadn't requested anyone scout the place. If her enemies were watching, she didn't want to clue them into her plans. The dragons should not have been aware of this particular location—it was an ancient Haven portal, unused since her own expulsion. None of the living generation of dragons knew of it.

But there was one dragon who most certainly would have remembered, as this had been one of their favorite places for a tryst. And Dion's balls if that very dragon didn't just rise up out of the water in front of her.

Meri blinked, sure the sight was a mirage. His wet hair was darker from the water, his naked body bronzed by the golden light of the setting sun. Her heart lurched into her throat at the sight. That body had been hers once, in all its immortal magnificence. She'd have happily kept a male body if she'd been able to hold onto his.

Gritting her teeth, she reminded herself that *he* was the reason she'd been expelled from her home to begin with. Her desire for his body had ruined her life. But that old connection still existed. Her small taste of his blood all those eons ago sparked to life with a vengeance.

CHAPTER 43

AODH

*A*odh's head whipped around, his pale eyes glowing fiercely as he scanned the gardens for the disturbance. It hadn't been a sound, exactly, just an oddly disjointed sensation, as though he'd forgotten something. Then he saw the movement near the path and a tall, dark-haired woman stepped out of the shadows.

She wore a filmy black kaftan over a similarly sheer gown that looked like it could have been conjured from dragon smoke. Something in her eyes sparked recognition, but that disorienting sense of being split kept him rooted in place, undecided how to act.

"Who are you?" he asked.

"Don't tell me you don't remember. You and your champion tongue were my favorite toys, once upon a time. Did you come for one last fuck before I destroy your world?"

Recognition flooded him with icy dread. *"She's here,"* he shot quickly to Neph. Vrishti and the satyr had to be close behind him, but he didn't dare turn and betray to Meri that he wasn't alone. Forcing a more casual expression, he still couldn't bring himself to actually fake a smile.

"It's been a long time, Meri. The gardens here aren't what they used to be, but your presence certainly adds a certain sinister effect it never had before."

Meri chuckled and took a step closer. He could scent the distinct aroma of sex that clung to her, so familiar and once so arousing. Now it only made him ill, and he hoped once again that Neph heard him and was keeping Vrishti clear until they figured out what to do.

"You were always shit at telling even polite lies. But I have no illusions. I'm going to fucking *destroy* the Haven tomorrow, once I secure the Source for myself. You ... perhaps I will keep you just for fun."

A dark chill slithered into his mind, the cold blackness of it searing like a blade and causing his vision to darken for a second. He stood paralyzed. The old sensation of that first time she'd taken control of him was something he had never forgotten, but this was far worse. His consciousness rippled and split as her power asserted itself, like a face plunging just past the calm surface of a pool to peer into the depths beneath.

He silently called to Neph, but received no reply.

A second later, the sensation receded, and Meri looked up at him with her head tilted.

"You're holding out on me, sweet, feckless dragon. Whose lovely essence is it that's filled your well today? She's left you practically glowing with all that power. Have you fucked a nymph? Where is she now?"

Meri's eyes flashed with greedy glee, as though she'd just stumbled upon an unexpected sensual feast. Within the depths of his secret soul, he shouted a message he knew only Neph would hear, if the satyr were even listening now. *"Keep Vrishti away! Get her out!"*

Just as the last syllable filtered through the ether, he saw them both appear, drifting in behind Meri. Neph's eyes widened, and he bent to grab Vrishti's arm as she pressed her hands to the ground and began her chant to call the power up from the earth. Vrishti ignored Neph's word of warning, too engrossed in her magic. Vines erupted from the earth around Meri's feet as the woman turned.

The vines swiftly writhed and twined in knots around Meri's legs and up her body, catching her off guard and cocooning her lower half within seconds. Meri let out a yelp of surprise as she glanced down, then her gaze shot to Vrishti and she stared.

"An ursa female, and so powerful."

Vrishti bared her teeth and laughed. "You have no idea."

Aodh's chest warmed with pride at the blast of pure power that filled Vrishti's aura. She pressed her hands harder against the ground beneath her. The earth rippled in waves between her hands and Meri's feet, and a fresh wave of vines burst forth, wrapping entirely around Meri's body.

He and Neph would have to recreate their temporal barrier here to trap her while Vrishti's magic held her. The satyr rushed forward, his hands already glowing with the prepared spell, and Aodh sank to the ground tracing the circle around Meri's feet. She seemed oddly fixated on Vrishti, completely ignoring what would be her downfall within moments.

"Oh, my dear, I am sorry. *You* are the one who has no idea how very, very perfect you are."

Aodh's ears popped and a rush of air blew past him. The vines where Meri had been collapsed inward, tightening around each other in a sagging column now that they had no structure to bind to.

He blinked, disoriented for a second. Prickling shock flooded him when he saw her reappear a second later behind Vrishti. She pulled back a fist and a glint of shining metal caught the waning light as her blow hit the back of Vrishti's head, and the pretty ursa sagged limply to the ground. A split-second later, they were both gone.

"No!" Aodh yelled, racing to the spot where they'd been. Neph let out a curse and followed him, then popped out of sight.

"She can't have gone far with a passenger," Neph said. *"Split up and search the island."*

"We should never have fucking brought her. Sweet Mother, why didn't I sense the bitch?"

He disregarded the dangers of revealing himself and shifted, then launched into the air with a surge of flapping wings. Soaring over the island, he felt a strange sense of déjà vu, only this time he was hunting for his lover, and not a way out.

CHAPTER 44

VRISHTI

*V*rishti came to with the taste of blood on her lips and a groggy sense of displacement. The light was wrong—closed in, artificial—and it made her itch. She hated tight spaces.

She struggled to move, but her limbs felt like lead weights and her head refused to turn. All she could do was stare up at the stark light above her in its mirrored, dome-shaped fixture. It looked like a dentist's light.

Where the hell was she? The last thing she remembered was the glorious surge of pure power as she harnessed her magic to help capture the woman she now knew was the enemy Aodh had warned her about. The leader of the Ultiori.

She winced at the sudden, sharp spike of pain that pierced her skull. A shadow moved nearby and she fixed her attention to it.

"Where are we? What do you want? They'll find me, you know."

"They won't be quick enough," Meri said. "We'll only be here for a little while, then we're going home, you and me."

Something cold and sharp jabbed at her forearm and pain

shot into her tender skin. Pure panic gripped her, cold nausea knotting in her belly. The woman came into view then, her dark eyes filled with chilly contempt.

"Fate has shifted in my favor. I have a perfect vessel for the baby and enough Source power to move an army, all in one fat little ursa package."

She adjusted something at the side of the table, and out of the corner of her eye, Vrishti saw a transparent bag begin filling with her blood. Blood-filled tubes lay along each arm, warming as her blood flowed out of her.

Somewhere from far above, she heard the sounds of a skirmish. Meri cast a worried look to the ceiling before moving to Vrishti's feet and pushing against the table. Wheels creaked to life somewhere beneath her, and a shimmering veil between her and the ceiling rippled as they moved. Whatever barrier Meri had erected around them moved with them.

Vrishti closed her eyes, forcing herself to focus. First she sent out a silent plea, hoping her melded connection to Neph and Aodh still worked, but all she sensed was that cold, wet darkness, as though her very own mind had become a sealed cell with no lights. Then she reached deeper for the power she knew had to be there.

"Oh no you don't," Meri said, tutting softly. Then a sharp tug yanked at her mind like a leash. She could feel the power swelling in her, a fresh wave of her estrous pulsed in her core with its urgent ache. A sudden painful spasm gripped her and she cried out involuntarily, hating herself for her outburst in this woman's presence.

"It hurts, does it? Well, I have the perfect solution to your little issue. This will solve both our problems."

The wheels of the exam table rolled across a smooth floor, the lights fading for a moment before brightening again. The temperature dropped several degrees, lending some relief from Vrishti's heated body, but not to the pulsing ache of need in her womb.

Behind her head something shifted, beeped, and she heard a soft scraping sound. Warmth rushed across her and the table moved again, turned in a tight arc, and then stopped. The soft whoosh sounded again and from her new vantage a door slid shut behind Meri, leaving behind nothing but a seamless, solid wall of steel.

"Where are we?" Vrishti asked, her voice shaky and brittle, her vision already swimming from blood loss.

"Allow me to introduce you to your new little passenger. My pride and joy."

Meri turned the table again until Vrishti faced the center of the room. In front of her stood a wide pedestal of circular steel, and on top of it was a cylindrical tank filled with viscous, clear liquid tinged light pink. Her breath caught in her throat when she saw the tiny creature inside. It was no larger than a mango from her father's tree, its tiny hands balled into fists as it floated inside the tank. Tiny wings lay along its curved back, the membrane so thin it was nearly invisible with delicate webs of blue veins crisscrossed within. A vivid blue cord extended from its navel, the end attached to a network of biomechanical nodes at the top of the tank where it was fed from a measured container of red fluid that slowly diminished.

The shimmering field around them flickered, and Meri cursed toward the ceiling.

"They found you, didn't they?" Vrishti asked. "Nikhil and the others."

"It doesn't matter now. Everything I need is right here in this room. By the time this temporal bubble catches up to them, we'll be gone."

She hurriedly began tapping at the console that rested atop the counter on one side of the steel pedestal. The entire contraption lowered several feet, leaving the container of blood suspended above with the baby's umbilical cord stretching up out of the fluid.

Meri's hands shimmered with blue light when she disconnected the cord, then pushed more power into the viscous liquid inside the tank. A glowing, egg-like membrane formed around the fetus.

Then Meri turned and placed her hands against Vrishti's bare middle, between her navel and her pubic bone.

"What are you doing? No!" Vrishti said, finally discerning some hint of what the evil bitch intended.

"Do you want this little creature to die? Because that blood up there is all that's left to keep her alive unless you take over. She'll know where to go as soon as I show her the way—her only instinct now is survival, sustenance. And you have exactly what she needs."

Tears streamed down Vrishti's cheeks, her chest aching at the perfect shape of the beautiful, tiny creature inside that bubble in the tank.

"Please …" Vrishti begged.

"Not that you have a choice, but would you actually refuse to save that life? Do you know how many other babies died to create this one?"

Heavy sobs racked Vrishti's body as she watched the baby move, unable to tear her gaze away. Its little foot kicked out, pushing clawed toes that resembled a tiny, oblong paw at the impermeable barrier that encased it. The movement propelled it in a circle, and it rotated until she could see it head-on in all its perfectly formed wonder. It was a little girl, and Gaia's tears if Vrishti wouldn't do everything in her power to save it from whatever this evil bitch had in mind.

She nodded, her vision blurry from tears.

"Good," Meri said, a hint of smugness in her tone. Her hands tightened over Vrishti's womb and warmth flooded into her like Meri had opened up a faucet from her palm directly into Vrishti's core. The ache of her estrous disappeared, and before her eyes, the baby shimmered and grew translucent, just the way Neph's body did when he began a drift.

Mere seconds after the baby disappeared, her body felt infinitely fuller, a sense of perfect well-being overcoming her, even stronger than the sensation imparted by Aodh's magic breath. Her consciousness faded just as the wild power within her found purchase and enveloped the tiny creature as though that were its only purpose all along. But at the same time her heart broke for the what she'd been forced to do just to stick to her own principles.

With the certainty that the sacrifice had to be worth it, she let herself slip into darkness.

CHAPTER 45

AODH

$\mathcal{A}$odh rematerialized inside the sandstone corridor, Neph already by his side breaking into a dead run toward the sounds of conflict. They rounded the bend to the sight of several hunters locked in combat with a pair of turul females, fully shifted with wings spread and talons dug into two of their opponents.

The turul's predatory shrieks echoed down the corridor, sending chills down Aodh's spine. He hadn't heard a turul battle cry in eons, and this pair certainly knew how to use their lungs to drive fear into their enemy's hearts. The Ultiori they were currently ripping to shreds had their arms raised defensively, and the two behind them turned and started to run. Aodh leaped forward, manifesting his wings as he moved to propel himself over the fight. He flew past the fleeing hunters, landed in front of them, turned, and released a lungful of blazing white heat directly into their faces.

The hunters didn't know what hit them, backpedaled only a step before bursting into flames. They flailed and yelled for a second before falling to the ground in a pair of flaming heaps that quickly dissolved into blackened coals, then pale ash.

Aodh raised his head in time to see Neph in full satyr form rip the head off one man, then turn to the remaining hunter just in time for the turul to tear out his throat with her massive beak.

The corpses at their feet, the pair of turul shifted into two lovely women. One was statuesque and dark-haired, the other a petite redhead. They panted and bent over at the waist to catch their breath. The dark-haired one nodded her thanks at Aodh as he approached.

"We had them dead to rights, but thank you," she said. "Late to the party, are you?" She gave him and Neph a once-over. "You're too clean to have been here from the start."

Aodh looked down his pristine body, then at her blood-spattered one.

"We had another mission. Has their leader shown her face? We need to find her quickly."

The woman shook her head. "No sign of her, but we haven't been to the lower levels yet. There's talk of a lab down there. Calder was working his way up, and we're to meet them once we clear the upper levels. Come."

She turned and strode quickly the other way with her smaller partner falling into step beside her, red hair a wild, untamed mess falling down her back. The redhead paused and stuck out her hand.

"She's terrible at introductions. I'm Viki, she's Anya. We're from the Black Mountain Enclave." As she walked, she eyed them both. "I remember him," she said pointing at Neph, then she narrowed her eyes at Aodh. "You I've never seen, but you must be Belah's other brother. The sweet one."

Aodh frowned, too focused on following Anya to care much about Viki's attempt at conversation, but he nodded and forced himself to make conversation. "Sweet, am I? Compared to what?"

"Dark and dirty," Viki said with a grin.

Neph let out an involuntary snort that made Aodh jerk his head to the side and stare at his mate.

"She's talking about Ked and Gavra. Do you disagree with her description of my brothers?"

Neph shook his head. "No, but she's never seen you in action when you're angry or horny."

Aodh scowled and pushed past them. There was only one corridor, and he could see another turn at the end that appeared to be lit with electric lights. Hearing more sounds of fighting, he broke into a run.

Behind him, one of the turul women whistled, the sound both beautifully melodic and loud enough to make his ears ring. Moments later, the sound of flapping wings filled the corridor behind them and they were overrun with more turul flooding past in a single stream, feathered wings brushing along both sides of the hallway as they soared over Aodh's head and down the steep staircase in front of him.

They fought again, making their way through throngs of hunters at each level and leaving more bodies and piles of ash in their wake.

He and Neph kept moving, the slow progress pushing his panic higher the longer it took to find any sign of Meri or Vrishti. Every so often, he and Neph would lock gazes, and his sense of frenzy would magnify with the sensation of Neph's own desperation flooding into his mind.

They had to find her. The longer it took, the more danger she was in, and they absolutely *had* to get her back to the Sanctuary the next day.

They emerged from the tangled corridors into a central room where several smaller groups converged, and he finally spied Nikhil. Beside him, Neph let out a triumphant yell and he turned to see about half a dozen other horned satyrs rushing in, pale-faced and weary, but their eyes all swirling with battle frenzy.

Calder was in the middle of the group and broke away. It was then that Aodh saw Aurum and Nicholas. Belah and Nikhil and their turul mates were in the center of the room, speaking with Ked and Marcus. Several other dragons and turul were scattered around, catching their breath, but there was no sign of Meri or Vrishti.

Aodh crouched and shifted into his true shape, then let out a roar of rage. He'd tear down the entire base stone by stone, if he had to.

Instantly, seven satyrs materialized in front of him, and Neph's huge horned shape reached out from the group to calm him.

"We think we know where Meri took her," Neph said and glanced at Calder.

Calder gestured toward the doorway he'd come from. "Meri has a secret lab the next level down. Now that we've cleared her base, we need to get back down there. She had something … a captive … in the lab we want to take with us."

"Not Vrishti …" Aodh said, barely coherent in his rage. Neph's hand rested on his brow ridge, the touch managing to calm him enough for him to shift bach to his human form.

Aurum stepped closer to her satyr mate. "A baby. Likely a product of her experiments, but an innocent nonetheless. We didn't want to disturb it sooner because we feared it wouldn't survive, but now that we have control here, we need to go back for it. Perhaps we'll find some clue down there about what she's done with Vrishti."

Aodh took a deep breath, struggling to find the calm that was normally innate for him.

"It was my fault she came with us," he said to Neph.

"We both saw the power she's capable of. We had to let her try," Neph replied, his tone comforting despite the obvious sense of wrongness Aodh saw flickering through his lover's aura. Neph had seen something—sensed something—and now doubted his own words as a result.

"What did you see?" Aodh bit out.

Neph pressed his lips into a tight line and moved to follow Nikhil and the others through the doorway Calder had departed through.

"Don't you fucking walk away!" Aodh reached Neph in a few quick strides and grabbed the satyr's arm, spinning him back around. "What the fuck did you see?"

"Nothing!" Neph's voice echoed through the cavernous room, the outburst causing their entire group to stop and turn. His eyes swirled wildly and his jaw clenched, but he didn't pull away. "I can see all times at once, if I look. Past, future … Right now, I know my sister is pacing in her cell in the Haven because she's sensed Nereus awakening. Your brother is on his way to talk to her, to calm her down. I see those moments because they have nothing to do with me. But I can't see a goddamn thing when it comes to who I love the most. All I see is blood, and it terrifies the fuck out of me. I don't even know whose blood it is. We have to go and hope to all that is holy that it doesn't belong to her."

The tangled knot of emotions Neph projected through their bond hit Aodh like a sudden burst of fire. He swallowed a painful lump in his throat.

"You love her as if you've already mated. How many times did you meld?"

"Only twice, but I would give anything to have had a third."

"I should have marked her when I had the chance."

Neph nodded. "We should have blood-melded her the

second we got back. We'd be able to find her, if we had. I don't even get a sense of her from our melding—not even with your power added to mine."

"I don't deserve her after today." Aodh's stomach lurched at the thought of what his overconfidence might have caused. What would Meri do to her? Why had she taken her to begin with?

"Come. We don't have time to waste on self-doubt." Neph gripped Aodh's elbow and the liquid sensation of the drift washed through him. A moment later, they landed at the end of the stairwell just behind the others and followed Calder through a huge steel door that he accessed via a keycard at a blinking panel on the wall.

This level of the Ultiori base was even more modern than the ones above them, and they found themselves in a concrete and steel corridor on the other side of the door. Several yards beyond the door was an alcove where a pair of steel lift doors stood open, three slaughtered Ultiori hunters lying in a pool of blood on the floor. Aodh resisted the urge to set them on fire, but the blood caught his attention.

"Was that what you saw?" he asked, directing Neph's attention to the pool on the floor between them and the opening to the lift.

"No. The quality of the light is wrong. I'll know it when I see it."

Calder motioned for them to move. "The lab is this way," he said. Aodh sped up, flanking the younger satyr with Neph taking up the corridor on the other side of his nephew.

They rounded a bend where a large door stood open. Aodh peered in through it where he could see a massive glass tank. Around it the floor was flooded with slick fluid and blood, and several other dead hunters lay near the four door-ways that led into the big room.

"That was where she kept us," Nereus said, the first words

Aodh had heard him speak since they'd reunited. "Meri charmed the suspension fluid somehow to block our connection to the River, but Calder and his mates had enough power to break through. Now that we're out, I can feel Nyx again. She is hurting … I must get to her soon."

"It won't be so easy," Neph said. "She's blocked all the Haven's portals from the inside. Not even I have enough of the Source in my blood to force one open."

"This way," Calder said. Aodh tore his gaze from the carnage in the other room and followed Calder into a smaller room across the hall. This room was more steel and concrete, devoid of signs of conflict and sterile aside from a tiny trail of blood that began in the center of the room. Slight scuff marks on the floor betrayed the absence of some kind of table that had once occupied the spot beneath a collection of articulating lamps attached to the ceiling.

Neph cursed and Aodh's heart rate picked up. He bent down to the blood, which was sticky and nearly dried. A small smudge clung to his fingertip and he lifted it to his nose. The pungent, fertile scent was unmistakable.

"Sweet Mother, no," he croaked.

Most of the group stood back, grim faces observing them as Calder led Aodh and Neph into a lit cooler to the other side. They reached a solid wall and stopped.

"The baby we discovered was inside the room beyond this wall. There must be a way to open it, but we haven't found it. We'll have to drift inside."

Aodh's heart felt like a lead weight in his chest, his gaze fixed on the trail of blood that stopped at the wall. Vrishti's blood.

"By Gaia's grace, please. No." Neph's tone was a mournful plea breaking through the buzz of helpless panic that had risen up Aodh's spine. A moment later Neph was gone, his shape fading into mist and disappearing as he drifted through the wall. Aodh forced himself to focus on the power to move and followed.

CHAPTER 46

NEPH

*N*eph's silent prayers to Dionysus and Gaia went unheard. He landed in the room beyond the steel wall to the overwhelming scent of green grass and wild-flowers—Vrishti's essence was so deeply imprinted on his soul he'd know that scent anywhere.

A choked cry caught in his throat as he fell to his knees in the pool of blood. Aodh appeared beside him, his roar instantly filling the room, but even the deafening volume of it couldn't penetrate the sickening din of Neph's own failure.

"Sweet Mother," Aurum whispered when she arrived. The immortal Gold's power flooded the room with a despair that only barely matched what Neph already carried deep within him. "Where is the baby?"

Neph was transfixed by his own dark reflection in the pool of blood beneath him. The indecipherable vision had been this, he was sure of it. He should have heeded his gut, left her behind in the safety of the temple. It took him a moment of self-flagellation before Aurum's words sank in.

"What baby?" He tore his gaze away from his macabre reflection to look up at the others. Aurum, Nicholas, and

Calder had joined him and Aodh and were staring up at the small transparent tank in the center of the room.

"There was a fetus in the tank when I scouted this room earlier," Calder said. "It was hooked to that supply of satyr blood. There's no way it could survive for long without that supply."

"We were going to find a way to save her," Aurum said in a shaky voice. "To protect her from the mad bitch's experiments. We're too late."

Slowly Neph gathered his wits and mentally reached out to Aodh to calm the raging dragon. His roar had cracked the tank, which now slowly leaked pinkish fluid that began to pool on the floor in a swirling mix with Vrishti's blood.

"Satyr blood … that's what was feeding the baby," he said, catching a whiff of the stuff.

"We were hooked up to tubes in the other tank," Calder said. "Father and the others had been supplying her with blood for ages, but this child can't have been more than a few months past conception. My guess is that her experiments never worked until this one, or she'd have acted long before now."

The fog finally cleared from Neph's mind and the truth fell into place with a sickening snap. "She needed the power of the Source for the child all along. Your blood was the closest she could get. Vrishti's blood … Gaia's tears, she's taken her for her blood."

"Where?" Aodh yelled. "Where did Meri take her?" The dragon hauled Neph up by his shoulders and shook him. Neph met the dragon's wild gaze and shook his head.

"She couldn't use the portal we cast the trap spell on, even if it were clear of the trap. She has to have a backup plan."

"But she can't get into the Haven, so where would she go?" Calder asked. "We've all been locked out since Mother went mad. She'd need the power of the Source to open it, and Mother's the only one who can do that. From the inside."

Neph gave the others a pained look. "Vrishti's at the height of estrous, or would have been when Meri captured her. Her blood is pure Source. Enough power to open a portal from outside."

"Then we shouldn't wait to do this." Aodh snatched the dripping tube that dangled from the side of the wheeled examination table and held it over his mouth. Several red drops gleamed in the dim light from the console as they fell onto his tongue. He closed his mouth and swallowed before handing the tube to Neph.

It would be only half a blood meld, but Aodh was right—having Vrishti's blood in their systems would grant them both a closer connection to her. And as long as she remained in the human world, they would find her.

Neph held the thin tube over his own mouth until the tangy taste of her blood hit his tongue. The second he tasted her, his body flushed with a surge of unexpected power. He instantly shifted back into his full primal shape, dizzy from an overwhelming need to find his female and mount her until she was ripe and filled with his seed. He shook his head until the feeling passed and inhaled deeply to settle himself.

When he looked up, Aodh regarded him thoughtfully.

"I used to do that to you with only my breath," the big dragon said.

"You still do. Trust me, if we didn't need to get to her, I'd mount you right here."

"Ah … Shall we go get her, then?" Nicholas asked.

"She's downriver several miles, near the coast. I know the portal, but we need to be prepared for a battle. Aurum, get a message to Nikhil to send everyone to our location the second he can."

"Done," the golden beauty said. "We're with you."

Neph reached out both his hands. Aodh twined his fingers between Neph's and Aurum took his other hand, her mates linking hands on her other side. As a unit they drifted, landing a moment later to the deafening crash of heavy surf on a rocky shore.

He stared around, disoriented, his eyes acclimating to the darkness. There should have been a cave entrance here, but there was nothing but a wide expanse of sand and rocks. He released the others' hands and ran in the direction his instincts told him Vrishti would be in.

Rounding a rock-strewn berm, he found the eroded cave entrance, repositioned after ages of ocean wind and waves had worn down the far side and collapsed the old entrance. Dim lights filtered out from inside. It was far too quiet, but he and Aodh picked up speed, rushing toward the entrance and clambering over broken boulders to reach the opening where they could see an ancient tide pool that reflected the light from several abandoned torches.

Abandoned. The place was entirely abandoned, but Vrishti's blood was everywhere. Meri had painted a circle of glyphs beside the tide pool that was surrounded by the kicked up dust and pebbles of hundreds of feet trampling through. The space was only a fraction of the size of the cavern Aodh had hibernated within, so barely a few dozen men could have fit in this cave at once.

Staring back out into the darkness along the beach, he saw the signs he'd missed. The shore looked like an army had recently trekked across it, all the way into this small space that still reeked of blood and sweat and piss.

"Where the fuck did they all go?" Nicholas asked.

"Meri's gone home," Neph said. "And she took an army with her."

"Can you see the Haven, Uncle?" Calder asked. "Do you know they've breached it?"

Cold numbness weighed down Neph's limbs. His mind rejected the idea of even looking—confirmation of their failure to protect their home was the last thing he wanted to see.

A warm hand gripped his shoulder and he turned to see Nereus and the other four Thiasoi soldiers. They'd drifted in with as many of Nikhil's soldiers as they could bring.

"Assana will know what to do," Nereus said. "But we need to find a way back in, and this route is not an option."

"Your reunion with my sister should not have to happen under such dire circumstances," Neph said to his oldest friend.

"I was Meri's prisoner for centuries. I never expected my homecoming would be easy. We'll beat her one way or the other. How can we get home to do it?"

"The Sanctuary," Nicholas said. "We made it through the Rainsong portal at the Solstice. We can do it again now."

"No," Aurum said. "Our entry last time threw the energy of the barrier off balance almost catastrophically. It took us weeks to repair the damage we caused. And anyone not an ursa would need to be immortal just to survive the passage."

"Aodh and I can survive it," Neph said.

"That still doesn't solve the power balance issue," Aurum reminded him. "While I'm willing to risk pissing off the ursa to protect the Haven, we don't know what will happen if that much power becomes unstable."

A warm wind blew through the cave, setting the torches flickering and carrying with it the scent of summer that proved a painful reminder of how he'd failed Vrishti. Would her mother know what had happened?

"I may have a solution," a smooth, melodic voice said from the entrance. Everyone turned as a petite, gray-haired woman entered, seeming to float on the breeze for a moment before her feet appeared beneath the hem of her wispy dress and settled on the ground beneath her.

"Sophia. I didn't expect to see you here," Neph said. Despite knowing how powerful a seer Sophia North was, she still made him nervous whenever she appeared out of the blue like this.

Sophia turned her stormy gaze to regard him. "My world is in danger of destruction as much as yours is, if Meri manages to control the Source. I have a very valid stake in seeing her brought down."

"How do you propose we do it?"

"Just as the ursa says. But you will not enter the Sanctuary by a single portal. Four immortals must enter at each of the four portals: Stonetree, Rainsong, Sundance, and Windchaser. Only then can the power toll be balanced and the integrity of the barrier remain whole."

"My brother will help," Aodh said. "Aurum, will you?"

"No," Sophia said. "Your brother should not leave his mate. My great grandchild needs Ked's power to survive, and no breeding female should attempt the passage. The barrier takes life as a toll—it would damage her baby."

"I can go again," Nicholas offered, but his mouth snapped shut when Sophia's words sank in. "Wait, her baby?" His gaze shot to Aurum, whose eyes had widened, her hands dropping to her belly.

"Yes, her baby. And you, my child, are not immortal. Your power is not fed to the barrier when you enter because you have a blood tie to it already as a Stonetree."

"Who else is there?" Neph asked.

Sophia called over her shoulder, her voice a cross between a songbird and the whistling wind. The crowd that had congregated around the cave entrance parted and a scruffy, but well-built blond man appeared.

"Grandmother, stop jerking them around," the man said.

"Sometimes you are so full of shit it's no wonder your eyes are brown."

Sophia scowled at the man.

"Who are you?" Neph asked.

"Ozzie West. Fate's bitch this year, it seems. No thanks to her." He shot a mockingly cheery grin at Sophia, who narrowed her eyes.

"Impertinent boy. Fine, you want me to tell them the truth, I will. My grandson's Zephyrus's chosen heir. The West Wind won't be left out of the coming fight and has decided to one-up his brothers this time around. He has a soft spot for the Haven, you see, where the others do not."

"Nanyo … tell him." Ozzie crossed his arms. The old woman glanced around the cave at all the interested faces, but seemed no closer to revealing her secrets.

Nikhil finally barked out the command to everyone unnecessary to leave, which was instantly followed. Moments later, the only ones left behind were Aodh, Neph, and the two turul.

Before Neph's eyes, Sophia transformed, her diminutive shape growing until she was as tall as her grandson, with flowing jet-black hair and storm-gray eyes. Her smooth skin glowed with an inner power the likes of which Neph had never seen, and tiny blue-green glyphs seemed to dance within the depths of her dark pupils. When she held up her palms, the same glyphs appeared in twisting patterns upon her skin, spinning in a swirling blur he could barely track.

"What the hell are you?" Neph asked, his skin prickling.

"I am exactly what you believed I was all along. Of all the higher races, the turul are Fate's chosen children. I am the agent of Fate who helps direct them on their paths. The dragons are my master's second-favorite children. They have typically had a longer leash. Nymphaea and ursa have always had much more freedom to choose. It was the balance agreed upon by Fate and its counterparts."

"I know several dragons and ursa who would disagree about their supposed ability to choose," Aodh said.

Sophia turned her glyph-filled eyes to the dragon and lifted one shoulder in a tiny shrug. "It's up to the one marked by Fate to convince the others of their divine bond. Neph and Vrishti could have rejected you. Neph *did* reject you once. You were always meant to love the two of them. Whether they returned that love or not was their choice."

Aodh tensed, a tiny puff of smoke gusting from his nostrils the only sign of his barely contained rage. Neph rested a hand on his shoulder, opening his mind to hopefully ease the dragon's ire. *"Focus,"* he said.

Taking a deep breath, Aodh finally nodded. "So this makes you divine. And Ozzie … Zeph? What do I call you, friend? I knew Zephyrus long ago, but he hasn't manifested in ages."

Ozzie lifted an eyebrow at his grandmother, and Neph directed his questioning look to her.

"Zephyrus and his brothers are no more than whispers now," Sophia said. "They are pure power the way the seasons are to the ursa. It was easier for them to allow the turul to decide for themselves how to wield their power, rather than rule over them. When you're as old as the Winds, life grows tiresome. I am sure you both would agree. This is the first time they've chosen a vessel to inhabit, but with Zephyrus's power, Ozzie can serve as the fourth immortal."

"Are you all right with this?" Neph asked the man who stood, silent and listening with arms crossed over his broad chest.

"I am Fate's fool. I don't exactly have a choice. But if it helps you get to the woman you love, it's worth it. There are some perks." He gave Neph a half-smile as a warm wind blew through the cave again, sending ripples across the tide pool between them. The surface swirled into tiny eddies and then stilled to a glassy sheen displaying images that hadn't been there before.

Within the depths of the water, Neph had a clear vision of what had been muddled in his own mind. The Haven was displayed with all its glorious grottos and waterfalls, the residents engaged in a ferocious battle against the Ultiori hunters who had been granted access.

An army of antlered nymphs and immense clawed bears stood between the hunters and the Source, blood spilling left and right. Meri's army was too numerous. The others could only hold out for so long without assistance, even with the throngs of ursa streaming in to replace the fallen nymphs.

"We need to get in there," Ozzie said. "Or we may as well give up now. Your mate is here." The image shifted to one of the many luxuriously appointed prisons scattered around the Haven, where he could see Vrishti's unconscious shape lying on the bed.

Neph cursed at the sight of the red stripes down her limbs where the needles had been torn from her flesh and she'd continued to bleed, but even more shocking was the way she seemed to curl inward, her arms wrapped around her midsection as though protecting something.

"Sweet Mother, she's pregnant," Aodh said. "That's what Meri did with the baby from the tank. Maybe this is a good thing. If we can get to Vrishti and control that child, we can control Meri."

Nikhil emerged from the darkness outside the cave and Ozzie flinched at his sudden appearance. "My first imperative is to kill Meri. Forget controlling her."

"Mine is the Haven's welfare," Neph said. "But I'll be damned if I'm going to let Vrishti rot while we figure out how to gain access to get more defenders inside. We have to go now. Equinox has only just begun. Aodh and I will try to find a way in for the rest of you once we are inside and Vrishti is safe. One thing I am sure of is that it will have to happen *today*, or all is lost."

"But there is no way to communicate beyond the barriers that separate the Sanctuary and the Haven from the outside world," Nikhil said.

"This is where I come in," Ozzie said. He waved his hand and another breeze blew through. The images on the surface shifted again, and this time voices audibly echoed from within the Haven. A huge red dragon breathed fire at a throng of hunters while a nymph atop his back roared a battle cry. But the clearest sound was that of a whispered prayer that came closer and closer as the image moved, panning around to focus in on an isolated grotto Neph recognized.

Within the grotto, Nyx rested on her knees atop the bed, her face raised up to the moonlit sky that shone through a hole in the cave above her. Her voice was barely a whisper, but her plea was as clear as a bell. "Nereus, come back to me. Nereus, come back to me. We need you."

Across the pool, Nereus fell to his knees and reached out a hand, stopping just before he disturbed the surface. "My love," he croaked, then swallowed harshly. In a whisper of his own, he said, "I am coming home. We will save the Haven."

Wind rustled Nyx's hair, teasing it around her face like a soft caress. "Hurry," she said, then nodded and lay down on the bed.

"Winds can travel where bodies cannot," Sophia said. "We will ensure the required messages get where they need to go. We must not waste more time, but Ozzie and I will need you to take us to the portals before we enter."

"I am ready," Aodh said. He immediately went to Ozzie's

side, leaving Neph with Sophia. With only the most cursory communication to settle their tasks, they drifted.

~

A FEW MOMENTS LATER, Neph deposited Sophia beside the Sundance portal in the southwestern desert. Somewhere in the far Southern Hemisphere near Patagonia, Neph sensed Aodh materializing to deliver Ozzie to the Windchaser portal before traveling on to the Rainsong portal.

Neph left Sophia with only a word before drifting again to the Appalachian forest where he'd spent the most memorable days of his entire life with the woman he loved. He banged on the door to the cabin, but received no reply from inside. Wanting to waste no more time hunting down Cade, he drifted directly to the portal.

There were signs of recent passage suggesting Cade had already gone home—was likely already inside the Haven aiding in the fight. With a silent prayer for the ursa's good health, he whispered, "I am ready," trusting that the West Wind's powers were as strong as Ozzie's vision had indicated.

Barely a moment later, he heard a whisper in return.

"We are ready. Enter the portal now."

He and Aodh needed no further encouragement. Through their blood connection, Neph sensed the dragon's eagerness, and it propelled him through the opening Cade had left primed.

CHAPTER 47

AODH

Barely a few seconds on the other side of the Rainsong portal, the air currents around Aodh's head shifted, carrying Neph's scent along with two others. Before his eyes the three of them materialized, carried on the drift with Neph's power.

"I knew we would want to start with Sathmika," Neph said. "We owe it to the Summer Spirit to tell her what has happened to her daughter."

Aodh nodded and linked hands with the others. Another drift carried them swiftly to the center of Sathmika's throne room. It was every bit as polished and resplendent as the current ursa queen's, but almost entirely silent. Aodh might have blamed the silence on the time of night when they'd arrived, but he sensed no auras of resident ursa aside from the one vibrant and impatient aura of the woman who now sat on the throne in front of them.

When they materialized completely, Sathmika stood and rushed toward them.

"Where is my daughter? Does the attack on the Haven have anything to do with her?"

Neph nodded grimly. "She is there. The Ultiori have captured her. They're holding her while they carry out their attack to reach the Source."

"We can't let them reach the Source," Sathmika said. "That much power in the Lamia's hands … she would destroy us all. The Queen has sent every ursa capable of defending into the Haven to aid in the battle, but it won't be enough if the reports I've heard are to be believed. There are too many hunters. How the hell did she get that big an army in?"

Aodh and Neph shared a look. "Vrishti's estrous …"

Sathmika cursed, cutting them both off. "Gaia's tears, I knew I should never have let her go, but she found you … got you back." She gave Aodh an appraising look and pressed her lips together with a nod. "She has far more strength and willpower than I ever gave her credit for. Let's get her home in time to complete the ritual. The Summer Spirit *must* be transferred today. This body of mine won't endure another full season. The next Solstice is too far away."

The sounds of running footsteps made Aodh turn. The door to the throne room flew open and three figures ran in, one of whom he recognized.

"Brother!" Numa called. "Sweet Mother, we thought you were lost for good."

His sister launched herself into his arms, enveloping him in her sweet evergreen scent. She squeezed him so tightly his ribs cracked, then pulled away, already intent on the dilemma. "We need to get the dragons in to help fight. Theron and Bekim and I have been agonizing over the problem for the last few hours—ever since we got word of the attack."

"I know. But we don't have time to figure that out right now, sister. My mate is Meri's prisoner."

Numa's eyes widened and her mouth dropped open.

"Summer's daughter? She was due to return home today, wasn't she?" She turned to look at Sathmika. "As your heir, isn't she bound to you—primed to receive the Summer Spirit when you release it, no matter what?"

"She is, but I won't release the spirit until I know she's safe. She must be brought home."

Numa glanced around the room at all of them. The pair of ursa behind her kept their gazes fixed on her as though waiting for her command.

"What are you waiting for? Go get her!"

"I'm going with you," Sathmika said. She gripped both Aodh and Neph by the hand and nodded. In Aodh's mind, he sensed Neph's focus shift back to the Haven, and for the first time since he'd been sent away from the place and into Nyx's temporal prison, he could easily sense the path back in. A second later, Neph's power pulled him along into the swiftest, most violent drift he'd ever experienced.

They landed at the base of Gaia's falls, the roar of the water pounding against the rocks around them. Wading out of the water, a trio of shifted nymphs greeted them with bows drawn.

"Who sent you?" one asked.

"Ephyra, lower your weapon!" Neph barked. The nymph's head snapped up and she immediately dropped her bow when she saw her leader standing to the side, himself shifted to his full height, glorious with massive horns and sturdy hooves.

"Sire, forgive me. Uh, welcome home?"

"What is the status?"

"Assana's managed to erect an anti-drift barrier protecting the Source, but it's only a matter of time before the enemy fights its way through and makes it on foot. The Thiasoi are holding ground as well as they can with the ursa's assistance, but there are just too many to fight for more than a few hours. We don't expect to be able to hold them off past tomorrow without help."

"Get word to Assana to release Nyx. Nereus is returning, but doesn't have a way inside yet."

He eyed the pools of the Source and turned around to face the line of conflict where the Ultiori soldiers were engaged in combat with the nymphs and ursa. For every hunter that fell, another swiftly took his place; even as durable and impervious as the nymphs and ursa were, they were still grossly outnumbered.

"We have to fight our way through to get to Vrishti," Aodh said, seeing Neph's calculations of the path they would need to take to reach the outer edge of the Haven where Vrishti's cage lay, according to the vision Ozzie had shown them.

"Not only that, but if Nyx is going to release the binding spell she put on the portals into the Haven, she needs to get to the Source herself. I can't do it for her since I wasn't here when she locked them. But we don't want to risk letting in more Ultiori, anyway. We'll have to hope your sister can figure out another way to get the dragons inside."

Aodh eyed the giant tree that rose up from the central pool of the Source. Neph frowned up at it as well.

"It carries an uninterrupted supply of the Source into the Sanctuary," Sathmika said. "A precaution I had to take when Nyx went mad. I can use it to create a stronger barrier around the area, at least. You two go find my daughter and get her home!"

The ursa woman stepped into the pool, wading deeper until she reached the base of the tree. Turning her back to its trunk, she manifested her claws and dug into the wood behind her. Clear water seeped out where she pierced it and she began to chant.

"Go!" she yelled once more between incantations.

Aodh turned and faced a shimmering green barrier several yards ahead. Rushing forward with Neph on his heels, they pushed past and the barrier snapped shut behind them. He turned once to look back and saw a honeycomb of woven magic wrapped around the entire area that encompassed the Source. The nymphs who had guarded it were now outside, aiming and shooting arrow after arrow into the throng of Ultiori fighting their way closer to the Source.

When Aodh pressed his hand to the barrier, it felt like an electrified wall, the magic burning his palm instantly and sapping his power in much the way the Sanctuary's barrier had when they came through.

"Come on!" Neph yelled. He charged forward, lowering his head and barreling through the gap in nymphs and ursa who had parted to make way for him. Aodh shifted and let out a fierce roar that echoed off the rocky grottoes around them before he followed suit, charging through the throng of enemy fighters, breathing fire and slashing out with talons and tail as he went.

There were thousands of them to get through. Their weapons were knives and swords that were easier to carry and required no ammunition. The Ultiori had always stuck to the simplest, yet most effective weapons, and Aodh wondered if Nikhil's influence was what had kept their skills so well-honed. Their swords weren't enough to combat an immortal dragon's fire, but even he wouldn't be able to prevail on his own against so many.

He and Neph barely made it through without being overrun. The dense foliage of the Haven's forests and grottoes made it nearly impossible to fly, so the second they were clear, he shifted back to two legs and ran barefoot alongside Neph, their taste of Vrishti's blood acting as a beacon to her location. The closer they got, the stronger that sense of a tether pulling him in became.

When Neph disappeared in front of him, he realized they must be out of the anti-drift zone. He instantly followed suit, landing within the latticework of roots that created the cage where Vrishti was being held.

The second the drift ended, Adoh knew something wasn't right. A deafening roar sounded, followed by an anguished cry. When his vision cleared, a blur of fur and teeth flew at him and he raised his arms up defensively before the massive bear tackled him to the ground.

"She's feral!" Neph yelled. Aodh spared the briefest glance to the side where Neph sat, half-leaning against the bars of the cage, his face twisted in pain as he held a bloodied arm tight to his chest.

"She tasted your blood! Can you meld her like this?"

"I don't know. Let her pierce your skin too."

Aodh jammed his arm into massive black beast's mouth and she clamped down. He felt his bones strain under the force of her bite, but not even her powerful teeth were enough to draw blood from his impervious dragon hide.

Fire. His flames could weaken dragon skin, but he'd never tried it on his own flesh. Turning his head, he raised his other arm while enduring the raking claws that dug into the flesh of his shoulders and pushed him down. Her teeth sank into one shoulder and he endured it, wrapping his long legs around the bear's massive torso and holding on, intent on keeping her there until he could make sure she'd tasted his blood.

He turned his head to the side and breathed a gout of white flame against his forearm, hoping this would work. Pain tore through his body, and it was all he could do to keep the breath going long enough for his skin to blister and sear away.

Heartbeat racing from adrenaline, he twisted around, lifting the arm up and brandishing the burned flesh in front of Vrishti's wild, snarling face. She immediately bared her teeth and snapped, biting down hard enough to make Aodh yowl in agony. Blood flowed as she tore at his arm, rending flesh from bone.

"Now!" he yelled, shutting his eyes and forcing himself to open his mind for Neph to take command of their bond. He tangled his free hand into the thick fur at Vrishti's neck, hunting for the pressure point that would enable the meld to begin. He was abstractly conscious of how silky soft her fur was, and could easily imagine he had his fingers tangled in her human tresses the way he had when the two of them had first made love.

He reached beyond the pain with Neph's help and found the secret garden within Vrishti's soul—the place where her spirit connected with the Source. She was there now, but instead of sitting silently by the shore of the water, she now sat upon a small island in the center, the waters of the Source like a moat around her, and she held a tiny infant in her arms.

"It's us, Vrishti. We aren't here to hurt you."

"I have to protect her! She is innocent. Don't let anyone hurt her."

"We won't," Neph said. "But you have to calm down and let us help you."

"Meri wants to hurt her," she sobbed. Tears cascaded down her cheeks, dripping onto the damp, dark curls of the tiny head that she held against her shoulder.

"We'll protect her, just please come back to us. We need to take you home. Both of you."

The pain in Aodh's arm lessened significantly. When he opened his eyes, he barely had time to register Vrishti's shift back into human form before she crumpled into a ball on top of his prone body. He sat up and wrapped his damaged limbs around her, ignoring the pain that lanced through his shoulders where she'd latched on, leaving behind painful bruises where he hadn't allowed her to break his skin.

"What happened, love?" Aodh said softly, his lips brushing the top of her head as she clung to him. Neph came to kneel beside them and pressed a hand gently to her back.

She shook her head. "Get her out of here. I don't care what you do, just get her out!" Lifting a shaky hand, she pointed to the sunken bath.

For the first time, Aodh saw the limp body floating on top of the blood-tinged water. Neph lurched to his feet and strode across the room, splashed into the water, and flipped the body over.

"It's Meri. She isn't dead, just unconscious. Mauled to within an inch of her life."

"Finish her off, for fuck's sake," Aodh snapped, tightening his grip around Vrishti's shaking form.

Neph hauled the body out of the water and knelt beside her, his continued ministrations sending Aodh's pulse into the stratosphere again. "If you don't do it, I will. Stand aside so I can burn her to fucking ashes."

"Bad idea," Neph said, shaking his head. "As long as she still draws breath, her spirit is tied to this body. The second we kill her without ensuring we can control where her spirit goes, we lose our advantage."

Vrishti let out a mournful moan and Aodh cupped her head, murmuring a soft whisper to comfort her that carried a dose of his breath for her to inhale. She quieted and he relaxed a little.

"So we complete the spell we attempted before. Trap her inside a barrier then send her spirit back where it came from."

Neph sat back on his heels and shook his head again. "That would only work out there. When a nymph dies outside the Haven, her spirit is sent to the winds. Inside the Haven, she'd become one with the Source. With Meri blood-melded to an entire army, if we just kill her outright, her spirit jumps into the nearest blood-melded creature. Blocked from those creatures, she goes back to the Source. Neither option is ideal. Keeping her body alive for as long as possible is the only way to control her."

"Well, then what the fuck do we do with her?"

"Vrishti," Neph said, looking at the whimpering girl on Aodh's lap. "When did you go all mama-bear on her and do this?"

"When I woke up inside this cage something snapped. She was about to tie me down, and I just couldn't let that happen. I remembered the story Nicholas told me about what happened to his mother. What they did to her. I knew I had to fight back, but after that, I … everything is fuzzy."

"So not long after you arrived. But we fought our way through armies still clearly intent on reaching the Source. Her spirit is still intact, and likely still has control of her army's minds too. We shouldn't let her closer to the Source, so taking her out of the Haven is not an option. Come on, let's see if Nyx has come to her senses yet—she might have some ideas."

Neph stood, hoisting Meri's unconscious body in his arms. Blood-tinged water dripped down his naked legs as he slung her over his shoulder.

"Kitten, can you feel our blood meld? When you bit us, it should have been completed. We each had a dose of your blood before we got here."

Vrishti wrapped her arms around Aodh's neck as he stood, and he could feel her slight nod against his shoulder.

"It's like the mind meld, only stronger—like my veins are filled with firewater. Hot, but … powerful."

"Good," Neph said, glancing back at them as he prepared to drift. "We may need all our power to get through this. Let's go find my sister."

They arrived outside Nyx's grotto to the sounds of strident arguments. Ephyra glanced up and scowled at Neph when he approached, Meri's wet body still slung over his shoulder.

"Sorry, sire, she won't leave."

"I never said I wouldn't leave, Ephyra," Nyx said. "I said I couldn't leave *yet*. I was waiting for my brother. There's something we need to take care of. Bring the body inside, Neph."

He followed his sister's instructions, laying Meri's unconscious body on the bed where he'd seen his sister praying in the vision. Nyx gripped the damp rips of Meri's shirt where Vrishti had clawed her and tore them open to reveal a deep gash in the woman's side.

"The bathwater she was in had just enough healing magic to prevent total blood loss, but this body of hers is at the edge of death. No doubt the little shit is wishing we would kill her." Nyx spat in the unconscious woman's face and stood.

"Do we need to heal her?" Aodh asked.

"No. She's transfused herself with enough blood from her victims that she's mutated into a creature who won't easily die. Her body is just a little too durable, but her spine took just enough damage to no longer allow her to control her own body. The human central nervous system is delicate that way."

Neph nodded. "That's what I thought. We'll secure her here until we can find a way to sever her power over her armies."

"That will be no easy task," Nyx said. "As you both know, the only way to break her hold on them is for a more powerful creature to blood meld her victims. But there are thousands out there. It's a less daunting task to simply kill them."

"Please," Vrishti whispered, catching Neph's attention. He strode back to Aodh's side and stroked Vrishti's cheek, brushing her hair away from her pretty face. Brown eyes gazed up at him, beseeching. "I don't want to be here. Can we go home now?"

"Of course, kitten. Nyx, can you secure her in here?"

"Yes. If you see Gavra, send him to help—he created the perfect prison for me before. I trust he'd be able to create one as impenetrable for her as well."

"Will do," he said, and they exited the grotto.

The Haven was a mass of carnage. They skirted the fighting as well as they could, Neph leading the way while Aodh followed, Vrishti securely tucked against him with his wings manifested and cocooned around her.

The Ultiori hunters were every bit as blood-hungry as they'd been before. As he ran, Neph pummeled their soft bodies with his huge fists and impaled them with his horns. Each time a body fell, he heard their death rattles and their final words. Before too long, the repetition began to haunt him with its promise.

"Death will never stop me," they all said, the words carrying the same intonation and cold certainty every time they were spoken.

Assana and two Thiasoi maidens met him halfway, flanked by a huge brown bear and Gavra in his fully shifted red glory. Fire shot over their heads at the hunters who closed in behind, turning their pursuers to ashes while Silas tore the ones ahead of them to shreds.

The maidens ran alongside with Assana leading the way straight back to the Source. Gavra and Silas held the line behind them, beside the rest of the nymphs and ursa, fighting a bloody battle to protect the Source.

Here and there a Hunter would make it through the line, only to be knocked back by the powerful magic of the barrier Sathmika had erected.

"Mama!" Vrishti yelled, leaping out of Aodh's arms and running to the barrier. She passed through it without effort and fell into her mother's arms.

"Baby, you can't stay here. Take my gift and go. We have no time for formalities tonight. You are the Summer Spirit. Go home and be safe."

"No! I can fight too. Look!" She turned around and pressed her hand to the ground at the edge of the pool her mother stood beside. Vines surged up from beneath her fingers, but they only tangled around the pebbles before falling back beneath the soil.

"The baby in your womb needs all your power now, Vrishti. Go home and keep the baby safe."

Neph stood just outside the barrier, avoiding contact with it while he waited for mother and daughter to say their farewells. Sathmika had a look of grim determination in her eyes, and with a sinking feeling he let himself see the path that lay before her.

"Vrishti, let her do what she needs to do and say goodbye. We need to take you home."

Vrishti shook her head, giving him a bewildered look. "We have to protect the Source!"

"No, kitten. We have to protect *you*. That baby Meri put inside you means something to her. We can't risk letting her have it again. If she survives this somehow, she'll come for you."

Sathmika bent and rested her hands on Vrishti's shoulders. She turned her daughter to face her and urged Vrishti to look up into her eyes. A flash of light surged beneath Sathmika's skin as she pressed her lips to her daughter's in a chaste kiss. In that instant the light flooded them both, blasting brightly from the sunburst tattooed on Vrishti's chest, and then Sathmika's skin returned to its previous deep brown.

The older ursa matriarch held her daughter's face for a moment longer, her gaze glassy with unshed tears. Then she nodded once and stood, wading back into the Source where she pressed her back to the tree once more.

"I have enough energy to last through the day. Find a way to preserve the barrier and let the others inside before my power is gone."

"Then you'll come home, right?" Vrishti asked. "I need you."

"No, baby. You don't need me. You have everything you need. Learn to trust the Summer Spirit and you will be fine."

"Vrishti!" Neph called, and Aodh echoed the call beside him. "We have to go."

Around him, a chilling chant was being repeated among the Ultiori hunters. *Get the ursa bitch. Keep her. Hold her.*

"Meri's in their heads still," Aodh said. "All of them."

Looking over his shoulder, Neph saw Assana, Silas, and Gavra still holding off the throng of hunters. When Vrishti finally passed back through the barrier protecting the Source, a mad surge pushed against the defenders. Half a dozen frenzied hunters rushed him and he turned, putting his body between Vrishti and the mob. Aodh's wings whipped out and wrapped around them, shielding them from the rabid attackers.

"Hold on," Neph said and Vrishti clung to both him and Aodh when they drew their collective power and drifted back to the Sanctuary.

CHAPTER 49

AODH

"She's going to die, isn't she?" Vrishti asked, still staring out the window of her dawn-lit quarters in the Rainsong Clan Lodge. She didn't cast a glance to Aodh or Neph, but Aodh moved closer to her anyway, needing contact as much for his own comfort as for hers.

"What do you see, kitten?" Neph asked softly.

"Don't ask her that," Aodh snapped. "She doesn't need the burden of your goddamn curse right now."

Vrishti gave him a sad look and tugged at his hand. He lowered himself to a crouch in front of her and looked up into her eyes.

"I suppose it isn't really a question I don't know the answer to. I can see it as well as you can. I hate feeling like we're just waiting for the inevitable."

Aodh squeezed her hand. "We aren't just waiting. My sister's working on a solution with Sophia North and her nephew. We can go help. Neph and I just want to make sure *you* are all right first. You and the baby."

Those words sounded so foreign coming from his mouth, and felt even stranger when the odd thrill surged through him at the idea of being a father again for the first time in several thousand years.

Vrishti gave him an odd look and a half-smile tugged at the corner of her mouth. "I felt that. You didn't even get me pregnant, but you're still happy about this baby? I'm not even sure if I'm happy about it. I just wish I'd had a choice."

"We're happy as long as you are, kitten," Neph said, lowering himself to the floor beside Aodh. The big satyr sat back against the wall to one side of the window with his knees bent and his arms rested atop them. "If we need to find a way to … take care of it … we will."

Her hands pressed tighter against her belly and she shook her head. "No! Don't you dare suggest hurting it!"

Neph expelled a relieved sigh. "We'll love and protect the baby as if she were our own. All our races care fiercely for our offspring. Loving your child is instinctual for us, regardless."

"Even if it's really *her* baby?"

"But it isn't hers, either," Aodh said. "No more than Nicholas was hers. No more than my brother Ked's child was hers—or might have been, if we hadn't rescued Evie from the Ultiori before they had a chance to steal it. This baby was an innocent victim, stolen from another Ultiori captive. We rescued her."

Vrishti dipped her head and rubbed her palms in a circular motion over her slightly swollen belly. "I wish we had more time to … to process all this. But we have to find a way to save the Haven."

Time. The bane of Aodh's existence would never cease to haunt him. Either he had too much of it, or not nearly enough.

"We can have a little bit," Neph said. "More than we think we have, at least."

Aodh's gaze shot to Neph. "What do you mean?"

"I wouldn't chance more than a few hours, maybe a day. But the Sanctuary is fed from the Source, so I have access to enough power now to literally give us time. Time I think we need. To properly mate, to decide what to do next. To help Numa and the others figure out how we're going to get Nikhil's soldiers inside to end this war."

"Will you be able to save my mother?" Vrishti asked.

Aodh felt the pang of Neph's uncertainty before the satyr could hide it. Vrishti's frown betrayed that she'd sensed it as well.

"I don't know. If we can find the answer soon enough, perhaps."

"Then we should start now," Vrishti said.

Neph stood and reached out his hands to them both. When they drifted, it was only a short distance to the lush courtyard in the center of the lodge. The Rainsong Lodge was largely deserted, aside from the three of them and a handful of guests, including Numa, her two ursa companions, Sophia North, and Ozzie West.

The courtyard they stood in was a huge garden spanning the large central wall of the throne room. The knotted pathways surrounded a clear pool with a big, round stone in the center that reminded Aodh of the pool in the center of the Dragon Glade, only this one was covered in verdant moss and dotted with tiny yellow flowers.

Neph shed his clothes and dove into the water, coming up on the island and motioning to the pair of them as he settled back. He appeared tense and ready for action, his brow furrowed. Vrishti dropped her robe to the ground and dove in after him and Aodh followed, admiring the pretty ursa's complete lack of self-consciousness that was so at odds with how he remembered her the first time they'd met.

"It'll only take a moment if you both help," Neph said when they settled beside him on the island. With Vrishti between them, they linked hands and their minds easily followed.

Within moments, the intention was as clear as if it had sprung from Aodh's own thoughts. They would create a temporal bubble, just large enough to encompass the lodge itself, that would speed up time inside and thus slow down the passage of it outside the bubble. They would feel no different, but for every hour that passed within their little bubble, only a minute would have passed outside it.

He sent his sister a brief warning that was met with an enthusiastic "hell yes" before they proceeded. With their three powers merged, it took a split-second for them to erect.

When Aodh opened his eyes, he met the gazes of the two people who had monopolized his thoughts for centuries, and it hit him like a tidal wave that *this* moment was finally the moment he'd been waiting for all that time.

For once, he believed time was on his side.

"Are you sure we have time for this?" Vrishti asked. Her body thrummed with desire for the two men beside her. After all they'd been through, after learning how much she could endure, she really hoped that this time she could just let go and enjoy the pleasure they gave her.

Her control of her own body had become a sense of pride for her since the first night she'd followed Neph's commands to discover her own pleasure. That control had been completely stripped from her within the past day after Meri's horrific invasion—of the Haven and of her own womb. She would do everything in her power to protect the child she now carried, but it would take more time for her to feel fully in control of her body again. Right now, she just wanted to trust in the pleasure her mates could give her and let her body enjoy what it needed to feel complete. And if this worked, she would hopefully be granted enough time to recover.

Neph nuzzled her neck on one side, inhaling deeply as though she were his only source of air. On her other side,

Aodh stroked her hair and cupped her cheek, tilting her head so he could gaze into her eyes.

"Our meld should tell you all you need to know," Aodh said. "What do you think?"

The meld. Of course. She'd felt the rush of awareness flood her in those moments after she'd tasted Neph's blood, followed by Aodh's, in her protective maternal rage. The link was still there, as strong as ever, and she closed her eyes and dove beneath that shimmering surface of their shared power. What she saw was akin to looking through the glass at an aquarium, but everything on the other side appeared frozen.

The entire Sanctuary outside the Rainsong Clan Lodge was in a kind of stasis, and when she let her consciousness fly over the landscape and down Gaia's Falls into the Haven itself, she found the same had happened there.

The chaos of the fighting had stilled completely. Arrows hung suspended in mid-flight and drops of blood hovered inches above the ground. Hunters remained at the edge of death while even more of their counterparts stood ready to take their place when they fell. From her vantage, she could see the vast scope of the battle that raged in the Haven and how terrifyingly outnumbered they were.

Vrishti let her mind explore this new landscape of frozen time while Neph and Aodh explored her body with lips and tongues and soft caresses. They pressed her down to the soft, mossy rock, and her body rejoiced in the pleasure while her mind still flew, separate from the experience yet fully aware and engaged just the same. It was as though she could exist everywhere at once, the way the summer sun can shine its light upon an entire continent, blessing the living creatures with its warmth.

Her consciousness reached her mother where she remained waist-deep in the crystalline pool of the Source, her back up against the sacred tree she'd tricked Silas into growing to save the Sanctuary. Her mother's power held strong in the moment, but without the Summer Spirit that now resided in Vrishti's soul, Sathmika would not last. It saddened her, but she knew her mother's decision had been the best one. To wait longer to transfer her inheritance would have been disastrous.

The other clan leaders appeared outside Sathmika's barrier, lending their own power to fortify it, but Sathmika called them off. It was not their time yet. Summer was due to sleep, to rest and rejuvenate to be reborn again when Spring had finished her reign. Vrishti recalled the lessons she'd learned about the ursa hierarchy. When she was at her full power after her first child, she would be ready to take over ruling her race for a season, but in ursa lore, a season could mean several centuries. She had time.

They could have more time, if she wanted. With her power merged with her mates, they had command of time— could manipulate it to their needs, but did they dare abuse that power? Could it help them win?

She touched Neph's head, reluctantly urging his mouth away from its slow passage down her torso. His gaze shifted to hers, eyes swirling and drunk with need.

"Can we take too much?" she asked.

Aodh lifted his mouth from her breast and glanced at Neph, his lips a tight line. "We'll take what we need to win," he said. "So it doesn't matter."

"But it does," Vrishti said. "I need to know what the consequences are if we don't take full advantage of the time we give ourselves. It can't be infinite, can it? There has to be a limit."

Neph leaned on one elbow, leaving his other hand resting lightly over her swollen belly. "There is and there isn't a limit.

The temporal bubble doesn't stop time. It simply shifts the parallax so time moves differently around us. It could go slower or faster, but we've chosen to make it go slower.

"The consequences can be catastrophic if we take too long. We are taking power from the troughs of the waves and feeding them to the crests. If we don't give the power back at some point, the crests become too big to control. Think of it like a tsunami. If we don't maintain control over the crest, it can destroy us. So we have a limit on how long we can let it build before it becomes too much power to rein in."

"How long?" Vrishti asked.

"With the three of us fully mated, we can buy ourselves quite a lot of time. The blood meld is only the beginning."

"I want enough time to save my mother," Vrishti said.

"Then let's not waste more time," Neph said. "The power isn't beyond our control yet—far from it. Look again at your vision, but pay attention to the very surface of it—the ripples at the edge of the bubble."

She closed her eyes and focused again, first acutely conscious of the way their hands still roamed gently down her body and back up, but they refrained from more distracting touches and soon she found their rhythmic caresses calming and reinforcing her focus on the rhythm of the waves that made up the bubble around them.

After some time, she saw the pattern rippling over its surface in a continuous flow like the tide traveling across the surface of the ocean. The ripples were tiny, but after a few moments, they grew. With the slightest effort of will, she discovered she could control their size. With each adjustment, she observed the world beyond the bubble. Time slowed down the larger the ripples became, and at a certain height, she was sure time had stopped.

"It isn't possible to stop time entirely, kitten," Neph said, sensing her question. "Nor can we reverse the flow. But it takes power to maintain this state. If we aren't diligent, the power feeds on itself, and the ripples grow larger until we no longer have the power to control it."

"But we *can* control it, can't we? The three of us together are powerful enough."

"Once we're fully mated, we can maintain the bubble long enough to work out a solution, but not indefinitely. A day of our own time is worth the years we give back to the lives we can save."

A day. Vrishti stared up at the cascade of hanging leaves from one of the big trees that arched over the pool. It was the beginning of Spring today, and the hanging tendrils were covered with tiny pink flowers amid the pale green leaves that signaled new awakening life. She would have given more if she could, but every second was worth taking advantage of if it meant she could protect the ones she loved, protect her home, and save her mother's life.

"All right," she said.

Warmth bloomed in her belly when Neph pressed his lips to hers again. She hummed into his mouth as their tongues slid together, caressing and tasting before he pulled away and Aodh took his place.

"I'm going to mark you like I should have done ages ago," Aodh murmured after breaking their kiss and leaving her breathless.

"Please," she whispered, not sure whether she was responding to his promise or to the teasing caress of Neph's fingertips as they moved back and forth along the juncture of her thigh.

Neph gripped her thigh a little tighter and she lifted it, letting him pull her legs apart while Aodh bent and pressed his lips to her sternum right over the glowing sunburst and moved lower.

The pale-haired dragon worked his way down, lingering at her breasts for an eternity until wet heat flooded between her legs. Neph murmured his approval, his fingers dipping between her folds and sliding back and forth in a lazy caress as he watched her from above.

"Don't tease me," she moaned. "It's not allowed anymore."

Neph smiled down at her and Aodh chuckled with his lips still wrapped around one nipple.

"Oh, but kitten, it's so much more fun when we make you beg." He pushed two fingers into her slick, sensitive opening and turned them, hooking the tips to rub against her inner wall until she arched and cried out.

Aodh wrapped his big hand around her other thigh and pulled it wide, hooking her leg over his hip. His thick, hard cock brushed against the curve of her ass, his tip tickling so close to her spread folds she tilted her hips in an effort to get him closer. But they both seemed content to simply tease, and she bit her lower lip to suppress a moan.

Aodh's cock disappeared from between her thighs as he moved lower, continuing to hold her wide open while he explored down her belly with his mouth and tongue. He paused at her navel, giving it a sensuous kiss, then darted his tongue out and tickled beneath it with the forked tips.

Vrishti's eyes flew open at the slight sting of lashes that seared her lower abdomen, right over her womb. Looking down, she saw white light coating Aodh's tongue that seemed to flow into a pattern he was tracing into her skin. He was marking her. And while it hurt, her heart swelled with the rightness of it. When the circular pattern was complete, he blew out a pale cloud of smoke that settled over her belly, removing the pain completely and leaving behind a beautiful glowing mark.

Aodh turned his gaze to her. "I am yours always, Vrishti."

She bit her lip again and could only nod due to the hard

lump in her throat. *"I love you,"* she finally managed to mentally blurt out when she remembered she didn't need a voice to tell them how she felt.

His tongue darted out again, swirling in smaller circles below the mark he'd just left, and his gaze grew heated as he made his way lower with those glorious wet caresses. His mouth found her clit a second later and sucked it in. Between that delicious stimulation and Neph's fingers still fucking deep into her, she gave up all restraint. The pleasure rocketed through her in a flood as she came, delicious aftershocks lingering between her thighs as both men drew out her pleasure for several more minutes before withdrawing to let her breathe again.

"Your turn," Aodh said to Neph. "Where do you want it?"

"Wherever you choose to put it."

Through their connection, Vrishti sensed a charge of uncertainty from Neph, as though he hesitated to accept that he was worthy of the gift Aodh was about to give him. She sat up and twisted around, pushing her hands against Neph's shoulders.

His gaze shot to her, eyes wide. "What are you doing?"

"You won't make the decision, so I will. Put it here," she said, pressing her palm over the half-healed bite mark she'd left on Neph's left pectoral when he came to rescue her.

Aodh obeyed, and as his tongue lashed over Neph's chest, she took the satyr's cock in her hand and stroked him to full hardness again. Neph's eyelids fluttered, his wince of pain disappearing as she pressed his thick tip to her entrance and sank down onto him.

In only a few slow strokes, her pleasure had risen to its peak yet again and she slowed, panting and biting her lip to avoid crying out. Aodh and Neph both watched, their gazes enraptured as she rocked her hips on Neph's cock.

"Don't stop, kitten," he growled, pushing his hips up into her. She let out a gasp and froze, digging her nails into his stomach.

"It's my turn to finish marking you both, but I need … need your essence first. All of us together, right? To seal my marks."

She gave Aodh a beseeching look and he raised his brows, a sly smile twisting his lips. "Say it, sweetness," he said.

Groaning, she rolled her eyes. "I want you both to fuck me. Come inside me together. Please."

With a rumble of approval, Aodh moved. His big body loomed for a second as he positioned himself behind her, straddling Neph's thighs. Then he wrapped his arms around her and pressed his lips to her throat.

"This is my favorite thing in the universe," he whispered, cupping her breasts and briefly toying with her nipples before resting a big hand on her shoulder and pushing her down against Neph's chest. The big satyr caught her head in both hands and pulled her into a kiss. She latched on hungrily, groaning in anticipation as Aodh fondled her backside before pressing his thick tip against her already filled opening. She lifted up off Neph's cock far enough that only his tip remained inside her.

"That's right, love, let me into that tight sheath of yours." Aodh gripped her hip, holding her steady while he added his tapered head to Neph's and pushed into her ready opening alongside the satyr. The thickness was only a slight adjustment at first, until both their tips were seated and Aodh gripped both her hips in his hands, pushing deeper.

Neph grunted into her kiss, tangling his hands in her hair as he lifted his hips and pushed deep in tandem with the dragon.

They held still for an agonizing second that seemed to

last an eternity, their thick cocks both pulsing with restrained need to fuck. And then they moved, their wild desire flooding her mind the only sign of what she was in for. But they knew her need so well they knew she would not protest the rough, wild fucking that followed. She held on for dear life as they pounded into her, their cocks filling her and stretching her so perfectly.

She clung to Neph's shoulders and he reached up and gripped her fingers, twining his hands into hers and holding them above his head. "Hold on, kitten," he said, and she nodded against his shoulder, panting and grunting with every punishing thrust. He released one of her hands, and a second later she felt it slip between them to find the tight, needy bud of her clit and rub.

"Going to come so fucking hard," he growled, and when her body spasmed with the first wave of her climax, he cried out. Her core clenched around both of them, and Aodh's fingers tightened to a painful grip at her hips as his own sonorous roar echoed through the courtyard and both their cocks erupted inside her, filling her with their essence even as her own gushed forth around them.

Aodh's panting breaths filled her ears and she felt herself being turned. Still sandwiched between them, their cocks buried deep, she found herself on her side with one man at her front and the other at her back, both so tightly wrapped around her she couldn't move.

"Never fucking letting you go again," Aodh said.

"I'm fine with that," she answered.

Gradually they relaxed and slipped out of her. She dipped her hand between her thighs to gather their mixed essence in her palm. First grabbing Aodh's damaged arm, she slicked the glowing fluid over the deep and still open teeth marks that remained there, then took another measure and rubbed it into the mark on Neph's chest.

With that complete, a gradual sense of calm and peace filled her entire being. They were one, complete and whole, and with that thought, she knew that anything was possible.

They'd only lain there for a few moments, basking in the afterglow of their lovemaking, when Vrishti heard footsteps. Several of them, in fact. Frowning, she clenched her eyes shut, hoping she could ignore the sound and savor the last few moments of solitude with her mates.

She knew better, and the Summer Spirit was the one who urged her up and alert, invigorating her the way the morning sun had always done in those days when she had enjoyed rising and heading to school. She'd arguably loved school more than most kids in those days, but that Vrishti had never known what kind of pleasure and comfort she'd be giving up by leaving bed as an adult.

But it only took a silent reminder of what was at stake for her to sit up and greet the group of individuals who approached her now.

Aodh's sister Numa led the group, her deep green eyes flashing with excited light. On one side were the pair of ursa males who'd agreed to stay behind and guard the Sanctuary while the rest of the ursa left to fight the battle to protect the Source. On her other side were the two turul who had helped

Aodh and Neph enter the Sanctuary. Numa was the only one Vrishti knew very well, but she appreciated the others' loyalty and dedication to their cause.

"What is it, sister?" Vrishti asked, the endearment slipping out before she could censor herself.

Numa beamed, her gaze shifting briefly to her brother before looking at Vrishti again. "I am so sorry to disturb you three, but we have what I hope is good news. I think we've found a way to open a portal that will allow the dragons and turul outside to come in to fight."

Vrishti stood excitedly, slipping back into the robe she'd shed when she'd come out into this idyllic courtyard to enjoy the company of her mates and complete their bonding. She crossed the small stone footbridge back to the other side. As she approached Numa, the dragon's aura flickered to life and she blinked, halting in confusion at the strange combination of glowing clouds that surrounded the five people in front of her. Confused, she glanced over her shoulder at her mates.

"You're seeing their auras, that's all," Aodh said. "We share powers now that we're blood-melded."

"Oh," Vrishti said, turning back to look at Numa. Something was odd, but she couldn't put her finger on it.

"What is it?" Numa asked. "Do you see something?"

"Just your aura, I guess," Vrishti said, shaking it off. "Let's go back to the library to talk."

But as she fell into step beside the dragon, she couldn't shake the sense that Numa's aura wasn't right. She looked back at Neph and Aodh again. Each of them was surrounded by glowing, golden clouds with clear, shimmering outlines.

Aodh's sister's was an ever changing swirl of colors.

"Has her aura always been like that?" Vrishti asked, turning her head slightly to glance at Aodh.

"What do you mean? It's as green as her scales when she shifts. What else would it look like?"

"It isn't green to me," Vrishti said. *"It's every color, like it can't settle down. Maybe I just don't know how to use that power properly."*

"It'll come to you. Let's hear what she has to say."

Once Numa spoke, Vrishti forgot about the anomalous aura that surrounded the dragon. They could save the Haven once and for all, and that was all that mattered.

Thank you for reading "Dragon Guardian"! If you loved it, please visit the retailer and leave a review!

But wait, there's more!
The Immortal Dragons' quests for mates is nearly complete. Read about "Operation Wildcard," the twins Neela and Naaz's quest for their mates, by picking up "Dragon Blessed" today, or keep reading for a preview.

And don't forget, subscribing to the Dragon Beasties mailing list gets you **two free sexy dragon shifter stories** not available for sale anywhere.

DRAGON BLESSED

DRAGON-BLESSED TWINS NEELA and Naaz have waited nearly three thousand years for their chance to awaken their fated dragon mates. On the brink of a war with the enemy who enslaved them, their commander finally sends them to do just that.

But the twins' mission isn't called "Operation Wildcard" for nothing. These dragons are unique. Zorion was sired by none other than The Void himself, and Asha is the product of an ancient union with the dragons' former enemy, who is now their most powerful champion in the war.

These dragons' powers are unknown, and Neela and Naaz will be the humans to reveal them and recruit them for their cause.

But their true enemy is ever watchful, and when Neela makes a risky decision to reveal her new lover's powers, it will take nothing short of immortal dragon fire to save her.

Read on for an excerpt, or buy now.

~

Chapter One

Australian Outback
Four Days Prior to Spring Equinox

"WE SHOULD HAVE BROUGHT a dragon with us, I'm telling you."

Neela gave her brother a sidelong look as she rifled through the pockets of the unconscious Hunter at her feet, finding only lint. "You keep saying that. If I'd known you were going to be such a whiner about walking, I would have invited Sterlyn and Zamirah to come."

Naaz frowned. "It isn't the walking. I'm just fucking sick of getting ambushed by Ultiori every ten miles. We could've flown and been there weeks ago." He finished his own inspection of another Hunter and stood, scowling around at the latest unit of mind-controlled mercenaries they'd come across on what had become the mission from hell.

Neela toyed with the hilt of her blade. "This is the same unit that attacked us two days ago, and they're none the worse off for it. It'd take ten minutes to make sure they don't try again."

"They're victims like us, sis. And no match for us, either. We get this mission done, we can free them from Meri's influence once and for all."

Neela let out a sigh and dropped her hand to her side, hoping that their mercy didn't come back to bite them on the ass. Again.

She turned her gaze back to the ocher landscape of the Australian Outback. At times a desolate wasteland, it possessed its own stark beauty. Today they'd hiked down into a canyon of iron-rich stone oxidized by the harsh climate into shades of red. She was surrounded by natural formations that reminded her of Red dragons in their sanguine majesty.

Reds weren't her favorite, though their closest friend was mated to one, and immortal Red blood ran through her brother's veins. The power that blood gave him was waning, as evidenced by the cut on his forearm he carefully tended now. One of the Hunters had landed a lucky blow.

Neela's own enhanced abilities wouldn't last, either. She'd been granted one last infusion of Belah's blood just before embarking on this quest, but that had been weeks ago, and while they'd managed to predict and fend off ambush after ambush on their way to the hidden dragon temple, it wouldn't last much longer.

Just two more days. That was all they needed.

"We have no choice but to walk, brother, and be on our guard for the next ambush, because I have a feeling this isn't the last we've seen of these guys. You may as well take a breath and enjoy the journey. Doesn't this landscape appeal to you?"

A trickle of sweat carved a path down her brother's temple, cutting through the layer of red dust to reveal the richer brown of his skin beneath. He was her mirror in so many ways, some identical and others her polar opposite. They could finish each other's thoughts, knew each other's deepest desires, and possessed the same unwavering determination to prove themselves. He was her best ally in a fight too, as their six unconscious enemies attested to.

Naaz turned his gaze to her, vivid blue eyes as much at odds with the dusty burnish of his skin as the bright, cloudless sky was at odds with the red landscape. "I wish I had your patience. When did you turn into such a wise woman?" The corners of his eyes crinkled, pieces of red flaking away with his smile to land on the dusty kerchief tied around his neck.

Neela couldn't help but smile back. "One of the necessities of being female, I suppose. It's a requirement to tolerate the men in my life."

Naaz's laugh was deep and rich. "Are we that much of a trial? Perhaps *he* will be different."

A knot twisted in Neela's gut and she shifted her gaze back to the path before them. Zorion was still an enigma, despite his occasional mental visitations that had begun not long after she'd first learned of his existence. She quickened her strides, impatient to end their journey and meet her dragon in the flesh.

"Zorion *is* different, but maybe not the way you're suggesting. He's nothing like you, and I doubt his sister is anything like me."

Naaz raised a brow as though he were about to make some quip. Then he pressed his lips together, thinking better of speaking the words. He was always better at holding his tongue than she was.

"They are ours, regardless," Naaz said. "I doubt they are like anything that exists in the world ..." His throat rippled with his effort to swallow. "Asha is ..." He trailed off and shook his head.

"She's your mate."

He nodded and gave Neela a small smile that betrayed his helplessness. She had the same feeling of desperation clawing at her, the same driving need to get there as soon as possible. Only part of it was due to the conflict raging between their allies and their enemies. The repeated attacks she and Naaz had endured during their journey didn't help. The dragons she and her brother were seeking could turn the tide of this war, but that prospect did nothing to diminish her and her brother's need to finally be with their mates.

They'd been forced to wait nearly three thousand years for this. Barring any more ambushes, they were only two days out from the temple where their dragons lay in hibernation. But two more days felt like two days too many. Marveling at the scenery was the only way Neela managed to pace herself on this trek through an unforgiving landscape.

The dreams didn't help ease her agitation. Zorion had been in her head ever since she and Naaz had come across their ancient temple long ago during a quest for their master. She'd been drawn to the chamber on some remote, desolate island in the middle of the ocean, and she and Naaz had drifted there, answering a call they'd both heard. But they'd barely had the chance to set eyes on the pair of statues—barely dared to touch them—before Nikhil had tightened the vise of his control on their minds and forced them to stand down.

That had been the beginning of the end of their loyalty to their *Sayid*, and their subsequent rebellion ultimately forced their master to imprison Neela just to keep Naaz under control. It had taken centuries before they understood that the man they saw as a second father to them was being influenced by something much stronger and more insidious than they could ever understand. It was only within the last year that they'd discovered the true identity of the creature who had kept them imprisoned and conducted vile experiments on them.

She and her brother were still complicit in Nikhil's vicious acts, though. They'd been his tools at the beginning, killing out of loyalty to him long before their minds were affected by the monster who controlled him. Dragons had died at their hands, though far more were imprisoned and tortured after Neela and Naaz had become slaves themselves, rather than soldiers.

There was a fine line between the two, she realized. That line was choice, and the moment Nikhil had hidden their mates away from them was the moment their choice had been removed.

Now that their beloved *Sayid* had his mind back, he had released them. And having their freedom restored, they had both chosen to remain at his side, despite that ever-present need to find their mates. Neela had managed to hone her self-control during her thousands of years of imprisonment. The urge to bloody her fists on the doors of an impervious prison never went away, but she learned not to act on those urges after discovering it did no good. Their true jailer was far too powerful a creature to fight alone.

WANT TO READ THE REST? **Buy now.**

ABOUT OPHELIA BELL

Ophelia Bell loves a good bad-boy and especially strong women in her stories. Women who aren't apologetic about enjoying sex and bad boys who don't mind being with a woman who's in charge, at least on the surface, because pretty much anything goes in the bedroom.

Ophelia grew up on a rural farm in North Carolina and now lives in Los Angeles with her own tattooed bad-boy husband and six attention-whoring cats.

Subscribe to Ophelia's newsletter to get updates directly in your inbox. If newsletters aren't your thing, you can find her on social media.

http://opheliabell.com/subscribe

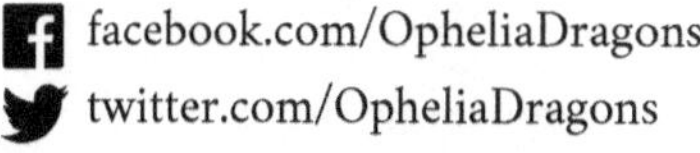

facebook.com/OpheliaDragons
twitter.com/OpheliaDragons

Immortal Dragons Series

Dragon Betrayed

Dragon Blues

Dragon Void

Dragon Splendor

Dragon Rebel

Dragon Guardian

Dragon Blessed

Dragon Equinox

Dragon Avenged

Immortal Dragons Box Sets:

Immortal Dragons: Books 1, 2, & 3 + Prequel

Immortal Dragons: Books 4-6 + Epilogue

Black Mountain Bears

Clawed

Bitten

Nailed

Stonetree Trilogy

Fate's Fools Series

Fate's Fools

Fool's Folly

Fool's Paradise

Fool's Errand

Nobody's Fool

Eye of the Hurricane

Fool's Bargain

April's Fools

Thieves of Fate

Aurora Champions Series

(Set in Milly Taiden's "Paranormal Dating Agency" world)

The Way to a Bear's Heart

Hot Wings

Triple Talons

Midnight Star

Once in a Dragon Moon

Second Skin Series (Romantic Suspense)

Mad Dog

Mile High

Valentine's Day

The Devil's Daughter

Marked Man

Rebel Lust Taboo

Casey's Secrets

Blackmailing Benjamin

Burying His Desires

Doubling Down

~

Standalone Erotic Tales

After You

Out of the Cold